MASTER OF THE ABYSSAL FORGE

Master of the Abyssal Forge

Forge

Volume 1

MARCUS K. CHRISTENSEN

Foreword

Frankly, I still cannot believe this day has come.

Bit of a strange introduction for my first published book, but I think it is quite fitting.

I have been telling stories for the better part of 20 years and writing for 15 of them. My earliest memory is of me telling my grandfather of these worlds I had made up while he was at hospice. All my life, I have said that I wanted to become an author. I started writing down those stories the very moment I learned how to write. First in Danish, then in English, as I started learning the language in third grade.

I have always been writing since then. It has always been part of my daily routine to get something done, writing-wise. Write a few pages, outline a chapter, or edit a dozen pages. It was important for me to keep going all the time. I knew I needed all of the routine and skills I could acquire if I ever were to publish something, let alone get to a stage where I could live off of what I had written.

Through the years, part of me had lost hope in that dream. Perhaps it was due to never producing something that lived up to my expectations. Perhaps it was due to my secondary obsession to do well at something else, so I have a backup plan. No matter the reason, the results are the same.

That was why it was such a surprise when I finally read through the newest draft of this very book and thought, "This is great." Frankly, that had never happened before. I finally had something good, something that lived up to everything I had dreamed of. Not only that, I was also very satisfied with the outline of the entire series. Everything felt too perfect.

From that point onward, I knew what the next step was. The results of this step are what you are reading right now. I had to follow this project to the end, and finally, I have reached that point. The fact that you are reading these words shows not only that I succeeded in getting the book published but also that you have found the concept of this book interesting enough to read it. For that, I am eternally grateful.

The story you're about to read is a bit outside my normal wheelhouse. Despite this, I still think it is a great story that I am all in on expanding.

Master of the Abyssal Forge is a fun amalgamation of a vast array of concepts. Its roots can be traced to my musings of historical revisionism and the concept of "history is written by the victors." That alone was insufficient to make much more than a semi-interesting thesis, not even close to an actually compelling story. However, combine this with 300+ years of history, two main characters with a complicated relationship, and now you are going somewhere.

Ultimately, this is a story of hope. For many of the characters, their stories are already finished. They have made their choices. Some regret them, others stick to them. One of our protagonists, Astolphos, falls squarely in the former category. He has dedicated the remainder of his immortal existence to atone for his past choices, a goal he deep down knows he will never achieve. He is stuck in an eternal loop of misery.

Lunarias' appearance is an opportunity. She is the key to breaking this eternal cycle he has found himself in.

On the other hand, Lunarias' story is one of accepting that the world she lives in is much more complicated than she has been told. She has grown up in a country that has "defeated" its enemies, who freely brands the remainders of their adversary nation as beasts that need to be exterminated. She has trained her entire life within this doctrine and has become incredibly efficient at this task. Now, she stands before someone who can show her what the history books have neglected. She cannot escape this confrontation, as she is bound by duty to escort the source straight to the capital.

To her, Astolphos is a wrench thrown into her worldview. Through Astolphos, she will need to face the truth of the world and those she serves, and even more importantly, what she will do with that information.

I hope you're going to enjoy this first volume of the series. The entire storyline for the series is outlined and ready. I have everything I need; all that is left is to sit down and write. In that regard, I am already well on my way, and hopefully, you will see the next volume at this time next year.

I hope you will find this story enjoyable. Many days were spent writing it, and even more was spent refining it using the help of those willing to read it.

And speaking of those that have helped me, I have a few mentions. First of all, I would like to thank my friend Kristian Harbo. He has always been there and helped me immensely throughout the many years we have known each other. Where it was difficult for me to gauge my writing and figure out if I was moving in the right direction, Kristian was always there to help me. I will always treasure the moment when I sent him the draft of this very book on a Friday evening, and he reported that he was done that same Sunday with the most detailed notes I have ever seen. This mention (and a trip to Flammen) does not make his efforts justice, but it will have to be enough until I figure out something better.

I would also like to thank my mother, father, and brother for their support throughout all these years. Without them, I might never have taken writing as seriously as I am doing now. I know that they are as excited to see where this is going.

No matter if this attempt at a writing career will turn into an Apollo 11 or a Hindenburg, I know they will be supporting me all the way.

Last but not least, thank you to Yomikkui for the cover. I hope this is the first of many projects where we will be working together.

And without further ado, thank you to you, the reader, for picking up this book. Know that this small gesture has not gone unnoticed, as checking the sales numbers will be part of my daily routine now.

Chapter 1

"Here you go. 16 horseshoes, just as ordered. That'll be 35 Merias," Astolphos said.

The last of the shoes had just left the forge and was still radiating heat. It was the last order of the day. Sunset had long passed, and the fire in the forge was nothing but embers, barely illuminating the terrace it was built upon. His customer, the village's local stabler, did not respond. He was too busy perusing the wares on display to see Astolphos in the doorway.

As Astolphos cleared his throat, he finally got his attention.

"Sorry," The stabler said, "Just looking at the sickles. Doin' a mighty fine job, I tell ya."

"Well, thank you. I'll throw one in for ten extra."

The stabler raised an eyebrow as he stared at the smiling blacksmith. Astolphos knew the reason behind the reaction was not too high of a price but quite the contrary.

"Ya' sure? If ya' took it to the city, ya'd get at least 30."

"But my services are required here. What'd happen if I just left for the city?"

"We'd indeed be swimming in shite, I tell ya."

"Oh, why not?" The stabler said, "Ten's a deal." The stabler took one of the sickles off the rough, wooden shelf.

Along with everything else in the shop, the shelves were made with whatever Astolphos had lying around. They were made of sticks and thin logs held together by his forged nails, while the forge was a congregation of rocks put together as close as possible. The floor, as well as the walls, were made of crudely carved floorboards, except for the one wall connected to the forge outside; that one was made of stacked stones too.

Though the interior was rustic, the wares were anything but. Forged with precision and an eye for their purpose. They were made with functionality as their one and only focus, ornamented only with Astolphos' logo burned into the wooden handles: a circle with a pair of tongs in the middle. If it did its purpose and would last a long time, it was good enough to sell; that was the ethos Astolphos lived by now.

"So, acquired a new set of horses?" Astolphos asked as the stabler scrambled with his pouch, far larger than usual.

"Nee, three from the Aurillian church came and asked for room. Paying me for keeping the animals well-fed and ready to run."

"Aurillian horses still in condition to ride?" Astolphos said, surprised. The knights and clergymen of Aurillia were notorious for taking their equipment to the limit and then some more, even if the equipment was a living creature.

"Condi... Oh 'Stolfos, ya' speaking funnily again."

"Sorry. Will the horses survive?"

"Yee. Rare indeed."

The stabler finally put 45 Merias onto the counter and took the horseshoes and his sickle.

"That's a deal," Astolphos said. "You know the rules."

"Ya' and ya' damn rules. Ugh... Fine." The stabler put his palm forward, and Astolphos shook it. It was less than two seconds, but it was more than enough for Astolphos to do his deed.

He usually drained only a few hours of life essence, perhaps one whole day if it had been a particularly slow day of sales. The stabler never felt anything. Through many years of practice, Astolphos made the process utterly undetectable for everyone but the highest-ranked clergymen. It was the perfect way to keep himself sustained.

"Oh," The stabler said, "One of them asked for the local smithy. I told 'em of ya, so they'll prolly visit soon."

If the clergymen were visiting, it could turn for the worse quickly, depending on their rank. Astolphos tried to hide his surprise, and the stabler stood as oblivious as before.

"One of the clergy?"

"Nee, a knight, and a lady at that."

"This just got stranger. See you. I've got to close up shop now."

"See ya."

Once the farmer closed the door behind him, Astolphos gave a relieved sigh. Though it was only a few of the clergy who could detect his true nature, it was still a threat to have one in the shop. The knights, however, were harmless in that regard. They were genuinely skilled in combat, but in their eyes, Astolphos was just a normal human being. Then again, if they could detect him, they would have found out as soon as they entered the village, and his shop would be in flames by now. So everything was probably fine.

He started closing the store for the day. First, he went outside with a bucket of water to quell the last embers. Second, Astolphos swept all the small metal scraps off the brick terrace before putting new wares onto the shelves.

The building felt too small, as always. Just a few more square meters, just a few extra shelves here and there. It was always too small, no matter how large Astolphos made it. Nevertheless, he always made do with what he had, organizing everything as neatly as possible. Farming equipment was to the right, weapons to the left, and everything not able to hang on the walls went to the shelves lining the floor in straight lines. Any store larger than this one would also be suspicious since it would require too much manpower for a single person to build. That was a slippery slope that could end in disaster.

Before he was satisfied, the moonlight shone through the translucent cloth stretched across his windows.

Just as Astolphos was to blow out the candles, the door opened.

"Sorry, we're closed. Could you come back tomo..." Astolphos trailed off as he finally saw the person.

It was a woman clad in plate and chainmail, with the steel breastplate proudly displaying a brass relief of a wolf with daggers stabbed into its eyes, the insignia of the Aurillian knights. Her hair, going just below the shoulders, was blonde and straight. Her blue eyes looked innocent, like she still had not been introduced to the horrors of the world, but the scar on her right cheek told otherwise. It was too long and precise to be from anything but battle, and with humans no less. Though it should break her visage, it just complimented her fair complexion.

As Astolphos looked at her, there was no doubt in his mind. She reminded him so much of a woman he had loved many years ago. She was a Hewris, one of his own blood.

Chapter 2

The man in front of her looked nothing like the black-smiths she was used to. He was tall and slender. His hair was almost a silver color, bordering on ethereal and translucent. He was cleanly shaven, very unlike the blacksmiths she met on her travels. She would have guessed they were around the same age if not for the wrinkles around his eyes. He smiled with a certain radiance. It was difficult not to smile with him as his amethyst eyes looked through her like he was reliving a memory long past.

If she had not seen some of his handiwork on the shelves, she would have said he was barely an apprentice, even considering his age. With such little muscle to show, he should scarcely be able to swing the hammer with enough force to dent the metal. Nevertheless, she was surrounded by proof; all she had to do was to look.

"Apologies. I'll return at dawn," Lunarias said.

"Well... Are you the knight I've heard of?" The smith asked, "The one asking for a blacksmith?"

"More a weaponsmith. I have a weapon in need of repairs."

"Let's take a look."

Lunarias grabbed her scabbard, but her hand only grabbed the air. With a heavy sigh, she flung the sack in her other hand onto the counter. Once she untied it, the eleven pieces of her broken sword reflected the candlelight unto her face.

The blacksmith looked at the content, visibly confused. It took some time before he arranged the pieces into their original shape. Once the parts were aligned correctly, Lunarias realized a piece was missing.

"What can even cause that kind of damage?" The blacksmith exclaimed. "Have you been fighting a horde of Abyssals?"

If only, then she had a glorious story to tell the others once she returned to the capital. Instead, she could only mutter the truth with a dampened voice, "Bandits in the Forest of Sorrows. I was careless and hit a tree."

The blacksmith whistled as he shook his head at the parts. The longer she stared at the remains of the sword that had saved her life on many occasions, the more apparent it became how impossible it was to put it back together.

The sword was an heirloom. One of her ancestors made that sword, and it was passed down to her. She was the newest, and now last, owner of a truly masterfully crafted weapon.

Though it did not have the ornamentation or the shine of a nobleman's heirloom, it greatly compensated with its ferocious cutting capabilities.

"Sorry," The blacksmith said. "Even if I had all the pieces, the result wouldn't be satisfactory. I don't think anyone can repair it, at least not anyone still alive. Besides, buying a new sword would be cheaper."

"That's what I feared. In that case, I need a new weapon. Can you forge anything of similar quality?" Lunarias knew it was a ludicrous question. She could go to the personal smiths of the royal family, and even they would struggle to deliver.

The blacksmith stroked his chin, deep in thought. "It would take time. Bland as it may look, this was a great blade. Something like it would be difficult for even the regal smiths of the capital to make." A smile grew on his face as his eyes grew distant. It was a smile of confidence. "Once I have my hands on the materials, I'd need a week."

His answer came as a shock. The wares on display were impressive, but they were still far from the quality of her previous weapon. He was either overconfident or thought his confidence would net him higher pay.

"I'd recommend a few adjustments to the weight, though," The smith said, "This sword was made for someone with a bit more mass than you. I think you'll find something lighter much better."

Though it was just a sword, having to replace it saddened Lunarias. But she had to remember her training. Material objects were replaceable. They would take damage and break. The things themselves had no value, the person using them had, and the coffers of the knights were brimming.

"But it's a bit too late for that at the moment," The blacksmith said, "Come back tomorrow, and we'll talk further." It looked like he wanted to say more, but instead, he turned around. She, too, turned around to leave. Almost as soon as she did, her stomach rumbled with great intensity. She froze that very moment. From behind, the blacksmith chuckled; he indeed heard it.

"Well, Care to join me for supper?" He asked, still chuckling.

Her embarrassment surely on display, she turned around. Though a kind gesture, she still found it suspicious for him to ask a complete stranger such a thing.

"It's just a way for me to welcome you to the village," The blacksmith said, "As well as thank you for your service towards our protection,"

She wanted to decline, but her stomach rumbled again. Frankly, she did not want to cook tonight. Riding on horseback for as long as she had was tiring, especially since they had not taken a break since they left Hybrik.

"And by the way," The smith continued, "Please, take one of the weapons on display until I've made you a new one. A knight without a weapon is like a castle without a wall."

His smile never faded. He gestured towards the wall with various weapons.

After a quick bow of appreciation, she studied the various weapons on display. The weapons were not just attention grabbers. They were functional. Swords, maces, axes, even a war scythe, all hanging on the wall. One of the swords stood out to her. It was much prettier than the others. Its scabbard had its wooden core exposed and blackened instead of covered by leather and linen, like many others beside it. The blade was of the same high quality as the rest, highly sharpened with a polish where her reflection laid undisturbed on its surface. The hilt had a simple finish; it was not ornamented in any way. The grip, pommel, and crossguard did their job but nothing else.

"This one," Lunarias said.

"Excellent choice. It's something I've worked on for some time. Though the hilt may look crudely made, this is because of..." The blacksmith continued talking about different materials and its shape, but Lunarias quickly stopped following his train of thought once it became too technical.

Though the sword was beautiful, it was still just a tool. It was made to be used and discarded once it became obsolete or unable to complete its job.

She removed her old scabbard and put the new one in its place. Once she was satisfied with its fit, the blacksmith led her behind the counter and through a doorway.

***

Lunarias had seen better living quarters at other fringe villages of the kingdom, but she had also seen far worse. His home had three rooms: the shop, a storage room, and the main living quarters. They first passed through the storage room, filled with various metal bars, lengths of wood, and whole hides of treated leather. It was kept orderly and tidy, with metal on one side, wood on the other, and leather hanging from racks on the walls. Not a speck of dust or cobwebs.

There was no door between the storeroom and the actual livable part. In fact, the only door she passed through was the main entry into the shop. Everything else was separated by empty doorways and the counter. Looking deeper into his home, Lunarias saw the embers of a fireplace about to go out. The blacksmith took some firewood from a stack at the back wall and threw it into the fireplace once the ash was dumped into a bucket.

"Anything I can do?" Lunarias asked.

"Just sit down and relax. You must've had a long journey. Where did you travel from?" As the embers ignited the new stock of firewood, the blacksmith chopped a bunch of vegetables. His living was simple. A bed and a small wardrobe were in the corner of the room, contacting a stone wall. A table was placed in the middle of the room, illuminated by an iron chandelier hanging in a simple chain from above. The only other furniture was a small kitchen counter in an L-shaped pattern, closed off to the side toward the fireplace. Lunarias sat at the table and looked at the blacksmith's quick knife movements. There was no reason to doubt his skill if he moved with the same precision and speed with a hammer.

"We traveled from the Capital."

"Long trip, I must say. Two months on horseback?

"Two and a half. We ran into some... trouble on our way."

On their way, Abyssals and bandits alike tried her prowess.

"Forest of Sorrows, or also before that?" The blacksmith asked.

"Not just that forest. We left a party of four, three clergymen and me. One took a hit to the stomach. She had no chance."

The chopping stopped as the blacksmith looked at her.

"Must've been tough."

"We got to Hybrik soon after. She suffered for three days before she succumbed. We had to take a break in the city; the sisters were too shaken to continue."

"Well... At least the remainder arrived in good shape, thanks to you, I assume?"

"Barely. Once the bandits ambushed us in the forest and I lost my weapon, we had no choice but to flee."

That day was a dishonor for more reasons than just her careless sword handling. If she had kept a better eye on the clergymen when they were escaping, they could have escaped with just a bruised ego, but now they also brought along a substantial financial loss.

Fearing for their lives, one of the clergymen unwound a saddlebag and threw it to the bandits as a distraction. Of course, it was the bag with the emergency rations and the vast sum of Merias. They were given that money to restore the monastery and care for the children arriving the following evening. She had to swallow her honor tomorrow and ask the knights escorting the children for help.

"So, where are you going to stay?" Astolphos asked, "Please don't tell me it has something to do with the old monastery?"

However, her silence was enough of an answer for the blacksmith.

"What are you going to do to the monastery? Isn't it too dilapidated to live in?"

That last sentence tipped her off. Normal villagers did not use words like 'dilapidated.' They would just say the church was destroyed or something along those lines. Those were the words of a noble, not some smith at the outskirts of the kingdom.

"You're very well-spoken for a blacksmith out here. Tell me, have you been attached to a noble house earlier in life?"

The blacksmith was busy preparing dinner. As her question left her lips, he went to the cooking pot with vegetables and venison. It took time before he answered. She was still determining whether he was that focused on the task at hand or using cooking as a pretense to make up an answer.

"Maybe this is a good time to introduce," The blacksmith said,

"My name is Astolphos Auriolis, son of a scribe and a seamstress. I've never been near the nobility, but my father's vocabulary may have rubbed off on me." He extended a hand toward her.

"Lunarias Hewris. Second generation knight of the new noble Hewris lineage. Knight of the second order." Out of habit, she rose from her seat and saluted with her other hand but quickly sat back down in embarrassment.

Astolphos chuckled. "Pay it no mind. I've heard of how they're drilling the training into your heads. Now, are you going to renovate the monastery?"

"We are, but we lost the Merias in the forest. That money was to restore the building and pay for the children's expenses."

"Children? So, it's going to be an orphanage?"

"Yes. They're scheduled to arrive tomorrow. Children from other outskirt cities up north. Those with many people going to the Abyss."

"Oh..."

The Abyss was the name of the areas under the control of the Abyssal King 150 years back. His creatures still roamed, even though he was long dead. Hunting them was very lucrative; a single party venturing into their territory could supply an entire village with enough food to keep the bellies full every night. But it was dangerous. Most of the new adventurers never returned from their first hunt.

"Still a large problem further north?" Astolphos asked.

"Far too great. Too many children end up without parents."

"And it's not even necessary. If they just left them alone, they wouldn't attack."

"They will not attack because we're assaulting them," Lunarias stated firmly. She was trained to combat Abyssals, ensuring their ranks were too scattered to mobilize any sensible army.

"We may never know," Astolphos rebutted. It was the usual sentiment. People never understood why the kingdom needed to constantly send troops out there. Some thought the Abyssals would stay away from the kingdom if left alone. Those were the people who had never seen the horrors of an attack. Lunarias still had to see such an attack happen, but she had seen the villages where such attacks had occurred. How houses were torn down to get to the villagers inside, how families were torn apart, limb by limb.

Before the citizens saw the sights she had in person, they would continue to spread their ill-informed, sowing discontent throughout Aurillia.

"But a knight of the second order," Astolphos said, "Are the clergymen high enough in rank to need such a valued knight?"

"Heh, valued..." Lunarias sighed. This man was certainly not a previous city-dweller, else he would know of her situation.

"No," Lunarias said, "they're both completely fresh out of tutoring."

"Then why send you? A single third order knight, or simply some mercenaries, could do the job."

Lunarias remained silent. Saying the reason aloud would only further convince her of its truth, and having the words come from her own mouth meant she accepted it. This was not an assignment; it was exile.

"Enough of that," Astolphos said, obviously seeing how fidgety Lunarias became of his questions, "If you wouldn't mind, I'd like to know a bit more about you."

"Why?" Lunarias said, suspicion at the forefront of her mind.

"You're going to live here as the protector of the abbey, might as well learn about each other now rather than later. You said you're a Hewris. Is that a new noble family?"

"Um... Sort of, we've been a noble family for some generations now, but we don't have the rich histories of the other families. Apparently, one of my forefathers helped immensely during the war and was rewarded with his aristocratic status."

"Sounds like he was a strong warrior to get such a reward. Wouldn't surprise me if he was part of the last assault." He gave her a slight smile.

"I never met him. He was dead long before I was born."

"I think he would be proud knowing one of his descendants had risen to second order."

"Maybe..." Lunarias had difficulties figuring out where this was going.

She yawned. It had been a long and exhausting day.

"Nevertheless, I have a suggestion," Astolphos said. "Since the children arrive tomorrow, what about bringing them here? You're out of money, so I'll supply a boar we can roast on my forge. Y'know, give them a hearty welcome and all that."

As with his sudden invitation to eat, he made up good deeds on a whim.

"How're you going to find a boar?"

"I'm a bit of a hunter in my spare time. Trust me, I'll bring in the goods if I have to."

Just like before, she hesitated to agree.

But did she really have any other choice but to say yes? She had no money to pay for food, and here was someone who extended a helping hand to her and the clergy.

"If you're sure," Lunarias said, "we'll bring the children here by sunset tomorrow. But I have to know," She leaned forward, "Why would you do this? What are you getting out of it?"

"Nothing at all. Just doing a good deed when someone needs it. Now, the food's done."

Talking to the blacksmith was illuminating. As much as he acted strange and impulsive, he did not feel like a bad person.

If everyone in the village was like him, it indeed was the perfect place for the orphanage.

Chapter 3

The dishes were barely cleaned before Lunarias rose from her chair.

"It's been nice meeting you," Lunarias said, "but unfortunately, I have my duties to tend to."

"There's no reason to patrol the village. We've not had any thieves or brigands in the last five years. But I understand, orders and all that."

"Thank you."

Astolphos followed Lunarias to his front door, where they bowed at each other before going their separate ways. Part of him was happy that she left as soon as she did; that meant he did not have to lie and feign being tired.

Thanks to his Gift, he no longer needed sleep or food. Even breathing was no longer required. He only breathed when customers were around and ate only in non-Gifted company. If not for the chance encounter, he would just have gone down to the hidden basement as soon as he closed the shop.

The hidden basement had features that would give him an appointment with the executioner if found. The flameless forge in the middle of the floor was the least of his worries. Altars devoted to an art form the kingdom thought eradicated, scarlet vials with liquid life essence nicely ordered by volume, and most important of all, one strongbox, locked by machine and magic alike to make sure nobody could touch it, let alone open it.

Astolphos unlocked the safe and pulled out a flask in the shape of a skull, he clenched his hand above its opening, and the precious red drops flowed and filled it to the brim with the life force he drained today. The strongbox was important not because of its contents, but because it would be the main focus of anyone finding the basement. The decoy phylactery was there for the same reason. Anyone seeing the eerie shape of the skull would think the flask was evil. And while an angry mob would be busy destroying it, Astolphos had enough time to pack the necessities and fake his death before anyone was any wiser.

It also helped a bit that the decoy phylactery was connected to the real one and extended its maximum capacity, hence the need to refill the decoy instead of the real one. Without re-filling either, he could live for one month, which fell to two weeks if the decoy was destroyed.

"So... what're you going to do?" His forge asked.

"I don't know. It's family. Should I really just keep this to myself?"

"'Stolfos, you gave up that life long ago, remember?"

"It's just...How the hell would you deal with this?"

"You do know you're asking a crystal for family advice, right?"

"But you're a Gifted too. What would you have done if our roles were switched?" Astolphos picked up the orange crystal from inside the fireless forge. It felt cold to the touch, much in contrast to its searing heat mere moments before. Every time the crystal uttered a word, the light inside of it pulsed.

"First, I'd probably drop everything I was doing to help my dear friend regain his body."

"Ha-ha, very funny."

"Then, I'd probably just keep it a secret and live with it. Is there even a good way to explain this? 'Hey, I know your career is to hunt Gifted like us, but I'm your great-great-great-great grandfather, who's also immortal, by the way." The crystal did its best to mimic Astolphos voice as it spoke, further hammering a stake through his dreams.

"Well, want to make something?" The crystal asked.

"Not tonight, Glaucos. I just want to think for a bit."

"Fine by me, that just means I get to conserve some more energy. Can you put me back on the pedestal?"

Astolphos put the crystal back on its pedestal on top of the safe.

"Can you see any way where telling her is going to end well?" Astolphos asked.

"If you tell her, I can guarantee we have to leave for Marados the next day."

And that was one thing he did not want to do so soon. He did not want to spend years waiting for the others in that decrepit castle. However, the temptation had not quelled, nor did he expect it to.

"Don't worry about it," Glaucos said, "We've been through worse."

Astolphos chuckled, "That's certainly true."

The light inside the crystal dimmed, showing his friend had gone to sleep.

Glaucos had not always had this form. His core was damaged back in the last battle against the Gifter, leaving him unable to regenerate his body. Feeling guilty, Astolphos swore to help his friend regain his body. Luckily, Glaucos was an elemental, so he got sustenance by being embraced by the elements. Throwing him in the fire once in a while was enough to keep him alive, and fire was a thing Astolphos had more than enough of.

However, there was no fire burning this night. Astolphos instead spent the time pacing the basement, racking his brain to figure out a way to tell Lunarias the truth. He, however, reached the same conclusion as Glaucos, and the next thing he knew, the orange rays of the morning sun illuminated the living room above. There was no longer any time to think; he had a busy day ahead.

***

The day started like any other, with Astolphos stoking the forge. However, today its purpose was different. It did not need to be hot enough to soften metal, just enough to roast some meat.

When he was done, Astolphos grabbed his bow and a few arrows before going to the forest south of the village. He promised to roast a boar tonight, and he always kept his promises.

The villagers greeted him on his way down the road, eagerly asking where he was going. Everyone praised his initiative and said they would help another day if needed. They were all much kinder than what someone like Astolphos deserved. Every kind word they said, every offer of help, they all stung deep in his soul. None of them knew what he was doing with every transaction in his shop. They all knew him as the kind smith peddling his wares to a price much lower than their actual value.

But the price they paid was not in Merias but in minutes.

An hour here and there was unnoticeable, something not causing weakness of the flesh nor any lack of feeling in the extremities.

But it kept him sustained. It kept him alive and able to continue repenting for what he did so many years ago. The question was, did his petty dealings really bring enough value to justify their cost?

Once the forest's darkness enveloped him and the smoke of the village chimneys disappeared below the canopy, he hid his bow and arrows in the foliage. They were nothing but a smoke-screen to mask his true powers.

Astolphos closed his eyes, letting all his other senses do the work. The sound of leaves rustling, critters squeaking in the trees and on the ground. The cold morning wind rustled his hair. One by one, he closed those out, too, leaving only one left.

He felt the life essence of all living beings around him, every animal, every insect. The life forces represented themselves as red mists inside his eyelids. The larger the creature, the larger the mist. Scanning the forest, ignoring all the smaller life forces, he finally found his target. The mist was larger than the squirrels and birds but centered closer to the ground than a deer. It was either a boar or an extremely short and fat donkey.

Making as little noise as he possibly could, Astolphos sneaked closer to the animal. He knew its location and felt its essence.

The animal was majestic, or at least as majestic as a giant pig digging in the ground could be. It stood, unsuspecting of Astolphos looking at it from behind.

He closed his eyes, extending his hand towards the animal, towards its essence. He grabbed its essence without a sound and let it flow into his hand. The boar squealed, feeling its life being sapped away. It thrashed around, looking to find and kill its adversary. Once Astolphos had a good grip, he closed his hand. All of its life force left its body in one fell swoop, jumping to his hand, where it dissipated into the air. A shame the life force of an animal was insufficient to sustain him; else, draining the villagers was obsolete.

The boar fell to its side with a thump. No movement, no damage to its hide. It just stopped breathing as its heart gave out.

"Thank you for leaving the world with such ease," Astolphos said to the lifeless body.

It was a prime example of a well-grown animal. Not too much fat, a practical mountain of muscle, but still light enough for Astolphos to carry it to the village without raising an eyebrow.

He grabbed its hind legs and dragged it back to the village in one hand. Once he found the spot where he hid his bow and quiver, he let go of the beast. He pulled out a knife-like object from a secret compartment in the quiver. Its blade parted in thirds, mimicking the shape of his arrows. Astolphos found the beast's heart and stabbed the knife down to the hilt, then pressed on its chest to make the blood flow out of the wound and unto its hide.

Once satisfied with his work, he flung the bow and quiver unto his shoulders and took hold of the boar with both hands. He staggered forward with the boar on his back. As the light of the sun shone on him once he exited the forest, a couple of villagers came to help carry the animal.

He only had one thing to do before sunset, prepare the animal for roasting.

Chapter 4

The blacksmith was right in his assessment. The night was as quiet as it could be, and the following morning was just as uneventful. Life in the fringe villages was much calmer than what Lunarias was used to. Back in the capital, there was never a slow night, be it a pickpocket or drunken disagreement. Here, she might even come to regret not bringing any books. But the quiet also brought along with it a seething feeling of unrest, a feeling of uneasiness reminding her of the moments before an ambush on the campaigns into the Abyss. The sight of the sea to the side did not help either, as it felt like she stood at the end of the world when she looked at the ocean far below.

But the view from the top of the old bell tower was beautiful. On one side, she had the village; on the other, she saw the ocean. The monastery was built at the very edge of the Aurillian kingdom. Any further, and you had a steep drop down an almost flat cliff side to the sapphire ocean, which depths were unknown to anyone.

Though it was challenging to climb the bell tower, the view made it worth the effort. The wooden stairs were rotten to the core, making every step hazardous. The rest of the monastery was no different. The roof was leaky in many places, and the plaster between the stones cracked long ago. It was a miracle that the walls still stood to this day.

Looking down from the tower, Lunarias imagined how splendid the monastery was in its prime, how sturdy it was built, and how high the peak was compared to so many others she had seen in her lifetime. The view from the top was spectacular. Even better, the wind carried the damp smell of rotting wood away, replacing it with the sweet smell of the budding forest to the south.

With the help of a spyglass, she saw how the villagers helped the smith carry a giant boar to his forge. Just seeing the creature made her mouth agape. The beast was at least half the size of the blacksmith.

Frankly, she would not have believed the villagers if she had not seen the creature with her own eyes.

It just showed the tenacity of the villagers on the fringes of the kingdom. They were able to train themselves to do amazing things because they did not have the luxury of the larger cities. Learning and living off one skill was not an option; you had to fill multiple roles. A smith training himself to track and fell such a beast was the perfect example.

"Lady Hewris. Would you have time to help us for a bit?" One of the nuns yelled from downstairs.

Lunarias sighed as she descended. The monastery was decrepit, but the nuns refused to abandon living in it. They were working tirelessly to make the place somewhat livable again. It was just limited to the kind of work they could do. They could only sweep away the stones and clear some of the rubble. For everything else, they needed craftsmen, and those cost Merias.

Last night was terrible. She had not seen the monastery inside before visiting the blacksmith, and now she wished she had never seen it. One side of the double doors had fallen off its hinges and lay smashed on the ground, half-digested by termites, maggots, and who knew what. Last night she took one look inside the building, one look at the sisters who struggled to find a place to sleep amidst the rubble before she gave up and pitched a tent outside. She said her nightly prayers and went to bed. She indeed hoped they would find an alternative;

letting the children live there was reckless, if not straight-up dangerous.

The sight of the nuns diligently clearing the floor of rubble extinguished that hope.

"Good news, sisters," Lunarias said, "The blacksmith upheld his word; we're eating at his forge tonight."

"That's great news, lady Hewris. We'll talk to the knights about lending their support if you could take care of the children in the meantime."

"I'll take care of the knights. They're my brothers-in-arms, after all."

On their travels, she let slip her relationship with the Aurillian knights. Many of them looked down on her because of her gender. Female knights were rare but not unheard of. The same could not be said of second-order female knights. As far as Lunarias knew, there had been three before her, all dying soon after the inauguration. As far as she knew, she had outlived all three combined already.

The other knights looked at her as a detriment, an accident waiting to happen. She was not going to make their prophecies come true.

"We'll not intervene then," The sisters said, flashing a pitiable smile.

They were simply trying to alleviate the damage such requests would have to her reputation. Asking her fellow knights for money since they lost their funds would only further reinforce their stigma, but what could the knights do? They had already sent her to a fringe city on babysitting duty, literally. She had led several successful campaigns into the Abyss, and for all of her accomplishments, she got this.

It infuriated her more than she would like to admit, but she would carry out her assignment as given, no matter how long it would take. But she had to wonder; sending her here was sudden and out of character from her commander, the very same man who had trained from when she first entered duty. He told her the command came from higher up the hierarchy, but it was still strange. Her track record did not warrant such a duty to a peaceful region. Her abilities were wasted here.

"Could you please help get these out of here?" The sister asked, "There's a shovel over there." She pointed at a reasonably large pile of rocks with a shovel sticking out.

The nuns were effective. Soon, they could walk on the floors again, as long as the roof did not collapse due to their walking.

"Are you two sure we shouldn't ask to use the dining hall until the abbey is renovated?" Lunarias asked as she shoveled rocks out through the broken door.

"Oh lady, have fate in the Ancestors. They'll protect us when we're inside their domiciles."

"Then why do you have cuts on your hands?" Lunarias asked. The nun quickly covered her hands with her long, blue sleeves.

"It's their will. They're reminding us why we should be grateful for their protection."

Lunarias had vowed to protect the kingdom and its inhabitants, but clergymen were always infuriating to be near. Aurillian knights were sworn to the queen, who lent some knights to the Church for guard duty. Still, their refusal to carry weapons and their complete faith made them somewhat disturbing. Their sister, who succumbed on the journey, went with a smile. She thought it was the plan of the Ancestors, the previous kings and queens of the kingdom.

Lunarias had to get used to it. She had to stay with them for a long time to come.

Shoveling the debris out was as exhausting as she thought. Her armor only hindered her, but she kept it on as she had to be prepared for everything.

Once she finished the pile, the floor looked to be in a somewhat livable condition. Still, she feared for the roof. The wooden support pillars had so much rot in them it was visible from two floors down. Part of it looked ready to fall at any minute, and what were the sisters' reactions when Lunarias told them?

'Have faith in the ancestors.'

Devout to the end, they were. Hopefully, their end would not be followed by the children they were responsible for.

"If that's everything," Lunarias said, wiping the sweat from her brow, "I must meet the blacksmith. He's going to forge me a new weapon."

"But haven't you already bought a new one?" One of the nuns asked, pointing at the wooden scabbard leaning against her breastplate.

"He lent it to me, so I could continue my duties. Once my new weapon is finished, I'll return it to him."

But him lending it to her without any collateral was strange. It was an expensive piece; something about it did not feel right. What he said might be true, that he wanted to help her, so she chalked her suspicion up to paranoia.

"Remember, the boar will be ready at sunset," Lunarias yelled to the nuns as she left the monastery.

***

It was surprisingly easy to find her way around the village. She saw every building from her vantage point on top of the monastery and remembered their placements. Many villagers were interested in what would happen since there had been no clergymen in the village before, a statement immensely puzzling to her. They had a church of the ancestors on that hill, after all, no matter the state it was left in.

Trying her best not to be too dismissive, she talked with them briefly before excusing herself. A simple walk from the monastery to the smithy took longer than she wanted, but she arrived at the sight of Astolphos preparing a spit above his forge with calm and mellow flames lazily dancing on the coals.

"Oh, hello, Lunarias," Astolphos said, "You're here early. If you're here to help prep the meat, you're a bit too late though."

"I'm here to discuss my new weapon, as we discussed yesterday."

"Straight to the point, I see. I've thought a bit about it since our conversation, and I'd like you to try a few swords first to get an idea of what you'd like."

"Can't you just make something like the one I brought?"

"Sure, I could try, but there are a few problems. First, though I have an idea of its weight, balance, and form, I can't be sure due to its condition. If I had to base it on what I'd seen, I can't guarantee the result to be sufficient. Second, that sword of yours was an heirloom, wasn't it?"

"It surely is. How'd you know?"

"I apologize if I sound patronizing, but from what I'd seen, the weapon didn't look like it was made for you, but instead, someone a bit higher and with more heft in their swings. Of course, I could be completely wrong. I've not seen your fighting style after all. If it's alright, I'd like to correct that. It'll help me tailor a sword to you, though the result might end up much different than what you're anticipating."

"And how can you, a blacksmith, evaluate my skills?" Lunarias asked, mildly offended. She had devoted her life to her craft, her entire being to her knighthood. How could a smith so far from the front lines judge her combat style and suggest her weapon was not suited for her?

"I'm not completely green either, miss. You inevitably have to draw your weapon when you're on the road. Though I'm far from your level in terms of experience, of course," Astolphos said with a slight smile. For some reason, that smile added further timber to the fire of irritation inside Lunarias.

"In that case, what about we take a match?" Lunarias asked, "You get to see my style, and I'll see if I underestimated you."

"Uh…" The blacksmith took a step back with a surprised expression. That look made her come back to her senses.

"Apologies. It was out of line for me to make that suggestion." She bowed to Astolphos, who let out a hearty laugh.

"I have to apologize too. I'd forgotten how proud you knights are of your fighting. Nevertheless, I accept your challenge."

"What?"

He scratched the back of his head, looking away with an awkward smile, "I think it'll be fun. Plus, it's many years since this hand has swung a blade. Getting the rust off once in a while is a great thing."

Lunarias hesitated. Though it was her suggestion, his enthusiasm felt a bit too genuine. Who knew, maybe that calm surface hid a battle-loving brawler? At last, she decided it would probably not hurt any of them as long as they were careful. With a slight nod, Astolphos vanished into the shop and came out moments later in an old gambeson. It looked like it had come straight from the battlefield, with several deep cuts all over and a few holes around the chest. Surely, he must have something better, for that thing would not withstand more than a few actual attacks.

"I know, I know," Astolphos said, "It's a bit worn. I use it to see how effective my sharpening is."

"You're not dependent on that thing in case of an attack, are you?"

Astolphos scratched the back of his head uncomfortably once more. "Well… I've wanted to travel to Hybrik and get something new, but I've been tied up here for a while now."

Astolphos drew his sword. It was a one-handed sword with a very delicate blade. It looked like someone had taken a dagger and stretched it to thrice its length.

"But never mind that," Astolphos said. "It'll still serve its purpose today."

"Let me just say it's not my fault if I break it." Lunarias drew the sword lent to her. It was longer and heavier than she was used to, but it had about the same profile as the one she had lost. She grabbed the hilt with both hands and presented the blade to her opponent.

"Don't you worry," Astolphos said, "I trust your skills."

Lunarias regarded the blacksmith. His techniques were evident from the start. He wielded his sword in one hand and extended it as far out as he could with his other hand hanging loosely at his side. The blade was too thin for a slashing-dominant style; it was made for thrusting. It was a risky choice from his side, all she had to do was to make it past the point of the blade, and her victory was ensured. The hand holding the sword was constantly fidgeting, trying to get a comfortable grip as his wrist bent in a way that would make the stance incapable of being upheld for too long at a time. The one thing which would stand up to scrutiny was his footwork. It was also the only thing that showed he had any experience fighting, but it also told her that the rapier was not his preferred weapon.

In total, she was confident it would be a quick match, with her victory all but assured.

Astolphos did not make the first move. It looked like he was too occupied with where the tip pointed, something Lunarias would take advantage of.

Considering that she had trained her entire life to fight, she felt bad for beating an apparent amateur, but it was for his own good too. The enemy, be it bandit or Abyssal, would never wait for him to get adjusted before attacking. They would take advantage of it to deliver a quick and deadly blow.

While slightly loosening her grip on her sword, she took the first step, then another and another. She set her plan in motion when she was four steps away from the tip of the blacksmith's weapon. She lowered her center of mass significantly and set off with a great stride. She passed his point in just two steps and prepared herself to deliver the first and final blow.

Astolphos lowered his weapon and pulled it back towards himself while his off hand went behind his back. It happened too quickly for her to react. With his left hand, he drew a dagger with multiple serrations on the blade and two hooks at the ends of the guard. The guard of the dagger caught the blade of her sword. She stepped back, retracting her sword as Astolphos twisted the dagger to the side.

"That's a dirty trick," Lunarias said.

Astolphos adjusted his grip on the rapier one last time; his grip steadied as he turned his body sideways, slimming his profile, "A surprise attack was my only option."

All the insecurity on display vanished. She was tricked from the start. The trick he pulled reminded her not of a knightly duel. It belonged in a back-alley fight against some rogue.

"But it almost worked," Lunarias said, flashing a cocky smile, "but it seems like you're ready to face me head-on now."

"We'll see. Perhaps I have another trick up my sleeve."

Astolphos took a small step forward and swung the rapier at her breastplate. She deflected the point away, but Astolphos continued to close in the distance, brandishing his dagger. Before he could use it, her left hand left the hilt and grabbed her scabbard. She released it from her belt and thrust it at the blacksmith's stomach. It pushed him back with a grunt as she realized she had done so at full force. However, the blacksmith recovered almost without delay. She took advantage of this and took a step forward. As she swung her blade, Astolphos swung his dagger but stayed his hand as Lunarias tried to block it with the scabbard.

With her sword touching the gambeson, the duel was over.

"I'm not the only one fighting dirty," Astolphos said.

She cocked her head at this comment, only realizing a moment later that Astolphos' eyes were locked on the scabbard. If he had hit the scabbard, it would, without a doubt, ruin the surface finish, rendering it unsellable.

"Sorry, I didn't think about it when I pulled the scabbard. It's just something I do when I'm under pressure."

She put the scabbard back onto the belt and sheathed her sword,

"But I must say, you almost won back then. I underestimated you."

"I'm honored, but this duel was determined from the start. Do you normally use your scabbard in battle?"

"Every time the battle grows tense. Most opponents don't know what to do, as it's not the most normal of techniques."

Astolphos took off the gambeson, put it on the ground, and then laid the weapons on top of it.

"That's true, most would anticipate either a shield or another sword, but the scabbard can throw them for a loop. Any reason for not using the other options?"

"Weight, mostly. The scabbard weighs almost nothing compared to a sword while still having decent range. I just find a shield clunky to have around."

"Then I might make a scabbard out of metal, or at least with a metal shell. I can't imagine a scabbard lasting long on the front lines like that."

Four fights were the usual life span of a scabbard in Lunarias' possession. She even had a few lying around if she knew she would be away from a blacksmith for a while. They were, however, made cheaply, as anything else would be stupid if they were going to be ruined anyway.

"You think it'll last longer that way?"

"It might be a bit heavier than you're used to, but it'll last a while longer, and you'll be able to bend it back into shape if you're in a pinch. Now for the sword itself."

Lunarias raised an eyebrow, "Did you really get enough info from that duel?"

"Not even close. I was going to ask if you would demonstrate your technique on a dummy?"

"That shouldn't be a problem."

"Great, could you please wait a few moments?"

Astolphos entered a small shed beside his home. From the outside, she heard him rummage through it, throwing stuff out onto the grass with haste. Until, with a loud sigh, he came out with a training dummy under his arm.

"Do your worst. It's old and easily replaceable," Astolphos said as he stabbed the dummy into the ground.

Lunarias regarded her new opponent, a training dummy high of age, with green discoloration at the right side of the burlap sack, comprising a rough head. She took the same stance as in the battle against Astolphos, with her hands pointed towards the ground but the blade pointing directly at her target. From behind, she felt Astolphos' stare.

At first, she kept it simple. Side-steps followed by a slash, cuts with both the true and the false edge of the blade, perhaps a thrust occasionally. Then she began on the fancier stuff. She imagined the dummy as a living adversary and showed how she would parry and block various attacks.

It continued for a while, only stopping once she was slightly out of breath.

"That should be enough," Astolphos said as he approached Lunarias. He stopped momentarily when his eyes locked on the dummy, torn to shreds in her last flurry of attacks.

"I must say, I thought you'd use a lot more thrusts than you did."

"Most Abyssals are unarmed, so great precision is not required. They also attack mostly in groups, so wide cuts are preferred on the battlefield."

"I've gotten a few ideas. Please follow me. I'd like to show you a few options of what I have in store at the moment."

Once inside the store, Astolphos grabbed a small chalkboard while rummaging behind the counter. He finally found what he was looking for. It was covered in a blanket. Before he removed the cover, he looked at Lunarias precariously. Looking at how the blanket curved around its contents, she had a good idea of what it was, and she did not like it.

"Before I show this to you," Astolphos said. "Please remember this is my own recreation. It's not original since those shall always be turned in to the Church."

He removed the blanket, revealing exactly what she thought it was. The sword was short and curved, with a very small handguard. Not as decorated as the ones she had seen on the battlefield, it was apparent this sword was made to imitate the swords of the Abyssals, the enemy of Aurillia.

"That's about the reaction I thought it'd get," Astolphos said,

"Just wanted to air the idea since this kind of sword is made with slashing in mind."

"In this case, function doesn't matter. That's the weapon of the enemy, and I refuse to carry anything resembling it."

"Understandable. In that case, what about this one." Astolphos went to the wall and picked up practically the largest sword he had. It was the same simple construction as everything else in the shop, but the blade was massive. It was longer than the one she was lending, and the blade was wide. The one feature that stuck out was the lack of a point. It looked like the tip was cut clean off.

"This's called an executioner's sword," Astolphos said, "It has some heft, but you can cut through anything living with it, and even some types of armor. The biggest drawback is the complete lack of a point, so thrusting is completely off the table. Try holding it." Lunarias took hold with both hands and prepared herself, but she was unprepared for its actual weight. Just keeping the 'point' still was an endeavor. She did not have to try swinging it. She instinctively knew what the blacksmith said was true; she could probably cut through light armor with it. This was a weapon that could get the job done.

"A bit too heavy for any precision," Lunarias muttered as she returned the sword.

"That's why an upper guard is practically required for this kind of thing. If you have plate pauldrons and a helmet, I recommend carrying it with the edge resting on the armor. The small edge damage is well-traded for the power it delivers."

If she had to be honest, she liked the executioner's sword. She was used to weapons with heft behind their attacks. Even the sword that broke was a bit on the heavier side. The problem was that the executioner's sword was only useful when fighting Abyssals, and not even all of them. She needed something lighter for her other duties, upholding peace by catching criminals.

"Though I like it," Lunarias said, "It's just not versatile enough for dealing with bandits, thieves, and their ilk."

"Good point, but keep this one in mind. I have an idea."

They did not look at any other weapons, but instead, Astolphos began drawing on a small chalkboard. He made some sketches of three different parts, a strange-looking scabbard, and two blades; only one seemed to have a hilt. The thicker one did not have a handle. At least, that was what she thought it looked like.

"I have an idea," Astolphos said. "But I have a question before I can go further. Would you have any problem carrying your weapon on your back?"

She thought about it for a moment. She had seen such scabbards before, but it was for weapons like polearms, axes, and the like. She tried drawing from such a scabbard when she went through heavy weapons training.

"I don't think so," Lunarias said, "I'd probably need some time to adjust, but it's possible."

"Good. That's enough for me. I will make you something never seen in the kingdom before!" Astolphos continued mumbling to himself, but as far as she could discern, he wondered loudly about materials and things outside of Lunarias' expertise. But how he listed the items off his memory alone told her of his experience just as much as his wares.

"Why is someone with your skill out here in the fringes? Couldn't you make a fortune arming the barons?"

"I could, but the barons already have skilled smiths; these people don't. They need weapons more than the barons. If I leave, they'll have to request arms and tools from the merchants. We both know the premium such people take for their service."

"I...I didn't think of it that way. Apologies."

Astolphos laughed, "No reason for that. Even the villagers think it's strange. After all, who would throw away a fortune just to do some good deeds?"

His hand still flew across the chalkboard as he talked. He wrote a few words around the drawing, but his handwriting was illegible. Her curiosity had not gone unnoticed.

"My father may have been a scribe, but excellent writing was a skill I didn't inherit," He said with a deprecating smile as he hid away the chalkboard.

"I think I've got everything," Astolphos said. "Could you help me mount the boar? After all, getting the spear through it requires at least two people."

Chapter 5

Watching the boar as it roasted was a task carrying the same level of excitement as patrolling the village at night. It reminded Lunarias of the many times she ambushed Abyssals at the borders, the long wait between the setup and the action. Neither she nor Astolphos wanted to be the only one to keep an eye on the animal, so they took turns. When it was Astolphos' turn at the boar, Lunarias spent the time perusing his other weapons on display. She had gotten permission to try anything she wanted as long as she sharpened them when she was done. His collection was far beyond the scope of what was expected of a village blacksmith, and many had such esoteric shapes that she had never seen anything like it before. Swords with even harsher curves than the weapons of the Abyssals, swords with hooks, Axes with large heads, and spiked hand-guards. She was curious about how some of them should be used in combat, and their appearance alone gave no hint. However, her eyes told her they all were made by the blacksmith. Their appearance was devoid of anything ornamental, combined with their highly polished surfaces, razor-sharp edges, and the embossing of tongs surrounded by a circle was the telltale sign of his making.

The exception to the rule was the sword at her hip and a knife on display close to the counter. The blade was engraved from pommel to tip with vines and leaves. The handle depicted a battle between two people, or maybe mankind against the Abyssal King, inlaid in gold into cherry wood.

"Looks like you like my recreational projects," Astolphos said.

His sudden address startled Lunarias, making her take a solid grip on the hilt of her sword out of habit. Quickly realizing what she was doing, she relaxed her grip, praying that Astolphos did not notice.

Either he did not notice, or he was good at hiding it. He stood in front of her with the usual smile on his lips.

"They're beautiful," Lunarias said.

"Thank you. I work on something like these in my spare time when I know no customers are coming."

As Lunarias' fingers slid across the engravings, she felt no jagged edges or irregularities. The closer she looked at the lines, the more she realized how much care had gone into even the smallest details. She did not dare to guess how long it had taken to make those engravings; her guess would be too low.

"I can't let you borrow both, so please leave this one in the shop," He chuckled, "Though none of the people here can afford it either, they're still nice to have around as a way to show off my craftsmanship."

"How much does it cost."

"1500 Merias."

The price was enough to make Lunarias' hands shake. Her hands held an object whose price went far above her yearly pay. It was a price fit for a Baron, maybe a viscount of a prospering mining town, not something found on the shelves of a smithy at the fringes of the kingdom.

"You do know the worth of your services." She had heard from the other villagers how low his prices were. How their tools never broke and how cheap Astolphos made repairs in the unlikely event.

"Indeed I do. It's a fancy blade, but it's no different from this one when thinking purely of the materials."

Astolphos threw her another knife. This one had no fancy engravings, no grip of exotic wood. This was a tool, the other was a piece of art. When held up beside each other, she saw how identical they were in shape. The ornate one had a higher grade of polish, but the shape of the handle, and the shape of the blade, were mirror images of each other.

"16 Merias for that one."

For a moment, she thought he had misspoken. Still, the look in his eyes told her that the price was that low. 6 Merias would cover food and drink for the average citizen for a day, so for a relatively small sum, the villagers could buy the tools necessary to keep their trades up and running. Prices such as these might explain the prosperity of a village of its size and placement.

In the fringe villages she had previously visited, the only regular visitors were soldiers and traveling merchants, and given this village was not connected directly to the Abyss, she doubted soldiers would visit unless prompted. That meant the only way to get things the villagers did not produce was through the merchants, who could raise their prices because they knew the villagers had no other way to acquire the wares. Despite this, it looked like the villagers had at least some disposable income. Their clothes were without stitches and patches, and she had even seen a few women wear jewelry, albeit without gems, gold, and silver.

"And what're your prices for the jewelry?" Lunarias asked.

Astolphos smiled at the question. She even felt like there was a bit of mischievousness behind it. There was only one place in the village where jewelry could be made: this forge.

"A bit more than for the tools, but those prices vary depending on the occasion." Astolphos took a strongbox out from underneath the counter and put it on top. He unlocked it using a key hanging from his neck. "If I know it's for a present, I sometimes adjust the price up or down depending on how the sales have been the past week. As long as they're happy with whatever I make, I'm fine keeping the prices fairly low."

He took out a few pieces from the box and placed them on the counter to show. It almost felt like he was trying to sell some to Lunarias. Rings and necklaces were abundant, but few were made of gold and none with jewels. They were far from the fancy things the jewelers in the Capital had on display, but she could imagine the prices being in the range where they could be bought as a luxurious gift, and everyone still could go to bed with food in their stomachs. Still, something was interesting about the simple designs compared to the intricate pieces of gold and gems she sometimes had to wear before she picked up the sword. She found herself looking through the strongbox out of curiosity.

"On the other hand," Astolphos said, "Custom jobs are a different story. For example, if they want something specific engraved, a tool made of a special material, or with a unique form, I'll charge them full price. Though those requests only come once or twice a year."

The strongbox stood in stark contrast to the rest of the shop. It was disorganized and messy, with more than a few necklaces being tangled together. She found another smaller box inside as she looked at the bottom. It was flat on all sides, and its colors blended into its surroundings. Lunarias picked it up and opened it before the blacksmith could protest.

What met her eyes was far different from everything inside the box. It was a tiara made of a blue metal far too recognizable to the knights. Several emeralds were embedded in sockets spread across its surface. It was beautiful, but Lunarias could only focus on the metal.

"Abyssal steel?" She uttered. The metal was not only scarce, it was practically impossible to purchase. The Aurillian kingdom never found a way to extract it; the metal in circulation all came from the Abyss.

"Where have you gotten this from?" *And how did you even forge this?* Lunarias wanted to ask, but she already knew the answer to the latter. Nobody could forge Abyssal steel. It was impossible to heat it up, no matter how hot your coals were. This was the first thing they learned during training.

Only relics of the war were in circulation. If someone was in possession of a weapon made of Abyssal steel, the knights had orders to arrest the person on the spot under suspicion of being an Abyssal in disguise. On the same note, all weapons of Abyssal steel had to be turned in to the knights. Baubles and trinkets, on the other hand, did not have the same negative connotations. The nobles liked to wear them as a symbol of power, as if to show that their knights had ventured deep into the Abyss and had found treasures, even though, for the most part, they were bought under the table from those of ill repute.

Knowing this, Lunarias wondered how a blacksmith possessed such a treasure.

"Oh...I apprenticed under the smiths of a duke many years ago. Sadly, his wife passed during my apprenticeship, and he blamed this tiara. He gave me the task of destroying the thing. If I failed, my apprenticeship was done then and there." Astolphos scratched the back of his head in shame. "I knew it was an impossible task, so I just hid the tiara and told him the job was done. What other choice did I have?"

His answer was quick and sincere. She was sure he was not lying; he had just confessed to a crime in front of a knight, after all. But she could sympathize with the man. He was given an impossible assignment. As they stood there, looking uncomfortably at each other, Astolphos' face contorted as if he just realized something before it quickly turned into una-dulterated horror.

"By the gi...king. I've forgotten the!" Astolphos was already out of the shop before ending his sentence.

Boar, Lunarias finished. She, too, realized what he meant. While they were leisurely chatting the time away, the boar still roasted. She followed him close behind.

*****

"Sorry about that." Astolphos said as he spun the spit, "The thought of this catching fire is just too much to bear."

The boar's skin had charred on the backside, but a few scrapings with a knife would take care of the worst. Besides that, it still roasted nicely, though its appearance had turned somewhat monstrous. Astolphos had only gutted and removed its hide before throwing it on the spit, so its head was still attached, and the heat had not been kind to its visage. Its ears were black and charred, its eyes boiled away long ago, and its mouth was open with a long metal pole poking out. Lunarias could easily imagine such a creature's effect on the children. Their screams and cries from the moment they saw it was vivid in her mind. To some extent, it even looked like an Abyssal of some sort.

"Is it alright to test the blade on flesh?" Lunarias asked; she had to do something about it.

"As long as you're talking about the pig, I've got no problem. Just be sure to keep the blade out of the center of the heat. Though I've only flared the forge somewhat, it can still mess with the temper if you're not careful."

She drew the sword and pointed it at the pig with the intent of decapitation. She took her usual combat stance, feet evenly spaced, one farther forward than the other. Her knees bent slightly, a solid grip on the hilt with both hands clamped as tightly as possible and the tip of her sword pointing directly outward. Her eyes followed her target intently as the neck slowly spun around its axis.

With a single, clean cut, the blade sliced through flesh and tendon at equal measure until the sharp tune of metal against metal rang in the air.

Astolphos immediately grabbed his hair as he stared at the blade; it had hit the spit with full force. She hurriedly pulled the blade out of its fleshy prison, expecting to see a dent or a missing chip. Contrary to her expectations, the edge was unscathed.

"Sorry, but the blade is undamaged!" Lunarias said to ensure the blacksmith.

"I'm not worried about the blade. I thought for a second you'd snap the spit and send the meat into the flames!"

Astolphos drew a knife and cut loose the remainder with an extended, circular cut to inspect the spit.

"Everything looks okay." Astolphos exhaled, relieved at the revelation. He did not look at the sword. Either he did not care what happened, or he had complete confidence in his work. Just to be sure, Lunarias examined the blade once again. There was no chip, crack, or dent; It was pristine.

"It's incredible," Lunarias said. "It surely cannot be steel."

"But it is, with something extra mixed in. Gives it one hell of a hardness, enough to eliminate all need for flexibility."

"And you learned this trade from smiths hired by the barony? They're more extraordinary than I thought."

"And a bit by traveling after my apprenticeship. You learn a lot when on the road."

Before she had the opportunity to ask further questions, the laughter and screams of children took her attention. The two nuns, two knights, and one and a half dozen children made their way directly to the porch of Astolphos' shop. At least the nuns and knights were; the children went rampant on the plains around the smithy. The sisters stopped a distance away as the knights approached them.

"Knight Hewris of the second order. The sisters informed us you wanted to talk. We're leaving today for another assignment, so is there a place we can talk in private?"

Before Lunarias got a word in, the knights turned their attention to Astolphos.

"Could you lend us your shop for a while, blacksmith?" The knight asked. Though it was phrased as a question, it was painfully obvious there was no choice. Astolphos looked uncomfortable, maybe even a bit nervous.

"It's free for you to use," Astolphos said calmly.

No time was given for her to interject before the knights went past her. She clicked her tongue in frustration. Her fellow knights always treated her that way, ignoring her and her commands. Judging by their leather armor, they were of the third order at most. She is their superior in experience and rank, but they would always treat her like they were higher in rank. Many years of this treatment had taught her how to ignore it. It was just another inconvenience on a truly long list. All because they saw her as a detriment.

Still, she needed their help. Asking for help would only further damage her reputation, but just this once, the damage was justified.

"Please excuse me," Lunarias said, "My colleagues are calling for me. I entrust the children to your care." But as she passed Astolphos, she whispered: "They'll stay away from the strongbox."

Chapter 6

The knights looked impatient. They seemed to look even less forward to this than Lunarias. Nevertheless, they knew the protocol and waited for their superior to initiate. She took her time, first looking at them to estimate their experience. Their armor was almost pristine, and their lax demeanor told her all she had to know; they were practically fresh out of training. Judging by the dignified look in their eyes, they were most likely of noble upbringing. Inexperience combined with arrogance; it was the worst combination to deal with.

"No need to salute, third order," She said to point out their unknightly attitude, "This is an informal meeting."

"Apologies, but we want it to be formal and on the record. We were told by the clergy you had a request." One of them said.

Lunarias sighed. Interacting with other knights was as infuriating as always, "Fine. As your superior, I demand all the Merias you can spare. You will leave yourselves with enough for the travel home but only enough for the cheapest inns."

The color drained from their faces. As she thought, noblemen by heart. Just thinking of not dining at the fanciest inns must be a nightmare for those city snobs. Looking at them, she tried to remember how she had acted when she was in their shoes. Had she been just like them?

"May we inquire why?"

"We were robbed on the way here. We lost the funds meant to repair the Church and feed the kids."

"Could you not have defended them against simple robbers?"

"My sword broke during the battle. We had no other choice." She omitted the part where the clergymen unwound the bag. She knew there was a higher chance of them accepting the order if she was at fault, but if they knew it was the Church's fault, the knights were not obligated to help. She intentionally tarnished her reputation, but it was for the greater good.

The knights whispered to each other, just quiet enough for Lunarias not to understand them. She knew they had money to spare; the question was whether they were honest.

"We only have 100 Merias to spare. Will this be sufficient for the time being?" They said once their convening was over.

"More than enough," Lunarias said, "Could you also send a request for funds on my behalf to Captain Gallados? It'll keep us afloat for a while, but it's not enough to start the repairs."

"Of course. We have to return to the capital with the envoy. We'll relay your situation to the commander, but we'll keep this exchange between us. We'd like a personal note, so we can get the amount from your household."

Lunarias could not hold back her sigh of relief. Though they acted roughly, they were much better than some of the knights she was used to.

She was already half done writing her letter, permitting the carriers to withdraw 100 Merias from the Hewris treasury when one peculiar detail struck her.

"A diplomatic envoy? Here?" Lunarias asked.

"We're wondering about that too. Someone close to the queen had a task here, and we escorted him along with the children."

As if his mention was a cue to enter, the door opened.

In came a stubby man, almost as wide as he was tall. His clothes were of high quality and made of green fabric, a sign of a nobleman's high status. A signet ring hung on his finger, showing the queen's seal with pride. The man before her was either close to the queen or a royal family member himself.

No matter his rank, just wearing those green clothes indicated a much higher rank than what Lunarias could receive in her lifetime. She saluted the stubby man, who just waved dismissively at her.

"Knight of the second order, I am here to find a person on behalf of the queen. I would like your help locating him."

Chapter 7

Keeping the children in line while ensuring the boar did not catch fire was just as tricky as Astolphos had thought. The children were unruly, messy, and brought chaos where order had reigned for so many years. The nuns tried their best to calm the rascals but failed, albeit with more grace than the blacksmith.

"Please, get away," Astolphos said, "You're going to hurt yourself if you go any closer!" One of the kids tried to touch the forge, but one of the nuns dragged him away before his fingers touched the hot stones.

"Listen to the man, little one." She flashed Astolphos an apologetic smile before dragging the kid away, a smile he could only return with superficial kindness. He knew they could not see his powers from the second Lunarias entered the shop without intending to kill him. If they could sense him, they would have known the second they set foot in the city square. They would have known where he was, who he was, and where his allegiances lay many years ago. Because of this, Astolphos liked to keep a distance from clergymen. The only reason he invited them was to spend time with Lunarias.

The kids kept the clergymen preoccupied for a while, but conversing with the nuns was unavoidable once they were all served and sitting relatively quietly. As one of them ap-proached him, he felt his day had just worsened.

"Thank you for all of your help," The nun said, "We wouldn't know what to do if you hadn't come to our rescue."

"But you would probably think of something. Taking everything into consideration, you're pretty lucky. Everyone in this little village will help as long as you ask."

"We'll keep that in mind. It may be some time before we can pay for the help, though."

"It wouldn't be help if they required recompense. Just try not to convert them while asking." As the words came out of his mouth, Astolphos realized he had initiated what he wanted to avoid.

"Are they not believers, then?"

"They're believers, alright, but not of the Ancestors." Astolphos walked to the end of his porch, enjoying the sunset.

"It's an old village," Astolphos said, "Their religion is far older than the war against the Abyss. They returned to the old ways once Aurillia reclaimed the land."

"Is that why the church is in such a condition?"

"Not exactly. I've been told it has never been a church of the Ancestors. First, it was a cloister for some harvest god, where bundles of wheat were given for another year of bountiful harvests. Then the Abyssals took the area and converted the cloister shortly after." Astolphos gave her a smile of dual meaning. It would look kind and compassionate for her, but he smiled with gloat. The church had never been for the Ancestors of the kings and queens. At one point, the Gifted even prayed in there. Those clergymen had to live there whether they liked it or not. He could not wish for anything better than that.

The nun took a step back in disbelief. "But...But the altar!"

"Was probably too wrecked for you to see effigies of the Abyss. I can assure you. Your religion has never been prayed for here."

He enjoyed this. He enjoyed telling her the truth about where they were going to live. Judging by her face, she would much rather have lived in ignorance.

"But we were told it was an old church of the Ancestors."

"It happens more often than you'd think. To most people, a building's a building. What happened there decades ago matters no more. Usually, the villagers kept silent since it ensured peace. I just wanted you to know the truth."

She remained silent for a moment, frozen in place. "Thank you," She finally said, but it was apparent she did not mean it.

"Not that it matters too much," Astolphos said, "When the villagers came back and began praying to that harvest god again, they tried to rebuild the old monastery, but it was in too bad a condition, so they just left it to crumble instead. I think the children will love the harvest festival when that comes around. Maybe one of them would be selected to sleep in the barn."

"You are very knowledgeable for a smith," The nun said, "Have you served one of the noble houses?"

"I'm the son of a scribe. One of his employers was a traveling scholar. I trained to take over once my father got old, so he brought me there to be taught. My habits dictate that I have to know the history of the places I visit," Astolphos lied.

"Sounds like you would've done well if you stayed on that path."

"Maybe, but we may never know."

Finally content, she left him once some of the kids became restless. Astolphos sighed in relief. He hated the clergy but had to get used to them now. They all had to live in this village together until the time came to travel back to Marados once again. It may still be a few decades before then, so he had to stay consistent and inconspicuous.

Lunarias and the knights finally left his shop, along with the noble who had forced himself inside before. They were all on the way to him, clearly indicating something was wrong. Judging by the nobleman in tow, it was much worse than he first imagined.

"You must be Astolphos Auriolis," The nobleman said, extending a reluctant hand to Astolphos. This was indeed worse than Astolphos had imagined. This man knew. Just as reluctantly, Astolphos shook his hand while looking nervously at Lunarias. It looked like she had yet to be told the truth.

"That's me. What's yours?"

"For my protection, I'll stay anonymous. For all intents and purposes, you can call me Monty."

"Alright... Monty. What business does a nobleman such as you have with this humble blacksmith?"

"I'm not here to meet a blacksmith. I am here to meet Astolphos Auriolis on behalf of the king, Regios the Seventeenth."

The purpose was all clear now; an old debt had come to be settled, one he had happily forgotten for the better part of his life.

"Your excellence," Astolphos said, "Forgive me, but I don't understand. What can the ruling power of this kingdom have of business with a blacksmith in the fringes?" He had become accustomed to lying during his lifetime. They could not discern the lies from the truth by looking at him. As long as he did not botch some of the common facts.

He apparently did botch the facts. Lunarias and the knights looked at him in disbelief, and Astolphos knew immediately his fate was sealed. The nobleman's smile said it all; it had been a trap. Had he really forgotten who ruled Aurillia at the moment?

"Regios has been dead for over five decades," Lunarias said, stunned, "How can you possibly think he's still reigning?"

Astolphos tried to laugh it off. "Oh, you know... I have been out here for a long time. I was never going to meet him and only talking to the lowest of noblemen at most. With all the history lessons, I must've mixed it up." But he knew his laughter fooled no one. Lunarias looked at him wearily. All the while, the nobleman sighed with impatience.

"Astolphos," The nobleman said, "I know everything, so please stop this charade immediately. Else I have no other choice than to be more direct."

Monty threatened to break the age-old treaty, though Astolphos already broke it by playing dumb. The nobleman must surely know who was the most powerful of the two. With a snap of the fingers, Astolphos could solve everything, but he swore to never use his powers on humans again unless absolutely necessary, not just to the king, but to himself too.

"Sorry," Astolphos said, "I don't know what you're talking about."

"Then let me be blunt. I have come on behalf of Queen Keiris the twenty-seventh to redeem the favor you owe the late King Regios the thirteenth."

"What's he talking about?" Lunarias asked, stepping back as her hand slowly moved to the hilt of her sword, the sword Astolphos had made out of his last batch of Abyssal steel.

"Dear lady Hewris. I'm talking about an old treaty made between the king and The Master of the Abyssal Forge, the personal quartermaster and armorer of the Abyssal King himself, Astolphos Auriolis."

The nobleman did it. He spoke of Astolphos' old title, airing it to everyone like it was simple tavern gossip.

Everything became silent. Even the kids stopped playing once the dreaded word was mentioned: Abyssal. The nuns, who had just been smiling at him for his hospitality, covered their mouths in shock as their eyes looked at him like he was some kind of monster. But what hurt the most was Lunarias' reaction.

She drew her sword and slid to the side in one fluid motion, blocking his way to the kids. Her eyes turned dark as she looked at a monster, something she trained her entire life to defeat, someone she still did not know she was related to by blood.

Seeing his own family draw their weapons against him with their intent clearly shown hit him worse than any blade.

With a voice hard and cold, Lunarias said, "Have you done anything to the children?"

No matter what he answered, he knew she would strike the moment his mouth opened. He would never get to say a word.

"Knight, control yourself!" Monty demanded, "The Master of the Abyssal Forge cannot hurt anyone as per the treaty with the king. Using his power under any circumstance, except for a few particular cases, will accompany his execution. And your attacks can't hurt him either."

Lunarias did not lessen her grip. If anything, she strengthened it.

"I vowed to slay any Abyssals," she said, "be it inside or outside our borders. I will carry out my sworn duty!"

"Killing a partner of the throne is a capital offense!" The nobleman said, "If you do not step down now, you will be charged with treason."

At the mention of the harshest of offenses, her stern expression lessened, and she lowered her blade with a sneer.

"What purpose has the queen for his kind?" Lunarias spat at Astolphos' feet.

"I don't know," Monty said. "But I know you'll accompany him to the capital."

"I'm what!?"

"As decreed by the queen herself, Lunarias Hewris is to accompany the Master of the Abyssal Forge on the journey from wherever he is located to the capital of Aurillia."

Chapter 8

Lunarias kicked the stone walls of the church once again. Yesterday's encounter had left her in a foul mood, not just on her own behalf but also because it affected the sisters and the children.

She had kicked the same wall the entire night as she had repeatedly paced around the room. Her greaves were dented and bent into an uncomfortable form, losing all the protection they had given. Usually, she would ask the local blacksmith to make her a new pair, except he turned out to be a damned Abyssal.

Once they arrived back at the church, the sisters rummaged around the altar, looking frantically for something, and unfortunately, they found it. They had told Lunarias everything the blacksmith had told them, and to their horror, the things they found among a particularly dense pile of rubble only lent more credence to his words.

Once they looked, the clues were everywhere. Effigies, engravings, and inscriptions on the densely moss-covered walls. Their search turned into a larger investigation of the entire building, which furthered a sense of dread for every cleared room.

If she had to point out one good thing about their predicament, it was that the sisters now wanted to get out of the building as quickly as possible. It was the only positive thing she could say because their search only affirmed her fear of the building being ready to collapse.

Lunarias had gotten the worst assignment of them all. She had to escort the enemy to the Aurillian capital, no less by the queen's orders. No matter how much she disliked it, she was forced by oath to carry out her orders, even if it meant living with the enemy. Anything less was treason, but the order still made her so angry that she lay restless for the entire night.

The sisters' frantic search had also kept them up all night. They may have thought living in a fringe village so far away from the Abyss would shield them from the horrors of the enemies. Now it turned out that the enemy had been living here for many years, acting like a wolf in sheep's clothes.

Even if their search proved fruitless and Lunarias was calm enough to sleep, the children would have kept them up all night. They, too, were shaken by the sudden turn of events. Many of them feared for their lives, while the bravest, or perhaps most foolish, asked if they could help drive the monster away.

Losing their parents to the Abyss was the norm where they came from. It was the easiest way to end up without parents; of course, they feared for their lives when such a monster lived nearby.

Just thinking of it made Lunarias kick the wall again, which at this point, was reduced to little more than a pile of rubble. The rivets fastening the steel plates onto the underlying leather creaked and broke, popping the plating plain off and sending it into the wall with a metallic cling. She sighed deeply at the sight. How far on horseback was there to the nearest blacksmith not out to kill all Aurillians? It was at least three days on horseback to Hybrik.

How would she even complete that journey now? The only weapon at her disposal was made by an Abyssal. Who knew what kind of curses roamed inside of it?

"...But what about that festive hall?" One nun asked the other,

"How long do you think we can use it?" They had been discussing where to move the children.

"But the blacksmith has the key. We have to visit that thing again," The other nun said, fear reverberating in her voice. They had not yet seen Lunarias, nor were they aware of being eavesdropped upon.

"What about we ask once the knight and the Abyssal leave the village? Once it's her problem, somebody else can give us the key."

"I have to talk to him today," Lunarias said, irritated at their willingness to leave her with all the tough jobs, "I'll get you the key."

The sisters looked down as they whispered, "Thank you."

"But why do you have to visit it?" They asked.

"It might try to make a run for it. I have to watch it if that's the case." Lunarias sat down beside the sisters. The children were all eating breakfast, but it was quiet compared to the rowdiness she saw through the windows of the smithy yesterday. Most were afraid, afraid of the sudden change of events. Their whispers were barely audible, but those few words she heard all entailed the blacksmith in some way, always with nervous reactions following shortly after.

"Have any of you heard of the Abyssal Forge before?" Lunarias asked the nuns. Such history was their field of expertise. Where Lunarias' training only covered the basest of history, theirs had it as an integral part of their function.

Remembering the horrors so the populace never forgot, that was one of their core assignments as clergymen. They looked at each other as if to confirm something, but their gaze soon parted as their lips followed.

"We've never heard of such a place before, but it carries the title of Master, so it's a very powerful Abyssal."

"What puts it ahead of the rest?" Lunarias asked, "Isn't it just an Abyssal?"

"Master was the title given to those hand-picked by the Abyssal King as commanders. They had powers far surpassing their brethren. Some legends say their powers surpassed those of the Abyssal king."

Their words made it run cold down Lunarias' spine. All knights had heard of the strength of the Abyssal king. How his mere presence on the battlefield was enough to make soldiers drop dead on the spot, how he could manipulate the terrain and bend the elements to his will. Something even close to that level of power was incomprehensible to Lunarias. The most powerful thing she had seen in battle was the occasional fireball, and even more rare, lightning shot from the palms of an Abyssal who still retained a slightly humanoid form.

The blacksmith looked entirely human. She would not have believed the nobleman if not for his reaction when accused. If he had acted surprised or disturbed by the accusation, she might have believed the nobleman had found the wrong person. But Astolphos just sighed in response. That was the same as a confession.

"But how's it even possible?" One of the nuns asked, "Didn't they all die along with the Abyssal King?"

"Apparently not," Lunarias said with a sigh.

"But moving forward," Lunarias said, "I want you two to keep its existence a secret from the village. We needn't aggravate it if it's as strong as you say. It may already be hostile. There's no reason to give it cause to attack."

The color vanished from the faces of the nuns. Lunarias only had a sword to defend them all; who knew how an assault would play out? Actually, she already knew from experience. Its powers were already out of her league if what they said was true. She might get a hit or two before perishing if she was lucky, but killing it was nothing but fantasy. If it fought from a distance, she did not stand a chance.

Something tucked at Lunarias' blouse. Looking to her side, she saw a boy no more than ten years of age. He looked frightened, and his eyes were misty and swollen. With a trembling voice, he asked, "Are we in danger?"

Lunarias had not thought of the children. They had heard her conversation with the nuns. Of course, their talk of how powerful an adversary they were up against unnerved them. Seeing the kid felt like having a bucket of water dumped on the fire inside her. She was angry, but it did not change her obligations or role in their small community.

With as smooth and mild a voice as she could muster, Lunarias said, "I'll protect all of you. It will never even come close to you, I promise." Lunarias flashed the boy a light smile. His mood had improved slightly, but the worry was still all too apparent.

"I'll visit that creature and make sure it's never going to be a threat to any of you," Lunarias said.

"Will you be alright?" The child asked.

"Of course. I'm trained for this." She ruffled his hair, finally getting a little giggle out of him, before leaving the church.

Chapter 9

Many years had passed since the last time Astolphos walked around clad for travel. His clothes were thicker than usual, and they scratched so much he wondered whether it was worth wearing them to uphold his cover. On his back was a backpack filled with the essentials: A bedroll, an extra set of clothes, the decoy phylactery, 2000 Merias in a pouch, several bottles of life essence hidden inside a few waterskins, and Glaucos.

Strapped to his right leg was a dagger for self-defense, another bag with the true phylactery, a telescopic staff with an elemental core on top, and a book of different techniques to accommodate the staff.

The villagers looked at him with the same banal curiosity as they had always done. His getup attracted attention, and they were more than willing to ask where he was going. It felt like any other day, but Astolphos knew nothing would be the same again.

No work was done that night. Astolphos was too busy talking with Glaucos about the new mess he found himself in.

Glaucos was a good listener when push came to shove, not that he had many other options in his current form, but he too found himself stumped by the predicament.

There had always been the risk of the royal family using the treaty for their own purposes, but after 150 years, Astolphos thought everybody had forgotten about it. He was the only one called upon, so Glaucos, Kennas, Nitris, and Heuristys looked to at least have been forgotten. To Astolphos, that was a good thing. That way, they could at least live their lives as they would, had they not joined him so many years ago.

"At least when we're on the road," Glaucos said, "there's a chance you'll discover something that could bring my body back."

One of the few abilities Glaucos still had was telepathy. Without a mouth, it was the only way he could communicate with anyone. Luckily, it also ensured they could talk in public without raising any suspicion.

Once we arrive in Hybrik, we're going to Kennas' workshop as quickly as possible. Maybe she's heard about this from Nitris, Astolphos thought.

"I doubt it. That girl is always busy burying her knives in her targets. She's probably not even been in Hybrik since our last visit."

Maybe, but we have to hope for the best.

"Hope for the best. Prepare for the worst."

Spoken like a true commander, Astolphos chuckled.

Traveling to the Capital would take at least two months on horseback, but Astolphos planned to take his time. If he counted on occasionally setting up shop for a few days when he passed through villages and towns, six months would be a reasonable guess as to the length of the journey. Who knew how long the queen's assignment would take? It might be months, maybe years. That was why he was going to Hybrik, a city a few days north of this village, to commission a carriage. There was a chance he would not return to the village before it was time to move back to Marados, so he planned on packing everything before setting off. He had to pack the entire basement and as much of his inventory as possible.

His carriage needed many hidden compartments, and he only knew one person he could entrust with its construction.

That was Kennas.

Kennas was a Gifted, just like Glaucos and Astolphos. Those of the Gifter's Hands who joined him in his rebellion kept close together but never lived too close as to not arouse suspicion. Kennas made a workshop in Hybrik, where she lived as an ordinary carpenter. It had been 25 years since their arrival and about ten years since Astolphos' last visit.

A long journey awaited if someone searched for a better carpenter than Kennas. Having more than 200 years of experience tended to result in that. Having her make the carriage was almost mandatory, though she may need a slight boost in the form of some extra years to her lifespan before that could happen. Not everybody was as lucky as Astolphos, getting the potential of immortality as part of his Gift. Astolphos, of course, did his best to use his powers to keep his friends alive and had been vastly successful in his endeavors.

"Come on 'Stolfos, it's still not too late to run. Instead of making that carriage, instruct Kennas to keep a low profile and to meet us at the usual spot when the time comes."

Do you want me to leave the timing to Kennas?

Glaucos grew silent for a moment, "Good point."

Besides, we discussed yesterday why we can't just run from this.

It was the core of their discussion last night. Glaucos wanted Astolphos to abandon the treaty and travel to Lumina, but the consequences of such actions were too severe.

If Astolphos ran, the Hewris family would no longer be considered a noble family. Their land would be seized, their titles revoked, and their positions sacked. His family would be back at square one if not even more behind, disgraced and unwanted for their fall from grace. What would happen to Lunarias? The title of knight was one only nobles could acquire. If she was lucky, they would keep her around as a squire, but more likely, they would just boot her out on the street, stripped of her armor, crest, and weapon.

In the end, they never reached an agreement. Glaucos meant they were no longer part of their respective families, so the obligations were no longer his. Astolphos could see his point, their descendants could no longer recognize them, and all of the Hands changed their surnames as part of the treaty. For all purposes, Glaucos was right, but it did not feel right to Astolphos. Deep down, they still had the same blood coursing through their veins.

To Astolphos, running was not an option. Too much ruin would be brought by it.

"What about that girl? Don't she have to know where you're going?"

The less involved she is, the better. We're visiting another Gifted, and having a knight with us would make everybody jittery, even if I could vouch for her.

Glaucos went silent. He probably agreed with what Astolphos said. Who knew what would happen if Lunarias drew her blade at Kennas? She may just swallow Lunarias whole. Worst case, Astolphos had to defend Lunarias against not just one of his own but one of his only remaining comrades-in-arms from back when he messed everything up.

A few villagers approached Astolphos, asking if he was leaving for business. He gave everybody the same answer: he had to buy special materials to make a new sword for the knight. Materials whose price and quality far exceeded what the merchants usually brought him on their passing-by's. It was only half a lie; he would look for some high-quality steel for a project, but the main objective was still the carriage.

Almost as soon as the staples were in sight, he heard the clanking of armor and the slight panting of a woman behind him.

"Where in the name of the ancestors are you going!?" Lunarias yelled.

"Looks like we stepped in shite, buddy," Glaucos said from the bottom of the backpack.

"I'm going to the next city to commission a carriage," Astolphos said, "Once it's done, we're ready to leave for the capital."

Astolphos pulled the backpack off and put it on the ground hard.

"Ouch, watch what you're doing," Glaucos said, "Are you trying to crack me all the way!?"

Shut it!

Lunarias did not look amused nor in any way to believe him. From her perspective, it probably looked like he was skipping town.

Who could blame her? Here he stood in front of the stables, clad for travel with a backpack filled to the brim. Frankly, everything but that conclusion was strange.

"It's going to be a long trip," Astolphos said, "We'll need shelter and a way to earn a living. I know someone who can make a carriage that fills both roles. I'll be back in a week, and we should be ready to begin the journey."

"Do you really think I'll leave you alone? You might as well just be skipping town to avoid this mess."

"Trust me, the thought sounded appealing at first."

Lunarias looked angry at his nonchalant answer. Her hand reached for her blade, but Astolphos raised his hands and stepped back. The scene had piqued the villagers' interest, who looked on in anticipation and wonder.

"But I have things on the line here too. I just have some preparations to take care of," Astolphos said before yelling to all the onlookers, "Don't you all have something else to take care of!? Back to business, nothing serious here."

Once the onlookers realized they were caught, they quickly looked away and mingled among themselves.

"Now," Astolphos said, "Could you please stay your hand. If you draw your blade, this may end very badly for everyone." His message came clean across. Lunarias' hand fell from the hilt, and she approached him in quick steps instead. This was the time he realized how damaged her greaves were.

"What have you done to your boots? There's no way to repair that."

"Don't mind it. Now, you said you're not running away?"

"I'm not! I'm just traveling to Hybrik to meet a friend who's a carpenter. Kennas can make the carriage we need in about two weeks. I just have to go there with some Merias to pay the commission and to buy some horses, and I'll be on my way back."

"We'll be on our way back."

Astolphos took another step back and looked at Lunarias in astonishment as she passed him on her way to the stabler.

"Excuse me, we?"

"I've got an order, and I'll follow it to the letter. I'll not leave you out of my sight."

"That's a problem," Glaucos chimed in. "Let's just hope Kennas has eaten as of late."

Astolphos kicked his backpack, which did not go unnoticed by Lunarias, but she did not remark on it.

"No reason to argue," Astolphos said, "Besides, the road quickly becomes lonely without a good conversation partner."

"Thanks for that," Glaucos said.

Shut it. She doesn't know you exist.

"Don't give yourself more credit than you deserve," Lunarias scoffed, "If it was up to me, you'd be dead already. I'll escort you as my duty dictates, but nothing else."

"Deal," Astolphos said with a smile, "By the way, we're taking your horses. They're faster than whatever else in there."

Lunarias sighed. "Fine."

Chapter 10

Night had arrived. Astolphos had forgotten how uncomfortable it was to ride for hours on end. His back ached, and the thorough beating his bottom received reminded him of the mandatory drills back when he was in the army of the Gifter.

Lunarias, on the other hand, looked to be a seasoned rider. She was busy making a bonfire while Astolphos could do nothing but lie on the ground, exhausted.

"You've been riding on horseback for two weeks straight and now this," Astolphos said, "How are you even able to move?"

No response from Lunarias. She mainly kept silent since they left the village, only occasionally asking for the general direction. The most vocal she had been since they left was mere minutes before they stopped riding for the day. Their place to stop was at the roadside surrounded by dense forest.

Only a small part of the forest was cleared for a gravel road, just for the road and a few meters to each side. They could barely camp there before either meeting the road or the dense foliage, but they made do. Other humans had camped there before them, evidenced by a burned patch of grass and a tree trunk Lunarias used as a bench.

Lunarias wanted to continue riding through the night, but Astolphos and the horses needed a break. Both horses fell to the side, exhausted once their saddles were off, with so little movement following that Astolphos checked their life essence out of fear of them being dead.

"I think you're wasting your time, 'Stolfos," Glaucos said, "Looks like she's pissed to a point beyond our understanding."

Might be true, but I still have to try. It's going to be a long journey ahead if it's in silence.

"Aye to that, but I don't think now's the time to break the ice. Try once we've arrived in Hybrik. Maybe everything will be better then."

We can only hope. Astolphos sighed. At least he still had Glaucos.

After lying on the ground for a while, he finally felt like he could sit straight with only mild discomfort. What he saw was Lunarias busily making dinner. He was about to tell her only to make food for herself before realizing that the portion she prepared was only large enough for her. It hurt Astolphos' feelings seeing her ignore him, but instead of remarking on it, he began reading through his book.

"Don't think about it," Glaucos said, "It's been a long time since we were in Hybrik. Ten years, right?"

That's about right. Last time, Heuristys was also visiting. That was a fun time.

"It indeed was. Remember how drunk he got? He was bragging so much about that big sale he'd made, only to drink up all his profits by giving rounds to the entire bar."

Astolphos snickered at the memory. *That was a good time.*

"And remember the day after? He passed out at the bar, and we had to carry him back to Kennas' shop. We had the bright idea of Kennas transforming into a hog and snuggle with him. Remember the scream he made when he woke?"

Astolphos laughed, drawing a strange look from Lunarias.

"Sorry," Astolphos said, "It's just a good book."

Lunarias shook her head and breathed an irritated sigh before returning to her cooking.

"You think she has any idea of my existence?" Glaucos asked.

Probably not. Does she even know of the existence of your type of Gifted?

"Good point. There aren't many of us left; if she had, she would not be sitting here now. Enough of that. Why're you reading through that old book? You think you'll need it?"

Hopefully not, but it never hurts to be prepared.

The book Astolphos read was one he had written. It was almost as old as himself, and constant mending was required throughout the years for it not to crumble.

The book was tattered and worn. When he had purchased it in the capital of the Gifter's kingdom, it was the most immaculate notebook money could buy. The gold-inlaid markings on the leather cover was worn away, and in some places, the leather was as thin as the paper it was to protect. The pages were yellowed, and the ink faded. Some pages were in worse condition than others, but it was overall still readable. The writing was intelligible for all but the most educated of Aurillians, and even to them, it would be unusable. The book explained how to use the staff in Astolphos' possession to its utmost potential. How he could direct his Gift to do things normally impossible. One such technique was how to transfer life essence from one being to another, provided they were of the same species, but that one did not require the staff. Another was how he could channel life essence into crystal and then cover a large area with it, or use it as a projectile against an adversary, a technique he had used far too often for his taste.

Other techniques required something more than just the staff and life essence. They may require certain incantations or materials. Some even needed a powerful elemental core to be on the staff.

In summary, that book was his self-defense. The dagger was only for show; the enemy would never come close enough as long as he had both the book and the staff, and in most cases, even without those.

Hours passed. Astolphos was busy reading through his book, refreshing on things he, for the most part, was unwilling to use. Lunarias swayed. It was apparent she was forcing herself to stay awake. Her eyes flickered constantly, and a few times, she nodded off before adjusting herself upright with a start.

Astolphos could not help himself chuckle at the sight. Humans still needed sleep. It was an instinct of self-preservation, one he had forgotten the feeling of through his many years.

She was diligent; he had to give her that. Diligence was just not enough when nature and instinct came into the picture, especially once someone could exert force over such systems.

Glaucos, she needs sleep. Could you please give her the final nudge?

"No problem, just a second."

Astolphos felt Glaucos use his Gift of control. Why a Gifted of the elemental type had the powers of telepathy was a thing even the Gifter wondered about. One thing was for sure, it had benefited Glaucos substantially since his uniqueness was part of why he was given his position of Warmaster.

Once Glaucos had established a connection, it was only a matter of seconds before the effects became visible. In this case, the result was instantaneous. Lunarias' eyelids closed, and she swayed. With a small gesture, Astolphos used his Gift to move his bedroll to where her head would land.

"Was that really okay to do?" Glaucos asked out loud.

"Compared to us old fools, she's just a child. Bedtime had arrived, so we just gave her the final nudge," Astolphos chuckled.

Chapter 11

The smoke from the chimneys of Hybrik appeared through the trees, and Lunarias exhaled in relief at a journey completed, only to realize she had been celebrating all too soon. They had yet to reach the capital. In fact, they were not even on their way there yet.

The four days of travel felt like an eternity. The Abyssal used as much time as possible to make her talk. At the same time, she had done her best to keep enough distance between their horses to make conversation impossible.

Complete silence was impossible, the Abyssal was simply too talkative, and it just grew worse the longer she ignored it. Being so close to your enemy without being able to strike against it had kept Lunarias in a perpetual state of paranoia. Her sword had not left her side since the village, and she was vigilant of her surroundings in case of an ambush.

While on the road, she realized a few strange things about her forced companion. It did not eat, though it had asked if it should cook for them both. Lunarias always made her food herself, and in return, Astolphos sat and read in that old book he always returned to.

Their target had finally come into view, and the city walls were finally visible in the last rays of sunlight. Just like their small nameless village, this one was situated at the cliff towards the ocean, but where the cliff edge was a steep drop in the village, Hybrik had a thick layer of scaffolding going the entire length down to the sea. Even from a distance, it was clear that many people were milling about on the countless layers connecting the city above with a large port at the ocean. The layers were lit up by the homes on them, where the workers' families were probably making dinner. If not for her duty, Lunarias might have stopped to admire the unique sight, but now she just wanted to move on.

"Hybrik sure is a weird city," Astolphos said, "Just 20 years ago, it didn't even exist. Now, thanks to trade with Ronasm, Meridia, and Chademokai, it's a bustling trading hub. Isn't it the largest of the port cities too?"

He had hit the nail on the head. Though being the largest port city in Aurillia was not that big of an achievement, considering there were only five in total, the sheer growth this city had experienced was extraordinary.

"Could we please move on?" Lunarias asked once it was apparent that Astolphos would be taking in the sight for a while.

"Look," Astolphos said, "none of us likes this mess, so how about we try to get the best out of it?"

"Be quick. The sooner you complete your business, the sooner we can end this."

Finally, it mounted his horse again, and they were on their way. The sun vanished during the last hours it took to reach the gates. The gate was lit by a single torch with a guard standing in its light, yawning as if to signal just how uneventful his shift had been. His boredom had apparently been so great he jumped as he saw the two travelers approaching.

"Who goes there?" He yelled, straightening his posture as he grabbed a tighter grip on his spear. Lunarias wanted to sigh at the sight. Obviously, the man in front of her had never seen any combat. His chain mail was whole, but the large splotches of rust speckled the iron. Though he had a semi-good grip on his spear, all chance of him using it efficiently went out the window once he stepped forward without lifting the spear, letting it point towards them with the shaft lazily planted in the ground behind him. As she looked closer, she saw the spearhead was bent and chipped. If he had to use it, it would do him little good.

"Knight Lunarias Hewris of the second order asks for permission to enter," She yelled before entering the light.

"Permission granted, but who's your traveling partner?"

"Astolphos Auriolis, blacksmith. I'm here to order the construction of a carriage."

"Anything to declare." The guard asked.

"None at all. I have nothing to sell, and all my gold is for spending inside the walls."

"Then you may pass at the usual rate of 7 Merias, for you and the horse."

As soon as the blacksmith had paid its rate, the guard showed exactly how his spear had fallen into such disrepair. He extended the spear as far upward as possible before knocking it against the stones around the door. You could hear the sound of metal against rock and see the sparks the impact created.

If that was their sign to open the gates, not only was it easy for the enemy to mimic, it even made sure the citizens were less protected by the guards, the city's only defense. What would they do when the Abyssals came knocking?

The blacksmith nodded at the guard as it passed, but Lunarias did her best to ride past him without giving him any attention.

The town was still lively when they arrived at the market square. The workers sat at the bars and inns, talking loudly as they imbibed one tankard after another. Once the bars were in sight, she wanted to get a drink if she had to continue listening to Astolphos' rambling.

They found a table at one of the bars in the circumference of a circular marketplace. It was one of the cheaper ones, the tables were old and sticky, and the clientele could mainly be described the same way. More than once did their presence at the table catch the attention of onlookers, who whispered among themselves.

"Sounds like they're talking about you, Lunarias. Though I must say their words mostly border at the obscene, I can understand someone like yourself drawing their attention."

"It's knight Hewris to you, and what do you mean exactly?" Lunarias said, irritated by the many stares. The comments of an Abyssal was the last drop as she brought down the contents of her tankard of ale.

"As I can understand between their obscenities, women in your employ are quite rare. Their fascination is, from my perception, far from unfounded."

"And what're they talking about in their obscenities?"

Astolphos grew silent momentarily, only to slowly mutter, "I would rather say that aloud in public."

She glared at the men, and their eyes diverted as their conversation faded.

"Maybe you should think about covering your armor," Astolphos said, "it draws their attention."

"As a knight of Aurillia, the armor symbolizes our oath and duty. Covering it up is off the table."

Astolphos sighed. "Then tomorrow's going to be a fun day. I can already see you and Kennas will not get along."

"Is she like you?"

Astolphos looked taken aback by the question but slowly answered in a cautious tone. "Partly, she's a bit more on the laid-back side and much more of a family person than I."

"That's not what I asked."

"...No, I met her at a bar here once. If I remember correctly..."

Lunarias interrupted, "Is this going to lead to our current case, or are you just rambling again?"

Lunari..." Lunarias glared, "Mrs. Hewris, we'll probably be here for the next two weeks. It will feel much longer than that if you won't talk to me."

"We have nothing of import to talk about. It'd be appreciated if you'd limit your speech to only when absolutely necessary."

Astolphos sighed, "I'm going to play some cards over there." Before Lunarias could say a word, Astolphos was already off the chair.

"Come back here!" She ordered, only to see Astolphos wave goodbye to her without a word.

She sighed deeply; why did she have to get the bad assignments? She had thought her main priority would be to keep it from escaping, but it had not tried yet. During the first few days, she tried her best to stay awake to keep an eye on it, but she was no match to the apparently sleepless target she had been given. If it wanted, it could just have run once her eyelids had grown too heavy, but the Abyssal was still there when she awoke.

His incessant talking made her duty demanding, or more specifically, the doctrine of never conversing with the enemy. She had heard the stories of the Abyssals whose mere words could enchant even the strongest soldiers, but its powers did not seem to be that.

Then the question was, what were its powers? Was it offensive? And if so, how powerful was it?

Before the day of their travels, she had never heard of an Abyssal with the title of Master, but according to the sisters, it was incredibly powerful. Maybe the local church here in Hybrik knew more? If so, she had the next two weeks to visit and ask the attendants.

From her table, she could see the table at which the Abyssal played, laughing out loud and cheering at the other players as well as himself. It was the life of the party. Just a shame it was also the enemy of their country and a creature that could potentially kill them all.

She raised her tankard to ask for another ale. She had to be at least a little bit tipsy to endure a night with his, no, *its* incessant blabbering. Though it was for the mission, she may regret how she insisted on sharing a room with the Abyssal. She had to ensure it did not flee, but now she thought the chance of that happening was close to zero. After those first two days of trying to stay awake, she had given up on the notion. She just slept through the night like she usually would. Even though it gave the Abyssal ample opportunity to escape, it just sat in the same place as it did before she went to bed, reading through the same old book.

The more she thought of her choice of accommodation, the more she regretted it.

It took some time for the men from before to find the courage to look at her again. Whether it was the fault of the alcohol or just her patience running out, she rose from her table and sat down at theirs.

"Well, hello there," Lunarias said, "Anything you want to share?"

One of the men looked nervously at the crest on her breastplate, then at her sword.

"Nothing at all, milady," One of them said, "We were just about to leave, right boys?" The man was bald except for three small splotches of red hair and the remains of a poorly-shaven beard. He had a large scar running from his right eye to his bottom lip. His clothes told her his employment was far from honest, clad black as the night and with many folds and crevices to hide weapons and stolen goods. His friends looked none the better. Some lightly moved their hands around as if to hide something underneath the folds.

"Come on, boys, we have work to do tomorrow." As one of the men rose from his seat, the other two followed, and they briskly walked away from the bar.

It was a shame she did not see a glimpse of the valuables underneath. She needed to see the stolen goods before throwing them in the dungeon. There had to be no doubt if she were to apprehend any citizen of Aurillia. It was one of the details that most knights forgot, and a fair amount of innocent blood had been spilled as a result. Even though those guys looked as much like criminals as possible, there was still a slight chance she was wrong, and it was a risk she was unwilling to take.

Her attention shifted back to Astolphos, who seemed to have won a large amount of Merias at the same moment.

"Barkeep, give these lovely fellows another round!" Astolphos yelled. "My treat!" The men cheered at him and raised their tankards as a salute.

Lunarias had to admit, she could see how that Abyssal could live in hiding for so long. It was charismatic and acted kind, doing its best to fit in. Everybody would be suspicious of the recluse who barely talked and spent most of his time inside, but few would suspect the man who casually sits down at a table and orders a round for everyone. Astolphos, too, raised his glass but did it in the direction of Lunarias with a smug smile. It was at that moment she realized her mistake.

By giving that round, he had solidified his position at the table. Removing Astolphos now would make her the most unpopular guest this bar had had for a while, and she knew she could not outlast Astolphos when it came to staying awake. Effectively, it had forced her into a position where her only choice was to leave it at the table.

"That bastard," Lunarias hissed.

Not completely ready to accept defeat, she sat at their table again. Two more tankards went down as she kept an eye on her target. Their looks crossed once or twice, but she had to capitulate in the end.

She had lost count of how much she had imbibed, but the world spun just a little when she saw the bottom of the current tankard. Finally admitting defeat, she stumbled back to their room.

Chapter 12

Part of Astolphos wanted to apologize to Lunarias for what he did last night, but another part thought it was a necessary step. The way she acted around him had the stench of delusional superiority. Astolphos thought letting the children play was acceptable, but they still had to respect their elders, especially if the elder was their "enemy." The gray hair was a sign of having overcome all kinds of adversity to reach that age. It was better to give her a lesson before the same happened to someone who was out to hurt her.

Once the last of the patrons at the card table had left or passed out, Astolphos counted at least 75 Merias of winnings. If he got the time, he would try to distribute his winnings to the poorer districts of Hybrik.

The types he played with were not the kind where their dealings were above board. Some of his earnings may very well have come from the pockets of those who called those poor districts their home. At least he knew some of the winnings were stolen since two of his comrades-in-cards let some tidbits of their shakedown slip once the tankards were stacked high. It also alleviated some of the guilt he felt for cheating his way to their ill-gotten gains. Glaucos' telepathy and a bit of sleight of hand carried them a long way.

Though justice had won at the tables in his eyes, it was not clear if Lunarias felt the same way, hence why he would keep his winnings a secret from her.

The first rays of sunlight passed through the shutters to their room, but she was still sound asleep. She had definitely gotten too much to drink last night. Astolphos sometimes forgot people got drunk from alcohol since his particular Gift made him impervious to its influence. As he thought back, he had probably not been drunk since he was her age.

The streets were peaceful back then. The war against the Gifted led the Aurillian kingdom to forcefully draft soldiers to their ranks. There was no one left to turn to banditry. Everyone was either at the front lines, helping in a profession, like what Astolphos did, or came from a noble family high enough to merit their removal from the draft.

Back then, he enjoyed the freedom of not being sent to the slaughter, spending his days doing minimal work while the nights were filled with brawls and beers. He would never have believed the responsibility he eventually ended up with back then. First, he became one of the regal smiths for the royal family, and later, he got an even higher rank amongst the Gifter's most trusted men.

Astolphos kept an eye on Lunarias the entire night. He saw how much she drank before stumbling back to their room. He had to admit, she fought for longer than he anticipated. Hopefully, she had learned that drinking to stifle boredom at a stakeout was a bad idea.

The streets were bustling with activity before Lunarias woke from her drunken slumber.

"Good morning. Looking forward to a productive day, I presume?" Astolphos said in amusement at her groggy state. Lunarias' eyes quickly found the pitcher of water Astolphos had prepared for her, which contents left almost as soon as it was filled.

For a second, Astolphos thought she would continue staying silent until her eyes caught his, and she angrily huffed at him.

"Look," Astolphos said, "I'm sorry about yesterday, but I just wanted some hours with more lively company."

No response.

Astolphos sighed, "I'll go and bring you some breakfast."

"I have orders not to leave you out of sight." Lunarias motioned to exit her bed, but Astolphos waved her down.

"I've had ample opportunity to flee. Though I don't like my situation, I realize running will only worsen everything. Sit down; I'll return soon."

"After that stunt yesterday, I'll not let you out of my sight," Lunarias said with determination in her voice.

Astolphos sighed once again. Letting the children play was fine, but a line had to be drawn somewhere.

"In your current state, you couldn't do anything against me anyway. If I wanted to hurt anybody, that headache would keep you unfocused. Trust me, you'll not have the same result as last week's duel. Just lie down and let me help."

"Why should I receive help from the enemy?"

"You're not. I lost the right to call myself an Abyssal long ago."

They stared at each other for a while. None of them wanted to back down, but the sudden resurgence of Lunarias' headache forced her head to the pillows.

"Go."

***

Most of the day was gone before Lunarias' hangover subsided enough for them to leave the room, and even then, it was apparent to Astolphos she was not feeling well. But she requested that the show went on, so Astolphos led them to Kennas' workshop.

Kennas liked to take in a lot of apprentices, primarily children who became estranged from their parents, to teach them the craft of carpentry. Her shops were always larger than what Astolphos had, partly because the projects a carpenter worked on were larger than those of a blacksmith, partly because those apprentices required space, contrary to Astolphos' almost hermetic lifestyle. Kennas was also a name well-known by the more civilized Gifted because she used her shop to integrate other Gifted into Aurillian society. Out of the unusually many apprentices working in her workshop, up to three were Gifted who wanted to live a more peaceful life.

The main building was four stories tall, with an enormous single-floor hall stretching from the side. The entire building was made of oak, though the varnish had faded with time in some areas. Above the door hung a sign Astolphos had forged. Written on it was simply "Kennas' Carpentry." Unoriginal, but it conveyed the intended message.

Far gone were they from the rowdy and messy city square and its adjacent markets. The workshop was located deep within the Craftsmen's District, where the sound of yelling and laughing was replaced with the sounds of horseshoes clicking along the cobblestone roads, the sound of metal against metal from the blacksmiths, and the all-encompassing foul stench of the tanneries.

Kennas' shop was right in the middle of the most established shops in the city. 25 years of business was usually far from the oldest in a city, but Hybrik was unique thanks to its astounding growth.

Lunarias did not look impressed by the shop. In the capital, even back when Astolphos lived there, many shops had passed through several generations. There was no way Kennas' place could look magnificent when compared to those shops, which have had hundreds of years to build the most impressive of facades. But when the time came to compare skills, even those old shops would get a run for their money.

Once they entered, an unexpected sight greeted Astolphos. The reception room looked the same as the last time he visited, with its ample counter parting the space in two equal parts. The counter had various pieces of parchment and writing implements strewn across it, with chairs on either side where both the carpenter and the customer could sit and discuss changes in design. The wall behind the counter had some of Kennas' special projects displayed on parchment, along with the official documents from the city and the carpenter's guild saying she had permission to do business.

What shocked him was that he had expected to see Kennas, with her messy red hair and dull brown eyes, standing behind the counter to welcome the new customers. Instead, it was a young lad, at least young enough for his hair not to have a stint of gray. Astolphos recognized him as one of Kennas' apprentices from his last visit, though he could not remember the name.

"Greeting, mister Auriolis. What brings you here?" The apprentice asked. Apparently, forgetting the name was one-sided. How long had it been since his last visit? Seven, maybe ten years?

"You look troubled. Is there anything wrong?" The apprentice asked with a smile.

"I'm just impressed that you can remember me. You must've been just a boy the last time I was here."

The apprentice flashed a smile, but something seemed wrong.

"It isn't every day you meet a man with white hair and no wrinkles. You make quite the impression."

"It just shows that Kennas has done a great job training you. Speaking of her, can you please go get that lazy lout? I'm here to commission a carriage."

He saw something strange in the apprentice's eyes for the tiniest of moments. As the smile turned to sadness, the eyes turned from bright blue to dull disks. It was for but a moment, just enough for Astolphos to even question if it was not his imagination.

"I'm sorry to bring you the news," The apprentice said, "Master Kennas was found dead not far from here last week."

"What!?" Astolphos yelled. He could not believe his ears.

"She was stabbed to death in an alley. Nobody has any idea why. In her will, she gave her shop to me, Ontrys," The apprentice said, making a slight bow.

That was impossible. Astolphos slumped down in a nearby chair in thought. It should not be possible for Kennas to die by simple blades and arrows. From Astolphos' pocket, the heat rose as Glaucos, too, fell into thought.

"Just to be sure," Glaucos said telepathically, "Did you also see Ontrys' eyes change for a moment?"

So that wasn't just me.

"It wasn't. You know what that means."

Yes, we just have to play along.

Astolphos covered his face with his hands to hide it from Lunarias. He could not afford for her to become suspicious, so covering his face, as if to hide his tears, was the only thing he could do.

"I'm very sorry to tell you this so suddenly," Ontrys said, "I never realized the two of you were so close until I saw the will. I understand if you want some days to process it, but she left you something in her will. I could go get it for you if you want."

"No, I'll come with you," Astolphos said, "Ms. Hewris, is it possible for you to wait here for a bit?"

It seemed like Lunarias would protest for a moment, but her hand slumped back to her side as she nodded. "I'll wait here. Just promise to come back when you're ready."

Astolphos gave her an appreciative smile before turning to Ontrys, who pulled up a part of the counter to allow him into the workshop. They turned to the right and entered the main hall. The spacious room was filled with people from children to teens working on making various parts out of wood with a precision that would make any teacher shed tears of joy. The smaller children, seemingly no older than 12, had the assistance of one of the teens. One girl, in particular, smiled from ear to ear at the boy helping her varnish an ornate chair. They went slightly into the shop, just enough so neither the apprentices nor Lunarias was within earshot.

"Want to tell me what's happening here, Kennas?" Astolphos asked, looking into the shop.

"Not here," Ontrys said, nodding towards the stairs leading to the upper floors.

They took the stairs past the two floors the apprentices called home, up to the fourth floor which Kennas had made her room.

It was the absolute top of the building, and as such, the walls were slanted to such a degree that you could barely stand straight a couple of meters from the center. This, of course, would not irritate someone in Kennas' condition. There was hardly anything in there but a bed, a table, and a couple of chairs, but everything was built to last. Anyone but those knowing Kennas' past would find the lack of any wardrobe puzzling, but everything else looked normal.

Kennas had never been the one who needed rituals and magic to thrive. Her powers were more...physical in nature.

"Now that we're alone, sorry for the masquerade, 'Stolfos," Ontrys said with a voice more fitting of a woman. Ontrys' face and body then melted and turned bluish-transparent.

"Kennas, you asshole. Couldn't you have given us a better hint?" Glaucos said, but would probably have yelled if he had a mouth. The puddle turned semi-humanoid before reversing its form back into a human, the body of the Kennas Astolphos knew.

With her red hair in a ponytail and brown eyes, which could not reflect any light whatsoever, she looked just like she did so many years ago. Her chin turned pointy as the last details fell into place, from the round form of her ears to the mole under her right eye.

The clothes did not change that much. It was the same brown pants with a leather apron; the only difference was that the patches on the pants and shirt had vanished.

Astolphos waited for Kennas' form to finalize before going in for a hug. Her slime did not leave the fibers, no matter how much they were scrubbed.

"Sorry about it all," Kennas said, "But things turned ugly last week, and my normal form had to die."

"What happened?" Astolphos sat down at the table and put Glaucos on it.

"Bastard Aurillians happened," Kennas said, but then Glaucos interrupted. "Did the knights figure you out?"

Kennas shook her head, "None of the sorts. Some thieves and other scum decided I was too rich and wanted to do something about it. They approached me one night on my way home from eating out, asking for money for 'protection.'

"Of course, I told them to sod off, which ended up with them cursing at me. The next day, another 'representative' came to see me, in my shop of all places, and gave the same offer at a higher monthly rate."

"Ya' chased him out with an axe, right?" Glaucos asked, laughing.

"You bet on it. I grabbed my axe, and out he ran like he got a bad case of the bowels. A few days later, I found myself in an alley, carrying some saws since I'd just gotten repaired at a blacksmith, fine guy, by the way. The next thing I knew, three guys approached me, faces covered by hoods and scarves. Two from behind, one from the front. Seeing the dagger in his hand, I knew what would happen. That guy told me, 'Let this be a message,' and then stabbed me in the ribs. That's where I 'died,' as far as everyone knows. How can you even deliver a message if you kill the recipient?"

"But what about the apprentice?" Astolphos asked, "I remember he was there on my last visit."

"Ontrys was a good boy. Smart and skilled he was, but I had to do something. That night, after those thugs had seen me 'bleed out' and left me in the alleyway, I returned to the shop and dragged Ontrys up here. I told him someone would do something horrible soon, and I would close the entire shop for good to keep everybody safe. I gave him 1000 Merias and a letter addressed to the carpenter's guild in Goralik, telling them he was ready to open his own business. When I was sure Ontrys had left the city the next day, I took his shape and told everybody Kennas was dead and that the shop was willed to me. Then everything returned to normal, though morale has been low the last few days."

"What a week you've had," Astolphos sighed.

"A week it's definitely been," Kennas said, "but everything's calmed down. As long as I can continue my work, I'm happy with whatever body I have to take. Speaking of work, is it time already? Where's Nitris and Heuristys?"

Astolphos sighed, "It is not time yet, but something has come up, and I have to speed up the schedule."

"The queen has called him to the Capital," Glaucos said.

"The contract, then?" Kennas asked, "That's mighty great of them to remember us after so many years, even more impressive of them to find you. Does that mean I have to come too?"

"Looks like they only remember me. No mention of anyone else, so let's not throw the dice."

"Which explains why you're the only one with a knight attached and why you're here for a carriage."

"Precisely. I think my time here is done, so I might as well pack up now. I need the usual thing, two four-wheeled carriages, one for living and one for working."

"Got it. It'll take a few weeks to get it done. Will you be in town till then?"

"Hopefully, but the knight might have other plans."

"That knight again?" Kennas asked, "Sounds like you've got one hell of a headache. Why don't you just use your gift to lose her? Who does she think she is to boss around the Gifter's right-hand man?"

"Her name is Lunarias Hewris. That should explain every-thing," Glaucos said.

Kennas' mouth went agape before she uttered, "Oh... That's indeed one hell of a headache."

Chapter 13

The walk home from Kennas' workshop was a quiet one. Though Lunarias was fine with the silent version of Astolphos, the reason for the silence left her with a sour taste. His visit to the shop had been long, and Astolphos brought only one thing with him: a dagger of his own making. It was given to him as a memento, which he now carried on his belt.

Letting an Abyssal carry a weapon was something she would never have allowed to happen. Still, considering its sentimental value, it would be far from decent of her to demand him to hand it over.

His silence continued back to their inn, where Astolphos returned to his book as soon as possible. Lunarias sat on her bed, doing her best to spend the time.

It did not go well.

She had previously seen people like this. On her campaigns into the Abyss, she had seen the grief the loss of a dear friend had caused. Even with her mostly loose connection with her fellow knights, she too had felt the sting before, more times than she would like to admit. She never knew what to say to her knights, just like she was speechless at the scene before her.

One thing she knew, the silence was killing her, or more precisely, the lack of Astolphos' attempts at breaking the ice.

Enemy or not, nobody deserved to struggle through the loss of a friend alone. This time, she was the only one around to fulfill the role. Though she still had doubts about his friend, silence at such a time was unacceptable.

"My condolences," Lunarias said. Astolphos closed his book and looked at her with a forced smile.

"Thanks."

"So... Was she a good friend of yours?"

"Very," He unsheathed the dagger and looked at the blade. It was made with the same care as the blade at her side. And just like it, it did not seem to have seen much use, if any.

"Kennas actually lived in the village many years ago. I made this as a gift when she told me about her plans to move to Hybrik. The roads were also safe back then, but traveling without a way to defend yourself was still a huge risk. Luckily, she never had an opportunity to use it. Would it have made any difference if she had carried it that day?"

"Depends on how many assailants there were. If it was just one, perhaps it would. But if there were more, it'll be hard to say."

"That's what I thought, but why would anyone attack her? She had worked in that shop for many years, never bothering anyone. Just why did something like this have to happen?"

"Sometimes people are just unlucky."

His mood seemed to improve momentarily, but silence befell as quickly as it had vanished. Now, Astolphos just stared at the dagger. The blade reflected the candlelight in a blue hue. It was a prime feature of Abyssal steel being present in its metal. The sight of this told her a lot about Astolphos, but it also confirmed her suspicions about his friend.

However, that friend was dead; that much was evident as she saw how the news had affected Astolphos. There was no need to ask further. That could always come later.

Astolphos continued fiddling with the dagger, looking at its features for a while before sheathing it. Something dripped from the ceiling and unto Astolphos' forehead. He tried to wipe it off, but it left a semi-blue residue on his forehead. A few more drops dripped before Astolphos moved his chair.

"Sorry, Mrs. Hewris, I'm not in the mood to eat tonight. I know you're not a fan of it, but could you leave me be for a while to collect my thoughts?"

Inside, she laughed at herself for how softhearted she had become towards this Abyssal. Just yesterday, she would have vehemently disagreed, but now, she thought hard about whether it was the right choice.

"I'll return when the sun has gone down," She said.

"Thank you."

Chapter 14

Though he did not think Lunarias would turn around and return to the room, Astolphos kept track of her life essence until she left the building.

"She's gone. You can come down now," Astolphos said.

The blue liquid suddenly grew from drips to a downpour of Kennas' viscous mass.

Astolphos knew it was Kennas from when the first drop hit his face, and he knew it would take more than a good scrubbing to get the color off his forehead. The wooden ceiling also had light-blue stains from where she passed through, but it was barely noticeable unless one actively looked for it. It took no more than seconds before the slime morphed into the shape of a body. Astolphos felt the slime on his hand move and writhe as it tried to get off his body. It felt uncomfortable, but nothing like what he had to do now would feel like.

He stuck his hand into still-forming Kennas and felt how tens of tiny tentacles picked off the smallest of drops. When he pulled it back, he saw several light blue circles on his hand.

The form changed color as its outer appearance began looking like fabric and human skin. Once the transformation was complete, there was no difference between the feel of the real deal and Kennas' illusion.

"Thanks 'Stolfos," Kennas said, "Sorry to intrude at this hour, but I need to speak to the two of you." She looked distraught.

"Of course," Astolphos said, "Please, sit down." He guided her to the only chair in the room. Kennas' usually cheerful smile was gone and replaced with worry. The dull eyes staring out into nothingness gave her a remote look that sent shivers down his spine.

"So, what's the problem?" Glaucos asked.

It took a few moments before she answered, "Those guys who stabbed me visited the shop after you left. Maybe an hour later."

Astolphos already had an idea of what had happened but kept quiet to let her explain.

"They went up to me and told me straight up they were the ones who stabbed the master a few days ago, right in front of all of my apprentices. They said that the price had now tripled, and if they didn't have the money by the end of the week, it'd end badly for not just me but all the apprentices."

"By the Gifter," Glaucos uttered, "Did they leave alive?"

"I'm not a fighter anymore. I couldn't do anything but keep the rest of the Gifted from pouncing on them and blowing our cover!"

"Oh, forgot about that," Glaucos said.

Astolphos felt rusty and sluggish when he fought Lunarias a few days back, and he trained a few times every month. Kennas had not held a weapon in more than 100 years, so Astolphos had no idea how bad it would be for her.

"I think we grasp the situation," Astolphos said, "and we'll help you no matter what. What're we talking about here?"

She squirmed a bit in the chair before she said, "If possible, I'd like them to leave us alone, but I also don't want them to die."

"That's unexpected from Kennas, The Great Devourer," Glaucos said.

"You know I've put that life behind me," Kennas said, irritated by her old title, "I don't want anyone to die just for me to live, not anymore."

"Even if it means losing your shop and those working there?" Astolphos asked. He knew where Kennas came from, for he felt the same way. Far too much blood was spilled because of them. He did not want anyone else to die so he could live anymore, but the difference between them was that people depended on Kennas. Those apprentices had a livelihood because of her, and nobody but she knew how many Abyssals had gotten a life in Aurillian society through her shops.

If Astolphos died, the only casualties would be himself. Sure, the remaining Masters depended on him to extend their lifespans, but he would leave enough life essence behind for them to live for at least 80 more years.

Kennas stayed silent for a while. It looked like his question was something she had not thought of herself.

"I..." Kennas said, "If I had the choice between killing someone or having one of my apprentices killed because of my inaction, I would raise my blade again, but that's the only reason. Killing them should be the absolute last resort."

"Then you also know how high a chance we have to use that last resort, right?" Glaucos said, "Because, to be honest, I can't see a way or reason to spare their lives."

"Of course, you don't. A peaceful resolution is too hard for the Warmaster!" Kennas snarled. Astolphos was quick to shush her.

"Both of you, calm down," Astolphos said, "Glaucos, there's no reason to talk about the worst as the first. For now, let's sit down and figure out a peaceful way to deal with this."

"That said," Astolphos turned to Kennas, "I can see where Glaucos is coming from. We're talking about bandits who'd kill somebody just because they stood their ground."

Kennas nodded and took a deep breath. Astolphos could only hope nobody heard her outburst.

"Alright," Glaucos said, "What do we know about those bandits.?"

Kennas grew silent.

"Nothing," she said, "I don't know their names, their faces were covered by their clothes, and I've got no idea where they meet."

"And there went the peaceful resolution," Glaucos said, "If we know nothing, then... Hey, what are you doing! Stop that! STOP!"

Astolphos threw Glaucos up in the air and caught him on the way down, only to launch him once again.

"I told you," Astolphos said, "Play nice. Let's at least try before giving up."

In the background, Kennas giggled.

"Alright, alright." Glaucos said, "Just stop this. I'm going to throw up!"

The thought of how a crystal could grow nauseous quickly appeared in Astolphos' mind but was shoved away to focus on the task.

"Have they tormented other business owners?" Astolphos asked.

"I've heard rumors but never seen them before last week. Maybe they've extorted seven other craftsmen the last month or so."

"That's good to know. That means they're operating largely in the city," Glaucos said, "and that they may have a head-quarters somewhere inside the walls."

"But we're still lacking a lot of information," Kennas said, "It'd draw too much attention to just start asking around town."

"Maybe that's exactly what we want," Astolphos said, "If we could just get in contact with one of them, then we can find a way to get the information we want."

"Maybe one of you could pose as an outsider peddling his wares at the marketplace?" Glaucos chimed in.

"That could work," Kennas said, "There's always a few spots for an outsider who'd like to sell their wares. The spots are a bit more expensive, and the organizers are picky about who gets them. You'll have to sell something special or valuable to get one."

"And no offense," Glaucos said, "But you can't call carpentry any of that. Nor blacksmithing, for that matter."

Silence fell over the room as all three thought for some long minutes. Finally, Astolphos got an idea. "There's nothing special or valuable about a blacksmith, but there's something valuable about a goldsmith."

"Good thinking 'Stolfos," Glaucos said.

"But we don't have any gold or jewels," Kennas said, "and I don't have enough unsuspicious capital to buy it."

"You have now." Astolphos threw the bag of Merias to Kennas.

"As long as I can just owe you for the carriage."

Kennas opened the bag and looked shocked at the content. "This's far more than normal. This covers so much more than the carriage!"

"It's also to fully equip it," Astolphos said.

"I may have to pay for half the carriage, but I don't care about that," She said, "As long as my life can return to normal, I'm fine doing that."

Her dull eyes never reflected her feelings, but Astolphos still thought he saw a shimmer in them for the first time.

Chapter 15

Not even a week had passed since she had gotten her new assignment, and she had already begun shirking it. Though Astolphos was grieving, and giving him some time to reflect was what her heart said was for the best, her brain still told her she had to keep him close. She felt silly for it, but some part of her thought that man was plotting something, an idea quickly dispelled by her memory of the grieving blacksmith staring reminiscently at the dagger.

Astolphos and Kennas were friends for a long time, that much she was sure of. The question was for how long. This Kennas was undeniably an Abyssal; the dagger told her that much. Whether it was a relic from the wars against the Abyssals, or Astolphos that made it, played no significant role. The important part was that the dagger had the shine of Abyssal steel, a material that had not been forged since the Abyssal King's demise. There was a high chance that someone carrying the weapon of an Abyssal was an Abyssal themselves.

Then a thought struck her. That apprentice, Ontrys, might have known of the identity of his master. Any sensible person would have disregarded the will and handed the weapon over to the authorities, as long as they knew the nature of the weapon, that is. There was a slim chance that the apprentice had simply not unsheathed the dagger and was oblivious to its importance. It was always possible, but as a knight, she had a duty to investigate it. Conspirators were as harshly punished as the Abyssals themselves.

If not for the clock being as late as it was, she would have returned to the carpenter immediately. She did not know why, but something told her the apprentice would still be there tomorrow and that she had something more important to do.

When she was done eating, the shops owned by the many craftsmen and peddlers began closing. The streets had a few moments of relative silence before they were again flooded with people, hungry for food and company instead of wares.

The place she had chosen to eat was a far cry from the sleazy tavern yesterday. The price reflected that, with one meal here being worth three courses at the other place. It was worth any price to keep a distance from the types she met yesterday. The local guards' job was to take care of the riffraff, but if she met those men again, they were all going to the barracks for a long talk.

Lunarias now had a choice. She could either return to their room at the inn or go to the Church of the Ancestors in Hybrik.

She chose to go to the church.

"Done eating? Or do you want another round?" The innkeeper said as he came to take her plate.

"I'm done. If you don't mind, is there a church nearby?"

"See, take a left over there and continue till you see the shit-brown house that looks ready to fall. From there, take a right, and you should see the church further down."

"Thank you."

The innkeeper took her plate and cup and left without taking any payment.

"Excuse me, how much do I owe for the meal?" Lunarias asked.

"Nothing. It's the least we can do since you're keeping us safe from the Abyssals."

"I must insist. How much?"

"Leave 13. That should cover it."

Lunarias left 20 Merias on the table. She had lost count of how many times she had had to insist on paying for what she ate. Even when they gave her a price, it was usually lower than what they charged other customers. Many would provide food and drink away as an act of gratitude, and most knights would partake without a second thought. Lunarias, on the other hand, meant the citizens deserved money for their services. After all, their jobs were just as important as hers.

The route she was given was relatively straightforward. Walking to the brown house, she saw firsthand the natural line between the normal city and the slums. It was a strange route to send anyone out on. As she walked past, the people around the street huddled together and left for the myriad side streets spread everywhere. Many shot her strange looks that turned to fear once they saw the crest on her breastplate. She heard whispers about a house but did not regard it too much. After all, if she saw or heard anything incriminating, she had to apprehend the person and drag them to the barracks for interrogation. Thus, she would not be able to reach the church this night and would earn the ire of the local guards in one fell swoop. No matter the city, unless knights were specifically requested, it always grew malcontent when a knight did the guards' job. She chalked it up to the guards feeling inadequate when the knights did their job for them.

She finally saw the brown house. It looked dilapidated and ready to collapse. It leaned dangerously to one side, where if you looked straight up when standing under it, it was possible to see the ceiling of the third story. No one stood around the building, probably afraid it could collapse at any minute. Lunarias, too picked up the pace when she passed under it.

It looked like she was leaving the slums when she saw the torches illuminating white stones. The churches of the

Ancestors were mostly made of white or bright facades, be it marble, limestone, or birch wood. It was something that made them easy to spot as long as you knew the general direction of them. Churches were always single-storied, in direct contrast to the monasteries and abbeys spread across the countryside, which were often two stories or taller. It made it hard to find churches when visiting a city for the first time, but for the most part, the citizenry was always happy to give directions.

The churches were open to visitors at any point of the day, but the priests expected a large tithe for their services past sunset. That is, for anyone but the knights. It is always possible for a knight to get a spare room at a church at any point.

Two torches lit the entrance, barely giving off enough light to see the reliefs cut into the doors. A slight glance at the carvings told her everything she needed to know. The priest here came from a family who participated in the siege of the capital of the Abyss. The carvings showed the castle with its barbed spires and crumbling towers, along with a robe-clad figure brandishing a sword at the knights of Aurillia. The gates were down, and out of them ran countless Abyssals, some of them had shapes she barely recognized as living beings.

She pushed the door, and it swung open without a sound. The church's interior felt both familiar and different at the same time. For the most part, if you had seen one Aurillian church, you had seen them all. Their benches, decorations, chandeliers, and confession stands were all made to be identical. The companies who produced interiors for the churches produced nothing but that one thing, and they had to be very picky about not only materials but also the skills of the people who worked on them. If there was one flaw, one inconsistency not excused in a very restrictive set of guidelines, the object would be discarded, and no compensation would be given.

Therefore, all the furniture was uniform across all churches, the same trite benches of darkened oak and the same altars of limestone imported from southern quarries.

There were no windows in the building. It was illuminated solely by a large chandelier encased in an even larger sphere made of myriad different colored shards of glass held together by a metal frame. The colorful illumination gave the church an otherworldly feeling, as if you had left the world you came from and entered one truly out of ordinary comprehension.

It still felt trite and boring to Lunarias because she had seen this environment so many times before. For the villagers who would enter maybe two or three different churches throughout their life, seeing the interior was as exciting and awe-inspiring as the first time they saw it as a child. Travelers, especially those who had to visit churches frequently, became immune to the effect after maybe the tenth or eleventh building, and she had seen many more than that.

The priest was busy dusting off the benches when she entered. It only took a few seconds before he stood before her.

"Greetings, knight. What brings you to the house of the Ancestors?" The priest asked. He was wearing the baby-blue uniform of the church with a copper crown reminiscent of the one worn by the queen.

"The pursuit of knowledge. Could you tell me about the Abyssal Masters?"

"That's an unexpected request. If you don't mind, could you explain why you want to know of a long-gone enemy?"

She had expected such a question. Almost every time a knight asked a priest for historical knowledge, their curiosity had to be sated first. You could deny answering, and the priest would still be obligated to tell you what they knew. It was common courtesy to satisfy their curiosity as long as it was harmless.

"In my previous campaign into the Abyss," Lunarias said, "We killed an Abyssal who talked about a Master. I was just curious about what he was talking about and if it's something I can encounter out there."

"If that's it, I can assure you there's no chance of you meeting a Master. They have all been dead for many years."

"Still, I want to understand why an Abyssal would bring it up as a threat to us."

"This's going to be a long tale. Please take a seat."

The priest led her to the living quarters of the church. The furniture was still made to be identical, but it was still a living area for people, so some things bore the mark of personality on it. Specifically, it was a small dining table and a set of chairs made of bright birch. They were simple, cheap in construction, but sturdy enough to be used for years to come. The room was illuminated by candles without any sphere encapsulating them, so it felt more normal than the ceremony chamber. The priest brought forth a pot of tea which he put over the fire, while he also brought two clay cups to the table.

The priest spoke only when they were both seated, and the tea was served.

"How much do you know about the Masters?" He asked.

"Not much. I know they're Abyssals more powerful than the ilk I'm dealing with."

"That's correct. Legends tell us of powers rivaling the Abyssal King himself. However, that's only a fraction of what a Master truly was.

"Though they've now devolved into nothing but feral animals, Abyssals were once an intelligent group of beings. They had their own civilization with their own lords governing territories. They had laws and rules, and their army was deployed with knowledge and expertise inferior to our royal lineage. If I had to equal the Masters to something inside our society, it would be the nobles closest to the royal family." The priest took a sip of his tea. All the while, Lunarias struggled a bit with comprehending what she had been told. She had met the noble families before. She was part of such a family herself, though one further down the chain than those in question. She had seen their behavior; it was nothing like the blacksmith she had spent the better part of a week with.

"Though I must say," The priest said, "we don't know the specific duties, only that the Abyssal King liked supervising everything himself. We can only guess their duties through the tidbits we've found and heard. We've heard of four Masters through literature and legends passed through generations. The Master of Assassination, the Warmaster, the Master of Law, and the Master of the Royal Guards."

"So they're leaders and administrators? That doesn't sound like capable warriors."

"But they were. There are no records of the Aurillian army ever killing a Master."

"What?" Lunarias looked shocked at the priest. Suddenly, her thoughts wandered to the blacksmith outside. What kind of assignment had she gotten?

"It's true," The priest nodded, "We have records of our army going to war against a Master and facing them head-on, but they were never able to slay it. We even have records of one battle where the Warmaster eradicated a thousand men alone. They were the worst kind of monsters, the kind who both had muscles and knowledge."

"But how could we have won against such power?" Lunarias was painfully aware of the strength of the Aurillian army. If just one of those Masters were capable of such achievements, how could the Aurillian military win the war? Their knowledge must be incomplete. Some facts must have been mixed throughout time.

"According to our recollections, the Masters vanished when the Abyssal King died. Maybe there was internal strife, and they killed each other, vying for the throne? We honestly don't know."

"And what if they're still alive?"

"Knight, the war's been over for 150 years now. There is not a soul alive that saw those battles."

"But that Abyssal said that a Master would avenge him. How do you kill something like that if one of them is alive?"

The priest went grew quiet. He looked to be in thought for a few moments before turning to Lunarias with a face drained of hope.

"Pray to the Ancestors none of them is alive. The only thing you can do is run away from it. There is no way to kill such a creature."

Chapter 16

The following day, Astolphos wanted to take a trip to the Scaffolds. The story the priest told Lunarias was still fresh in her mind, and when Astolphos proposed to spend the time exploring the city, she did not think she had any other choice but to say yes and go with it. If that priest was right, the creature before her was far more powerful than anyone knew. She could not afford to anger it because she did not know what it could do. For all she knew, that creature could destroy the city with a mere thought. That is at least the impression she got from the priest. This also meant that she had decided that staying as quiet as possible was off the table, as she did not know if it would be angered by being ignored.

And as such, when she awoke that morning to the creature having brought her breakfast for some reason, she had no choice but to go sightseeing with it. They started at the top of the scaffolds, where a market had formed at the city's edge, bordering the steep drop down the cliff. The stalls were all placed on solid ground, ending on the line where the cobblestoned ground turned to wooden planks. The last stalls, before going onto the platform, all served food, and benches were set up so that you could enjoy the sea view while eating.

It took an hour before she regretted going to the priest for information, as her answering a few of the Abyssal's questions resulted in a barrage of conversation. It was so talkative about everything, and it seemed to have quite the knowledge about the city and could explain a bit about its history. Far more than what she was ever going to need.

"Have you ever been to Hybrik before?" Astolphos asked.

"Besides the short stay on my way here, no. The Abyssals are not attacking this part of the country for some reason, so there isn't much reason for us knights to be here."

"That also explains why you've become quite the attraction." The blacksmith flashed a grin.

Lunarias clicked her tongue and went to one of the stalls to look at the wares.

Their first stop was a market selling various fruits from inside and outside the kingdom. She picked up one such fruit. It was green with thorns all over and had a hole in the middle. It felt like it had a tough shell too.

"How would you eat this thing?" Lunarias asked.

"That's a pinwheel," Astolphos said, buying a few and putting them into his pouch, "They're very sour, but they kill all kinds of filth in the water. Cut a few slices and put them into your waterskin, and you don't have to worry about your water becoming stale. They'll be great for our journey."

"Isn't it too early to buy them then?"

"They're supposed to be yellow. Give it a week, and you'll see the color change."

She looked at the fruits and then at the merchant, who nodded to Astolphos' words. She was going to see if they worked on their journey then.

It only took her a few minutes at the market to figure out that Astolphos was buying resources for their journey. The empty backpack he brought along was slowly being filled with various tools and a pile of papers with pre-paid orders for food stacked up in his hands. She looked through the orders as he gave her the documents for safekeeping. She could get behind most of it, as it fell into the basic necessities she would have bought. There were, however, other things on the lists that she was looking at questioningly. The blacksmith was, of course, more than happy to answer her questions. His answers fell into two categories: One was that they did not have a set budget and, as such, were allowed to splurge on things like honeyed fruits and expensive meats. The other being tools of the trade, as it seemed like it wanted to continue peddling as a black-smith on their travels.

The amounts of Merias that changed hands that day was staggering. She wondered how a blacksmith could have the money to spend so much, and then she was reminded that she was not dealing with an ordinary blacksmith. That creature had had more than a century to accrue wealth; of course, this was like a drop in the bucket for something like it.

She kept an eye on the blacksmith, and on more than one occasion, she caught herself thinking of it as a human, but the thought was quickly shut down by the rest of her being. It might look like a normal human, but that creature was danger-ous, even if it was laughing along to a bad joke from a merchant who was more than happy to display his wares.

However, the sight of this laughing Abyssal was better than the sorry sight she saw in their room yesterday.

The sun reached its zenith as they were done with the market atop the cliff.

"Was that all?" Lunarias asked, her eyes darting to the wooden platform and its stairs leading further down.

"Not yet. I still need a few things, and I can't seem to find them here. Not that I expected to, but it was worth a shot. I think we can be lucky at one of the lower markets."

The blacksmith walked onto the platform and towards one of the busy stairwells, only turning around once he realized Lunarias stood still at the transition.

"Is there something wrong?" The blacksmith asked.

"No, nothing," Lunarias answered shortly, her eyes fixed on a gap between the planks. A feeling of vertigo gripped her tightly. If she took that step, there would only be a few centimeters of wood between her and a steep drop.

"Scared of heights?" The blacksmith asked.

She shook her head, but still, her feet betrayed her.

"You're welcome to go back to our room. I'll manage to carry all of this alone. It'll only take an hour, I think."

"I'll come along. Just give me a second."

And more than that passed. Astolphos stood patiently, waiting for Lunarias to take her step. And eventually, it happened, although with great reluctance.

"There's no reason to be afraid," Astolphos said, "These are only scaffolds in name. The construction is as sturdy as any house. There have not been any accidents of that kind since it opened."

"How do you know?"

"Because Kennas was part of the team that designed it."

She did not know how that knowledge was supposed to help, knowing that one of the designers was the enemy of Aurillia, but then she remembered that Astolphos had not yet realized that she had connected the dots. She let out a light chuckle at the thought of her enemy trying to calm her nerves.

The wind howled constantly from all directions at once. Combined with the chatter of the many people moving up and down the floors, the sound was deafening. Astolphos walked purposefully as if he knew exactly where he would find this missing item. The waves came closer for every floor they went down, and they had gone down at least 15 floors before Astolphos stopped and looked around.

It seemed like each of the floors had some kind of theme. Some had restaurants, others had craftsmen, and some had merchants peddling imports from other continents. She had realized that the further down they went, the more expensive the wares being peddled became. The materials improved, the craftsmen became more skilled, and the food grew more exotic.

However, the floor Astolphos stopped at had no shops. Instead, many small houses leaned up the cliff. The wooden facades and slanted roofs seemed only a few meters deep.

"What're we doing here?" Lunarias asked, "I thought you were looking for something to buy."

"I'm looking for a particular merchant, and I hope he's home."

Astolphos knocked on the door of the largest of the houses, and a burly woman opened the door and looked Astolphos up and down before awaiting him to talk.

"Do you have a merchant named Vina lodged in your fine establishment?" Astolphos asked.

"I'm not answering any questions about my guests." The woman made ready to slam the door when Astolphos blocked it with his foot.

The following discussion was one Lunarias did not want to listen in on. Instead, she looked into the house and realized it was much deeper than it seemed on the outside. Just like where the scaffold met solid ground on the top, the wooden platform stopped to make way to a rough stone floor. The house continued deep into the cliff's surface, turning into a hallway with doors to the sides. A large metal pipe connected all the rooms and ran to the front, where thick smoke blew out into the wind.

Somehow, Astolphos got the woman to tell him where this merchant was, and then they were on their way again, further down towards the bottom.

"We're in luck. He arrived last week," Astolphos said.

"What's so special about this merchant?"

"He's a seller of gemstones from Ronasm. You can't find these anywhere else, and I need them for a project and our trip."

Almost at the bottom, the scaffold extended outward, becoming as wide as the market at the top. The tendency still held as Lunarias could not identify most of the things sold at the stands. Food was still the most prominent of wares, but there were a lot of different materials. Pelts with patterns she had never imagined an animal to have and scaled skins coming from lizards so large she thought she would need a team of knights to take them down. The sellers all looked ordinary. Not even their clothing seemed too much out of place. She had imagined that there would be a larger difference between cultures entire landmasses apart, but this seemed to be a false assumption.

They wandered between the booths. The merchants howled at the top of their lungs in broken Aurillian to draw attention, which they got from Astolphos. They had gone through three rows of booths when Astolphos stopped to look at the ships coming to port.

"How much do you know of the other two continents?" Astolphos asked.

"Not much. That's not the responsibility of the knights."

Seven ships approached the harbor. Four carried a flag with a silver eagle on a blue background, one eye yellow, and the other green. The other three had Green flags with five pentagons, each in a different color. Each ship had a different pentagon highlighted with a golden outline, while the others were outlined in white.

"The four with the eagle come from Ronasm," Astolphos said, "and the other three come from Chademokai, the golden outline showing which part, in particular, they come from."

"And you've been to both of them, right?"

"Yeah, what gave it away?"

"We've only had open trade with Ronasm for five years, hardly enough time for a blacksmith to learn the language, let alone when he says he's not been to the city for more than ten years."

Astolphos shrugged, "Well, the cat's out of the bag."

The ships moored into the harbor below. Astolphos and Lunarias went so far down the stairs that the masts were now at eye height.

"How is it over there?" Lunarias asked.

"For Ronasm, the climate's a lot colder, that's for sure. Not to the degree where you need thick woolen coats in the summer, but the winter brings with it snow to the shins and biting cold. Else, the culture seems a lot like ours. Their houses are a bit shorter, but that's the most significant difference I can think of appearance-wise. There are some other things, but you wouldn't believe me.

"For Chademokai, I wasn't there long enough to say anything with certainty."

"I just find it strange that we can be from different continents, and everything seems the same down to the clothing."

"That's intentional. The two countries are at war. If no one can distinguish who comes from which country, you can circumvent the embargos."

"So Hybrik has become some sort of middle-man for trade between the two?"

"Seems like it."

Lunarias turned around to look at the market with no particular purpose. If she listened closely, she could identify three distinct languages being spoken, the least prevalent being Aurillian, strangely enough.

"And might I ask why you were overseas?"

"Of course, I was sent by the Abyssal King to create diplomatic ties."

And now Lunarias' disinterested look turned wary, scanning the crowd to see if anyone intercepted that information. She half expected to see some servant with their mouth covered and eyes filled with fear, but no one had even budged.

"Relax, no one within earshot can speak Aurillian well enough to understand what I'm saying." But despite his words,

Astolphos leaned closer to Lunarias, who instinctively did the same.

"The Gifter, as we called him, wanted to create allies overseas. He hoped it would help end the war for good, so he sent me and some of the other Masters to negotiate some treaties. It wasn't exactly a success."

"Wait," Lunarias interrupted, "You knew of Ronasm and Chademokai back when the Abyssal King was alive? We only figured that out twenty years ago."

"And they were the ones establishing contact, right? Do you know who they asked to speak with when they arrived?"

Lunarias shook her head. All she knew was that the sight of an unfamiliar ship had caused quite a stir. It was the first time in many years that the knights were called to this part of the country. Sadly, she was only sixteen when it happened.

"Never mind then. Anyway, neither Ronasm nor Chademokai was willing to make any alliances with us. They feared that we were agents from the other and quickly turned us away. We were practically chased out of the port in Chademokai. They also thought it was laughable to propose a third continent, so I somewhat understand their suspicions. We did, however, hear about some internal strife inside Ronasm and went to talk to their leader. He was a strange fellow, always dressed in blue and wearing a crown, like he had been given the call by God. But he was a bit more open-minded and was willing to hear us out."

However, Astolphos stopped speaking at that, looking down at the table as if a bad memory resurfaced.

"What then?" Lunarias asked.

Astolphos hesitated but sighed, saying, "Let's just say that I had to go home on short notice, and everything fell through. I think it's time to move on. We still have one more stop before returning to our room."

Chapter 17

Lunarias raised an eyebrow at Astolphos' change in topic, but he did not want to talk about what made him and the other Hands withdraw from Bluecoat's camp. He could not be sure how much Lunarias knew of her family's true story; divulging too much could make it possible for her to connect the dots. Why that was a bad thing, Astolphos still debated, telling himself that the time would come eventually. But that time would not be today.

He still had to find that gemstone merchant. He needed those gems for his plan to help Kennas, but he knew that the seller also sold special kinds of gemstones from the Western parts of Ronasm.

His sight returned to normal after the first step, and the red haze of life essences washed away to be replaced by actual human beings. He had stopped at the railing not to admire the view but to scan the surroundings to see if he could feel a familiar essence. Ten years was a long time, and it was an essence he was not that familiar with on top of that. Combine this with the fact that tracking the essences of non-Gifted humans was more of an instinct than something measurable, and you got an unreliable tool more likely to mislead than guide you. It was, however, still better than running around the market, looking for someone whose appearance could have changed drastically in ten years.

The only reason for Astolphos being sure that the essence at the dock belonged to the merchant was one unusual aspect, rebellion. Opinions, emotions, and choices subtly change the color of one's essence. Happiness and sincerity made it burst outward, anger compressed it, making it ready to burst out at any second, while sadness and regret made it dimmer. However, self-righteous rebellion, as Astolphos called it, made the aura bright and compressed. Everyone in Bluecoat's insurgency bore its traits, and that was why Astolphos approached that particular merchant in the first place. He knew from his aura alone that this person was allied with Bluecoat, which meant a kindred spirit and hopefully a hefty discount.

Astolphos did not try to mask his knowledge to Lunarias, electing instead to go in a direct line to the nearest staircase. She followed close behind, like a steadfast dog unwilling to let its owner roam alone.

The docks were the busiest part of the Scaffolds, with boxes being moved to and from the ships, most of them not even going up to the markets, instead being stowed away on the ships bearing the opposing nation's flag. Under-the-table dealings at their finest. Those wares lucky enough to go on display were sent up by elevators being pulled by bulky dockworkers using thick rope.

"Which way?" Lunarias asked, stepping out in front of Astolphos.

He closed his eyes, seeing all of the essences for but a moment, enough time for him to reacquire the merchant. They found him waddling down a gangplank with a large box in his arms. He was swearing in Ronasian, something about making the captain shove the box somewhere if he is asked to carry his own merchandise again.

"Good day. Are you the gemstone merchant I've heard about?" Astolphos asked in Ronasian.

The merchant immediately seized up and took a firmer grip on his box. His eyes darted up and down Astolphos, followed by Lunarias, where his eyes fixed on the sword on her hip.

"Depends on what you've heard," The merchant said. He was a thin man, the kind of person that did not seem to be prepared for the world outside of a study. No fat, but no muscles, either. He was still dressed in Ronasian clothing, in this case, a purple robe with gold silk lining. His hands were covered by thick leather gloves fit for travels in colder regions and when you move heavy wooden boxes and do not want splinters. His cheekbones became visible when he talked, and his green eyes were sharply focused on Astolphos. Every step he took rang with the sound of coins colliding, probably coming from a pouch hidden beneath the robe.

"Don't worry, I'm a customer. Do you need any help with that thing?"

Astolphos took hold of the box without waiting for an answer and let the merchant guide him. They went past the elevators, instead steering towards the staircase.

"Do I know you?" The merchant asked.

"You probably don't remember me. I bought a bunch of uncut gems from Aurum from you many years back."

That was the truth. Astolphos needed a bunch of gemstones in an attempt to restore Glaucos' body. The result of the ritual was non-existent, but the quality of the gems was above and beyond. Just what Astolphos needed this time.

After just a few steps up the stairs, the merchant was out of breath. Lunarias approached to help move the merchandise, but the merchant shook his head.

"Tell your bodyguard to stand down. I've got this," The merchant said in Ronasian between breaths.

"He says he's fine, but thank you for offering."

They eventually got it up the last of the steps. The trip to the merchant's booth was a cakewalk compared to the stairs, or at least that was how it seemed. After all, Astolphos did not feel his lungs burn or his muscles fatiguing for something like this. It also helped that their destination was roughly in the middle of the market, just before the point where the sun cleared the scaffolding and cast its rays on the booths. His neighbors also sold exported materials; one sold wood and aggressively pushed his maple stock onto an Aurillian businessman. The other was selling pelts, but he looked out from his seat in boredom, and jealously at his competition, who all seemed to get the customers.

Once the merchant regained his breath, he almost immediately went into business mode.

"Thank you for your help. I just hope you don't expect a discount for it."

"Don't worry, it never crossed my mind," Astolphos lied, "I have a list of gemstones I need."

He pulled a list containing 20 different stones. The list was hopefully legible, as it was more than 60 years since Astolphos last wrote in Ronasian.

The merchant looked at the note momentarily, cocked his head, but eventually nodded.

"That's a big order. It's going to cost 24000 Merias." He said.

Astolphos raised an eyebrow, "That much? I can get the stuff for half up in the city."

"Import fees. Besides, why would you come to me for this? No one would know the stones come from Ronasm."

"I came here because of a common acquaintance," Astolphos said in a hushed voice, careful of the bored pelt salesman. The gemstone merchant, however, leaned back in his seat and flung his arms behind his head, stretching.

"I don't know what you're talking about. I don't think we're in the same circles," The merchant said, his voice so sincere that Astolphos would not have doubted him if not for their prior transaction.

Astolphos leaned further forward, needing to put a hand on the booth to avoid falling over, and whispered, "From the port of Chrysner, go north until you reach a small logging village. Then go east into the forest and pray to Nocta and Vitalis that the guards expect you."

The merchant initially looked shocked, but his business face returned as he nodded.

"I remember you now. Long time no see. Seems like we misunderstood each other. The price is 1000 Merias."

"That sounds more like it," Astolphos pulled out a small piece of parchment containing instructions to find Kennas' workshop,

"Deliver the stones to this shop. Ask for Ontrys; he will have your payment."

Chapter 18

The last evening rays were upon them when they reached the top of the scaffolding. However, the crowd showed no sign of thinning out. On the contrary, more people had arrived at the upper levels as the tables and chairs were put out in front of the booths selling roasted vegetables, meats, and alcohol.

"Want anything?" Astolphos asked, his attention drawn by a stand selling what seemed to be skewered lamb. Lunarias looked at the same booth and said, "I'll get us a spot to sit."

And thus, Astolphos went to the queue alone. He could see from his spot how a group of people rose from their seats as Lunarias approached, only for her to smile awkwardly and gesture them back on the bench. What caught his gaze, however, was something sitting at the wall of a house beyond her.

"Don't even think about it," Glaucos said.

About what?

"You have a mission, don't compromise it for the sake of a few Aurillians."

Leaning up against the wall was a father and a mother cradling their shivering child. However, the shivering had nothing to do with the cold temperature; he was sweating and coughing.

"I know what you're thinking. But you need to keep a low profile, or else you might need to fight Lunarias."

Astolphos knew Glaucos was right. There was no reason to even debate it. But still, Astolphos was unable to look away.

Then someone shoved him, "Your turn," said the guy behind him in the queue.

"Ahh, five skewers of lamb, two plates of grilled vegetables, and two cups of ale."

"Coming right up! Where are you sitting?"

"I'm with the knight. We'll be difficult to miss."

And right he was, as Lunarias had not only found them a place to sit but an entire table built for at least ten people.

"Quite the table for us," Astolphos said with a smile. Lunarias, however, massaged her temples.

"I told them we could share, but they wanted me to have the entire table. Gratitude for my valor in fighting the Abyss."

"They truly hold the knights in high regard."

"We're fighting the Abyssals for them, but I just wish they would keep it down. There's no reason for this." She gestured to the empty chairs, one of which Astolphos sat on. He put one seat between them to give Lunarias the space she surely wanted.

"I know that feeling too well. Sometimes you don't want their gratitude. You just want their company."

Lunarias shot him a questioning gaze.

"You're not the only one who's had a position where people looked up to you. Frankly, I sometimes thought it wasn't out of respect that they kept their distance, but fear."

Lunarias sat silently momentarily, "Most don't want to say it out loud. But we knights can be some stuck-up assholes at times. You saw the knights back in your shop, right?"

Astolphos could only nod. He remembered clearly that dignified look they shot him when they took his shop for the meeting. They wanted him to be grateful for them to use his 'lowly' dwelling for their business.

"Most of the knights are noblemen," Lunarias continued, "with a few coming from lineages of wealthy merchants. I know some who would look at this table and think there were still too many people around and order them to take a wider berth around it."

"You'd think those kinds of people would stay far away from the frontlines," Astolphos said, "opting instead to stay in their castles with a silver spoon up their rear."

"Aurillian noblemen need to have served as a knight for at least five years before they are allowed to inherit their estate and the taxation rights that come with it. That's practically the only perk of being born a woman. You can get all of that without serving at all."

A waitress then approached their table, putting their food onto it, with the addition of a fruit platter.

"I think you're at the wrong table. We didn't order any fruit," Astolphos said.

"We decided it was only fair to give a dessert for the knight's service to our country. It's on the house." And after a quick bow toward Lunarias, the waitress left before they could interject.

"I see what you mean," Astolphos said.

"You'd think the worst part of the job was the campaigns to the Abyss. I would say I've fought with the innkeepers and cooks about whether I have to pay or not more than I've been in combat with Abyssals."

"We'll just leave a bunch of Merias on the table when we leave."

"They'll chase you down to return it. I've tried that before."

Lunarias sighed as she took one of the skewers and immediately started coughing at the first bite.

"That's spicy!" Lunarias exclaimed.

Astolphos took one of the skewers and dug in too. Though spicy, his reaction was to soundlessly grab the ale.

"I thought you nobles would be surrounded by spice from the moment you were born," Astolphos said with a smile.

"I've not been back at the Hewris estate since I enlisted seven years ago," Lunarias said when she grabbed her tankard of ale.

"That's a long time. Family issues?"

"Nothing of the sort. I've just been busy. Six campaigns into the Abyss and several missions around the country."

"Is that a lot?"

"The nobles we talked about before usually only experience the Abyss once during their five years. The inheritance laws only dictate that you have to go once, so that's what most of them do."

A slight smile crept up on Lunarias' lips as she let out a light giggle.

"What's so funny?"

"It's just, I forgot for a moment what you actually are."

"I'll take that as a compliment, coming from someone as seasoned as you. Why did you join the knights, to begin with, anyway?"

"There are only three reasons to join the knights. You're going to inherit your family's estate, you're a hothead going in for the glory, or you think you can actually do some good for the country. The first group leaves as soon as possible, the second ends up dead sooner rather than later, and the third rises the ranks, losing their drive for change when they finally have the power to do so."

Astolphos finished his second skewer and began digging through his vegetables, "And I guess you fall into the third category?"

"You contest that?"

"I haven't known you long enough to make that assessment."

Lunarias shrugged. That was apparently a good answer, "I'm going to go get us some more ale. Want anything else?"

"Thank you."

Lunarias headed for the booth. The line was even longer than when they had initially arrived. This gave Astolphos time to look around the busy plaza. They had reached the point where the families were all leaving, as the wine and ale flowed freer to the dockworkers celebrating a work well done. But despite how much he tried to distract himself with the bustle, his eyes and mind wandered back to that family with the sick child.

The more he stared, the more he realized they had been down on their luck for quite some time. Their clothes were ragged and unpatched, and the lack of meat on the father only showed how little they could afford to eat.

"Don't think about it," Glaucos said, "Lunarias has just begun trusting you. You shouldn't throw that away for the sake of some people you don't even know."

Astolphos took one more look at Lunarias. She was busy standing in line, convincing the citizens not to let her in front of the line. He then rose from his seat, keeping his head low in case she looked his way.

Easy for you to say. You don't have the power to do anything about it.

"Just turn around. You can't save everyone."

But I can save them.

Glaucos sighed but went silent as Astolphos pushed his way through the crowd.

"Spare a coin?" A father asked as Astolphos approached.

The man looked ragged, like he had been awake for many days, and his unkempt beard covered half of his face. The wife was only slightly better fed, and her clothes were patched in some places, but there were still several holes and gashes in the garment. The child took labored breaths and looked to be only half-conscious. Whatever sickness he had gotten would lead to his demise within a couple of weeks unless he saw a doctor soon. Astolphos looked at the child's essence, and what he saw confirmed his fears. It was not a question of weeks, but days.

Astolphos crouched and looked to and from the questioning parents.

"May I see the boy?" Astolphos asked.

The couple looked at each other, "I don't think that's a good idea. His illness can spread," The father said.

"Maybe I can do something to help." Astolphos did not wait for the parents to give permission. He clasped his hands tightly around the child's and closed his eyes. The essence in his body flowed into the child's, lengthening however long the boy had left. He gave the boy about two weeks' worth of life essence, though the illness might shorten that to some degree.

When he opened his eyes again, the parents looked at him with wonder, confusion, and horror. He had tried to shield the red glow of the essence being transferred, but it was unavoidable for them to have seen it. They knew exactly what he was. The question then was what they wanted to do with that information.

However, the boy's eyes shot open momentarily and locked onto his fathers. Even if it was difficult to evaluate, Astolphos was quite sure his coughing had also lightened.

"I can't do more, sadly," Astolphos said, "You still need to get him to a doctor, else his condition will worsen again. This should cover the visit and the medication, at least for some time." Astolphos counted 100 Merias and handed it to the mother, who reluctantly took it with shaking hands.

"Now, I must be on my way," Astolphos said, "I wish I could do more, but now the rest is in your hands."

The father looked at him for a moment but then flashed a grateful smile before he said, "Thank you, kind stranger. It's nice to know some Aurillians are kind enough to help those more unfortunate."

As Astolphos rose to return to their table, he sighed.

"An Aurillian, huh?"

He fought his way back to the table, where Lunarias had returned with more ale. It did not seem like she had been sitting there for long.

"Where've you been?" She asked when he sat down.

"Just wanted to stretch my legs."

Chapter 19

Lunarias locked the door to their room as soon as they entered, turned around, and pointed an accusing finger at the blacksmith.

"What in the name of the ever-loving Ancestors did you do to that kid?!"

She had barely been able to contain her anger on their walk back from the market. Only the thought of some random person hearing them had kept her from pulling him into an alley and yelling at him. Now that they were alone, she could no longer keep it contained.

Astolphos sighed, sitting down on his bed, "So you saw it."

"Of course I did! Did you seriously think I wouldn't keep an eye on you? I left the queue the moment you snuck away from the table. Now, what did you do!?"

From her place among the crowd, she had been unable to see anything but the smith crouching at the family and the looks they suddenly gave him. Even a peasant could figure out that he had somehow used his powers. The question was just what it did.

However, the blacksmith did not look her in the eyes. His eyes pointed at the floor, seemingly debating whether to lie to her again.

"I swear, if you did anything that will harm the citizenry, I will strike you down here and now!"

Her hand was already on the hilt of her sword, the sword it had borrowed her. But Astolphos extended a hand to stop her as he took a deep breath.

"I didn't hurt the kid. And besides, nothing bad happened."

"They can still tell the guards. Did you even think about what would happen if they did that?"

"Who would report the guy that helped your son survive?"

"...What?"

"Did you really think I'm that kind of monster? That kid was living on borrowed time. He had less than a week left to live. With what I did, he might make a full recovery. So what if they know? I at least saved a life by doing so."

She could feel the rage from before being quelled as her brain processed Astolphos' words. She had no idea what he had done and had automatically assumed the worst. There was still a chance it was lying. After all, it had lied to her back at the market about just going for a walk.

"What? Don't tell me you disagree with what I did?"

Astolphos' words struck deep because it was the truth. She did not know what he had done or how he did it, but if it saved someone's life, everything would be great, right? There should not be any wrong sides to saving someone, especially when that someone was so young. But some part of her disagreed, and it was something that had been persistent throughout her entire life, her duty.

"Whatever plans the queen has for you, they will inevitably improve the lives of the citizens much more than you alone can. But you must hide who you are to be part of that plan. The benefit of the many outweighs the life of the few."

"Easy to say when you're not one of the people whose life is deemed 'a necessary sacrifice'. I admire your belief in the queen, but that belief just shows you have never met anyone governing a country."

Astolphos rose from his bed, putting his hands into his pockets, "Let me tell you something I've learned throughout my life. I have seen regents come and go. I've outlived dynasties. I have personally known people you've never heard of that owned larger parts of Aurillia than any of the duchies currently alive. And let me tell you, I have only met one compassionate person who actually had the power to do anything. It's just like with your commanders. Their resolve to change the status quo crumbles when they finally have the power to do so, all because they realize the only reason they have that power is because of that very same status quo. Look at the streets of Hybrik, and you'll realize your queen is no better. Today, I have done more for the citizens than your royal lineage has done for generations."

"You didn't even know the queen's name a week ago. How can you make that assessment!?"

"Because I have already seen enough by just being in this city! I hate being in large cities because I can see that nothing is changing for the better, even though I've been here for more than 100 years. The only thing that's not stagnant is the amount of homeless populating the streets."

"That's rich coming from an Abyssal."

Silence befell the room, with Astolphos looking at her sternly, opening and closing his mouth as if he was struggling to find the words.

"Besides, why do you even care?" Lunarias asked, "You're not an Aurillian. You're from a country of monsters hell-bent on our destruction."

Something changed in Astolphos, he looked furious for a moment, but then he took a deep breath, and the eyes that locked onto hers were no longer the kind eyes he had persistently kept up. What looked on her was more animalistic, perhaps even malicious. She had imagined seeing this in an intelligent Abyssal, and now that she had seen it, part of her wished she had never said those words. Out of instinct alone, she took a step back.

"How dare you!" Astolphos said, "I've dedicated my entire life since the end of the Gifter's reign to improve the livelihood of the citizens of Aurillia! Did you think I continued smithing for almost nothing out of the kindness of my heart? I have a debt to those citizens you noblemen have forsaken. What I do for them is the least I can do to pay for my past actions."

"And yet, you can regret joining the Abyssal King's army all you want. They'll turn on you the moment they learn the truth."

And once again, they both grew silent. It was only natural for an Abyssal to regret its choices when its King was killed by Aurillia. They had chosen the wrong side and would pay for that decision for the rest of their lives. She meant every word she said to Astolphos. He did owe Aurillia a debt so significant he could be working for four of its lifetimes and still not be halfway.

But Astolphos only chuckled at her comment, looking at her with those steely eyes that made her body scream to pick up her weapon.

"Seems like I have a misunderstanding to correct here, Ms. Hewris. It's true what you said; the citizens of Aurillia will never accept me. They will heartily take my wares for almost nothing, but I'm not doing this because I regret joining the Gifter. Quite the contrary.

"Not a day goes by where I don't regret betraying the great Gifter, the only regent I have met that was both able and willing to change everything for the benefit of his subjects. I am the reason Lumina, what you call the Abyss, crumbled. And as an extension, I'm the reason why the citizens of Aurillia live in squalor."

Lunarias was speechless. Many things clicked in place, especially the part as to why the regents of Aurillia permitted an Abyssal to live among them.

"You're wrong," Lunarias said, "if not for the death of the Abyssal King, we would all be slaves to his regime!"

"Were you there?" Astolphos asked, taking a step closer to Lunarias. His anger had quelled, but instead, deep sadness enveloped his eyes. Sadness so vast Lunarias had never seen anything like it. She preferred the anger.

"No, you weren't, but I was. I saw the Gifter's kingdom at its greatest. I saw how every single citizen, no matter their position in society, could live a life free from disease and hunger. A society where doctors could use their Gifts to cure even the worst of afflictions, a society so strong that nothing could topple it as long as our immortal leader guided our future. Look out the window. Look at how dirty the street is. Look at the people going past that homeless man trying to sleep with a moth-eaten blanket! I never saw anything like that in the 200 years I lived in Marados, and that was the capital! Here, I'm pressed to think of a moment I have not seen such a sight in a city even half the size of this one. If you had the knowledge I have, you would be ashamed of what you just said."

Lunarias looked down the street. Sure enough, a homeless man was bundled up in a blanket with more holes than cloth. They must have gone right past him on their way in.

"But let me guess, this is the first time you've seen him? This is the first time you've actually spent a few seconds looking at someone beneath your status as something other than a criminal. You noblemen are trained from birth to ignore the suffering of your citizens, and your training as a knight told you to only look at them as potential criminals. Isn't that right?"

There was nothing Lunarias could say. She did not even know where to begin, with what was wrong, or with what was right. She just knew one thing. There was nothing more to say now.She turned around and opened the door. She would not stand another second of that thing lecturing her on things it did not know anything about.

"Lunarias, wait-"

But it did not get the chance to say anything more before she shut the door in its face. Damn be her duty. She was not going to stand this any longer.

Chapter 20

"So, is that all?" Kennas asked, still in Ontrys' body, "Did she mention anything about telling the guards about you?"

"I don't think she would," Astolphos sighed.

After his argument with Lunarias, Astolphos could not stand being at the inn. He did not want to wait for Lunarias to come back. There was a chance that she would not come back at all. After giving her half an hour to cool down, Astolphos packed his stuff and left her a note telling her she could find him at Kennas' workshop. He then paid the innkeeper for the room two weeks in advance and left.

Kennas was a bit bewildered with Astolphos knocking at this time of night, but a quick explanation once they returned to her room cleared that up. Now, Kennas sat in her candle-lit bedroom with a frown.

"Not only did you anger a knight to such an extent that she ran away, you even admitted that you still support the Gifter. Even if she knew you two are related, I wouldn't put it past a knight to still report you to the garrison."

"She's ordered by the queen to escort me to the capital. Pulling together a lynch mob of soldiers would go against that order entirely, as they are more likely to try to kill me than put me in chains."

"She already went against her duties the moment she left you in that room," Glaucos interjected.

Kennas nodded, "My thoughts exactly. I need to gauge the chance of this coming back to me. Note or not, she knows of your connection to this place, and I will not let risk my shop for this."

"I can find somewhere else to stay if that will help."

Kennas hesitated, "That's not the problem. If she tells the guards, they will search the entire city for you. They will search this shop, and if they do, it just takes one misstep from the Gifted here to blow our cover."

Kennas' gaze went to the table, "Are you sure she will not tell the guards?"

"...I think so." Astolphos.

"And will you take responsibility for the outcome if she does?"

He knew well what Kennas meant with responsibility. She did not mean it would be his job alone to clean up the mess, but that whatever would happen, no matter the amount of bloodshed, it would be on his conscience for the rest of his life.

"Want me to tail her? To find out what she's planning?" Kennas asked.

"No, I think it'll be best to leave her alone. I have faith in her."

Astolphos and Kennas silently looked at each other for a moment before she exhaled and left her chair.

"Thank you for taking this risk," Astolphos said.

"Don't think about it. I should be the one apologizing for my questions and for the fact that I can only offer you the basement to sleep in. Now, for something different," She said, her voice a bit more cheery, though he could feel it was forced.

"A merchant came by a few hours ago, leaving this bag here. Is this what you ordered?" She threw the bag at him, its contents emitting the sound of glass shards hitting each other.

He took a few out of the back and brought the candle closer. Gemstones: not too expensive, but not cheap ones either. The ones he grabbed were an amethyst and a topaz, each pre-cut into flat hexagons. Their colors shimmered in the light of the open flame, revealing a pristine inside. He did not want to examine them all, but the few he did lived up to his expectations and were worth far more than he paid.

"These are great. He delivered just what we needed."

"I also got the rest of the stuff you requested, equipment and everything. I've got my apprentices to set up a spot for you in the basement."

"Great, I'll probably have enough wares ready by the end of the week. How's it going with the carriage?"

"We've not yet begun. Got quite the backlog thanks to too many ships and too few shops capable of working on that scale. We might need a few more days than initially anticipated, but we'll get it done. Now, what's next?"

"We need a spot to put up a stand at the market. It has to be somewhere visible for the thieves, but not the guards. Do you have any ideas?"

"Second floor of the scaffolding. A lot of traveling craftsmen set up shop there when visiting. A jeweler will stand out a bit, as they normally sell stuff like clothes and the like."

"Perfect, if everything goes according to plan, get me a spot for Tuesday. I'll probably need a few of your apprentices to help man it, though."

"I'll get it done."

Kennas sat down at the table again, sighing again, unable to hide her worry. Astolphos grabbed her hand.

"Nothing bad will happen. We've got everything under control."

"It's just, why does all of this have to happen now? Everything's been fine for decades, and then someone tries to kill me, and you get called upon because of that stupid contract."

Astolphos leaned back and put his hands behind his head, "That's just how things go sometimes. Frankly, I'm surprised we're the first ones to encounter problems this time."

Kennas giggled, "That's true. Heuristrys is not going to let this one go, is he?"

"Probably not for the next few centuries, that's for sure."

"I can already imagine what he's going to say. 'I told you Luminis had my back."

And with a deep exhale, everything was back to how it was before.

"Kennas," Astolphos said, "Do you regret what we did? Would you still have gone against the Gifter?"

Kennas was silent.

"I think we've all had ample time to think of it 'Stolfos," Glaucos said, "But... I don't know. I fought against the Gifter because Balacastrys' plans would've led to too many casualties, but part of me thinks we're far beyond what that kill count would've been by now."

"What we did was a mistake," Kennas finally said, "If I had just remembered how Aurillia had been, if I had not listened to the people telling me that everything would be better, perhaps everything truly would have been. If I knew of the misery commonplace in Aurillia, I would've been on the side of the Gifter."

"Even if it meant becoming one of Balacastrys' pawns?" Glaucos asked, "Remember, he exploited what happened to you for political favor, and that plan afterward was monstrous."

"I know. I might be known as the scourge of Lumina for the rest of my life, but it would've been a fair sacrifice to have made paradise."

***

Kennas went to bed soon after, and Astolphos went to the basement. The entrance was a door on the far side of the workshop, lit by a sconce about to burn out. He heard giggling from the inside. Kennas told him he would share with the three Gifted apprenticing under her, but Astolphos thought they had gone to bed long ago.

Inside, the room was lit up. The basement was a medium-sized storage room converted into a living area when the upper floors were too crowded. It consisted of three bunk beds, a table in the middle, and some desks to the side, one of which had all of Astolphos' requested tools lined up. The room was lit by an iron chandelier above the table. The three apprentices were playing a game of cards on the floor and looked up at Astolphos, stunned.

It did not take long for Astolphos to realize why, as one of the apprentices' cards hovered in the air in front of her. The cards fell to the ground a moment later, but it would have been too late if it had been a guard. The other two apprentices, boys between 10 and 15 years, let go of their cards as they rose from the floor. Astolphos, however, gestured for them to sit down again.

"Let me guess, you learned how to control your gift a few weeks ago?" Astolphos said.

The girl nodded, still on guard along with the other two. Astolphos cupped his hands and let the energy flow through them. The effect was immediate as the air around started to shimmer and cool, forming a small levitating ice ball. The moment he moved a finger, the ball vanished in an instant.

"The Aurillians don't appreciate our Gifts. Next time, it might be an Aurillian that enters through there. You need to be faster at shutting it off. I'll give you a few lessons tomorrow if you want."

Seeing his abilities in action made the apprentices sigh in relief.

"So you're the guest Kennas talked about," The oldest boy said.

"And it seems like you know Kennas is still alive. How much do you know of the current situation?"

The apprentices looked at each other, silent.

"So not that much. We'll keep it that way. No reason to mix you all up in this mess. Well... We'll share this room for a while, so I hope we can all get along. Why don't we start by introducing ourselves?"

"How about we do so over a game of cards?" The youngest boy asked.

"I think it's already quite a bit above your bedtimes, right?" Astolphos asked, "I'll start. I'm Astolphos Auriolis."

"As in, the Hand of the Forge?" The girl asked.

"I see you know your history. That was my title a long time ago."

"But wasn't your last name Hewris?"

"Please don't use that. It has some other connotations nowadays."

And since those connotations involved a noble family and a high-ranking knight, it would be best to ensure that anyone never uttered it. Astolphos sat down on one of the beds, looking at each apprentice.

"So, what're your names?"

The youngest boy was the first to speak. "I'm Cyrillys; nice to meet you."

Cyrillys was a short boy with curly red hair and blue eyes. There was not much meat to his bones, and he looked more like a scholar than a carpenter. His clothes were the same as all the other apprentices, hemp-colored pants with suspenders and a white wool shirt.

"And I'm Intros," The older apprentice said, "I've been here for three years now." And that was something that showed. Though only of average height for someone his age, his muscles had gotten quite the built-up thanks to the back-breaking work. He even had the slightest stubble on his chin, which would, without a doubt, grow into a magnificent blonde beard in a few years. However, His eyes were a thick auburn, almost reaching to the deepest browns. The look he gave the blacksmith told him everything he needed to know. Intros did not yet trust him.

"I'm Inaris," The girl said, seemingly not wanting to say anything more. She was a bit of a special case. Like Astolphos, her hair was downright platinum, with a pair of eyes so grey that anyone would think she was blind. Platinum hair appeared when a Gifted had exceptional powers that would not be expressed through their body changing, unlike what had happened to Glaucos and Kennas. The Gifted was lucky that Aurillia never figured out the connection. Whether she kept being a carpenter or not, she would have a fantastic future ahead, as Aurillians were captivated by the platinum hair, and business somehow always came their way.

"It's nice to meet all of you, but I think it's time for bed for all of us. Though I've not yet cleared it with Kennas, I'm sure you three will be helping me with a little side project from tomorrow onward. I hope this isn't a problem."

"What kind of project?" Intros asked.

"We're going to make a bunch of jewelry."

Chapter 21

Lunarias woke up to the sound of the garrison's morning guard shift echoing through the stone halls. The sounds felt nostalgic as memories of her days in training ran through her mind, of how her peers had groaned and bickered when they were woken early in the morning, only to quickly put on the armor and go to combat training.

That was a long time ago now. She was now accustomed to waking up in a solitary room in an inn, with at most a few comrades with whom she was going on an assignment with.

She put on her armor, making a mental note to ask the quartermaster for a new pair of greaves, and went for the cafeteria. She got the same response wherever she went. The soldiers first looked confused at the sight of a woman clad in armor walking the halls, at which point their gaze went to the ground when they recognized the sigil on her breastplate. She even got a table all for herself in the crowded cafeteria, as the guards went out of their way to avoid sitting with her. The cafeteria was not much more than a linen tent at the far end of the walled courtyard, with a few tables where some servants were mechanically putting the same food in each bowl. All the soldiers were sitting rank and file at long splintered tables that had been out in the rain one too many times.

The food was exactly as she expected, rye bread with a side of unidentifiable salted meats. The surrounding soldiers ate it with the same disinterest as they mingled with each other, their tired looks telling her these were the ones who had just left their shift and were going to bed as soon as they were done.

But despite how crowded the 'cafeteria' was, she was surprised by how few people were coming off their shifts. Hybrik was a large city where foreigners were constantly coming and going. It would stand to reason that they would have their fair share of work for the guards, but there were surprisingly few, less than 40. She had expected at least 70, even if this was only a small part of the entire garrison.

Sitting with no one to talk to gave Lunarias time to study the guards, their movements, and their gear. Like the guard she met at the gate a few days ago, their equipment was rusting away. It was the same for everyone she looked at, and not a single one seemed to have a problem with it. She glanced to the other side of the courtyard, where a set of rotting training dummies jotted out of the ground. If they did not even train, they would genuinely not stand a chance if the Abyssals invaded.

"Miss Hewris?" A nervous-looking guard said.

Lunarias shot him a disinterested look. He was far up in age, probably at the cusp of retirement, and likely without ever seeing combat. He did not even bother with his armor, only wearing a thin gambeson.

"The captain wants to talk to you. Could you please follow me?"

She wordlessly picked up the remainder of her breakfast and followed the elderly man. They entered the keep, if you could call two towers with a small two-story building in between a keep, and went up to the second floor. The door stood wide open and revealed a lavishly decorated office with a kind-looking man sitting behind a desk. He was also not wearing any uniform, instead electing to wear a finely tailored blue coat atop a green shirt and brown pants.

"Miss Hewris, pleased to meet you." He rose from his seat and went to her with an outstretched hand.

"You must be the captain," Lunarias said, at which he nodded.

"That's right, I'm the one in charge of the security of this fine city. I'm terribly sorry to encroach on your busy schedule, but I'd like to discuss why you're here."

The captain gestured for her to take a seat at his desk. Lunarias did so out of courtesy, even though she wanted to keep the visit short.

"I've just not been informed of a knight coming to Hybrik. If we were, I would've been able to give you a better room."

"Don't think about it," she said, waving his concerns away, "My mission has nothing to do with Hybrik. Being here was not even part of the plan, honestly."

"But is it possible you can tell me a bit more about your mission? Since it brought you to Hybrik, part of it might be important for me to keep my citizens safe. I know you knights like to keep your secrets, so I'm not asking for details, just whether I need to prepare for Abyssals."

For a moment, Lunarias thought about telling the captain the truth. She could tell him that there already was an Abyssal on the loose inside his city and that this Abyssal could be dangerous beyond anything he had seen.

"My mission is secret, but rest assured, it has nothing to do with Abyssals in or around Hybrik, nor anything about an imminent invasion."

But she did not do it. Despite everything she had heard last night, that Abyssal was still her responsibility. Telling the guards would only rile them up and result in them ransacking the city to find any trace. That last part might be a bit of a stretch, considering the guard's looks, but it was a risk she was unwilling to take. Besides, if that blacksmith indeed was a Master, she doubted the entire garrison could do anything.

"I'm glad to hear that. We're hard-pressed enough as is. Mobilizing the entire city guard would put quite the strain on our resources."

Lunarias kept her silence at that. She wanted to tell him that his guards would be worthless in battle, but there was no reason to make an enemy of him. Instead, she took a deep breath and said, "I would like to discuss something with you. Who's in charge of the guards at the gates?"

"Well, I'm the one organizing everything, so that must be me," He said with a smile.

"When was the last time you went and inspected their work?"

"What's this about?"

"I think you would find some issues with how they do things. First of all, they're not taking proper defensive positions when someone is approaching, and they're damaging their equipment by knocking it against the gate."

"Thank you for the notice. I'll send someone to evaluate it. Is there anything else you want to make me aware of?"

"No, but since you are short-staffed, do you have any pressing assignments I can take care of?"

The captain looked at the old man, who took a step forward.

"There have been some problems at some of the farms outside of the city," The old man said, "Their tools are breaking at night. We think it's just some animal problem, but they persistently say that someone is breaking it."

"And you've postponed it because you think it's some animal doing it? I get the gist of it. Give me the directions, and I'll be going."

Chapter 22

Out of the corner of his eyes, Inaris focused on three floating gemstones, trying her best to keep them calmly in the air. Astolphos held a hammer in one hand and a metal tray in the other. Through a few demonstrations in the early morning hours, Inaris had shown Astolphos the extent of her abilities. Consistency and speed; that was her weak points. Right now, she trained her consistency; Keep the gemstones levitating at a certain height, do not make them waver.

Astolphos swung the hammer into the tray, and a dull ringing sounded across the small basement. Inaris opened her eyes immediately, followed by the three gemstones falling to the ground. She looked dejectedly as a garnet bounced on the wooden table and came to rest.

"I canceled it as soon as I could," Inaris said, "but they didn't fall."

"How are you canceling your gift?" Astolphos asked.

"I imagine the wind underneath them vanishing."

Astolphos gave her a slight smile, "Let me show you something."

He cupped his hands together like he did yesterday, this time, an ice crystal at the length of a finger formed. It spun lightly in the air, its sides reflecting the environment. He saw Intros and Cyrillys working at a small forge, looking on eagerly as the first clay mold hardened.

"Now, I will do what you are doing," Astolphos said.

He imagined the crystal heating up instantly, returning to the vapor from which it came. The change was instantaneous in his mind, but reality was anything but. The crystal first turned cloudy before thin vapor streams emanated from its surface, slowly reducing its size until it vanished.

"Your gift might not respond as quickly as you want because our world prohibits it, just like with this crystal. But take a look now."

He formed the same crystal again, but he moved his right little finger outward this time. The crystal vanished almost instantly, releasing its vapor into a large cloud before dissipating at an impossible speed.

"When you use your thoughts to cancel your gift, you let the speed be up to the world around you. But what if you instead reverse what you have done? Instead of imagining the wind vanishing, imagine a wind pushing it downwards."

"But what about your pinky?"

"That's because I've trained myself that moving my right little forward means reversing all active Gifts. I normally have a staff in that hand if I'm in combat, so it's unlikely I'll make that movement by mistake. But don't focus on that right now. Just try to reverse your gift."

Inaris nodded and closed her eyes once again. The three gemstones left the table, levitating at head height. Then they vanished. The was a sharp sound as they pierced the table and shattered on the stone floor.

"Sorry!" Inaris said.

"Don't think about it. I've got more gemstones than I need, but let's switch to playing cards instead, alright? I'll go buy you a new deck later today."

And with Inaris practicing on her own, Astolphos returned to his work. He was making a clay mold for a pendant, and was just done carving in the general shape when Inaris wanted his help at practicing. His tools for this carving were a dull knife and a spoon. It was a simple trapezoid with a small circle on top for a gold chain.

"Master Astolphos, may I ask you a question?" Cyrillys asked.

"You don't need to be that formal. I lost my titles a long time ago. What is it?"

"I'm just wondering, why does a blacksmith, and such an esteemed weaponsmith like yourself, know how to make jewelry?"

Astolphos turned around to look at the two Gifted and Glaucos, the latter currently serving as the heat source used to fire the clay.

"Boredom mainly," Astolphos answered, "When you've been working with metal for as long as I have, you eventually want some variety in you're making. Goldsmithing was a welcome change of pace."

"Come on 'Stolfos, don't make it sound so noble," Glaucos said,

"We both know you started back during your midlife crisis in Lumina."

"What're you talking about?" Astolphos said.

"Don't you remember? You began making your own jewelry about the same time you tried changing your style."

"I have no memory of that," Astolphos said too hastily, turning away to hide his blushing cheeks as the awkward memories flooded back into his mind.

"In that case, let me describe the most extravagant thing you chose to wear back then."

"Please don't..."

"Kids, take a good look at the blacksmith in his brown pants and apron. Now imagine him wearing a deep green robe with frilly sleeves and a cape made of peacock feathers."

"And should we now air your dirty laundry, Glaucos?" Astolphos said, turning back at them with a mischievous smile.

Glaucos remained silent, probably realizing his mistake when he brought up their time back in Lumina.

"Back when I was going trying out something new, and let me tell you all, that peacock cape looked stunning, Glaucos was going through an episode on his own. Do you remember that waitress?"

"Don't say any more!" Glaucos said in as threatening a tone as a crystal could muster.

"You proposed to her on the spot and then went to get some wedding bands made. Do you remember helping me forge that wagon wheel of a ring? We spent several months making that thing, but it melted during the wedding!"

"I was nervous!"

"Several months of work, and it was gone a few minutes after you first wore it."

"You were crying behind the church because of that!"

"Who wouldn't? Such a masterpiece reduced to a hot pool on the church floor!"

Intros and Cyrillys broke out laughing at the scene in front of them. Inaris was barely able to contain herself as the cards fell to the floor, as she, too, stifled a giggle.

Astolphos cleared his throat, "Truce?" He asked Glaucos.

"Truce. And the first mold is done."

The mold above Glaucos cooled down, but it took an hour before Astolphos removed the finished molds and put on a new set. The finished mold was for a simple ring. Usually, he would never use molds for any of this, instead electing to use his hands and tools to shape the metal. But that process would take time, and that was a limited resource at the moment. Using a mold meant less work at the cost of reduced quality.

With the finished form, he went to another table-sized forge with a few small pieces of charcoal inside. He lit it with a firestarter and went to prepare the gold as it was heating up around a small crucible.

"Does anyone know where Kennas put the gold bars?"

"I think she put them under the unused bed," Cyrillys said.

And true to his words, three gold ingots lay underneath the bed, covered in linen.

"That's Kennas for you," Glaucos said, "hiding the valuables even when a common thief would stand no chance against six Gifted."

Astolphos pulled one of them out, realizing it was far too big.

He sighed, "Do you know if you have any saws that can cut through metal?"

"No," Inaris said, "But I have an idea. Can you put the ingot onto the table?"

Astolphos did as he was told, and Inaris stepped up to the table. She raised her hand above her head with fingers outstretched. The air whirled around the room, intensifying as it all moved toward her fingers. It wheezed as she chopped down onto the ingot, the table creaking and bending as if it was about to break. But it did not, and when Astolphos looked, the ingot was cut into six pieces.

A chill ran down his spine, and his eyes went to Inaris, beaming with pride.

"It worked!" She said, giggling.

"Kennas has told you not to do that!" Cyrillys yelled, making Intros clasp a hand on his mouth.

"Shut it. We don't want Kennas to hear you."

That fact frankly did not surprise Astolphos. That Gift Inaris used was one for offense, not utility. Kennas would not want anyone to lose Control like she had many years ago.

"What did she tell you?" Astolphos asked.

"She said that nothing good could come out of that Gift, and it was best to forget it."

"Has she explained why she thinks that?"

The three apprentices all shook their heads.

"Then that's not my story to tell. But let me tell you something else. She's been through a lot; you should not take her word for granted. But I'll tell you this, she can be very protective of you. She wants to ensure you get as good a life as possible, but her way might not suit all of you. Listen to what she says, and think about it. Some of it will make sense, some might not, but you should never take anyone's word as law.

"Inaris, that Gift you just used can be dangerous, but it might also be just the defensive tool you might need at some point. Having it up your sleeve might not be that bad of an idea, right? Besides, what you have is granted to you by the Gifter himself. Forgetting about it is the same as abandoning everything he stood for."

"Quite something to come from you," Cyrillys said.

Astolphos took that one on the cheek, he deserved it, and they all knew that.

"So, what about you two?" Astolphos asked, "What're your Gifts?"

"Bulwarking," Ontrys said shortly. He rolled up his sleeves and showed his bare arm. The skin thickened and deformed, eventually graying as it turned as hard as stone.

"Anything regenerative?"

"Not yet, unfortunately. But perhaps I'll get it later."

"Perhaps you will. Those two Gifts tend to cling together."

Astolphos then turned to Cyrillys, who silently looked down at the ground.

"He's not yet gotten his Gift," Intros explained, putting a hand on Cyrillys' shoulder. Astolphos approached and rustled Cyrillys' hair.

"Don't overthink it. You'll get your Gift eventually. As for Inaris, I think I have a task where you can put that Gift to good use."

Chapter 23

Lunarias set off as soon as she knew where she was going, mostly because she was afraid that staying would make her say something to the captain she would regret. A garrison captain should not send someone out to make reports for him when a knight makes an inquiry. He should have gone there himself. But right now, she did not have any other place to be, so it was necessary not to rock the boat too much.

She could be sure of one thing for certain. Looking at the other guards in the garrison, this problem was not solely for the gate guards. She had to send a letter of this to the capital, informing her superiors of this fact and hopefully get some improvements made.

But the walk to the farms was long, and now that she had closed that topic, her mind wandered to her conversation with Astolphos last night. She knew she was just running away from her duty, involving herself with the garrison and taking their assignments, but she did so because she simply did not know what else to do.

She had cursed herself all night for not knowing how to respond to the Abyssal. She had heard Abyssals swearing their allegiance to the Abyssal King before, but that was while blades were drawn and lives were on the line. This was the first time she had heard it come up in a somewhat calm conversation. From the mouth of someone somber, not furious. The face that said the proclamation was not painted in anger and bloodlust but sadness and regret. Much worse, she heard the arguments, and part of them resonated with her.

Walking through the streets, she finally saw the homelessness and misery surrounding her. It was precisely as Astolphos had said. She was truly taught not only to ignore it, she only looked at them as potential criminals.

And she also knew she took this case for the same reason. Perhaps some form of atonement, but she shot the thought down, half of the fear for where that rabbit hole would take her. Focus on the task and nothing else. That was what she filled her head with instead.

She was so caught up in her thoughts she had not realized that not only had she passed through Hybrik's gates, but her destination was right in front of her. She was halfway down a narrow dirt road sandwiched between two wheat fields. Ultimately, she saw three straw-thatched houses arranged in a horseshoe, with four people bickering in front of a small shed.

"And what're we supposed to do!?" One of the farmers yelled, "We can't put food on the table if we can't borrow your scythes!"

"And we can't give them to you because then we can't get our crops harvested in time!"

Their argument, however, ceased when they spotted Lunarias. Their eyes fell to the crest, and they bowed.

"What's this about?" Lunarias asked.

"Nothing important, m'lady," A farmer said, "Just some peasants falling on hard times, nothing worth your time."

"I've come here because I've heard reports from the guards that your tools are breaking every night. I'm here to investigate this."

The farmers looked at each other, "We didn't think they'd send anyone, let alone a knight."

"But I'm what they could spare. Could you please tell me what's been happening here?"

"It's going to be faster to show you."

One of the farmers opened the shed beside them, gesturing to a pile of wood and iron lying on the ground. Lunarias entered and picked up the remnants of a shovel. The metal still looked usable, but the handle was broken in three places. The breaks, however, were clean, straight lines that no animal could produce.

"Every morning, we check the shed, and something new is broken. Every day. We asked the guards to investigate weeks ago, and now we don't have the equipment to tend the fields fast enough."

"The metal seems usable. Can't you fit new shafts to them and bring the tools inside your houses?"

"We tried both. But then, parts of our crops started dying instead. Larger and larger patches every day until we put the tools back in the shed."

Lunarias looked around the shed. The doorway was wholly visible from the house on the opposite end. There even was a window looking directly at it.

"Have any of you tried staking out the shed? Perhaps keeping an eye on it from that window?" She asked, pointing at the house.

"My boy did once," One of the farmers said, "He says he saw rustling around the shed but could not see anything."

"Behind or to the sides?"

"Behind the shed."

Lunarias rose from the ground and felt around on the shed's back wall. It did not take long before she felt loose planks that could be pushed away to create an opening. She could pass through the opening with ease. The farmers looked at each other, perplexed.

"Has these planks been like this for a long time?"

"I fixed up the shed two months ago. They weren't loose back then."

"That means that we've found out how they enter."

"So you believe us?"

Lunarias nodded, "An animal isn't able to remove nails. Now we just have to catch them."

"Are you going to call the guards?"

"I don't think that's going to work. They'll make too much noise and scare the thugs away. We'll deal with this ourselves."

Lunarias exited the shed and went to stand in the middle of the houses. There were only two roads in and out, one leading to Hybrik and one leading south. To the east, behind the furthermost house, was a forest. In between was another wheat field. To the North was a field of cows, while the south had a bunch of large apple trees.

"Does that forest end up becoming the Forest of Sorrows?" Lunarias asked.

"That's right," One of the farmers answered.

"And is there a fence behind that house?" She pointed at the house to the east, at which the farmers nodded.

"Alright, I have a plan. I need you to dig up the part of the fence obscured by the house."

Chapter 24

It had been a hard day of work in the basement. Everyone had fallen into their own rhythm, each with different duties that worked together to make the production as smooth as possible. Astolphos looked up from his workshop to look at the apprentices at work. Intros stood at the forge with Glaucos, heating the gold to pour it into a mold for a ring. The skin on his hand hardened before he grabbed the searingly hot crucible and poured its content like it was a pitcher of wine. Cyrillys was busy with the molded products. He sat at a desk with a pan on the table and a set of whetstones. He sanded and polished the molded gold pieces. He then gave it to Inaris, who would cut the gemstones to size using her Gift and hand them to Astolphos, who would fasten everything together and take care of the final fit and finish. In the downtime between rings, he would work at the other forge, making gold links for necklaces. Astolphos thought it was an overall great setup they had going. The jewelry might have been better quality if Astolphos had taken care of the entire process himself, and quite a few slip-ups resulted in remelting rings and throwing away gems. Still, the speed at which they worked was far greater than Astolphos could ever have imagined. It was so great that he thought about getting a few apprentices for his next shop.

There was a knock on the door. Astolphos had locked it so that the apprentices had time to hide their Gifts in case some other apprentice had any business with them. He only opened the door when Intros' skin was normal, and Inaris had no levitating gemstones around her.

"How's it going?" Kennas asked, having taken the shape of Ontrys once again, "I've not heard anything from you all day, so I thought I'd check in."

Kennas locked the door behind her, returned to her real form, and walked for the pile of gold rings.

"You've done so much?" She picked up a ring and examined it. They were all relatively simple, a bare gold band with one-to-five stones on top. The gemstones were chosen randomly from the pile of garnets, amethysts, peridots, and opals. They were perfect for their purpose. The gold and gems would attract attention, but the craftsmanship would deter most sales. Combine this with a ludicrous price tag, and they would end up in the situation they hoped for."13 rings, 6 pendants," Astolphos said, "Half of the rings are ready for market, while the pendants still need chains. Your apprentices are naturals at this."

Kennas giggled, "I'm sure they're happy to hear it. I hope my emphasis on versatility makes sense to you three now."

Kennas put down the ring, flashing a grin to each of the apprentices.

"I'm sure 'Stolfos are going to reward your hard work. Remember the competitions back in Lumina?"

"How could I forget?" Astolphos said, smiling at the old memory,

"The other Gifted in the forge would work themselves to exhaustion for a chance to win. But I'm not going to do something like that here. How about we go out to get some dessert after dinner tonight?"

Inaris and Cyrillys were beaming at this, while Intros asked,

"What was the reward back then?"

"I was responsible for the city smiths across the entire country. Win the competition, and you'd get your own smithy where you would be the master."

"Quite the reward," Intros said.

"By the way," Astolphos said to Kennas, "How's it going with getting that booth?"

"We got it on Tuesday, so now we need something to sell. And judging by these, we don't need to worry about that."

"But that doesn't mean we can relax yet. We're going to put in the same effort tomorrow, right?"

The three apprentices nodded, all seemingly looking forward to tomorrow.

"Dinner's about ready," Kennas said, morphing back into Ontrys,

"Let's go up and get something to eat."

They all followed Kennas up into the workshop, where a long table fashioned out of several smaller ones was set up in the middle. Two apprentices were yelling at each other.

"Please excuse me," Kennas said as she went to the two apprentices. They immediately quieted, but Kennas sat them down and started talking to them.

"That sight brings back memories," Glaucos said.

"We've been in that situation far too many times, though our topics probably were a bit more serious."

"And don't forget the times when Nitris and Heuristrys really got going."

"What're you two talking about?" Inaris asked.

"Just two old friends we used to journey with."

"Isn't that the names of the Hand of Assassination and the Hand of-" That was all Cyrillys got to say before Astolphos shushed him and pushed everyone further away from the crowd. Astolphos crouched at a frightened Cyrillys. "You need to make sure no one can hear you when discussing these things, understand? If the wrong person hears it, you will die."

The frightened boy nodded frantically. His eyes scanned the room to do what he was told.

"It should be fine here," Astolphos said, "The focus of the crowd is all centered on Kennas at the moment, and it'd probably be fine before anyway. It just never hurts to play it safe.

"But yes, Nitris was the Hand of Assassination, and Heuristrys was the Hand of Commerce. They're old friends of Kennas and me."

"Does that mean they're still alive too?"

"That's right. The five of us are the last remaining Hands."

"Are you sure?" Intros asked in a tone far higher than Astolphos was comfortable with.

"Keep it down. But yes, they rely on my Gift to live for this long. I've not met anyone else, so they probably died of old age long ago."

"What about Balacastrys?" Intros asked.

"That's quite specific," Astolphos said. Intros' hands grasped his clothes tightly, his eyes filled with a certain intensity rarely found through pure curiosity alone.

Balacastrys was also a unique case. Technically, he was not dead, just permanently incapacitated.

"There's no way Balacastrys is still around, that's for sure."

"And you're sure of this?" Intros hands let go of his clothes only to grab hold of Astolphos'. The grip was solid, pulling Astolphos up from his kneeling position.

"I saw it with my own eyes," Astolphos said, leaving out the detail that he was the reason for it.

Intros lips wavered before he released his grip.

"What's this about?" Astolphos asked.

"Nothing." Intros turned around and headed back to the basement door.

"Intros, dinner's soon ready," Kennas yelled.

"I'm not hungry." And with that, he closed the door.

The eyes of the many apprentices were now squarely on the group of Gifted, their gazes making Astolphos shift around uncomfortably.

"Back to work, everyone!" Kennas yelled, "You know your tasks. I'll take care of things."

She approached Astolphos briskly, "What happened?"

"He asked about Balacastrys."

"We'll talk about this after dinner." And she was gone once again, busily giving orders to the apprentices. A few were staring angrily at Cyrillys and Inaris, who was still standing with Astolphos in the corner.

"Is there something wrong?" Astolphos asked the two apprentices.

"We've been taken off all duties as long as you're here," Inaris answered.

"They're probably wondering why we were the lucky ones," Cyrillys said, then shrugging, "It's just a hunch."

Chapter 25

Everything was silent around the small shed. Despite the farmers being just ordinary people, they knew the importance of following orders. If they had to catch those thugs tonight, they had to follow them exactly. Night fell long ago, and Lunarias had sat in the corner of the shed for hours now, obscured by a holed cape and a small pile of hay. The temperature had dropped substantially since then, her armor doing nothing to contain the escaping heat.

But this was not her first ambush, far from it. She knew the drill and toughed it out in silence, waiting for her prey to come in range before striking like a viper. Her fang was ready, the sword drawn and in her hand with a loose grip. However, her objective was not to kill whoever entered but to capture them. Therefore, she had sealed the scabbard onto the blade using tree sap, just enough to keep the scabbard on during a swing but still be able to rip it off in case she needed the sharpness.

At long last, something happened outside. She heard hushed whispers accompanied by careful footsteps. They approached the shed; she was sure of it. However, she could only listen to fragments of their conversation, which contained nothing helpful. The footsteps reached the shed, but instead of going for the actual entrance, the steps reached around, approaching the loose planks on the back wall.

"Think they've found out?" One of the voices said.

The planks moved slowly to not make the wood creak, "Not yet, at least."

Lunarias could not help herself from smiling. These idiots were in the bag soon enough.

Two entities dressed in baggy clothes sneaked into the shed, their faces obscured by what seemed to be a scarf but might as well be another fold. Their attire was utterly black, and Lunarias would not have known they were there without their voices and the pale blue moonlight shining through the ceiling.

She waited for both of them to enter. Even though this seemed to be an open and shut case, she needed to be sure, and the way to do so was to witness the crime itself.

They did not see Lunarias. They did not even look in the direction of the pile of hay not there the previous night.

"Think they'll pay soon?" One thug said to the other.

"I don't even think they can afford it anymore, but boss' orders are boss' orders."

One of the assailants drew a small hatchet from his many folds while the other grabbed a shovel and held the shaft with both hands. Once again, they did not realize that fewer tools were present than usual, especially of the sharp variety.

The hatchet-wielding thug raised it over his head and swung it down, cleaving the shovel shaft in two. That was her call for action. She pushed away the cape and the layers of hay on top of it, the sound of her armor taking the attention of the two thugs instantly.

"What'd we here?" One of them asked, "What're you doing up so late at night?"

"My word is that of the royal family itself. By the orders of the knights of Aurillia, surrender your weapons and get on the ground now." She presented her blade to the thugs, who grew silent. She knew it would not be that easy, and sure enough, the two ran through the planks of which they entered, ripping out the final nails that kept them on. But her command was not for them. It was for the villagers.

She heard the two thugs curse, probably as one of the villagers exited the wheat field and blocked their southern route. Lunarias exited through the actual door, knowing her plan was set in motion.

Sure enough, the two thugs ran to the center between the houses. The children inside heard the commotion and lit the candles to fool them into thinking the villagers were leaving their beds. The two thugs looked around, their eyes settling on the east, only to quickly look to the west. Lunarias stepped back, letting the two thugs see the unobstructed path westward toward Hybrik.

They did not think straight anymore as they made a mad dash for the road, a dash that would make them pass Lunarias at full speed.

She capitalized on it, stepping forward and swinging her sword across her shoulder. The two thugs could not stop, knowing full well that doing so would lead to their capture. They ran past her, and she swung her sword at the closest one's head, hitting him with all her might and sending him to the group with a dull thud.

"NOW!" Lunarias yelled.

Another two villagers stepped out of the wheat, blocking the thug's road back to Hybrik.

"Secure this one," Lunarias said to the villager blocking the southern road, pointing at the unconscious body on the ground.

She then took a step forward. The thug looked around for a way to escape. His eyes met the newly-planted fence to the northeast. The way southeast, however, was still unobstructed, covered in wheat that he could hide in. That was exactly where she wanted him to think.

He fell for the trap, sprinting straight through the wheat, lowering his stance to hide in the stalks. Lunarias followed him at a leisurely pace, counting her steps as her feet reached the wheat. After five steps, she heard a scream, followed by the sound of a body hitting the ground, and then the yells of the villager that jumped on the thug.

She counted ten more steps and kicked ahead lightly. Her shoes hit the low fence they had put in the field earlier. She took a high step to get over it, and immediately, she was inside a small circle of cleared ground, where the villagers wrestled with the thug.

"You all did well!" Lunarias yelled to the villagers as she grabbed the thug by the collar and dragged him up, punching him hard in the head with her steel-covered hand.

"Let's get these guys dragged into the house."

Chapter 26

The night soon passed underneath the dim light of a small candle. Hours upon hours were spent evaluating the finished wares and setting their prices. All was done quietly to allow the apprentices to get their well-deserved sleep. Intros did not leave the room yesterday for dinner, instead electing to go to bed early. He did not budge when the other apprentices and Astolphos returned. Astolphos suspected part of it was a ruse, but he did not remark on it nor try to test his theory.

Eventually, his work was done, and he lied in bed and talked with Glaucos for hours. Not having to sleep certainly had its benefits, but those quickly vanished when around someone who had to. But those hours went by, morning arrived with a couple of swift knocks on the door, and Kennas yelled that breakfast was ready.

Cyrillys was the first to get out of bed. He was down from his bunk at the first knock. His task was to drag both Intros and Inaris out of the grasp of sleep. Inaris did so with complaints and attempted negotiations but eventually yielded. Intros got out of bed without a word, something that, by the faces of the other two apprentices, was highly abnormal. He still wore the same clothes as yesterday and was the first to leave. However, it no longer seemed like he was angry, just in a bad mood.

"You coming to get breakfast?" Inaris asked Astolphos.

"Thanks for the offer, but I think I'll be warming up the forges instead. Just take your time out there. I'm not stringent on work hours."

And the two apprentices exited the basement, leaving Glaucos and Astolphos alone.

"You think we can have it all done for the market?" Glaucos asked.

"I'd say we already have what we need to get the job done, but the more we make, the higher the chance of getting noticed. If everyone's working as efficiently as yesterday, we'll probably be done with two and a half gold bars before stopping for the day."

There was a knock on the door, and Kennas entered. She did not change from Ontrys' form this time. She sat on Intros' bed, right beside the desk Astolphos worked at.

"Not hungry?" Kennas asked.

"I thought this was the perfect time to talk about what happened yesterday."

Astolphos readjusted his seat, looking at Kennas, whose eyes stared deeply into his own. Despite how alive the disks seemed, Astolphos knew it was all a ruse. This was Kennas when she was serious.

"So, what did you tell Intros yesterday?" Kennas asked.

"Not much. Inaris asked about the other Hands. She wanted to know if there was anyone else still alive. Intros asked about Balacastrys, and he acted like that when he got the answer."

"You said nothing more than that?"

"Nothing more than that. Do you know what that's about?"

Kennas was silent for a moment, struggling to find the words, but eventually, she looked up, took a deep breath, and said, "He thinks his father is Balacastrys."

Astolphos was at first ready to laugh at that idea, but he knew well that this was not a laughing matter. Kennas was too serious for this to be a joke.

"There must have been a mistake," Glaucos said, "There's no way Balacastrys got out of the crystal, right?" Astolphos knew that question was directed at him, but he did not know how to answer.

"...There is a tiny chance. I'd say we'll see a late Aurillian king strut through the street naked, covered in tar and feathers. But there is a chance."

"I tried talking to Intros about this," Kennas said, "Tried asking about the appearance of his father, how he speaks. He truly thinks his father is Balacastrys, our Balacastrys."

"Have you gone to check?" Astolphos asked. His thoughts were a whirl of wonder and a looming feeling of death.

Kennas shook her head.

"Why?" Glaucos asked, his tone more accusatory than questioning.

"I-I've been busy here with all of the apprentices and all of that. A-and the orders have increased-"

"You've always been a terrible liar," Glaucos interjected, "Just tell us the truth."

Kennas sighed, her head slumped down, "I'm afraid of knowing the truth. It took all of you to seal that bastard away. What chance would I have alone."

"But if he's escaped, we can be sure he's somewhere back in Lumina,"

"But what if we're wrong about that too? I took in Intros because his mother wanted him to live in Aurillia. But what if he's sent here as a lure?"

"You think he might be waiting there to finish what we started?"

Kennas nodded.

"Then I'll go check once the carriage is done," Astolphos said, "I'll send the phylactery to the next city by a fast horse. Without it near me, It'll be a stalemate."

"But you can't take him on alone!" Kennas rose from her seat, looking down at Astolphos with an exasperated expression.

"I'm not trying to, I'll go to see if he's still encased in crystal, and I'll report back once I've gotten to the next city. Have you heard anything from Nitris or Heuristrys?"

Kennas shook her head.

"Then we can be sure that we can contact them through the normal channels. I'll send all of you a letter about my findings."

But Kennas did not at all look assured by Astolphos' calm demeanor. Sure, it was only a front, Astolphos did not like the thought of that monster being free to roam once again, but he needed Kennas to be focused. One problem at a time, they had to take care of those thieves first. He put both hands on Kennas shoulders and looked her in the eyes.

"Don't worry, I'll be careful."

"It's probably just some imposter trying to cash in on Bala-castrys' name anyway," Glaucos said.

Astolphos agreed, nodding along. It seemed like that reached into Kennas as she dried her eyes and shook her head.

"Promise me you'll be careful."

"When am I not careful?"

"All the time,"

"Agreed."

There was a knock on the door. One of the apprentices opened it, telling Kennas about some conflict that had arisen at the table. With a sigh, Kennas told the apprentice that she would soon be there and told him to shut the door.

"And please don't talk to Intros about any of this. He has kind of a short fuse."

Chapter 27

The following night was one of many interruptions and uncomfortable sleep. Not only had the thugs taken up the bedroom in the house closest to the forest, but their screams also made it impossible for anyone to sleep in there. As such, the inhabitants had huddled with their neighbors, eagerly anticipating the moment their unwanted guests were no longer their problem. But even then, they all still had to wake up during the night. Lunarias and the grownups were taking turns going to the house and knocking on pots and pans to keep sleep away from the thugs as they sat bound in total darkness.

The morning after, everyone seemed to be internally begging to go back to bed, but there was work to be done. The peasants had to go to the city to fashion new shafts for their tools, while Lunarias had to harvest any information she could from their uncooperative guests. But first, it was time for breakfast.

Their breakfast was eaten in silence. All the peasants had collected inside one of the houses, eagerly awaiting to hear what Lunarias' plan was. She knew what had to be done next, but that was probably not something anyone wanted to see, less participate in. She tried to keep her mind away from it by focusing on the bowl of rye gruel in front of her, a thick, paste-like substance filled with half-broken seeds of rye. It tasted bland at best and had a repulsively sour taste at worst.

Frankly, she looked back at the food in the barracks with fond memories.

The peasants had insisted on sending someone to Hybrik to get something better, but she refused without giving an explanation. However, she knew very well why she had done so, and it was not because of her usual disinclination towards the gifts of the citizenry. It was because she wanted to try the peasant's life, or at least as close as someone in her position could. The blacksmith's words truly struck a chord, but saying that out loud was something she could not do. Speaking to the peasants that she wanted to try their lives would be conceding defeat to the enemy she had been fighting for so long.

As such, she sat in the tiny house with the peasants, eating the same food they had eaten daily for years. The silence dominated the crowded room, and all eyes were on her. One particularly sleep-deprived, grumpy man gave her a stern gaze, perhaps because his wife had forced him out of his bed to make room for the children of the currently occupied house, and he saw this as Lunarias' fault.

"So why wait so long to go to those bastards?" The man asked. His wife did not look amused by his bad temper, but Lunarias smiled slightly as she put down her empty bowl.

"When lacking sleep, you're likelier not to think of what you're saying. Keeping them awake all night makes them more likely to slip up."

"You knights surely are impressive. We'd never think of what you did yesterday, nor about how to deal with the bastards after."

"It's part of our training. All knights of the Second Order have to participate in battlefield tactics and interrogation techniques classes."

"Still, thank you very much for your help."

"It's all part of my duty. Now, let's get some information out of those thugs."

***

The two thugs were tied to chairs facing away from each other. All shutters were closed, and the candles were blown out. They had sat like that all night, unable to move and sleep because of the clanging of pots and pans. The door to the out-side was the only way in and out, and Lunarias held the only key. At first, the thugs screamed insults at them, but as the hours passed, the insults turned to negotiation and then again into pleading for their release. Now they were silent, or at least that was what Lunarias was thinking the entire time. As she approached the door, she heard that they were, in fact, talking to each other in exhausted tones.

She opened the door, and the thugs groaned as the light hit their eyes. In Lunarias' hand was a bucket of cold water, which she placed beside the door. She walked briskly to the shutters and flung them open, letting further sunlight blind her prisoners.

"Why're you here?" Lunarias asked pointedly.

The two thugs snickered at each other before one said, "Because some crazy bitch ambushed us."

Lunarias raised an eyebrow and sighed. Everything was as she expected, but the stupidity of the common thug still managed to fall flat on the low bar that was her expectations. That fact was all too oblivious to them as they looked at her disappointment with smiles.

She had not come to make friends or be the main bit of a comedy routine. She walked in front of the thug closest to the door. Their snickering faded with every step. The other looked from side to side to see what was happening, but the ropes did not allow so, just letting the periphery glimpse her armor. She put a hand on the shoulder of the thug in front of her and pushed back. This was the first time she had seen anything resembling fear on his face. She looked into his eyes, seeing him grow increasingly nervous by the silence until she clenched her fist and hit him in the stomach. He wheezed as the air was forced from his lungs, but Lunarias wasted no time, releasing her grip and finding a comfortable pace to walk around the two.

"I'll ask you again, why are you here?"

This time, her question was met with silence. The one she hit still gasped for breath, but he dared not meet her eyes. The other put up a front, but his hands shook as his eyes darted from her face to her breastplate. He knew full well of her position and what that allowed her to do. That told her one thing, she had to focus on the other one, as this one would talk.

"Last chance," She said, walking over to get the bucket. When she was again met with silence, she put the bucket onto the lap of the one she hit and grabbed the back of his head. He realized what would happen when she forced his head into the water.

He struggled against the ropes, his fingers stretched and clenched as he desperately tried to break the hemp forcing them to the armrests. He tried to raise his head, but Lunarias was stronger. The water sprayed from the bucket foamed and bubbled from his struggle and breath. The sounds he made reminded her of the death throes of a deer. She gave him 15 seconds underwater, but the time felt like an eternity. Lunarias could not look at the scene for disgust at her actions. His partner in crime was, however, of another mind. He twisted and turned to see what happened, what she was doing to his colleague, all to no avail.

At last, she reached 15 and pulled his head out of the bucket. He gasped for breath, but she gave him no time before she slapped him with her free hand and said, "This's the last time I'll ask nicely. Why are you terrorizing these peasants?"

But they still did not budge. This was not what she expected or hoped for. She was never the one taking care of the interrogations. She did not have the stomach to treat humans like this, nor the sense of immorality necessary to usually spare an Abyssal, let alone talk to them. That was, at least, how she had felt until last week, but she was somehow relieved her stance on the former had not shifted. But that meant she was not looking forward to what came next.

She grabbed the head of the wet thug. He screamed as he went underwater again. This time, she did not count the seconds. His partner screamed, yelling obscenities at her, but they, too, died down as the seconds passed. This time, her target was not a time but the point where his struggle veined.

"You can't do this!" The other thug screamed, jumping in his chair without moving an inch, "You'll kill him!"

She ignored his outburst, filing everything down as him reaching the breaking point. Her focus was on the one in the bucket. Then she felt it, or more aptly, stopped feeling it. His head thrashing about slowed, and that was when she grabbed him by the hair and pulled him up. It took a second before the water spouted from his mouth like a fountain. But still, there was no room for a break. She put the bucket back on the ground and circled the two. At first, she was silent as she stared down at the two. One seemed too tired, or perhaps he had given up. The other was afraid. He stared her in the eyes, but there was no antagonism in his gaze, only a silent plea that screamed of a last-ditch effort he did not even believe in.

She then put a hand on the pommel of her sword.

"I'm a knight of the Second Order. I'm only answering to those of the First Order and Queen Keiris herself. Of those, none will even raise an eyebrow at the mention of two missing low-lives like yourselves."

She then pulled her blade from the scabbard, letting the tip hover slightly above the ground, pointing its sharp edges at their feet.

"You were caught at the scene of the crime. Not only that, but I personally witnessed you commit it. Whatever punishment I deem fair is law, and your lack of cooperation leads me to only one conclusion."

Their eyes were fixed on the blade. They did not see Lunarias' other hand loosen one of the two straps keeping the scabbard fixed.

Her pacing stopped at the side of the one who had been through a lot this morning. He looked up at her with a surrendering look, almost telling her to get it over with. She checked on the other one. His eyes were strained because she was barely outside of view. Just enough for him to see her swing the blade but not enough to see it hit.

Her grip stiffened as she lifted the blade above her head. She swung it down towards his foot but adjusted her aim at the last second for it to miss. Her other hand reached for the scabbard and drew the end into his foot.

He screamed in pain, but Lunarias put her forearm to the back of his head and forced it into the bucket once again. As he struggled, Lunarias let go of the scabbard and grabbed the sword with her other hand, letting her get a proper grip on the head.

"I'm done asking nicely," Lunarias said, "I'd say you have about 20 seconds to answer me. Why are you here?"

The other guy stopped struggling, instead electing to sit as still as possible. He was shaking, and if she looked at his face, she was sure to see his lips wavering and his eyes darting. She was sure he was at the breaking point, but she had hoped he would have cracked by now. So far, everything she had done was reversible with a day of rest. The next thing was not. The guard would treat them as burglars, and only two punishments were available: forced labor or the loss of a hand.

She pulled the man's head out of the bucket to give him a moment to breathe, but this was only to make sure he had the air to scream. She lodged her sword in the space between his right hand and the armrest and twisted the blade before drawing it back slowly. Her eyes were on the edge, rotating it to ensure blood stained the metal. The screams were as intense as if she had lobbed it off completely. The weak facade of his companion broke down once again.

"What the hell are you doing!" He yelled, his eyes having caught sight of the sword slowly vanishing back towards her.

"Last chance to speak," she said coldly, her eyes not leaving the blade for a moment.

"I'll be dead the moment I'm out of here if I say anything!"

"But you'll be dead in here if you don't."

At that point, the sword was free. She examined it for a moment. The polished steel reflected a scarlet mirror image of her face.

"Suit yourself," she then said. She curled her fist and hit the man in the back of the head, knocking him unconscious. The bucket fell to the ground, its half-empty contents spilling on the floor.

Then silence reigned. There was no screaming, no gurgling, nothing but the slow dripping of water off the unconscious man's face and the hyperventilating breaths of the other.

"Kantos? Kantos! You there!?"

He continued to ask like that for several minutes, but eventually, Lunarias tapped her blade to his neck, and his calls immediately faded.

"He's gone, and you'll be next," she said as she walked before him, the tip almost touching his skin.

His eyes saw the bloodstains on the blade and thrashed against his binds, once again to no avail.

"Please, anything but that!"

"Then start talking, or you'll see the Ancestors. Last warning."

"We're here to intimidate the farmers into paying protection money!" He yelled.

"Now we're getting somewhere. Is it just the two of you, or are there others?" Lunarias drew back her blade but kept it ready if he regained his nerve. Her mere gaze was enough to send him stammering, but eventually, he composed himself enough to continue.

"We're a group of mercenaries that ran out of jobs. Our commander got an idea to keep our men paid."

"And that was to extort it from the citizens. I take it that you're doing this across the city?" It was only a hunch, but something told her that Astolphos' friend had been a victim of these criminals, Abyssal or not.

"What else are you doing?"

"Theft, fencing, smuggling, you name it. But I'm just a grunt, nothing but a low-ranker! I can't tell you much."

"Where's your hideout?"

He held his breath and looked away. A slight twist of her sword was all it took to make him change his mind.

"It's in the slums!" He yelled, "It's the-"

The door to the living room was kicked open, and eight of Hybrik's city guards marched in with their weapons brandished.

"What's the meaning of this?" Lunarias asked.

"We've been sent by the Captain to check on you." One of the guards said, "He grew worried that something had gone wrong since you didn't return to the garrison yesterday." The eight guards lowered their weapons at the scene, but something stroke Lunarias as odd. It was hard to place, but something about their eyes told her there was more to the story than that.

"Then you have done so now. Please return to the commander and tell him everything is fine, and he can expect my return this evening."

"Lady Hewris, please let us assist. We'll be able to get something out of the prisoners back at the garrison."

"And how did you know I was interrogating them?"

The guard was silent momentarily before clearing his throat and saying, "It's obvious that you were trying to do so. The fact that you are struggling with it too is obvious since one is knocked out cold, and the other is completely untouched."

"Knocked out?" The thug said, now looking at Lunarias with a smirk, "You bitch."

"Guards, out of the room, now!"

Lunarias marched out of the room, grabbing the talking soldier by the sleeve and dragging him out. The other seven followed closely behind. When the door was locked, she turned around with an ice-cold glare as she slapped the group leader.

"Do you have any idea what you've just done!? Just as he had started talking, you idiots stormed in and ruined everything!"

"I'm sorry," was the only thing he could say.

"Know your station! You have no right to talk back to me or disobey my orders, and you've just done both. I'll tell the captain of your conduct and will personally make sure to reinstate your discipline. Do I make myself clear?"

The soldier nodded but did not seem unnerved in the slightest. It almost seemed like he did not care at all. It unnerved Lunarias, but she did not know how to act. For a moment, she questioned if they even were soldiers, but then she recognized one of them from her breakfast in the barracks.

"Good," Lunarias said, "Now leave this place. I have to pick up the scraps of your mistake, if even possible."

"Lady Lunarias," The same soldier said, "I insist we bring them back to the barracks. We'll be able to get more out of them that way."

"Are you intentionally being dense?" Lunarias barked, "I just told you that you have no power to disobey my orders. Now leave!"

The other seven soldiers took a step forward.

"We insist."

At that moment, one thought went through Lunarias' head. She felt threatened by them, and she knew she could not win a battle against all eight simultaneously. There was only one thing to do.

"On one condition," she said, "I will help you escort the prisoner back."

The soldiers nodded, and two went in to retrieve the prisoners. Lunarias poked her head out of the main door and yelled to one of the housewives, "Go get everyone. We're going to Hybrik to replace the tools you've lost. The bill is on the city guard."

There was one thing she knew, and that was that she did not want to be alone with those guards right now.

Chapter 28

It was time for days upon days of hard work to finally pay off, and unfortunately, it seemed like it was going to. It had never been the plan to actually sell any of the jewelry. It had all just been the facade used to draw the attention of the undesirables they wanted. But while working with the apprentices, Astolphos would say they had managed to create quite some pretty pieces. He especially liked the necklaces, with the thin chains holding a square embossed with simple vines and four gemstones, one in each corner. But as Astolphos and Cyrillys stood at the booth, they had gained little interest, much less a single sale. Things had gone exactly as predicted. Some aides approached the stand to look but were gone at the moment of a close inspection. Everyone else looked on from a distance, knowing full well that they did not have the Merias to buy a single piece. Their time was spent looking around, but not too well, as that might detract the thieves.

"This went worse than I'd anticipated," Astolphos mumbled.

"Cheer up, sir. There's still more time left before we close," Cyrillys said.

Astolphos chuckled, "That's right, try your best."

But as the uneventful hours passed and the morning turned to early evening, Astolphos felt someone watching them closely. He did his best to not look in that direction, instead trusting Glaucos to do the task as he lay on the counter among the other pieces. Soon after, Glaucos remarked that another person had joined.

Are they still watching the booth? Astolphos thought.

"They are," Glaucos said telepathically, "They've moved a bit but are still watching. A boy ran between them, likely delivering messages."

The two possible assailants never looked at each other, and judging by the fact that one was wearing baggy clothes while the other was dressed like a nobleman, it did not even look like they should know each other. However, that kid running between them was the link.

Tell me when they make their move.

He did not have to wait long before Glaucos said, "Now."

Astolphos almost looked in their direction but stopped himself at the last moment. Though he knew they were up to something, it was important they did not seem suspicious of them, or else they would disengage and go their separate ways.

Cyrillys was preoccupied with talking to a potential customer. In fact, he was having the longest conversation of the day about one of the rings with a single garnet.

The nobleman approached first, but Glaucos kept an eye on the kid, who slowly inched closer to the booth from the side.

"Ahem...smith?" The nobleman said.

"What can I do for you?" Astolphos said, putting on a fake smile.

"What's the most unique piece you have on sale?"

"That should be this one." Astolphos had hidden a few rings under the table for this occasion. There was no difference in quality between the ones he pulled out and the ones on the table, but it still created an illusion of increased worth. The ring was as simple as all the others, but it had a lapis lazuli on top, starkly contrasting the warmer colors on the table.

"Take a look at this one. The ring itself might be unremarkable, or at least as unremarkable as gold can be, but I can do anything you want with it. The gemstone is a sapphire. Rumor says it comes from the Abyss, found among some of the Abyssal King's original treasure."

That was a lie. Nobody had found the treasury of the Gifter yet. Not even the Hands knew of its location. The knowledge of its whereabouts was lost along with the life of their leader, and the only way to find it was to travel to Marados Castle to the north and break it down floor by floor until there was nothing left.

The nobleman took the ring and looked at it carefully.

"I like what I see, but what can you do to the ring?"

"Well...Anything really. What do you want?"

As the nobleman talked about what he wanted of changes, Glaucos constantly told Astolphos the location of the kid, who was now visible at the corner of Astolphos' eye.

"That should all be possible," Astolphos said while still struggling to make heads and tails of the various strange requests this 'nobleman' wanted, "but that'll take more than a few hours. What about I'll have it ready tomorrow at this time?"

The kid had gotten close enough to touch the table, and with a motion almost too quick for even the unblinking Glaucos to see, one of the necklaces on the table vanished into his sleeve."

"He took the bait," Glaucos said telepathically.

"That'll be sufficient," The 'nobleman' said, "I shall return tomorrow, and I'll bring ample payment."

And with that, the 'nobleman' vanished into the crowd in a different direction than the kid.

"Have his scent?" Glaucos asked.

Of course. Astolphos focused on the life essences around him and singled out the one belonging to the kid. He struggled his way through the crowd at a leisurely pace.

"Cyrillys, can you take care of the booth momentarily?" Astolphos asked, but he was already outside the booth before he got an answer.

Many people were at the market, far too many for singling someone out with sight alone. Nobody of their right mind would think they were followed through such a dense crowd. Astolphos had to shove and maneuver through the sea of people but never lost sight of his target. The road led to some unpopulated side streets, leading to an area stricken with poverty.

Astolphos did his best to keep his distance from the kid and hide himself to not raise suspicion, and for a time, it seemed like it worked. The kid looked back on several occasions but walked onward.

However, just because the kid could not see Astolphos, it did not mean both were blind to each other. Astolphos wondered about the kid's age, and he concluded that the boy was no more than eleven years old. It was an unusually low age for a thief, but it showed something fundamental about the organization they were dealing with. They were recruiting orphans to do their dirty work.

Astolphos did not look at his surroundings; he focused only on his target. It was a long route they walked, and Astolphos thought, on several occasions, they had gone around in circles. On more than one occasion, Astolphos was tempted to drain some life essence from the thief, just enough to make him grow weak and collapse, but the age of the thief was enough to make the thought leave as quickly as it came.

Suddenly, the thief stopped in his tracks. Astolphos hid behind a stack of rubbish, watching the essence as it stood still.

Then he felt a knife at his throat.

"You should've just let it happen," The 'nobleman' said.

The thief quickly turned around and walked to Astolphos.

"I thought someone was following me. Glad you helped me, boss," The kid said.

But Astolphos was calm. After all, it was just a knife. They could slice and dice all they wanted; he would not care.

"I'm worth so much more to you alive than dead," Astolphos said. He did not try to fake panic or fear. He kept his tone neutral as he stared the thief directly in the eyes. The 'nobleman' yanked him about, adjusting his grip around the knife as he pressed it closer to Astolphos' neck. He could feel the edge, how it dug into his skin. He was afraid that the 'nobleman' would slit his throat. Because then he would have to kill both of them.

"And why do you think so?" The 'nobleman' said.

"Because I know you've been robbing and thieving about in this city for some time now and that you're probably sitting with a lot of hot merchandise you want to be sold. I can help you with that."

"And how do you know that?"

"Words travel fast in our kind of circles. Once I heard of your band of misfits, I thought you may need the services of someone like me."

Astolphos initially planned to follow the thief home to their base. Never had he thought he might end up like this. Still, he thought there might be a way to salvage. Maybe he could get on their good side and talk them into telling him what he wanted to know. It was a long shot; he knew that all too well, but in the worst case, he still had other options, though less peaceful in nature.

"But you're just a market merchant!" The kid said.

"Did you not find it strange? A traveling goldsmith setting up shop in a market for the commoners?"

The two assailants looked at each other in confusion. It was evident that the thought never crossed their minds. Inside, Astolphos sighed heavily.

"Now," Astolphos said, "Could you please let go of the knife, so we can talk business?"

As per his orders, Astolphos felt the pressure lift from his throat.

"Alright, what're you offering?" The 'nobleman' asked.

"I'll take all your hard-earned gains and transform them into wares you can sell everywhere. Once I'm done, there'll be no sign of their origin, just a nice, no-risk payday for everyone."

"And what're you taking for your service?"

"Either ten percent or 1000 merias, half upfront and half when the job's done."

"1000 merias!? You're insane!" The kid said. The 'nobleman' glared at the kid, and he cowered and looked to the ground.

"I assure you, my services are well worth it. No need for a black market or smuggling. Full price for everything. The merias you earn for this is enough to retire on."

Astolphos was now sure the 'nobleman' in front of him was the leader of their racket. His eyes shined with greed, a look that told Astolphos his plan had worked.

"750," The 'nobleman' said.

"950."

"...850."

"Let's meet in the middle, 900. Else, we can say I'll take 500 grams of silver and the 850."

The kid looked exacerbated by the amounts being thrown around. The amount they were currently negotiating about was likely larger than what that boy would earn before the thieves had used him up. It was a shame. Who knew what that kid had been through. Now, his future might be forfeit, for no children could stay in that business for long. Either they grew up becoming worse than the ones raising them, or they did not grow up at all. It was these kinds of kids Kennas liked to take in as apprentices, kids whose circumstances could lead them down dark paths. A shame their paths had to cross like this. Even worse for the kid was that the men mentoring him were imbeciles. Astolphos did not think this plan would work because he had thought he was dealing with somewhat competent thieves.

"800 and the silver," The 'nobleman' said.

"Deal. I'll meet you here at sunrise for work. Oh, and I want my necklace back."

***

Astolphos returned to a closing market. The stalls were being taken down, and the crowds slowly thinned out. Cyrillys was busy packing up the wares.

"Master, welcome back. I made one sale while you were gone," Cyrillys said.

"Really? I didn't think we'd sell anything. Thank the Ancestors you only pay for the stalls for one day, else I'd be looking at a huge loss. What price did you sell it for?"

"50 merias."

Astolphos stopped in his tracks. The boy had also cut 30 percent off the price. He made a mental note to tell Kennas not to allow Cyrillys to stand at the counter.

"That's great," Astolphos said with a fake smile, "Was it a nobleman who bought it?"

"No sir, it was an innkeeper with some money to spare and a wife who's mightily mad at him."

"At least I hope she's happy with his purchase..."

Chapter 29

"You can't do that!" The guard yelled as Lunarias pushed him aside and kicked open the door to the captain's quarters. Just as she had expected, the captain was not in some meeting, unlike what the guard proposed. Instead, he was busy biting down on the leg of a turkey while playing a game of cards with two other guards and the old man who seemed to always be around.

Her entrance had not gone unnoticed, all eyes were on her, and none seemed more surprised than the captain, putting his cards back on the table and raising from his chair.

"What's the meaning of this!?" He asked.

"I can ask you the same! You have been avoiding me ever since I returned to the garrison; why?"

"What're you talking about?"

Lunarias sighed. The commander was a lousy liar. His eyes darted around as he tried feigning innocence. But even had he gotten a flawless delivery, the two soldiers giving each other a coy smile would have blown the story anyway. But none of that was of any interest to Lunarias. Her eyes were on the old guard, silently sipping on his ale as if he had no care in the world. She had not paid any mind to him until now, but something about him rubbed Lunarias the wrong way. At that point, she realized that he was, in fact, caring, as he seemed to intently listen to what happened around him.

"I've been to your office three times a day since I returned. Your guard outside always turns me back, saying you were having some kind of meeting."

The commander pointed at the table, "Can't you obviously see that that's true!?"

"Please," Lunarias said, "Not even the knights of the first rank are that busy with all of their politicking. And besides, none of you seems to be the guildmaster of the tanner's guild."

A glare was shot at that guard, who could not escape the room quickly enough, closing the door behind him. That was the last sound in the room as Lunarias and the captain stared each other down. She could see on his face that he knew his story was done for, but no one wanted to be the one to point it out. However, he was the first to break eye contact, but only because his gaze went to the old guard, who glared at him.

"I'm sorry about that, Lady Hewris. It seems like I've not done a good job of instructing him about my schedule. It'll not happen again."

"Spare me. Just tell me why your men refuse me access to the prison."

"Are they?"

"And while you're at it, I demand an explanation as to why they're saying there are no prisoners awaiting interrogation."

This time, there was no response at all. The captain just looked back and forth between her and the old guard, who still unhelpfully sipped on his ale.

"Well?" Lunarias asked, her fingers drumming on her bracers, "Speak up."

But he still stood dumbfounded. At that moment, the old guard put down his cup and cleared his throat.

"We've gotten no records of you bringing in any prisoners for interrogation."

"Shut up. I wasn't speaking to you." There were now two pairs of eyes on the captain, those of Lunarias and the old guard, both expectantly waiting for his following words.

"It's just as he said," The captain finally said, "No one has informed me that you brought prisoners back from the farms."

"Strange, the soldiers told me they would inform you about this."

"Are you sure you weren't fooled, Lady Hewris?" The old guard asked, "Perhaps you mistook some charlatans for soldiers and gave them your prisoners?"

"It's Knight Hewris to you, and I was with them the entire trip to the garrison and saw with my own two eyes the prisoners being led into the prison. The men posted at the prison entrance even greeted the soldiers by name. If you think I was tricked, you have a big problem on your hands."

"In that case, I have no idea what is happening."

Lunarias was speechless. Even though her expectations of this captain were low, she had expected him to at least put up a fight. Instead, he displayed his incompetency for all to see. He might as well have gone and claimed he had no control over his men.

"You're a disgrace to everything Aurillia stands for and unfit for your duty." And with that, Lunarias turned around and flung open the door out of his office.

"Where are you going!?" The captain glowed red, but she could sense fear in his voice. He knew exactly what she was going to do.

"I've deemed you unfit for duty. I will write a letter to my superiors with my assessment and request your replacement and a full investigation of the Hybrik garrison."

The red immediately turned pale. Even the old guard rose from his seat with surprise on his face. But the fear on the captain's face only lasted as long as it took Lunarias to reach the stairs. He came running from behind.

"What in the name of the Ancestors are you talking about?!" He yelled at her, "What makes you think that!?"

"Every single word you've uttered in my presence. Your ineptitude has been on display with every answer you've given me. You clearly have no control of your men, and worse, your hands-off approach has led to the decay of your soldiers' skills and lack of respect for rank."

"That's a downright lie!"

Lunarias stopped on the stairs and turned around to face the captain. Even though she looked up at him, the glare she gave made him flinch.

"Then let me ask you some questions. When was the last time you inspected the armory?"

And already at the first question, he lacked the words, trying and retrying to push out a sentence that was an excuse at best and an unintelligible mess at worst.

"And now that you've had almost a week to go and investigate, what's your assessment of the gate guards, and frankly, what about the rest of the lot? When was the last time you checked on their training regimen? For the love of the Ancestors, just tell me how many guards are on duty right now! Just answer one of the questions satisfactorily, and I'll give you one last chance."

It seemed like the old guard would open his mouth for a moment, but one sharp look from Lunarias was all it took to make him shut up.

Eventually, the captain said, "There are no problems with the training regimen."

That statement was laughable. Lunarias saw those training dummies every morning, and mold was the only thing attacking them. The old guard exhaled deeply. The captain was the only one who did not know how stupid an answer that was.

"Really?" That was all Lunarias could say. She could not fathom how that could be his response.

"Yes, we can go down and check on them right now. The archers should be in full swing."

"Captain," The old guard said, "Perhaps that's not such a good idea."

"I know what I'm doing! To the courtyard!"

Lunarias sighed. At least the idiot had confidence, she thought as he almost flew past her down the stairs. He walked with the spirit of a fool who did not know his routine had gone too far. Lunarias, at times even struggled to keep up with him. Surprisingly, that old guard kept up with Lunarias. He was perhaps the only guard in this garrison with the stamina for actual conflict.

Once again, Lunarias saw the lax attitudes of the guards as they exited the building, as not only were they not saluting their captain, they laughed at him behind his back. At that moment, the captain realized his mistake, as he saw no archers in sight. He stopped in his tracks, but Lunarias was not to let it stop there. She gave him a hard slap on the shoulder and said, "Come on, perhaps they're on break."

They went straight to the training dummies. Not only were they falling apart, the rotten straw inside stank so badly Lunarias removed a bracer to cover her nose with the sleeve. The captain did his best to tough it out, keeping a fake smile on his lips until he gagged.

"Do these seem worn out to you?" She asked.

"Of course. Look, they're so worn they're falling apart."

"Come and take a closer look then. There's not a single visible cut or arrow mark on them. They're falling apart because they've been standing here for months. A garrison where the guards are training will run through a set daily. Can you tell me how these are rotting away if your men truly keep up their regimen?"

The captain took a few steps back and took a deep breath. His smile had turned deprecating as he looked at Lunarias.

What had happened had not gone lost on the soldiers, who all approached them.

"I must admit, I've been quite preoccupied as of late. I might not have been keeping an eye on my men."

"It must've been more than a year, I guess. Look at your men's armor. What do you see?"

"Everything seems fine to me."

"So you're fine with their armor being dotted with rust?"

The captain became quiet.

"And let me ask you this again. Do you know how your guards signal each other at the gate?"

And the captain once again struggled. Even the crowd looked around uncomfortably.

Lunarias sighed, "They're hitting their spears against the stone walls. That guard I met at the gate did not have a spear. It had been dulled so much that it was practically a stick with a metal cap at the end."

"I'll send some men to look into all of this."

"Don't bother. Your replacement will take care of that for you."

"Please," The captain pleaded, "Give me one more chance."

"Alright, one last chance," Lunarias said, "And every single one of your men is more than welcome to help you. Where are my prisoners?"

Just at the edge of her vision, she saw movement as one of the soldiers tried his hardest to get away from the crowd.

"Halt! You in the back!"

And he instinctively knew she referred to him. He turned around, and she quickly realized why he tried to escape. This was one of the guards that had gone to the farms to get her, and not only that, he was one of those that had led the prisoners into the prison. Their eyes locked, and he knew the game was over.

"Get over here, now!" Lunarias demanded. He dutifully followed her order and soon stood surrounded by the crowd along with Lunarias, the captain, and the old guard.

"Perhaps you can tell me where my prisoners are? You escorted them into the prison after all."

"Are you sure you're not mistaking me for someone else," He started to say before the captain cut him off, "For the love of the Ancestors, tell her the truth."

The guard hesitated, looking around at the crowd for a moment before lowering his eyes, "We tried to interrogate them ourselves, but we couldn't get anything else out of them. We released them the next day."

The captain looked at him in horror, but Lunarias just sighed. She did not believe him one bit. Frankly, she would not be surprised if the guards had some kind of agreement with those thugs at this point.

"I've seen enough," Lunarias said, turning around again, this time with the garrison's main gate as her destination.

Then she heard the captain scream, "Who do you think you are, coming here and bossing me around?! You're half my age! What do you know of running a garrison?!"

"Let me remind you, I'm a knight of the second order. I outrank you by far. Frankly, I could elect your replacement right now, and you could do nothing about it. But I want the capital to know what's going on here. I'll let your insults slide as a last measure of goodwill, do not test me again."

She did not stop to look at the captain. The guards stepped back as she approached, giving her a clear path to the gate.

"50.000 Merias," The captain said, "I'll give you 50.000 Merias if you leave Hybrik, and don't mention a word about this to anyone."

That brought a smile to Lunarias' lips. She turned around to look at the desperate captain. "Now there's something I regret," she said, "I regret that I sent the letter this morning. I'd have loved to add bribery to my list of condemnations."

When she turned around once again, two guards stepped up to block her path. They drew their swords and went to strike her, but Lunarias was faster. She pulled out the sword with her right hand and the scabbard with the other. She redirected the one on the right and let the other bite into the wood of the scabbard. While the one to the right regained his posture, she reversed her grip on her sword and stabbed it clean through his neck. She wrenched the scabbard downward and put her foot on the other one's blade while simultaneously releasing her grip on the scabbard to grip her blade with both hands. In one quick motion, the head of the other guard hit the ground with a dull thump. It was just as she had expected; they were amateurs at best.

Those two were the only ones who tried to stand against her as she grabbed the scabbard and left the garrison.

Chapter 30

It was early morning when Astolphos got out of bed and quietly exited the bedroom. Waiting at the desk was Kennas, and they left the building quietly.

They were met with the sight of Hybrik cast in orange from the rising sun. But the city was already bustling. Carriages came rolling through the city, loaded with food and skins from far away. Their owners looked like they were riding all night long to finish their route and sleep in a proper bed.

"You sure the shop can take care of itself?" Astolphos asked Kennas. Several of the men out on the street greeted her as Ontrys, all oblivious to the fact that they were, in fact, kindly smiling and waving at what they would call the enemy. The irony was not lost on either of them, as both gave each other a deprecating smile.

"I've left them a note about what's to be done. They'll manage, though they might not be as fast as normal. So, are you sure about this?"

"I'm quite sure this is our best shot. These guys seem to be the types to demand protection money. If they weren't the ones who tried extorting you, I'm sure they know who did."

Kennas nodded and waved to another shop owner, this time a tanner who wanted to talk about a set of skins he had gotten in that would look great on some chairs, but Kennas excused herself, telling him that she would come by tomorrow.

"You're popular," Astolphos said.

"What can I say? Experience pays off. That, and some connections to the different guilds."

"So, you've been playing some politics?"

"Not by design, the quality of my work had apparently spread a bit, and before I knew it, I was responsible for delivering a full set of tables and chairs for the Merchant's Guild, and things spiraled from there. But enough of that, what's the plan?"

"I'll tell you when you have to disappear, then you'll just watch from the shadows and try to gather whatever information you can."

This was just small talk to keep them from getting too serious. They had done this routine so often that they knew what to do without exchanging a word. Glaucos still remained silent. He looked intently around from a bracelet around Kennas' arm, trying to keep an eye for whether they were followed. His silence was a sign that everything was as intended.

Before they knew it, the cobblestones turned uneven, and the walls were rugged and washed out. Aurillian slums always surprised Astolphos. It never was a gradual change into disrepair; it was a sharp line from one part of the street to the next. The houses grew smaller, and the foot traffic changed from wagons and merchants to people lying on the ground in ragged clothes. Once again, the populace followed the linc dutifully; not even a tattered sleeve crossed the boundary. It was truly the point that showed precisely where the nobility stopped giving a damn. They might as well just build a wall around it. That would just manifest what was on everyone's mind into reality.

It was challenging to find an empty street, but they eventually did so, which allowed Kennas to change into a puddle and move along the walls unnoticed. From there, they soon arrived at the alley from yesterday, where two masked men looked to be waiting for him.

"Are you the smith?" One of the thieves asked as Astolphos approached.

"That's me."

"Put this on." He handed Astolphos a burlap sack.

"Is that necessary?" Astolphos asked.

"It is if you want to do business."

Astolphos sighed. It was nothing but an inconvenience to him since he could get a pretty good idea of his surroundings by looking at the different kinds of essences, not to mention Glaucos and Kennas following at a distance. The sack came on easily; the thieves tucked on it to ensure it would not fall off. Its fibers were weaved tightly, allowing not a slimmer of light to pass through.

As Astolphos used his Gift to orient himself, he saw a third man approach from behind. Taking their indifferent reactions into account, Astolphos was sure it was another accomplice, maybe someone stationed to 'take care' of Astolphos should he have chosen to walk away from the deal.

"So," Astolphos said, "How long will we be walking?"

"That depends."

"On what?"

"On how long you're going to be talking."

"...Understood."

Astolphos hoped he could get some information from the thieves while they were walking, but it seemed they had orders that made that difficult.

That just meant Astolphos had to pay more attention to where they walked and what the thieves told each other.

Chapter 31

Lunarias did not exactly know what to feel when she returned to the inn only to find their room paid for and deserted. Going there in the first place was difficult, as she knew it had been wrong of her to just storm out. The circumstances did not matter. However, she felt relieved when she opened the door and discovered the note on the bed. Even if it was only a postponement until they were going on the road again, it gave her time to think about what to say.

But her thoughts kept her up that night, and it was not only because of the awaiting conflict with Astolphos. It took some time before what had happened in the garrison registered with Lunarias. She walked out of there, carried only by shock, adrenaline, and a feeling of impending dread of what would happen if she stayed there another second.

Only two guards had attacked her, but the rest did nothing to stop them, that included their captain, who probably hoped that his soldiers could spare him a headache. That could only lead Lunarias to one of two conclusions, both bad. Either she had pissed off the captain so much that he did not care whether she died, or he had something to do with her prisoners going missing.

No matter what, everything leads her to the same conclusion. The garrison was no longer a safe place for her. She could not rely on any of the guards either, as some surely wanted her dead. That meant one thing, she had to get to the bottom of this alone. It was either that or wait for at least the two weeks it would take for the knights to arrive, and she was not sure if she would have to leave the city before that anyway.

That left her with only one way forward, try to figure out what was happening and send a report to the knights before the carriage was built. Astolphos told her that it would take about two weeks, meaning that she, at most, had one week left by now. It was not a lot of time, which meant she had to act quickly.

She woke up by herself at the first rays of dawn and had already donned her armor before the swift knocks came to the door.

From there, she went to the market and slowly moved to the slums. From her botched interrogation, she remembered that the thugs had mentioned their base was somewhere in the slums. That did not help that much since the slums encompassed an area large enough for her to prowl each day for weeks and just barely covered the streets. As such, she started at the part of the slums closest to the market, as the market seemed to be their favorite prowling ground.

She spent hours on the streets of the slums looking for those mercenaries. Her theory was that as soon as the market kicked into full gear, the thugs would come to see what they could steal and who to extort, but that did not seem to be the case. Instead, all she was met with was what she had expected of the slums, dirty streets, and homeless lying on them. She gave them a quick look, primarily to see if they threatened her or her mission. Other than that, she did not give them a second glance.

It was at that point she caught herself doing precisely what Astolphos accused her of, reducing the peasants into those of threats and those of irrelevance. She, however, told herself that it was necessary to do, as she was working with limited time.

At that time, she saw four people walk past the end of the street. Three of them wore those baggy clothes she looked for, and the fourth had a burlap sack on their head. The three surrounded the fourth, making them unable to do anything but follow their lead. Finally, she had found what she was looking for, and at the same time, she could even stop a kidnapping in progress. With a hand on her sword, she ran towards them. She was about to yell for them to stop when something grabbed her foot. It felt sticky momentarily, but then it turned solid and yanked her back. She lost her balance and was dragged in a shower of sparks as her breastplate abraded against the cobblestone. She managed to turn around, pull out her sword and chop at whatever grabbed her leg, but she hit nothing. She then knew what had happened; she was attacked by an Abyssal, a type she had never encountered before.

She stuck her blade between the cobblestone and gripped it as hard as possible. The tentacle let go, and Lunarias rose from the ground. There was a clear trail of blue mucus where it had held on to her, but there was no other damage. She pointed her sword forward, looking for any indication of the creature. There was nothing but a blue trail on the ground ahead of her.

"Show yourself!" Lunarias yelled, knowing full well that it was unlikely to happen. It only showed that she did not fear the Abyssal. There was no one else in the alley. She followed the trail until it just ended at a perfect point. The hairs on her neck rose, and she turned around. Behind her stood a semi-humanoid blob of blue slime, slowly changing color to browns, whites, and skin. The next moment, a woman stood in front of her. A pair of dull brown eyes stared at her as if trying to absorb the light around them. The red hair fell flat momentarily before it rose, and a band materialized, finishing a ponytail. The Abyssal wore an apron with several tools in its pockets, all hinting at one profession, carpentry.

"Leave the slums and never return," The woman said. Her words were cold, but her face showed nothing but hatred.

Lunarias looked down at her blade; it bore the same blue marks as her leg. She indeed had hit the creature, but it did not seem to be hurt in any way. The spot was not even close to the blade's tip; it was a clean passage in the middle. Not only had she hit, she had sliced clean through it, and there was nothing to show for it.

"What's happening?" Lunarias asked but was met by nothing but the creature clicking its tongue at her and turning to leave.

She thought of her options but concluded she did not have any. That creature was some kind of shapeshifter. Not only that, it was seemingly impervious to her sword. Perhaps because it was made by that blacksmith, she could imagine an Abyssal giving her a sword that could not hurt other Abyssals. No matter the reason, she had no recourse against that creature; it might as well be invulnerable. There was something about that word, invulnerable, as it passed through her mind.

"Kennas?" Lunarias asked. The creature stopped momentarily, telling her that her hunch was correct; this was Astolphos' friend. The one that was presumed dead. Kennas realized her mistake as she sighed.

"What else has Astolphos lied about?" Lunarias asked, "And what business do you have with those mercenaries?"

But Kennas just continued her walk out of the alley.

"Or perhaps you two are leading that bunch of degenerates? It would fit right up along with you Abyssals." She knew she was pushing limits, but Lunarias thought they knew more about this than she did. She needed more information to act on. The next line of pointed questions was right on the tongue when Kennas appeared right in front of her instantly, making her freeze.

Kennas no longer attempted to hide her contempt, and her eyes, still as dull as ever, told her everything she had to know. She would not even be a hindrance. Kennas could kill her here and now, and it would not even be much of a delay. That mix of hatred and confidence made it hard for her to speak.

"The only reason you're alive right now is because of Astolphos. You know too much, and it will only become a larger problem. I cannot afford you messing everything up, so I'll spare you this one time out of respect for him. Cross me again, or approach my shop, and I'll be less lenient."

Kennas' form turned blue once again and seemed to flow into the spots between the cobblestones.

Chapter 32

Astolphos knew immediately that something had happened. Glaucos had updated him about their location at every turn, but then there was nothing. It took a good five minutes before Glaucos established contact once again.

Glaucos! Where in the name of Luminis have you been?!

"We ran into some difficulties; everything's been resolved. We have overall moved closer to the eastern part of the Craftsmen's District, about halfway between the market and the wall."

Now he at least knew where he was and knew they were back looking out for him. There must be some reason why Glaucos did not give any further details, but he trusted that it was a good one and, as such, did not ask for more.

They walked for another ten minutes, which most of the time was not even used to lead them to their destination. Instead, they went in circles to disorient Astolphos. After the last turn, they stopped as one of the thieves fumbled with what sounded like keys. A door with some old, creaking hinges opened, and Astolphos was guided inside. The burlap sack was only removed from his head when the door was closed and locked.

The room he now found himself in looked to be all the building encompassed. It was cramped, with only enough room for a bed, a small pantry, and a bench where he could do his work. On the bed was a tall pile of metal trinkets. Jewelry, utensils, cups and plates, and things Astolphos could not clearly identify.

This is not their base.

"Got it," Glaucos said telepathically, "We'll monitor from the outside. We'll follow them if anyone leaves to see where they're going. Hopefully, we'll get closer that way."

He had not expected to be led to their base. He had hoped for a safe house with at least a little activity so he could eavesdrop. Through that, maybe find someone whose essence he could use to find the actual headquarters.

There was no way any of that would happen now. The thieves who had escorted him probably had gotten orders not to speak in his company, so everything now hinged on someone leaving so Kennas could tail them.

"You should have everything you need to work. Knock on the door if you need anything," One of the thieves said.

With a sigh, Astolphos nodded and turned his attention toward the workbench.

The tools they had brought him were of shoddy quality. The forge was a small transportable one, and the tools looked either cheaply made or heavily used, probably both. A small stack of firewood was on the floor beside the bench, and Astolphos went to work immediately. Though all he did now was a waste of time, he could not back down now, taking his show yesterday into account.

Once the fire was lit, Astolphos turned his attention to the trinket-filled bed. Some things, particularly the plates and candelabras, were too big to come into the portable forge, so he sorted things into two piles after what was currently smeltable and what needed to be broken down first.

In the meantime, the thieves had gotten enough of watching Astolphos rummage through the pile and showed themselves out of the door.

The lighting was terrible in the room, with the only light sources being a few candles on the walls and the glow emitted from the heating forge. However, even without proper lighting, Astolphos knew something was wrong with the ill-gotten goods. Many things felt too light to be silver. The difference was minute but grew in proportion with the object's size.

Holding one of the lighter plates up against the candles revealed why. As with the weight, the plate looked too bright as the flames danced on its surface. He knew from appearance alone this was not silver he was looking at. It was nickel.

Nickel, when polished, looked like silver, a fact many swindlers took advantage of. Because nickel could, in some cases, have an even brighter and more lustrous hue than genuine silver, some of the lower noble ranks liked nickel more since only a trained eye would realize the difference during dinner.

However, if a person takes hold of the plate and already has some metallurgy experience, they would realize something felt wrong. They may not see the brighter hue, but they would think something was wrong. It could be the weight or how the metal felt after being used for a while and the polish wearing off.

The pile was huge, but after Astolphos moved a candle around it to see the reflections, few things looked to be of genuine silver. He could not stop himself from chuckling at the thought that their targets turned out to be such amateurs. If the thieves could not see the difference between silver and nickel, they were nothing but bandits that tried to be something more than they were. That also made sense, considering they were willing to kill Kennas for not paying protection money. However, it also meant that the chance of a non-violent solution to their problem was pushed further away. Thieves could be reasoned with; he had done so before. Bandits and robbers, on the other hand, only understood one thing: force, something he, regrettably, also had experience with.

But that was a problem for later. He still had work to do here as to not arouse suspicion. The only difference was that now he also had to sort through the wares to separate the worthless from the silver.

It was truly tedious work examining so many trinkets with only a candle. But the low amount of silver told him quite the story. Hybrik was a prosperous city, meaning the nobles could afford silver, let alone gold, after the imports from Ronasm. This meant that these thugs did not target the rich but those in the middle between craftsmen and noble, who wanted to look more affluent than they actually were. As to why, he could only theorize that their rowdy behavior made the nobles hire a bunch of guards, and their thieving skills were so bad that a violent confrontation was assured.

Only a few rings and necklaces were made of silver, barely enough for Astolphos to get his share. That was his highest priority because he could sell that silver and give away the money. First, to Kennas to cover some of the cost of this operation, and then give the rest to the less fortunate in the slums. He was not giving any of the silver to the thieves; they may have stolen it, but they did not deserve to own it.

The only work he had done was to sort through the trinkets. His sense of time had left him, as there was no way for him to look outside. Maybe he had only spent an hour. Maybe the day was almost over.

At first, he had kept time by counting how many times he had stoked the fire underneath the furnace, but that did not work, as it seemed that the wood burned for different durations.

The time had finally come for Astolphos to melt the silver. Making bars would be faster than making actual pieces out of jewelry, and it would probably satisfy the thieves, as they would be easier to sell. It seemed like the thieves had the same thought, as there only was a mold for bars among the haphazardly thrown-together pile of tools.

From there, he began the tedious work of melting down the pieces and filling up the mold, only to quench it in water, loosen it from the mold, and repeat the process. He frequently checked in on Glaucos and Kennas, every time being answered with a negative. The three thieves just stood outside the door, not interacting with anyone or leaving for anything longer than a piss.

After a while, the door opened, and one of the thieves entered with a burlap sack in his hands.

"Work's done for the day."

"Good to know. I'll need more firewood tomorrow, and it'll probably take me five days to get through that pile."

"We'll add more to the pile. This is only the beginning."

Chapter 33

Despite Kennas' warning and the inherent danger, Lunarias staked out the workshop. She waited until the city was quiet and then found a place behind a stack of boxes to hide. She was sure the two Abyssals were involved with those mercenaries, though she was unsure how much and whether they were allies or enemies. She needed answers for her investigation, and since asking them was with her life on the line, she had to watch the shop instead. The sun had already gone down when she took her position, and by now, she was sure that few were still awake in the entire district. She looked out for those people wearing baggy clothes and whether or not they were interested in that workshop.

She knew that something was going on. She had seen guards patrol the Craftsmen's District. However, no one seemed to approach this part of the street. She had even seen some guards walk down towards the workshop, only to turn back before they even got close enough for their torches to light up Lunarias' hiding spot, much less the actual building.

Her suspicions were rewarded not soon after another patrol turned around. Two figures approached the entrance with the moonlight illuminating nothing but their silhouettes. One of them stuck a hand into the fold of their clothes to get some object and jiggled it around in the lock. The door soon opened, and the figure entered the shop while the other seemingly kept watch. A few seconds later, the figure emerged from the shop once more, and they closed the door behind them.

The thought of stopping them then and there passed her. She decided against it because she could not risk waking up the Abyssals, knowing there was no chance she could fight against them and win. Instead, she would tail them until the Abyssals were out of hearing range. Then, she would intercept them and, hopefully, get some information she could send to her fellow knights.

Tailing them from a distance proved to be easy. They seemed not to expect anyone to follow them, much less a knight of Aurillia, notorious for always wearing their armor. Lunarias, however, had been in situations like these far too often on the campaigns to the Abyss. She had become adept at keeping down the noise as she crept through the streets.

The two figures then met up with a third, and they stopped to talk for a bit. Lunarias was out of hearing distance, but she heard they were amused by something. They turned their back to Lunarias, and that was when she decided it was time to strike.

She released her sword, still in the scabbard, from her belt and quietly sneaked up on them. She knew there was a huge risk for her armor to give her away, but it did not matter if she could get close enough to knock one out before they had time to react. Her movements were steady and short, especially her steps, as she could not afford her feet to slide and the greaves to grind against the stones.

But she did not get close enough. If, by accident or acute senses, the newcomer turned around to see her and drew a shortsword from within their clothes with experience and intent. That movement alerted the other two, who turned around to do the same, one drawing a dagger and the other a mace. Even in the darkness of night, the metal reflected at her in the dim shimmer of moonlight.

There was no dialogue between them or time to size up their opponents; they all went into combat stance as they approached. Lunarias kept her hands down, pointing the tip at each of them in turn. Their approach was unyielding and in sync. She thought of removing the scabbard but shook her head at the idea. She needed them alive.

Lunarias was the first to go on the offense. She pushed her sword forward, jabbing the one wielding the mace in the neck. The hit landed perfectly, and he fell to the ground gasping for breath. She felt a push on her bracer. It had caught a slash from the shortsword wielder, who sprung back the moment their eyes locked.

Her eyes immediately went to the last one, who ran at her with his dagger, ready for a stab. Her body reacted on its own, twisting the sword around to hit the dagger and force its trajectory to the ground. She continued the movement of her sword, drawing it toward her body. Her left hand let go of the hilt, instead grabbing the scabbard as she drove the pommel into his stomach. Not even a grunt; the clothes must have blocked it. Adjusting her grip back to the hilt, she swung the sword above her head and drove it into his. The guy fell to the ground. Then she saw it, the shortsword came with too much speed, and she could do nothing against it. The edge collided with the breastplate, and sparks flew toward her head as the sword deflected back. Her breastplate pushed the air out of her lungs, but it did its job and kept her ribs and skin unbroken.

"Damn," The person said, the voice distinctly female, "A knight."

"Surrender now, and I'll spare you," Lunarias said, only to be met with laughter.

"Your threats run hollow when you don't even want to draw your blade."

Lunarias clicked her tongue, not that she had expected it to work anyway. She looked at the ground, thinking whether it was time to draw her blade. One mercenary was all she needed for the interrogation, and she had already knocked two out.

Her eyes could only find the one with the dagger, the other one was no longer on the ground. She jumped back as she heard a scream to her left. The mace swung down in front of her, just where she had stood moments before. The mercenary did not waste any time. The mace swung upwards towards her head. She blocked it with her scabbard, the wood creaked and shot splinters splinter at her face from the force, but it held. This was no longer a viable strategy, Lunarias thought as she pulled off the scabbard and pushed the blade forward. It passed through the layers of clothes and continued through after some resistance. The mercenary howled in pain and woke the houses surrounding them. The shutters flew open with curious and angry citizens, all silenced and astounded when they saw what had transpired beside their homes. The lights from the candles illuminated the alley, and Lunarias could finally get a good look at who she fought. She saw the light leave the eyes of the one she stabbed as he slid forward and off her blade. She did not take long to collect herself and prepare for the third opponent. That opponent ran away from the light. Lunarias was about to run after them when she heard the sound of fully armored warriors running. A moment later, that very exit was cut off by four guards. The woman stopped running, but she turned around with a smirk instead of running the other way to avoid them. The guards passed her, drawing their weapons as they approached Lunarias.

"Lady Hewris, you're arrested for terrorizing the fair citizens of Hybrik and killing two guards."

Lunarias just sighed as she saw the last mercenaries turn the corner from which the guards had come. She did not want to say anything to the guards, but she was not going to be caught by them.

The guards yelled at her as she ran away, but that was all. She did not hear their armor ringing as it would if they were running after her. Three streets away, and it already seemed like they had given up. Something was up, but she could not figure out what. Only when she had stopped running to get her breath did she recognize the sound of leisurely footsteps emanating from where she had run. There should not be any regular citizens out at this time, and there was too little noise for it to be a guard. The only conclusion she could reach was that it had to be one of the mercenaries.

She leaned up the wall at the mouth of that street, eager that her plan might not have failed anyway. The footsteps grew louder, and she turned around with an outstretched hand and a blade pointing at the ground. Her fist grabbed a handful of cloth, and she wrestled the mercenary into the wall, pulling her sword up to their throat.

It was at that point she realized it was not a mercenary. It was instead Astolphos with its scrawny build and white hair.

It looked at her with a dumb smile held as a weak shield to hide its nervousness.

"Is it possible you can lower my blade?" It asked.

"Why're you here?"

"I was just worried about you. It was quite a scuffle you were involved in."

"Do you have anything to do with the guards not following me?"

"It'll be easier to talk if I didn't have a blade at my throat."

That only made her put the blade even tighter at its throat.

"Did you kill them?"

However, Astolphos did not answer. The fake smile on its lips washed away as it grabbed her hand and pushed the blade aside. As it happened, it felt momentarily as if the edge found purchase and sliced through the skin, but there was no blood.

That sensation surprised Lunarias into not putting up any resistance.

Now free, Astolphos cleared its throat and tucked its shirt further up.

"You seem to have been busy. What's that about you killing two guards?"

"That doesn't concern you."

"It does since those very guards let those thieves get away."

Lunarias kept silent, still unsure what Astolphos was doing, but she knew she could not trust it. Not as long as she had not found out what role the two Abyssals were playing.

"In that case," It said, "let me just air my theory. The guards are in on the extortion and burglaries. Since you had been into combat and killed two of them, and the fact that four random guards running to you instantly tried to apprehend you for it, I think many of them have taken bribes, perhaps even some of the garrison management. I can't be far off, given your expression."

Lunarias turned around. She was shocked by how close Astolphos had come to her own theories.

"But my question then is, why are you involved in all this?" Astolphos then asked.

"Those bastards are hurting the citizens. It's my duty as a knight to stop them."

"In that case, we're on the same side. You're trying to shut them down because their rackets are hurting the city, and I'm trying to do the same to ensure no one ends up like Kennas. What about we help each other? We might already have all the pieces; we just need to assemble them correctly."

Lunarias was silent for a moment before saying, "I don't think Kennas will approve of it. She made that obvious earlier today."

The blacksmith looked at her momentarily with a blank expression before it seemed like understanding washed over him.

"I'll take care of Kennas; she'll listen to me. Meet me at the shop in the evening tomorrow. I'll have things sorted out before then."

"I can't trust you," Lunarias outburst, "I can't work with your kind,"

Astolphos opened and closed his mouth several times, struggling to get anything out but an "Oh." Without giving another reply, he turned around and walked away.

"Kennas said you asked her not to hurt me," Lunarias said, "Why?"

Astolphos turned around. Something was brewing in him; she saw that from his conflicted expression. Eventually, he looked at the ground and said, "If anything happens to you, it'll jeopardize my contract with the royal family. I can't afford that."

And with that, he turned around again, this time sprinting down the streets before Lunarias could get another word out.

There was something more to that answer. She was sure of it.

Chapter 34

Though he left Lunarias seeming calm and collected, Astolphos cursed at himself for such a blatant lie. Though her comment about not trusting him did not surprise him, it still cut him deeper than he anticipated. So much that it was still on his mind when her next question came and took up his thoughts that such a thin-veiled lie could leave his lips. There was nothing more he could do, much less if he wanted Lunarias not to see the cut her blade made in his neck or, even worse, his true appearance.

The only saving grace was that Glaucos was not around, or else he would chastise Astolphos for doing such a half-assed job. 'Either tell her the truth or keep up the lie, don't make it teeter on the edge like this, he could imagine Glaucos' words. Instead, his walk home to Kennas' shop was quiet. He did not meet a soul nor hear the guards' armor clang in the adjacent streets. They were probably too preoccupied with the mess he had made to save Lunarias. Tomorrow was going to be interesting, that was for sure.

When he neared the workshop, he realized that the lights were on. Inside, Kennas waited on him. She had even gone and retrieved Glaucos. The letter the thieves had delivered was in her hand. It was crumbled and had five burn marks, each corresponding to where Kennas probably held it while reading. Her rage was barely contained; it emanated from her in waves that made Astolphos' whole being scream danger. One more little push, and he knew Kennas the Devourer would be back.

"Did you find their base?" Her voice wavered as she walked the thin line keeping her anger at bay.

"No, Lunarias intercepted them before they even reached the slums. She had apparently been watching the shop in case something happened." There was no reason to even try to lie to Kennas. They had known each other for so long that she would catch on immediately.

"Damn that girl!" Kennas yelled, "Why can't those Aurillians not keep to themselves and let us take care of our business! By Luminis, if I could get my hands on-"

"On who?" Glaucos interrupted, "Are you talking about the thieves responsible for this or 'Stolfos' relative?"

Kennas' eyes went wide before darting to the ground, "Sorry, my anger got the better of me."

"Don't think about it," Astolphos said, "But let's remember who the enemy is. Lunarias is just trying to handle the problem in her own way. We're two parties wanting the same thing."

"So you talked to her?"

"I wouldn't exactly call it talking. She didn't say too much. She's not trusting of our kind after all. She did let something-" Astolphos stopped himself too late. Kennas had caught on and looked at him expectantly for a piece of information he knew he should not give her.

"She's been attacked by the guards for digging into this. She did not say so clearly, but I think she suspects that a large part, if not the entire garrison is in on this."

"That would at least explain why no one had looked into Kennas' murder," Glaucos said.

However, Kennas remained silent. Her expression grew grimmer by the second. Then she cracked a smile, her eyes lit up with nothing but sheer bloodlust. Kennas, the Hand of Infrastructure, was gone once again.

"Then we know what to do," Kennas said, her voice revealing anger mixed with amusement, "The guards must know where their base is. We'll raze the garrison to the ground, find out which rats will talk, and exterminate the rest."

"By Luminis, Kennas!" Astolphos said, grabbing both of her shoulders. He was about to continue when he felt a stinging pain in his hands, followed by the sickening sound of burning meat. He pulled his hands away in a grunt of pain, only to see that all the skin was dissolved down to the bone.

"Kennas!" Astolphos yelled as he grabbed a pair of work gloves and covered his hands before turning off his disguise. Doing so cut off all sensations of pain, but he could no longer bear to see his true self.

Seeing her friend in pain snapped her out of her fury.

"I'll not stand idle as you throw away everything you've built from lack of self-control," Astolphos said, "This workshop will turn into the center of all of this. Think about it, how will it look that right after killing the owner of this shop, all the criminals responsible and half the garrison turns up dead for reasons that can only be caused by us Gifted? The knights will be here in no time, and there will be no excuse. You'll have to abandon everything and flee to Marados!"

"When did you join the side of the Aurillians?" Kennas said.

"I'm saying this because I'm on your side. What're you going to do when the knights come knocking?"

"I'll kill every one of them."

"And then what, return to being Kennas the Devourer? The Abyssal terrorizing the Aurillian fringes for 30 years? Is that what you want!?"

The last of the fire left Kennas' eyes as she looked down. Her gaze landed on Astolphos' gloved hands. "No, I'll never want to lose Control again."

"But you just did," Glaucos said, "You had that very same look, the unquenchable bloodthirst not much different from a feral animal."

Kennas fell to her knees, "I'm scared 'Stolfos," She gave him the note, now carrying even more burn marks.

The message was straightforward, Pay 3000 Merias by Friday, or end up like the old owner.

"I don't know if I can keep Control if they come here again, threatening my apprentices. I'll do anything to keep them safe."

"Then pay," Astolphos said. Kennas looked up in confusion.

"If you pay them, they'll leave you alone, right? Then pay the Merias and be rid of them. That'll solve everything."

"We're beyond this point now. That amount is not something I can pay every month. This is them sending a message. They don't want the workshop to be open anymore, to send a message to anyone thinking of standing up to them."

"So, our options are to find them and bring a stop to their dealings, have you close up shop and flee back to Marados to lay low, or let the Devourer return?"

Kennas did not nod, but Astolphos knew the other two agreed with him. There was only one real choice, find the thieves and end this before things had to turn violent.

"We need to know what Lunarias knows," Astolphos said, "She's the only one who knows how it is inside the garrison. Perhaps she has the missing pieces."

"But we don't know where she'll be,"

"We do. We'll wait for her at the inn once we're done melting their goods tomorrow."

Chapter 35

It did not take a genius to realize that things were escalating quickly. After the occurrences of yesterday evening, the atmosphere of the entire city changed. Everything was as expected at dawn, but then the whispers started, and the joyful tones quieted down. At around lunch, traffic thinned out, and there were more guards on the street. Whatever Astolphos had done to those guards, the signs could only have pointed toward the presence of an Abyssal.

This state of affairs, however, did not deter Lunarias, who walked through the streets, fighting a fierce battle against the uncomfortable feeling of the dress she wore. It had been quite some time since she was last forced to wear anything other than her armor on top of both a gambeson and a plain set of clothes, but she was a marked woman now. The guards were out for her blood, and that armor would make her stand out like a sore thumb. However much she reviled the idea of leaving her armor, the proof of her duty and allegiance, at the inn, she would not be able to carry out her duty with it on.

In its place, she had gone through the few other outfits she had brought along on her journey. Among the three outfits not dependent on the armor, she chose a plain teal dress, a thin leather belt around the waist, and a dark green scarf around her neck.

It had been months since she had last walked around without the weight of her armor slowing her down, and she felt it. This was particularly true with her legs, as the lack of the greaves meant that she automatically walked around much faster and with more force than a woman of her stature should. But the dress had the exact effect she wanted. Both commoners and guards took one quick look at her, identified she was a noble, and diverted their gaze immediately to not cause offense to the lord she was surely married to. It was quite lucky, as that meant she did not have to rely on the only weapon she had brought along, a short dagger strapped to her left forearm underneath the sleeve.

For every run-in she had had with those mercenaries, she learned more and more about their organization. She knew their headquarters were somewhere in the slums, and something told her it was in the upper part, somewhat close to the Craftsmen's District. That was, however, still a large area, and without her arms and armor, the slums were too risky to visit. Her target for the day was the markets, where she hoped to see some of those mercenaries participate in their 'trade.' For that, she knew the perfect location.

The tavern she visited when she had looked for the church was the perfect vantage point. She opened the door and saw the barkeep with crossed arms looking at three men in baggy clothes. None had drawn their weapons, but it seemed like she had arrived just before the conflict escalated. The three mercenaries looked at her with a surprised look.

"What's the meaning of this?" Lunarias asked, raising her nose to look repulsed at the scene.

"We'll be back," one of the mercenaries said before going past Lunarias for the exit. The barkeep immediately fell to the ground with a sigh, and Lunarias ran to his side, his wife not far behind.

"Are you hurt?" Lunarias asked, her eyes already scanning every inch of his body for any red spots.

"I'm alright," The barkeep said, getting back on his feet with the help of the two women, "The fear just got a bit too much for me."

Lunarias and his wife helped him to a seat at a table with a view of the outside. The wife then left, only to return with a pitcher of water and three cups. They both sat down beside the barkeep, who still breathed heavily. Lunarias got a seat facing away from the window. The tavern was empty, a rare occurrence even for this time of day. It had given the owners ample time to clean, as everything was spotless, from the rustic wooden floor to the polished tables, to the nicely ordered counter. Behind the counter was a slit that led to the kitchen, currently enveloped in the dark. The place was lit up by the sunlight streaming in from the windows.

The barkeep grabbed the pitcher with a shaking hand, and his wife put her hand on his when the shaking got the water to spill.

"Thank you, knight," The barkeep said, "I don't know what they would've done if not for you coming in here."

"Knight?" The wife asked.

"Lunarias Hewris, Knight of the Second Order, at your service. And there's no reason to thank me, I didn't do anything."

"You saved my life. Those thugs were about to kill me."

"If you don't mind, can you tell me why that is?"

The barkeep looked out the window before continuing in a hushed voice, "Those bastards have been extorting all kinds of business for protection money. Most of us didn't take them seriously, but then they killed some carpenter who had lived in this city for a long time. After that, no one resisted. Now, they're trying to raise the amounts, and I can't pay what they're asking. They've been coming here for a week now, and I think they want to make me another example."

"It's all because of this damned ring," The wife said, clutching a gold ring with a garnet on top, "If they hadn't seen it, they would've believed you."

"It's never your fault," Lunarias said, "It's the criminals that are in the wrong. Is it always the same three guys that are coming here?"

"I don't think so, though I didn't go out of my way to remember their faces."

Lunarias had hoped for another answer. This just meant that the group was large and well-organized. Still, this was vital information she could give to her superiors. It was also the one thing she had feared. This was too big for one person to resolve alone. Her opponents were men willing to kill just to pad their coffers. A single knight would not stand a chance. She would need an army.

Or two Abyssals. She remembered how Astolphos asked her if they could cooperate. She still did not trust those two creatures, but were they really worse than these thugs threatening the citizenry? Despite what they were, they seemed to only want to live a peaceful life.

"First this and now Abyssals in the city," The barkeep said, "I don't suppose that's why you're here, to begin with?"

"That's information I can't divulge. But is it possible that you can tell me what rumors you've heard?"

"Of course. This morning, some patrons told me several guards were found unconscious on the street yesterday. There was no sign of a scuffle. They had just collapsed in the middle of battle. If that alone wasn't weird enough, some people had heard the commotion outside and looked out of their windows. They were found knocked out too. It seems like they woke up some hours later but with one hell of a hangover."

"Is it truly an Abyssal that did this?" The wife asked.

Lunarias remained silent. She had to be careful about what she told this barkeep, as the rumors could quickly spread and lead the guards to them.

"I thank you for your time," Lunarias said, rising from the seat, "I have some business to take care of."

"Please come again when all of this is over. We'll give a few rounds on the house!"

Lunarias left the bar smiling at herself, knowing full well she would hate that as much as always.

Chapter 36

The route back from the tavern gave Lunarias time to collect her thoughts. With a large organization of thieves and thugs, along with a large part of the garrison, it would be no easy feat to clear the corruption, even if she had the support of the Aurillian knights. For her alone, it was impossible to do anything. Her initial thought was to go to Astolphos and Kennas, swallow her pride, and ask for their help. The only thing that held her back was Kennas, as she had no way of knowing if Astolphos could convince her. And then there was Astolphos himself. From what she heard, he spared everyone yesterday despite the circumstances, so she was sure he was at least not overtly an enemy of Aurillia. But that did not do anything against the fact that he kept secrets from her. Whatever the reason, it made her wary of the Abyssal.

The inn had suffered the same fate as the tavern, the citizens did not want to go eat with an Abyssal on the loose, and that was not going away until they were assured that the Abyssal was brought to justice. That was why most sizable cities always had knights at the barracks, partly to vanquish the Abyssals and tell the citizens to calm down. Hybrik was a special case, as the entire eastern part of Aurillia had seen no Abyssals for almost five decades. That was the problem with becoming complacent; resources get allocated elsewhere and cannot be found when needed. That was now her problem, as a city of this size could not wait for her reinforcements to return to normal. It would cripple the entire area for months.

Her thoughts were seeking a solution as she entered her room.

"Can't you knights respect fine craftsmanship?"

Surprised, Lunarias pulled out the dagger at the sudden address and brandished it at the intruders. She soon identified them as Astolphos and Kennas. Astolphos sat on the bed with the scabbard for her sword on his lap and a piece of linseed-soaked cloth in one hand and a rasp in the other. Beside him sat Kennas, who was busy reading a book.

"Why're you here? I don't think it's just to fix up the scabbard," Lunarias asked, returning the dagger to her sleeve.

"I want to give it another try to get us to cooperate. Fixing up the scabbard was just a bonus." Astolphos looked down at his work, gave the wood one more wipe, and nodded in satisfaction before putting the sword back in and laying it on the bed.

"I know it's difficult for you to trust Abyssals, as you call us," Astolphos said, "But our interests not only align this time, they're the same down to the core. I think sharing what we have learned will bring us closer to solving this problem."

Lunarias remained silent, her eyes locked on Kennas. She did not doubt that Astolphos was sincere, but the same could not be said about Kennas. Just yesterday, Kennas threatened her with death if she interfered, and now she was here, asking for Lunarias' help. Lunarias did not exactly know what she looked for on Kennas, some kind of tell that would illuminate what she thought about Astolphos' proposal. But she just sat there with tight lips and dull eyes that made it creep down Lunarias' spine.

"In what way," Lunarias said, "Do our interests align?"

She then looked squarely at Kennas, "Particularly, what changed from yesterday to today?"

But Astolphos was the one who answered, "The fact that those murderers are targeting Kennas' shop once again," He took a note out from his pockets and handed it to Lunarias.

The writing was fine and elaborate, not at all what she had expected from a group of thugs but perhaps fitting for some mercenary captain of somewhat noble birth. The message was clear; pay an unreasonably high amount of Merias three days from now, or they would come and kill Ontrys.

"Is this what they delivered yesterday?"

Kennas nodded, "And I will not let them touch my shop again."

"And I'm here to avoid this escalating into a tragedy."

"Tragedy? In what way?"

But Lunarias' question remained unanswered. Astolphos looked her in the eyes and twice glanced at Kennas. Lunarias understood; clearly, Kennas was the catalyst of that tragedy. The thought of all this being a ruse passed through her mind, but Astolphos seemed sincere, just as sincere as when he proclaimed his allegiance to the Abyssal King before her.

"But why? You're Abyssals; why care about us Aurillians? You said it yourself. You regret going against the Abyssal King, so why are you trying to protect us Aurillians?"

"I'm not," Astolphos said.

The answer rang through the room and made Lunarias just as speechless as their last conversation in this room. Only this time, she knew there was no room for the cowardice she displayed last time. She had to stand her ground. Hiding away the shock with a layer of indifference, she stared at Astolphos, who took her gaze head-on.

"The time for me to protect the Aurillians passed long ago. The only thing I can do now is limit the damage."

The same sadness was displayed, a deep-seated regret that would never vanish. It was the only thing revealing the vast difference in age between them. That Abyssal had seen and done things she could never imagine, and as she stared into that abyss, she did not want to imagine. But though their intentions were different, their goal was the same: bring down the mercenaries extorting the citizens.

"Alright," Lunarias said, "But you start. Tell me everything you've learned."

Chapter 37

Both parties were done sharing what they had learned. Astolphos sighed. He had hoped they could have pieced together something useful, but that was not the case. Frankly, everything he had learned confirmed his worst fears. There was no way to reason with these people. He had hoped it was just a bunch of stupid thieves with one or two impulsive members in their ranks. If they genuinely were a bunch of mercenaries, they would all be hardened killers, knuckleheads that only understood one language, force. Their ace would not even work either, as almost all mercenaries had once been sent into Lumina on one of Aurillia's 'campaigns' to harass the remaining Gifted. The mercenaries were more likely to take up arms when facing a Gifted. They could probably not leverage their title of 'Master,' as the Aurillians called them, to scare them away, as they likely lacked the education to understand the connotations anyway.

It just gave more credibility to the threat they left yesterday. One thing is to kill some carpenter. Killing her apprentices, children, was another thing entirely. A thief might talk up a good game but falter when it comes to actually following through. Mercenaries were like soldiers with less morality. They would obey any order given by their superiors without hesitation.

And to make everything worse, they were no closer to finding the headquarters than before. Sure, Lunarias had narrowed it down to somewhere in the slums, and her theory placed it somewhere on the border to the Craftsmen's District. But that did not give them much to go on. Her information that their leader goes by the 'commander' did nothing either. There was nothing special about it, so nothing could tie them to a specific mercenary company. Asking around town would do nothing either, as it was likely just a name used by the mercenaries internally.

That was as generic as it would come, and you would get nothing by asking around town.

On the surface, Kennas seemed to take the news in strides, but something told him that had more to do with her freezing her face into one expression while the contents within stirred violently in frustration.

"Please excuse me," Kennas said, bowing her head, "I have to go back to my shop to watch over my apprentices. Pleasure making your acquaintance, Lunarias."

Her voice was cold, and the purposeful look in her eyes as she went for the door made none of them say a word. Even Glaucos was silent as he was carried out of the room, still swirling around in Kennas' insides.

That left Astolphos and Lunarias alone with an uncomfortable silence. Astolphos' thoughts went directly to the last time they talked here, where Lunarias left the room in a rage.

"Is there anything you can do about Kennas if things worsen?" Lunarias asked.

Astolphos thought for a moment about what to say. Technically, there was a way for him to stop Kennas, but doing so was off the table. He had the power, but his mind would not allow him to even think about doing it to a friend as close as Kennas. Even if he were to lose her for another 30 years, that was much better than forever.

"There's nothing I can do to stop her," He finally said.

"And how bad will the damage be?"

"...Somewhere between half and the whole city, if not more."

Her eyes widened at his answer, but then she sighed, "And if that happens, Aurillia will lose our only large port city."

"Not to mention the lives of everyone living here."

She sent him a piercing gaze but diverted her eyes to the ground. And then there was nothing more to be said between them. Though this was still an improvement to the last time they spoke, there still was a long way before they were back to talking like when they first met.

"Come to the workshop if you learn anything else or need our help. I'm always awake, so I'll be there to open the door."

And with that, he rose from his seat and went for the door, but before he could get there, Lunarias rose from her seat. He turned around, only to see her stare at him with determination.

"That regret you speak of," she said, "How much of it is real, and how much is a lie to cover up whatever you're not telling me? Do you truly think Abyssals would've made a better world than this?"

"Everything I've said is the truth. You might look at us Gifted like liars, cheaters, thieves, and murderous beasts, but that is far from the truth. Under the rule of the Gifter, Aurillia truly would be better than this."

"But there is something you're keeping from me. Why?"

Astolphos opened the door to the outside, "Because, at this point in time, you'd never believe me."

And before Lunarias could say anything more, he closed the door behind him. A bit further down the hallway, he saw Kennas leaning against a wall, deep in thought.

"I thought you'd return to the workshop."

"I decided to wait for you instead."

Only when they exited the inn did Kennas say another word.

"That was a waste of time. That girl did not know anything useful."

"Nevertheless, she was closer than us. We had not even narrowed the headquarters' location to a specific district."

"But it's still not enough. We only have three days."

They walked a bit more and entered the Craftsmen's District before Kennas stopped walking.

"I still think we should go to the garrison."

Astolphos turned around and saw Kennas with her hands clasped and shaking.

"We've already talked about that. Nothing good will come of it."

"But nothing but disaster will happen if we continue like this."

"You can't know that. They'll slip up at some point, I'm sure of it."

"I'm not going to bet the lives of my apprentices on a hunch."

"But dooming you all to a life on the run is not an acceptable outcome either, right? Besides, you know my intuition is good. I'm rarely wrong."

"But when you are, it always ends in disaster."

He thought of something to say back, but there was no way to combat the truth. After all, his intuition led him to make a deal with the Aurillian King, and look at how all of that turned out.

"We have three days. Give me two more. If we have nothing to go on, we'll take the thieves as prisoners and ask them directly. If we then don't learn anything useful, we'll target the garrison. How does that sound?"

Kennas thought of it but eventually nodded.

"Alright, let's get ready for tomorrow. We'll have to be on the top of our game to find that headquarters."

"But do you think leaving the apprentices alone is a good idea? Perhaps I should stay back to watch over them."

"They're not going to do it in broad daylight. Being back at dusk should be more than enough."

"You still believe that? Despite What Lunarias told us of that barkeep?"

Astolphos paused for a moment, "Yes, I'm sure."

Chapter 38

The following evening, Lunarias knocked on the door to the workshop and was greeted by one of the apprentices. She was led to the workshop, where a large table had been set up, and the many apprentices ate their dinner, along with Astolphos and Ontrys.

Almost as soon as she entered, she felt all the eyes in the room on her. Only then did she realize the scale of what Kennas did. More than 20 children were seated at the table, most of which she could see on the scars on their exposed arms had already lived a pretty difficult life. Three, in particular, stared hard at her. A large boy even stared at her angrily while the two beside him looked at her worried. The girl, in particular, grew quite pale.

Lunarias at first looked around for Kennas but picked up from Astolphos that she had taken the form of the new clerk.

"Kids," Ontrys said, "This is Lunarias. She's helping me figure out what happened to Kennas. Can I trust you to not fight while I'm gone?"

The children nodded, and the two Abyssals rose from the table and led Lunarias into the kitchen. Kennas returned to her womanly form the moment she closed and locked the door. The kitchen was a spacious room. Its floor was made of stone, and various tabletops were put in neat rows from one end of the room to the other, only interrupted at the middle, where a large fireplace stood. The tabletops were a mess, with the knives strewn about and the remnants of many cut vegetables being pushed to the side. An almost sweet aroma emanated from the large brass pot, still being held warn by the embers of the charcoal.

"I didn't realize you had so many apprentices," Lunarias said, "It mustn't be easy to teach them."

"They can be quite a handful at times," Kennas said with a wry smile, her eyes caught on a particularly messy tabletop, "but nothing beats the moment when they go out to start their own lives."

"She's been running shops like this one in every city we've made a living in. A third of the carpenters in Aurillia can trace their origins back to one of her apprentices by now."

"Do they know about you..." Lunarias was about to say Abyssal but stopped herself as she did not know if the apprentices could hear her through the walls.

"...No," Kennas said flatly, "I'm just a normal citizen in their eyes..." It seemed like there was something more she wanted to say, but her gaze fell to the ground, her mind caught in a stream of uncomfortable thoughts.

"Anyways," Astolphos said, "Did you learn anything useful about our mercenaries?"

Lunarias shook her head, "Nothing, not even as much as running into one of them."

The fact that she could not wear her armor still excluded her from drawing too much attention. What she could do with a simple dagger was no small feat compared to the average citizen, but she would still be easily overpowered if she ran into any group of armed malcontents. Going anywhere where she was an easy target was too dangerous, so she could only walk around the markets, the Scaffolds, and the better parts of the city. She hoped that because of her fine clothes and the fact she did not go around with guards, someone would have tried to pickpocket her, but nothing happened. She did not see anyone wearing the usual baggy clothes, so she could not even try to provoke them to follow her.

"Same here, Astolphos said, "but was it just me, or did they seem a bit jumpier today?"

"That wasn't just you," Kennas said, "Something seems to have spooked them, and by something, I mean the fact that an Abyssal has shown up in the city."

"The question then is what to do next," Kennas said, her eyes for a moment getting a glint of emotion, but what Lunarias saw sent shivers down her spine.

"We're sticking to the plan, one more day, then we'll go to plan B."

"Plan B?"

"We'll take the mercenaries guarding me during work hostage and try getting their headquarters' location out of them."

"But wouldn't that require you to reveal you're Abyssals?"

Astolphos nodded. "I want to avoid that, this is why I want to get them to slip up instead, but we're running out of time."

He did not say why, but Lunarias could figure it out. From the brief times she had known Kennas, Lunarias was sure she would not take any chances at protecting her apprentices. Astolphos was not protecting Kennas from the mercenaries. It was the other way around.

"Alright then," Lunarias said, "I'll be back tomorrow evening. If we haven't learned anything new by then, we'll talk about how to best take the mercenaries by surprise."

"Do you want to stay and get something to eat?" Kennas asked, "We've made more than enough."

"Thanks for the offer, but I'll get something back at the inn. See you tomorrow."

***

Barely had she closed the door to the workshop when her attention was taken by some rapid movements at the corner of her eyes. She immediately pulled her dagger as she briskly walked to the spot.

She found nothing, not the slightest clue that someone had been there.

"Any problems?" Astolphos asked, appearing at the doorway, startling Lunarias.

"I thought I heard something."

He closed his eyes and turned his head around, "It does not seem like anyone awake is close to the shop. I think it's just the pressure of everything making you a bit jumpy."

"How can you be sure?"

But all he did was raise his eyebrow, and Lunarias realized he had used his powers as an Abyssal to survey the surroundings.

"Good night," Lunarias said, walking back to the inn.

She was, however, not wholly convinced of Astolphos' conclusion, and took a long and convoluted way home, stopping and hiding on occasion to see if anyone would reveal themselves, but nothing happened. She eventually reached the inn and went to bed, telling the innkeeper on the way to inform her if anything suspicious happened outside.

***

The sun had barely risen before someone knocked frantically on the door to Lunarias' room. She was immediately on guard, drawing her sword as she opened the door, only to hold her blade at the throat of one of the maids.

"There's a bunch of guards downstairs saying they're here to arrest you."

"Shit."

Lunarias quickly put on her armor and grabbed as much as she could. There was a lot of noise coming from downstairs, the innkeeper's voice booming as he said over and over again that he knew nothing of a knight staying at his establishment, all while the guards continued to threaten him. The maid led Lunarias to another staircase at the back of the building, it was crammed and dusty, but it seemed like no one but the staff knew of it.

"Why're you helping me?" Lunarias asked.

"The owner has been extorted by some brutes, and the guards have done nothing to help. You're here to put a stop to it, right?"

Lunarias did not answer. Her thoughts were already cursing at herself for not doing a better job yesterday. This proved that she had been followed, and whoever did so had tipped off the guards. She had to reach the workshop as quickly as possible, as she mused that if whoever it was had informed the guards, they were most likely part of that mercenary company. That meant they knew not only about Astolphos being con-nected to that workshop they were trying to extort, but they also knew that Lunarias, the knight that had been interrupt-ing their operation several times, were allied with them. She knew that if this was true, the apprentices were in danger, and through them, the entire city because of Kennas. She had to get there before anything happened.

They soon reached a back door. Luckily, the guards had just gone to the front door, so Lunarias sprinted away at full force toward the Craftsmen's District. She passed multiple guards on the way but could easily outrun the out-of-shape buffoons the garrison produced. She reached the workshop winded, gasping for breath but pushing on as she ripped the door open, only to see a man in baggy clothes come running towards her, his face contorted in horror.

Another person rounded the corner to the counter. It was the apprentice that stared her down yesterday. Her eyes wid-ened as she looked down at his arms. They were gray and scaly and had swelled to almost double their usual size. The apprentice also saw her simultaneously, and his arms returned to normal a second later, his eyes locked onto the crest on her chest as his face lost all color.

"Are any of you hurt?" Lunarias asked.

The apprentice shook his head, still as pale as before as he knew Lunarias had seen his ability, but Lunarias ran out the door after the mercenary. She had to catch him before he could tell anyone what he saw.

Chapter 39

Their traversal through the slums was slower than usual. Astolphos frequently checked in with Kennas and Glaucos, but they could only confirm that they kept to their usual route, albeit at a much slower pace than previously. His escorts were also much more silent, though they had not been that much for small talk to begin with. It all left Astolphos with the feeling that something was wrong, but he could not pinpoint what it was.

Then the familiar click of the lock, the sound of rusty hinges, and Astolphos knew they had reached the building.

Astolphos entered the store, but Glaucos immediately sounded in his head.

"Two of them are entering with you."

Astolphos ripped off the hood just in time to turn around and see them lock the door behind them while drawing their weapons. One pulled out a sword, while the other a mace.

"You shouldn't have lied to us," one said.

"I don't know what you mean."

"Quit playin' dumb. We saw you inside the shop of that carpenter we offed a few weeks ago."

Astolphos sighed; the gig was up, "So... what now?"

"We can't have anyone get bright ideas," The one with the mace said, "the boss wants us to make an example out of this. This'll hurt."

"You're not leaving this room alive, but that doesn't mean it'll be painless."

"I admire your optimism, but better people than you have failed trying to kill me before."

Astolphos closed his eyes and felt for their life essences. Several red hazes occupied his vision, but he focused on the two in front of him. He would need them to keep talking as he connected their essences.

"You're not going to resist us," The one with the sword said, "Not if you want us to keep some of the apprentices alive."

His focus faltered. He stepped back, his hands reaching for the telescopic staff out of nothing but reflex. The moment it left its concealed holster in his pants, the small rod extended to a length reaching above his head. On top of it was a large green crystal. It reacted to his touch, glowing with a soft light. The mercenaries took a step back, their sadistic grins twisting into horror as they realized just what kind of wasp nest they had kicked.

"What have you cretins done!?" Astolphos yelled. The mercenaries fell to the ground at his voice, their weapons falling to the ground with hollow thunks, mimicking that of their owners. They raised their hands to shield their faces as if that would help.

"T-The commander wants us to make an example. Three men have gone to kill them all. Please, we didn't know you're an Abyssal! We're just grunts! We beg you, spare us!"

"Kennas! Leave Glaucos here! Get to the shop as fast as possible!"

The confirmation came as screams from outside as all they saw Kennas' true form, as the gelatinous mass accelerated down the street at speed unseen ever since the fall of the Gifter.

"I spare no monster," Astolphos said as he grabbed hold of their life essences and pulled it out of their bodies. Without his special sight activated, all he saw was the two mercenaries shaking, struggling, and coughing as their literal life force left their body through all orifices as a thin, red mist. He felt a pulsing sensation in his free hand as their essence condensed into a scarlet liquid. Their hearts gave out seconds later, unable to keep beating as the years were forcefully yanked from their being, and they collapsed on the floor without a sound.

Astolphos looked down on the liquid and dumped it on the ground with a grunt of disgust at his own frivolity. He needed both hands free much more than 60 years of essence. He then pointed the scepter at the door, which blew it apart in a rain of splinters. Where the third mercenary had stood was only a blue spot on the stone and a single, pulsing crystal.

That third mercenary was given a fate much worse than his compatriots, but Astolphos did not want to think about it as he picked up Glaucos and ran back toward the shop. He once again thanked the Gifter, as his lungs did not hurt from sprinting, nor did his muscles ache.

The streets were deserted. Despite Astolphos running through both the slums and the Craftsmen's District, he never saw a person. He only heard their screams as the air filled with morose bells rocking from side to side at the tempo of his steps. It was the alarm telling the citizens that an Abyssal was sighted in the city and for all of them to get out of the city as quickly as possible.

He did not even run into one of the guards, though that did not surprise him particularly much. They would not be able to do anything anyway. It was for the better, as he did not have the time to stop and answer questions about his scepter or why he ran in the opposite direction of what one was supposed to do.

The shop soon appeared in his vision. The door was wide open, and silence dominated the interior. Expecting the worst, he turned a corner and entered a scene he had never imagined.

The Aurillian apprentices were nowhere to be found. Only three people were present in the room. A crying Inaris sat in a corner, embraced by Intros, who whispered for her to calm down. Kennas paced in circles around a mount of bloody chunks of skin. When she turned to Astolphos, her eyes were full of hate.

"What did you teach Inaris?"

Chapter 40

Lunarias arrived back at the workshop, winded and infuriated.

She had lost sight of her target. She had failed, and she did not want to think about what that meant to the citizens of Hybrik. She would have to rely on Astolphos to calm Kennas when she shared the news, but even that might already be a lost battle.

The door to the workshop was still wide open, and when she turned the corner, she saw Kennas staring at Astolphos in barely-contained anger. To the side of them, she saw the Abyssal apprentice from before hugging another apprentice, the girl that had grown pale last night. She cried and mumbled to herself, but the other apprentice held her tight, telling her over and over that everything was going to be alright.

"I'll ask you again," Kennas said, "What did you teach Inaris?"

Lunarias followed Astolphos' gaze to the floor. It was initially difficult to figure out what the pile was made of, but the scent of iron in the air and the remnants of bone told her everything she needed. That had been a person at some point. She had never seen anything like that done to someone before, be it Abyssal, Aurillian, or animal.

Astolphos remained silent, his eyes intent on the pile, his hands clenched and shaking.

Kennas' right hand became transparent as it extended and grabbed some chunks. She stepped forward and pushed them into the face of Astolphos.

"Tell me what shape these have!?"

Lunarias took a step closer to get a better look. It was difficult to see, but the chunks had all been cut in different patterns, but they all had something in common. They had been cut into the common shapes of gemstones. Squares and triangles with cut corners, diamond-shaped, and semi-circles. Whatever that cut it had passed through muscle, tendon, and bone as easily as the air.

"I told Inaris that ability was dangerous for a reason!" Kennas yelled, "This is what I wanted to avoid! She is too young to control it when under pressure!"

She threw the chunks back into the pile and turned around with her hands covering her eyes.

"But this is what saved everyone," Astolphos said.

Kennas turned around, her eyes locked onto Astolphos again, screaming 'How dare you!' without saying a word.

"Inaris should not be chastised and admonished for this," Astolphos continued, "for if not for her and the other Gifted putting their Gifts into use, we'd be looking at many more corpses, and none of them belonging to the mercenaries. Is that not true, Lunarias?"

Astolphos turned around and acknowledged Lunarias' presence for the first time.

"Intros told us that he ran into you. Would you have been able to stop the mercenaries in time?"

"She wouldn't," The male apprentice said, "Inaris had already unleashed her Gift before the knight arrived."

"What if her Gift had not been pointed at the mercenary? What if it'd been one of the other children during some argument?"

Their argument continued, but Lunarias tuned it out. There were more important things to do than to listen to them. She approached the two apprentices carefully. She was sure they were both Abyssals, and the girl was, without a doubt, the one they were discussing. Her power was able to cut that mercenary into tiny pieces, and despite the extra toughness granted by her armor, there was no doubt in her mind that it would not be of any help if those powers were aimed at her.

The male apprentice followed her steps with vigilance as if he waited for her to draw her weapon, but Lunarias went to her knees before the two.

"Did any of you get hurt?" She asked. The girl shook her head, but the male cleared his throat.

"They didn't get to that point. They tried attacking me, but my skin is too thick for those weapons. But it made Inaris here react on instinct."

"I'm s-sorry," Inaris said through her tears.

"Listen," Lunarias said as she touched Inaris' shoulder. She felt the wind around her fingers stir for a moment, but it faded as soon as the startled girl looked at her.

"Don't listen to what those two are saying. What you did saved a lot of lives. You have nothing to be ashamed of."

"But aren't you going to drag us away?" She asked.

Lunarias shook her head, "Any other knight would probably have done so, but... things are a bit different right now. You just acted in self-defense, nothing more, nothing less."

Despite the gravity of the situation, Lunarias could not stop herself from internally laughing at herself. If someone had come up to her two weeks ago and said that she would, in the near future, console an Abyssal for killing an Aurillian, criminal or not, she would probably have dragged him to a cell to sober up. But here she was.

"Did you catch the escapee?" Astolphos asked.

Lunarias snapped to attention, "...No, he got away."

"By Luminis!" Astolphos yelled, "Everything's falling apart. We have one dead, one escaped, and one we have no idea about!"

"He's in the basement," Intros said.

Astolphos cocked his head, "What did you say?"

"Cyrillys got his Gift. He can control people with his mind. He's keeping the third one captured in the basement."

"Damn it!" Kennas exclaimed, "Why didn't you tell us sooner!"

But she did not wait for an answer. She ran along with Astolphos towards the basement, but halfway there, the door opened. Out staggered a man dressed in baggy clothes, only these were dotted with crimson.

Chapter 41

"Lunarias! Get him!"

Astolphos wasted no time. He ran past the mercenary and headed for the basement. Kennas was faster, but they needed his Gift to heal whatever had happened. Lunarias could take care of the mercenary. She was more than capable of it.

He jumped down the stairs, his feet sticking to the landing, as he quickly found Cyrillys lying on the ground in a pool of blood. He was unconscious, and his breathing had stopped, but Astolphos could see he still had a little essence left, but it was dwindling fast. There was no time to assess his wounds. He had to transfer essence immediately. Kennas was already emptying Astolphos' belongings onto his bed, rummaging through until she found a small case filled with red vials.

Astolphos poured years of essence into the boy, slowly but surely finding the wounds with his eyes as Kennas emptied one vial into Astolphos' mouth. But the essence left Cyrillys' body as quickly as Astolphos could transfer it, and worse, it picked up speed.

"Cauterize his wounds," Astolphos said. He pointed at the wounds, and Kennas' hands turned to liquid as they enveloped them. Steam erupted from the liquid as Kennas heated her mass to temperatures rarely seen outside a fire.

But it was still not enough. Cyrillys was in bad shape, he had been stabbed countless times, and many had found their way into vital organs. Even as Kennas worked through the wounds, the essence poured away from the boy.

He downed two more bottles and used both hands to transfer their combined 200 years of essence. Cyrillys' light flared up for a moment.

And then it extinguished.

Astolphos' hands fell to his side.

"No..." Kennas said, her tendrils fumbling with his case to retrieve another vial. She brought it to his mouth, but Astolphos grabbed it, shaking his head as his eyes misted. There was nothing more he could do.

Kennas dropped the vial on the floor, turning her body back to human. She held Cyrillys' body tightly. "Cyrillys... Please come back." Was all she could say as the tears streamed down her cheeks. She howled, invoking Luminis, demanding Cyrillys' soul back, but nothing happened. There truly was nothing more to be done.

And then, her cries for help turned to curses, first at Luminis, but then.

"Damn the Aurillians," Kennas said, her voice dripping with poison as her sadness transformed to anger, "Damn their greed, their inhumanity. They came here for money, but I'll only give them war and death! I'll never rest until every single one of them lie dead at my feet!"

Chapter 42

"Lunarias! RUN!"

She barely registered Astolphos' yell before a torrent of blue liquid barreled up the stairs toward her and the mercenary. She pushed him away, jumping to the side just as the wave reached them. She was too slow. The wave struck her feet, sending her spinning as it collided with the mercenary and carried him away. He barely had the time to scream before liquid enveloped him on its trajectory to the wall.

Lunarias got back on her feet in time to see the impact, her armor had gotten a new set of scratches, but nothing was broken or hurt. The entire building shook with the power of the impact. The wooded walls bulged, barely holding together as several candles went out from the rousing wind. The mercenary swam around in the liquid, opening and closing his mouth like a fish dragged onto land. Air bubbles slipped to the surface, and then it all retracted. Kennas returned to her human shape, her hands clasped tightly on the mercenary's shoulders as she shook in anger. He struggled against the woman's grip, he screamed for help, but nothing came of it. He flung his fists, but they only sent ripples around her skin, as if he had hit a pool of water.

"I hate your kind!" Kennas screamed, "I sacrificed everything to save you! EVERYTHING! And this is how you repay me!? By extorting me and killing my apprentices, my children!?"

The mercenary looked at Kennas' face, his own standing agape as he looked at a true monster for the first time in his life. Then he screamed as a haze surrounded Kennas. He clawed at her hands, the only result being his hand turning red as they came into contact with Kennas' scalding liquid.

"I'll repay every single one of you back in kind! You hear me!?"The haze turned downright into steam as Kennas' image sputtered and faded as bubbles erupted from her center. Kennas would cook him alive if not stopped; Lunarias was sure of it.

Her hand found the hilt of her sword, but there it stayed. She remembered her last encounter with Kennas, how her blade had sliced through her tendrils without effect. There was nothing Lunarias could do to her. And then she still drew her sword, but her target was not Kennas, but the mercenary. She could do nothing to save his life, but at least she could make sure he did not suffer.

And then Astolphos reached the top of the stairs. He took one look at Lunarias, her hands, her disheveled hair, and his expression grew cold.

He adjusted his grip on the strange staff with an orange crystal on top, taking hold of it close to the top, and dragged the rest along the floor as he went up to Kennas, grabbed her shoulder and turned her around forcefully, and slapped her along the cheek with his free hand.

"Pull yourself together!" He yelled, "You could've hurt Lunarias!"

Kennas looked Astolphos in the eyes. The flat disks were unchanged, a fact sending shivers down Lunarias' spine.

"Why should I care for some Aurillian?"

At which Astolphos slapped her again, "You know damn well why! And what about all the apprentices upstairs? What about them? Do they also deserve to die just because they're not Gifted?"

Kennas grabbed Astolphos by the collar.

"How dare you!"

He raised the staff, the crystal resting up against Kennas' neck.

"You too?" She asked, looking at the crystal.

"We can't afford the Devourer to return. Please don't force us."

"After all these years, why are you going to their side now?"

"Because there is no other side anymore, we killed the other side ourselves back in that forest. It's this or nothing, and I can't let you run amok, devastating any city you come across once again."

And then, the two were pushed apart and landed several meters away from each other.

"E-enough," A timid voice said from behind. Lunarias turned around to see the girl standing with her arms stretched in front of her. She shook with fear, but Lunarias could not figure out what, or who, that fear was directed against.

"Please stop fighting. You're friends, right?"

Lunarias stepped in between them, using her body as a shield for the young girl in case Kennas was going to do anything. Lunarias would not be much of a hindrance, but perhaps it would give Astolphos enough time to do whatever he talked about. The girl grabbed her from behind, Inaris' legs seemingly giving out as the fear won over, and tears streamed down her face. Lunarias directed her sword forward, its point centered on Kennas, who had just risen from the ground. The same could be said of Astolphos, who used the staff to get back up. He shook his head at Lunarias, who in turn sheathed her sword.

"Have you calmed down?" Astolphos asked.

Kennas nodded, "Sorry," she said, hanging her head.

"Don't say that to me; say that to Inaris. She had to witness this mess."

Inaris took a deep breath as she let go of Lunarias' waist. The girl was exhausted but still stood on her own as she forced a slight smile on her lips, "It's alright."

Kennas ran to her side and fell to her knees in front of her. She put both hands on her shoulders and brought her close.

"No, it isn't," Kennas said, "I lost control. I shouldn't have. But you brought me back. Thank you." She then brought her in for a hug.

Lunarias went to Astolphos' side.

"You alright?" She asked.

"More or less, I'm just happy things didn't get worse than that."

"Does this happen often?"

"Thank Luminis, no, but it didn't end this well last time. But that's a story for another time. We have to get back to the mercena-"

Astolphos grew silent as he looked around the room. The mercenary was nowhere to be found. They had been too pre-occupied, and the slippery bastard had exploited that.

"He's right here," The other apprentice said from the entrance to the shop. His skin was hard and gray, and he dragged the mercenary along at the leg. He tugged hard, threw him into the shop, and blocked the only exit.

"Good job Intros," Astolphos said, sighing in relief.

"I'll deal with him," Astolphos said, "Lunarias, can I get you to go up and look after the Aurillian apprentices."

Lunarias nodded.

"Great. Kennas, stay down here and calm down. Right now, we need the carpenter, not the Hand of Infrastructure, and certainly not the Devourer."

Chapter 43

With the help of Intros and some rope, they got the mercenary tied spread-eagle between two bunk beds in the basement. He struggled wildly, but Intros and Astolphos had enough of the mercenaries' antics and tied him down using brute force alone. Astolphos could only admire Intros' toughness. Despite everything, despite the anger Astolphos saw flare up in his eyes when he saw the pool of blood and Cyrillys' covered body lying in his bed, Intros kept his cool throughout the ordeal. But everything had a breaking point, and Intros' came to his when the mercenary was tied up.

Astolphos saw his skin harden the moment Intros took a good look at the mercenary. Astolphos held Intros back as he clenched his fist. There was no knowing how strong Intros was when his Gift was active, but if he truly were a descendant of Balacastrys, it was a death sentence for the mercenary if Intros got his hands on him.

"Let go of me!" Intros yelled, "He needs to pay for what he did to Cyrillys!"

"And he will," Astolphos said, struggling to keep the apprentice at bay, "But we need to know where his accomplices are. The future of this shop rests on it."

Intros hesitated for a moment. His skin turned back to normal as he looked down and sobbed. Underneath his tough exterior, he truly cared for Cyrillys.

"Promise me he'll not leave this basement," Intros said.

"That's not up to me, but Kennas. Now, I don't want you present for what comes next, so go to Lunarias and help her with whatever she needs. Don't worry about her, she might be a knight, but she's on our side for now."

"And will she still be when all of this is over?"

Astolphos paused. It was a question he had thought of before, but he did not want to think it to its conclusion. Lunarias seemed to truly despise him only a few days prior, but now she just seemed to be wondering instead. He shook his head to get the thought out once more. Whatever happened next would happen no matter how he reacted to it. That is a problem for later.

"Just go up to her. I'll take care of this."

He then gave Intros a slight slap on the shoulder towards the door before turning his attention to the mercenary. He did not make a move before he heard the door upstairs close. The mercenary held his head high and stared directly into Astolphos eyes, almost as if to say, 'I have already won, do you worst.'

And it worked, as Astolphos' grip tightened around the scepter as he felt around with its end for a gap in the wooden floor.

"Relax 'Stolfos, he's trying to provoke you," said Glaucos, his voice also hanging at the precipice of anger.

The unknown third voice made the mercenary's facade crack as he suddenly looked around the room to the best of his ability, his shock clearly displayed.

"I'm not going to try diplomacy or negotiation," Astolphos said,

"A shame for you that my friend Heuristrys isn't here. He would've tried to make an agreement that would leave you unharmed and satisfied with the terms. Unfortunately for you, I'm just here to get this over with as quickly as possible. I'm going to give you one chance, and one chance only. I need the names of your associates, the locations of your bases, and the names of all the guards that your organization has in their pockets."

The mercenary struggled against the ropes, but nothing budged,

"Why should I give you anything? You're just going to kill everyone!"

"That's right, but that's actually your fault and the fault of the guy who ran away. You see, I actually tried to figure out a way to solve this peacefully. That's why we tried infiltrating your organization. But no, you just had to go to this shop in an attempt to punish us for trying.

"I can't keep any of you alive now; you know too much. But here's the thing, there's a fast way of killing, and there's a slow one, and you just wasted your chance at the fast one."

Astolphos raised his scepter and brought it down into the floor. It split the wood and continued down. He felt the instant it hit the soil.

The collapsible scepter had small slits at every segment where you could look through. That was on purpose. The insides of the scepter glowed with a faint blue hue, slowly rising from the bottom until it reached the top right underneath Glaucos.

"Ready?" Astolphos asked, looking up at the crystal.

"Fully charged and ready to cast, do your worst."

Back when Glaucos had his own body, his incredible destructive powers had come from the earth itself. It gave him an almost unlimited amount of energy. Now that he had lost his body, he was limited to the simpler parts of his Gift, and even then, what he could cast was limited by the energy stored inside. Astolphos' staff functioned as a direct conduit, letting Glaucos' energy perpetually refill just like in the old days. It also meant that Astolphos could tap into Glaucos' energies and use them to fuel his own Gift.

"You stand before Astolphos, the Master of the Abyssal Forge. Here's your punishment for your insolence!"

He raised his free hand and pointed an open palm at the mercenary's ankle as he thought of the most heinous spell in his repertoire, one he never wanted to use again. Glaucos glowed with an intensity dwarfing the candles lighting the basement. The mercenary screamed before anything became visible, but slowly, his boot grew blue, then cyan growths of crystal pierced through the leather.

"You know about the Forest of Sorrows?" Astolphos asked rhetorically, his voice booming louder than the screams, "Those very crystals are now growing inside your veins. They will slowly work their way through your body, millimeter by milli-meter, but the pain will never stop. It will continue to grow in intensity every second. But..." Astolphos flicked his wrist and snapped his fingers. It was not necessary, just part of the show.

He stopped screaming instantly and took deep, labored breaths.

"I can stop it at any point, but all I need to do is snap my fingers again, and everything will continue just like before. So, are you ready to talk?"

But the mercenary kept quiet.

"Then I'll give you ten minutes of pain." He then snapped his finger once more and left the room.

Chapter 44

Despite there being two floors between Lunarias and the basement, the distance was still not enough to quiet the intense screams of the mercenary. She did not know what Astolphos was doing and did not want to know.

It at least seemed like she was the only one who knew what was going on down there, as none of the apprentices reacted to it. Then again, they might have heard it all and were just too shocked from seeing Inaris use her powers. Judging by the remains of that corpse, it was a sight where Lunarias could not predict her own reaction.

Their actual reaction was far removed from what she had thought. Some were crying, some stared straight ahead like they were still processing it all, but the teenagers were reasonably calm. They comforted the younger apprentices, talking to them, reassuring them that everything would be alright.

It was far removed from the response she had seen back in the village since Astolphos' identity was exposed for the first time. There, everyone was paralyzed in place. Even the adults that supposedly had been the responsible ones just stared in horror. She expected to be greeted with the same scene, if not worse since they had just learned that some of their friends and family were Abyssals.

But this was different even from that, as not only was there nothing she could do, the older apprentices scowled at her while others looked wary of her presence. But no one talked to her. They only talked among themselves in hushed voices low enough for her to only make out the tiniest of parts.

She racked her brain as to something she could do to help, to take their minds off what was happening, but this was far beyond her usual duties. Her first thought was to get them all out of the building and take them somewhere where they could get their minds off the events. But that was off the table with what was happening in the basement. All she could do now was to shield them from the screams of the mercenary, meaning she blocked the only way in and out, with her sitting on a chair in front of it.

"What's going to happen now?" One of the older apprentices asked. He looked to be in his mid-teens, still a bit on the skinny side. Though his clothes were new, it did not look like he was used to them yet, as he more than once adjusted his shirt, though it looked to be a perfect fit. He looked nervous, like he did not want to ask but was somehow forced to do it anyway.

At first, she did not answer. She looked at each of the apprentices. There was something that just did not connect with her. She had seen the rage in Kennas, and even experienced it firsthand, but that Abyssal truly cared for these Aurillians. All their clothes were new and made to fit them, and everyone looked well-fed. It costs a lot of Merias to keep so many children healthy, far more than what a carpenter should be able to provide. And she had not seen any other adult in the shop. Kennas was the only one to keep them all in line; no, she was the only one there to raise them. How could a creature like that even exist?

Extraneous circumstances, that was her conclusion. Kennas cared for her apprentices, and the rage she had seen was because Cyrillys had passed away.

"I don't know," Lunarias said.

It was the truth. No matter how she twisted and turned her thoughts, she could not predict what the future held.

"Are we in danger?" Another one asked. Everyone turned nervous at the question. She had not expected it to come up. It was one question she knew they all had on their minds, but it was another thing entirely for them to say out loud.

She had to make a decision now. Did she tell them that they were in danger, or did she tell them they were safe? If she decided they were in danger, she would have to get them out of the shop before Kennas and Astolphos figured anything out. That would then lead them to live at an orphanage like the one currently being established at the village at best, and at worst, they would live on the street, living off the charity of the wealthier population, the ones that never set foot in the slums. More likely, they had to turn to crime, perhaps even joining the very mercenaries they were trying to dismantle.

On the other hand, if she told them they were safe, she would bet that her portrayal of Kennas was correct. She had only met that woman a few times, and most of the time, Kennas had either been cold towards her or downright antagonistic. Only once had Kennas smiled in Lunarias' presence, which had been when she asked about the apprentices. The question was just if that still counted. Astolphos tortured that mercenary to get information out of him, all because of the chance that their secret would come out. If someone as mild-mannered as Astolphos would stoop to that level to keep their identities secret, what other lengths were the two willing to go to?

"...I don't think so," Lunarias finally said. She chose to believe in what she could see right now. These children were cared for here, and she felt Astolphos would help her keep the apprentices safe if things turned sour. After all, he had stood up to Kennas before.

"Has Kennas not treated you like family up until now?"

"Kennas?"

"She's alive?"

"She is. She's an Abyssal and has the power to change her shape. She sent the kid she was posing as away and took his identity to continue leading the workshop. That's at least what I've pieced together."

None of the apprentices said another word. They all looked shocked at their peers. It was a lot for them to take in, with everything that had happened on this day alone.

"I need to ask all of you," Lunarias said. All eyes returned to her.

"How was Kennas treating you before all of this?"

It took time before anyone responded. They all seemed lost in memories. Some smiled with tearful eyes. A few even shook their heads with a self-deprecating smile on their lips.

"She reminded me of my mom," One of the younger apprentices said. Many nodded in approval. They told their opinion of Kennas, but none were negative. Even the apprentice who had first raised his concern agreed.

She knew she had made the right choice. Despite what Kennas was, she loved these children; they would be safe with her.

"Where is she?"

"Yeah, we want to talk to her!"

"She's downstairs," Lunarias said.

"Can we go see her?"

"That's... not the best idea right now. She's assisting Astolphos and needs quiet and focus."

And with those words, she saw the enthusiasm dampen.

"You know what," Lunarias said, rising from her chair, "How about I go down and see how far they are. If you promise me you'll stay put while I'm gone, I'll return to tell you when you can go down."

Chapter 45

The ten minutes were almost up. The screams had been harrowing. The door to the basement was not nearly enough to keep in the noise.

Astolphos spent the time looking through his spellbook, refreshing his memory on what other tools he had at his disposal. There were ample options within its pages, but few were of the kind he would ever want to use again. He could only pray that this had been enough.

But focusing on the book had not been enough to drown out the screams. They constantly reminded him that this was his doing, he was the only one responsible, and he felt it eat away at his soul. It had been centuries since he last had to do anything like that, but it did not feel anything like the last time. Back then, he had looked at his deeds as a mix of necessity and revenge. Now, necessity was mixed with doubt as to whether he could have done more to ensure a peaceful resolution. But the doubt also took a different form. He looked back at Kennas' actions not even an hour ago. Had they even become better through the years, or was it only a thin veil of civility hiding what Astolphos had degraded them to? Kennas was right at the edge of becoming the Devourer once again, and he internally justified what he was doing as a necessity. No matter how he twisted and turned his actions, he could not figure out another way to resolve everything without Kennas losing her shop, and with both Gifted looking at her now, he knew that had never been an option.

Despite her behavior earlier, she returned to her usual self. She sat and talked with Inaris and Intros since Astolphos exited the basement. He could see that despite how mad Kennas had been about Inaris using her Gift, she showed a level of restraint the Devourer would never have been capable of.

Inaris finally sat on her own again, looking and listening to Kennas tell her how important it was when one possessed such a dangerous ability to use it responsibly. Though she still admonished its use, she let Inaris know it was the right choice this time and that she had saved many lives. But on the other hand, she also sternly told her to learn restraint, and on more than one occasion, she said that Astolphos would be the one to teach her. It was a small price to pay if that was all it took to make Kennas forgive him.

But now it was time. Astolphos closed his book and took a deep breath, trying not to think of what he had to do now.

"'Stolfos," Kennas said, "I want to go with you."

Astolphos turned around to see Kennas already walking to his side.

"I don't think that's a good idea."

"Because you fear I can't keep myself back?"

Astolphos nodded, "If you lose control, I don't know what to do."Kennas grew silent and looked at the ground before taking a deep breath and looking him in the eyes.

"You know exactly what to do."

But Astolphos did not want to acknowledge that, he did not want to imagine the possibility, but he knew well that if Kennas lost Control, he would have to drain her essence. They no longer had Glaucos to restrain her, nor Cannos, the Hand of Communication, to track her down. If he let Kennas the Devourer escape, there was no way to stop her.

"All the more reason for you to not come with me. You have your apprentices. You can continue this peaceful life. Why risk it?"

"It's already too late. They know what I am. I wouldn't be surprised that the only thing keeping my Aurillian apprentices in place right now is the fear of me, Intros, and Inaris. I will have to go back to Marados castle and wait for the rest of you. I need to do this because I almost lost Control back then. If not for you pulling me away, I'd gone back to how I was in those dark years. I need to know that I'm not a threat to my apprentices if I am to open another store."

"...Glaucos?"

"I...think you should let her do it."

But despite being outvoted, Astolphos still thought it through. If Kennas lost Control, would he even be able to do what must be done? Would he be able to raise his hand and kill Kennas to save Aurillians from devastation? He did not know, and no amount of time pondering would lead him closer to an answer.

"What're you two talking about?"

Lunarias entered the room without any of them noticing. She went straight up to them, and for the first time, she did not have a hand on her blade as she approached Kennas.

Kennas bowed, "I'm so sorry about what I did to you before and for what I said. I wasn't myself back then."

"You're forgiven. I don't think I would've reacted differently if I'd been in the same situation," Lunarias said.

Her answer was far from what Astolphos expected. He would not have imagined Lunarias, of all people, to forgive an Abyssal for anything.

"What is it?" Lunarias asked, looking at the surprised Astolphos.

"Why're you down here? You should keep an eye on the apprentices."

"It doesn't matter," Kennas said, her hands shaking and barely holding back the tears, "They know what I am. If they want to run, they're free to do so."

Lunarias put a hand on Kennas' shoulder and gave her a wry smile.

"I'm actually here because they want to see you."

Chapter 46

At first, the apprentices looked happy to see Kennas, but their smiles were replaced with indecision as they realized it was true that Kennas was an Abyssal. Kennas, too froze when she saw their reactions. The only one who did not look fazed was Astolphos, who found a spot where he could lean up against the wall and survey the scene.

"Is it true?" One of the apprentices asked, "Are you an Abyssal?"

Kennas nodded, sitting on the chair Lunarias used to block the door. Her shoulders shook, but she looked at her apprentices with a somber smile.

"Yes, it's true."

Her smile cracked, her gaze hitting the floor. She opened her mouth to say something more, but only the slightest sobs escaped.

The apprentices were taken aback. It did not seem that they had expected her to just confirm everything. Lunarias, too, could do nothing but stare at the scene, unable to figure out what to do.

"Kennas and I are both very old Abyssals," Astolphos said, carefully looking at each apprentice as he talked, "We both served the Abyssal King as his advisors and administrators. I was responsible for our kingdom's forges, while Kennas was responsible for the infrastructure: Maintenance of roads, construction of new ones, redirection of trading routes, and the like."

Lunarias would have called them a liar if anyone else had said those words. Astolphos told everything like it was a matter of fact and with the authority required for someone carrying such a title. One thing was to hear about the Masters through priests. Another was hearing the very person proclaiming it before one's eyes.

"But shouldn't you be dead then?" One of the apprentices asked.

"Correct, but my ability, my gift, is that I can transfer life essence between people. Using that, I can extend the life of anyone I want. I stopped counting the years long ago, but I think I'm about 330 years old by now. Kennas had already been in the service of the Abyssal King for 30 years when I arrived, so she's even older than that.

"But both of us decided to go against the Abyssal King," Astolphos looked away. Lunarias saw the regret painted on his face as he continued, "We started a civil war, and it ended up razing the entire kingdom to the ground. When we realized the damage, the Abyssal King was no more, and most of the others in our position had either gone into hiding or perished along with him. Both Kennas and I were granted permission to live in Aurillia by the regent back then."

It was a lot to take in, even for Lunarias. Most of all, she now knew why he did not flee when that noble approached him in the village. He was far from the only one in that deal, and his fleeing would only result in the others being hunted down. But it still felt like he left a lot of details out. She would have to ask him about it later when no Aurillians were around.

"But I need to stress this," Astolphos said, "None of you are here because you're part of a cover. Kennas' love for every single one of you is genuine. You're no apprentices to her. You're family."

And silence befell the room once again. Astolphos words stung deep. More than a few apprentices looked at the ground in guilt. Lunarias, too was conflicted. Looking at Kennas now, she knew it was wrong of her to have doubted the children's safety. Looking at Kennas, moments ago a mighty Abyssal, she now only saw a sobbing mother scared to death about what her children would say. She knew she would stop at nothing to protect those children.

"Everything Astolphos said was true." Kennas said, unable to keep the tears at bay, "I'm sorry to have lied to all of you for so long, but if I told you the truth, I was afraid you'd all leave."

She stood up from the chair, but halfway up, some of the apprentices flinched. She stopped immediately at the sight, falling back into the seat. She produced a rust-covered key from her apron and let it fall to the floor. All eyes were on it.

"Inside my room, under the bed, there's a safe. It contains all the Merias I've saved up for many years. I can understand if some of you want to leave Hybrik. If so, take as much as you think you need, but please be mindful of the others who may want to do the same thing. I know it just sounds hollow now that you know the truth, but even though you've seen my true form, it does not change the Kennas you've all known. Living with you, working with you, it has been a joy I can't put into words."

Kennas rose from her seat and passed Lunarias to get out the door.

Chapter 47

The moment they opened the door to the basement, Astolphos knew he had messed up. Where he had planned for the crystal to claim up to the knee, it had instead taken the entire leg. He snapped his fingers immediately to stop the spread.

The mercenary was unconscious. All the pain was too much for him. His essence was still somewhat healthy, though it was weakened by the loss of a leg. But that did not mean the essence was gone. It was frozen inside the crystalline structures, giving it a slightly red hue in the light of the candles on an otherwise blue-hued disorderly surface.

He heard a gasp from behind. Lunarias' eyes locked on the crystal. She recognized it immediately. Not that he had expected anything different. After all, from what he had been able to piece together, she had quite a bad encounter while surrounded by that very same crystal.

"Is he still alive?" Kennas asked, her expression surprisingly peaceful, taking the deeds of the mercenary into account.

"Just unconscious," Astolphos said, "I'll fix that now."

It only took a light slap across the cheeks to jolt the mercenary awake. At first, the mercenary looked around as if he had forgotten where he was. Then the memories dawned on him, and he yanked at the ropes once more. Then confusion dawned on him, and he looked down on his legs.

This next scream was one of fear, pure fear of the kind that would give anyone pure of heart nightmares for a lifetime.

Luckily, there was no one in earshot living up to that description.

"I've stopped the spread, for now, at least. Test my patience, and my leniency will stop. Now, do you remember what I want to know?"

"Why are you here?" The mercenary asked. His eyes were squarely on Lunarias, who at first looked taken aback by the sudden address.

"You're supposed to protect us from those monsters, not help them. What happened to you, knight!?"

"It seems like you've not understood what I said. Let me give you a demonstration instead."

Astolphos lifted his hand, his fingers ready to snap. The mercenary pleaded when he realized what Astolphos was about to do, but then his hand was lowered by Lunarias.

"Please, save me from these creatures," He pleaded to Lunarias.

"Even if I wanted to save you," Lunarias said, "I couldn't do that. You see, I'm under orders to escort this Abyssal to the capital. This is under the orders of the queen herself. Do you know what that means?"

You could almost hear the mercenary's confidence crack as he lowered his head. He had truly exhausted all options, and they all knew it. The question now was just what he was going to say to it.

"We have five safe houses."

"Kennas, get me some paper."

The mercenary had cracked, and once that happened, the information flowed out of him like a busted dam. Though far from all being relevant, such as information about how they picked their victims or about what they did before turning to banditry. But among the torrent were a few important tidbits. Though challenging to point on a map with both hands bound, they got the safehouses marked on a makeshift map.

Five safehouses, four being satellites, and the last one being their main headquarters. Three in the slums, of those was the one Astolphos frequented, one in the craftsmen district, and one on the Scaffolding. Their locations did not surprise Astolphos. Having a place to lie low right in the hunting ground made a lot of sense, especially if one had to stash away stolen goods. But with the definite location pointed out, they knew what their next step would be. The one who got away must have run to one of those locations. The question was just which one. Astolphos hoped it was one of the satellites, which meant he might not have spread the discovery yet. It was, however, a different story if he had gone to their headquarters. Then the battle might be dangerous, and he would have to ask Lunarias to stay back, as she would have a much more adverse effect from their blades than the two Gifted.

"And the garrison," Lunarias said, "How much of it have you bribed?"

"We have about half of it either bribed or blackmailed. The others know what's happening, but no one wants to do anything about it."

"Why?"

"Because the commander is there to supervise."

"Your commander?"

The mercenary tried to nod, but the lack of energy amounted to only the weakest movements. He was genuinely drained of both physical as well as mental power.

"Is he the old man always close to the captain?"

Once again, the mercenary nodded.

"So, you know where the leader is?" Astolphos asked.

"Yes," Lunarias said, "I've seen him a few times. I've never seen him leave the garrison, so he's probably still there."

"That's good to know," Astolphos said, "Now, we're probably going to have a very long day, so how about I'll take care of the last bit here, and I'll meet you up there in a moment?"

Despite his proposal, Astolphos did not look forward to the experience. He did not want to kill anyone anymore, but he had no other choice anymore. This mercenary knew the truth, which endangered Kennas and her apprentices. He had to do it.

"No, I'll take care of him," Kennas said, her eyes fixed on the blanket-covered lump on Cyrillys' bed.

"Are you sure that's a good idea?" Astolphos asked, "You've already proven you can keep yourself in Control. There's no reason to tempt fate further, especially on the same day you lost Cyrillys."

"You're right. It's not a good idea," Kennas said, "but I have to do it. After talking to the children, I truly think some will await me tomorrow. I don't have time to wait. If I can do this without losing Control, I know for sure that my apprentices will have nothing to fear."

"I'm against it," Astolphos said, "Glaucos, please tell her why this is a horrible idea."

But Glaucos remained silent.

"Glaucos?"

"...I think we should let her do it."

"Wha-" He could not believe his ears.

"Think about it 'Stolfos. If she can't prove to herself that she can keep the Devourer chained, she will fear running amok for the rest of time. Right here, we can stop her if things go out of hand. This is not something that can wait."

Astolphos paused for a second.

"Are you sure this is a good idea?"

"Certainly not, but I don't see any other way forward."

Not a word left his lips as Astolphos climbed the stairs out of the basement. Lunarias was close behind, looking like she did not fully grasp the situation, but she knew full well that whatever was going to happen was not something she wanted to witness.

"Please, Kennas, rethink this."

But he did not wait for an answer because he knew none would come. He instead let Lunarias out and closed the door behind him, leaving Kennas and the mercenary alone.

It took less than half a minute before the screams began anew.

Chapter 48

The sight of that mercenary's leg was burned into Lunarias' retinas. She would never be able to forget that crystal. She was surrounded by them during her travels to this part of Aurillia. Everything in the Forest of Sorrows was made of that same type of crystal.

It was a damned place, a forest where everything living was encased in blue-tinted crystal long ago. Where the grass was as brittle as glass and just as sharp, and no tree had even a leaf on its branches. No one knew precisely when or why it came into existence. All that was known was that it had suddenly appeared at the end of the war with the Abyssals and that everything of metal that touched the crystal would shatter like glass.

But perhaps she had finally solved that mystery, and as she looked up at the one she theorized was responsible, the sweat ran cold down her spine.

"Don't think about it," Astolphos said, "She's going to stay in Control, I'm sure of it."

It took a second before she realized that though he looked at her while talking, those words were addressed to himself. He kept up a slight smile, but it was nothing but a thin veneer used to hide away his fear. She felt sympathy for the Abyssal momentarily, but then the screams returned to the forefront as Kennas did whatever to their captive.

"Did you get what you needed?" Intros asked. His eyes darted to and from the basement door, twitching as the screams increased another octave.

"More or less," Astolphos said, "Where's Inaris?"

"She couldn't stand the sound, so she went into the kitchen to make supper."

"Alone? For so many apprentices?"

"I wanted to wait out here in case you needed some help."

"I think we'll manage. Go help Inaris."

"But what about Kennas? Why's she still down there?"

"...You don't want to know. Please, go help Inaris, and don't wait for us. This is going to be a long night."

As Ontrys closed the door to the kitchen, the screams quelled. Astolphos winced as if bracing himself for something unpleasant.

And then it hit, the sickening smell of burning flesh carried to them by a cloud as black as the reaper's cloak escaping through any crack around the basement door.

Lunarias gagged and covered her airways with a sawdust-filled rag lying on a workbench. It was not the first time that unpleasant stench grazed her nostrils. Few knights came as far as her without walking at the border of the Abyss and being met with the smell of charcoal and burnt meat, only to be greeted with the harrowing visage of a village burned to the ground, residents at all. One should never become used to that smell, which was why she raised an eyebrow as she looked once more at the Abyssal at her side. He made no move to cover his mouth, and if not for the tears around his eyes, it would have been no different from their other exchanges.

"Is this what you meant by her losing control?" Lunarias asked.

"Something along those lines at least, just on a larger, in-discriminate scale."

"By the Ancestors, why are you keeping such a creature alive?"

Astolphos took a huge step towards her, his face for a moment contorting in anger, before returning to the depths of an ocean of calmness. She just let it happen, and once the moment had passed, he took a deep breath. She wondered why her hand had not flown to her weapon, why her reflexes had not taken steps to protect her from the threat.

Fear had frozen her in place. Her body did not know what to do against a threat as large and unknown as the one in front of her, or perhaps instead, knew exactly what the danger was and knew full well that there was nothing she could do to stop it.

"Sorry," Astolphos said, "It's been a long day.

"Where you see a monster, I see an old friend, a product of circumstance and time. We were all warriors once, following every order from the Abyssal King, no matter how impossible or improbable it would seem to be. We did it because the King was righteous in his cause.

"Kennas, more than anyone, embodied this. She would follow him to the ends of the earth to protect him and his vision of the future. And she paid the price for that. She was the Master of Infrastructure. Her responsibility was constructing new roads and keeping them maintained and safe. During the war, the routes close to Aurillia were always filled with scouts and regiments, and if the army was not needed to deal with their numbers, Kennas and her underlings were the ones who were expected to get the job done.

"None of us know exactly why Kennas lost control, but we all think it was all that violence. She never told us anything about her duty, of the actual number of soldiers she had killed. All we could see was a slow descent hidden beneath her devotion, and then one day, she never came back. We searched for her and eventually found her terrorizing both the Aurillian and Abyssal border towns, leaving nothing alive in her wake.

"But we found her at some point 30 years later and, through great effort, got her down to earth once more. But when she came, she looked down at her hands and was disturbed by the bloodstains. We learned later that her body count had been the highest of all Abyssals, every single one close quarters, as that was all her powers afforded.

"That was why she joined our side when some of us Masters turned our backs on the King and his empire. She didn't want to devolve back into that again, but the King would not allow her to step down from her position, or more aptly, the majority of Masters recognized her efforts as too necessary to lose. That was why when the late king of Aurillia promised salvation, she followed us without hesitation.

"But even though so many years have passed, she still only sees those stains when looking at her hands. It's the reason why she chose to become a carpenter. That way, she could keep her distance from conflict and war. Raising and educating less fortunate people is how she's chosen to atone for the sins she's committed. So, when you ask why I'm keeping a creature like her alive, I'm not. I'm keeping alive a dear friend who has had a tough life and wants to better the lives of everyone around her."

The smoke stopped billowing out from the basements, and moments later, the door opened. Kennas was still returning to her human exterior when she reached the top of the stairs. In her hands was the crystallized leg of the mercenary, nary a bloodstain nor remnant of skin present at the joint.

Despite everything Astolphos had said, Lunarias could not see it the same way. As Astolphos exhaled in relief, Lunarias' body tensed as she once again saw a monster that even Astolphos was afraid of going up against. This monster could be cruel. The screams and stench were more than enough of a testament to that. The leisurely pace she walked with as she threw the leg at Astolphos did not help the image either.

"Got it out of your system?" Astolphos asked.

"I'd say so. Thanks for letting me do this," Kennas then nodded at the leg, "Can you do something about this? I don't want my apprentices to see the remains."

"Of course," The leg instantly crumbled into dust, falling to the floor where it seemingly passed through the planks and disappeared into the soil. And with that, Lunarias mused, there were no remains left of that mercenary. The thought of the many who had suffered a similar fate made her shudder.

"So, what now?" Kennas asked.

"I have a plan," Lunarias said.

Chapter 49

"And remember, if I'm not back by dawn, take from the safe and leave Hybrik as quickly as possible. Find the closest city with a trader's guild, and get them to send a letter to Heuristrys in my name. Got it?"

Ontrys and Inaris nodded at Kennas' words, albeit reluctantly. But who would not? She had not only given them instructions to leave the city but indirectly told them that she would risk her life tonight to keep them all safe. They both looked at Astolphos, who stood close to the door to the kitchen. He knew they were trying to figure out whether the threat was credible or if this was Kennas being overly cautious.

He could not afford to give them false hopes, even though he was conflicted about the possible outcomes. The chance of those mercenaries figuring out Kennas' one weakness was slim at best, which left Astolphos as the biggest threat to Kennas' survival. He made her a promise and intended to keep it, no matter how painful it would be to carry out. A light shake on the head got the message across, as both looked down at their cutting boards and wished Kennas luck as she gave each of them a hug before leaving.

Only when they shut the door to the kitchen did Astolphos stop.

"I think you should sit this one out," Astolphos said.

Kennas turned around, a wry smile on her lips, "I can't do that, you know that. I'd not be able to live with it if I had to leave all of this behind because I just sat on the sidelines."

"But what of all your apprentices? What are they going to do if you don't come back?"

"And what will they do if all of this gets exposed. I can change my form. I can fit in wherever I end up. They can't! And a carpenter can't just relocate with so many apprentices without arousing suspicion. This way, we have the greatest chance of success. But we don't have the time to talk right now. Lunarias and Glaucos are getting in position as we speak."

They left the shop together and continued down the road. They had gone some distance before they split up.

"She certainly didn't like you butting into her plan, did she?" Kennas asked.

Astolphos chuckled, "I just think it was the part with her carrying Glaucos around as assurance. I think she's quite comfortable taking care of the garrison."

"You think it's going to work?"

"As long she doesn't have to get Glaucos' assistance. If there's any of us that will be able to get the guards to turn on each other, it's her."

"You think she's going to succeed at that?"

"Do we have any other choice? She has to convince them not to listen to their corrupt comrades, or else they all believe the story about you."

They walked in silence for a bit. It was incredible how the Aurillians reacted to the threat of Abyssals. The streets were practically empty, and those that peered out from their homes did so either with arms at their side or with their head on a swivel. The hustle and bustle of the busy craftsmen's district were reduced to hushed whispers, and the store owners stood around with far more inventory, waiting just at the cusp of their doorstep for someone to come and carry away their orders. It was a sad sight, just another testament to the fact that the Aurillians would never have won the war without Astolphos' rebellion.

They had reached the point where they had to part ways.

"I know it's tempting to create some express orders for your shop, but please do this without damaging the support pillars."

"Sadly, we're not the ones that run maintenance on the Scaffolding, but we do houses, so no complains here if a bit of collateral happens, alright?"

"I'll keep that in mind."

It was nice to see that Kennas still had her humor despite the circumstances. It gave Astolphos a bit more confidence. It meant she did not worry too much about the risks of this, though the same could not be said for Astolphos. The fear of Kennas losing Control was still at the forefront of his mind. She had not done anything like this since before the rebellion, and even back then, they had to restrain her more than once. The years might have mellowed her out, but her display earlier gave him no confidence. He prayed to Luminis that Kennas would be met with an empty safehouse and would be waiting for him and Lunarias in the tavern Lunarias told them about.

But he had his own mission to take care of now. He was to be the catalyst, the one that had to make the entire populace panic, and he knew exactly how he was to do that. But first, he looked around for a shop selling traveling wear, preferably someone some distance from his destination, the safe house inside the Craftsmen's district.

Luckily, he found one stowed away down an alley. It was small and far away enough that this guy could never piece two and two together. He bought a heavy winter cloak made of cow leather and a wide-brimmed hat perfect for hiding his face. The price was high, something the store owner tried to sell off as hazard pay. It was not worth it to haggle. Time was not on his side.

With his newfound anonymity, Astolphos took a deep breath as he looked at his surroundings.

His destination was an unassuming townhouse of three floors sandwiched between a cobbler and a weaver. It looked so ordinary that the thought of the mercenary giving him false information passed through his mind. Nothing told him that this was the right place, there were no bodyguards, and the essences inside revealed nothing out of the ordinary, just six guys sitting around a table on the top floor, playing a game of cards.

It was only when one of them rose from the table and opened the shutters that Astolphos got a glimpse of the far too familiar baggy clothes.

"Listen well, feeble Aurillians!" Astolphos yelled, drawing his dagger. His statement got the attention of not only a few people on the street but it also got a few houses to open their shutters and look at what was happening.

"I am the Master of the Abyssal Forge, and this marks the start of a new era. Cower in fear upon my power!"

He pointed his dagger at the door to the building. A crystal formed above his arm, long and thin like a spear, before it flew through the air, impacting the door to the safe house and ripping it off its hinges.

The citizens stood frozen to the ground, mouths wide open in shock as they probably saw the powers of one of the Gifted for the first time in their lives.

It suited him fine, though it did mean he had to be extra careful with not revealing his face.

The mercenaries were quick to react. The door had not been off for more than ten seconds before three of them exited the building, weapons drawn, while the remainder stood right at the door.

Astolphos looked at each of them in turn, none seeming to have connected two and two yet, compared to their inside companions, who took a step back as they looked at the door and saw the spear peering out of it. It seemed like they would warn their companions, but they were too late. The first one ran out, a sword held forward to the side with excellent control. These were indeed mercenaries, warriors with proper training, as he maneuvered his blade up to guard before reversing and striking for Astolphos' neck.

Astolphos twirled his dagger once, and immediately, it was encased in crystal as the blade lengthened to that of a rapier. He swung it up to block his opponent's attack, and immediately after, a loud crash emanated from the sword. Then the sparks flew from the mercenary's sword, as it shattered and the pieces fell to the ground. He looked at his hand in surprise, giving Astolphos ample opportunity to grab the man by the neck and lift him off the ground. Direct contact was more effective for draining, which was precisely what Astolphos did. At first, the mercenary thrashed about, but as the years left his body, the movements became limber and limber.

Then, the world spun around Astolphos' head before it hit the ground with a thump.

Astolphos did not even realize what had happened before the mercenary that decapitated him screamed in horror and fell to the ground.

Astolphos' body remained upright and continued draining the captured mercenary before it threw the carcass away and picked up his head. He always hated it when this happened, as, despite his current lack of a stomach, he could not help but feel slightly nauseous at the erratic movements his head made as it was put back in its place. He then stretched his neck and looked at the remaining mercenaries in turn.

"Now you've pissed me off."

Chapter 50

First, the ground shook as a loud crash blew through the streets. Then the screams began, and words such as monster and Abyssals were thrown about in abundance by the fleeing citizens of Hybrik. Lunarias, however, had expected this exact outcome and barely took her eyes off the garrison gates from her hiding spot.

"What was that!?" One guard exclaimed as he looked at a large black cloud forming from the explosion's origin.

"It came from the craftsmen!"

"Not the breweries!"

"We need to evacuate the area and help extinguish the fire!"

"The bells haven't rung yet, so it's probably nothing. Our orders are to protect the garrison."

"But what about the citizens!?"

"They'll manage. If you have any problems, go talk to the captain."

And that was the end of the discussion, as the guards who wanted to carry out their duties to the citizens took one look into the courtyard and turned back to look out, not saying another word.

It was both an uplifting but also a depressing display for her to see. It at least meant her intuition was good and that she did the right thing when she pushed back on Kennas' propositions. Now, she had to figure out how to make the clean guards turn against their corrupt comrades.

"Truly an outrageous display," Glaucos said. Lunarias jumped at the sudden foreign voice inside her head.

"My men would've rebelled long before the corruption would've come this far."

"How are you sure?"

"You don't have to speak. I can read your mind."

...*Lovely.*

"It certainly is. It makes communication during infiltrations so much easier. And I know that because it's happened before. It's always easier to root these things out internally. Before the weeds have taken root. It's always difficult to figure out who's good and who's lying when outsiders butt in."

If you have experience with this, what do you propose?

"My usual methods are a bit outside of reach at the moment, but the second best would be to surprise them and force a confrontation. If you don't give them time to make a strategy and get their story straight, it's much easier to pull out the weeds."

So, what's your primary method?

"Get a good friend to rummage through their memories and confirm their stories. And if we find out who started all of it, that friend could just scramble his memories to make an example."

...*Lovely fellow. I'm glad that kind of creature is no longer among us.*

"Actually, he's working as a mediator at your capital's trade guilds. You might have even met him."

But you said forcing a confrontation should work?

"Yes... What're you planning?"

That gave her an idea, one she thought was crazy enough to maybe work.

Lunarias stepped out, drawing her sword in the process. It took no time for the guards to spot her. They yelled at the garrison and then rushed at her with brandished weapons.

Reinforcements arrived shortly after, and Lunarias was surrounded.

"What in Luminis' name are you doing?" Glaucos yelled, "I promised Astolphos to keep you alive, and you go do something like this?!"

You said forcing a confrontation would work. That's precisely what I'm doing.

"With an army! An ARMY!"

The captain and the old man were not far behind. They kept their distance, standing close to the gate as they surveyed the situation. She looked at the old man, whose eyes locked on hers. The smile on her lips slowly made him pale, and he whispered something to the captain.

Everyone was tense. Lunarias felt her heart beat faster, thinking whether this was the right decision or if she had thrown her life away. The guards changed their grip on their weapons more often than she thought necessary. The legends of the Aurillian knights were probably circling in their heads, causing unrest as they surveyed an opponent they considered superior. But even then, some looked determined, and those were the ones she watched in turn, wondering how their reaction would be had they known she also had an Abyssal by her side to protect her. Just for insurance, she grabbed the small wand Glaucos was fixed to the end of, but she would not draw it, fearing that the mysterious device would make them nervous.

"D-Drop your weapon and surrender peacefully!" One of the guards yelled.

"I can ask you the same. You're threatening an extension of the Queen herself. That alone is enough to send you all to the executioner!" Lunarias yelled back.

"What happened to our comrades!? Those that you have killed!?"

"They did not drop their weapons."

The guards faltered, their position weakened, and their weapons wavered. For some guards, she saw fear in their eyes. In others, regret. But still, some occasionally looked back at the captain and the commander, but they were busy whispering. She knew those were the ones that were paid off, and in turn, she knew everything was over once those two had reached an agreement. She had to think fast if she were to solve this without relying on Glaucos' help.

"Some of you have forsaken your duties to the citizens of Hybrik!" Lunarias yelled, her voice took all of the attention, even from the ones that had looked at their boss moments before, "They have taken payment from a group of mercenaries that have devolved into nothing but common thieves and murderers. Earlier today, those very bastards killed the carpenter's apprentice for simply standing up for their racket! I know not all of you are yet lost, but you're all letting this happen. You are enabling this to continue.

"But let me give you some news: the knights of Aurillia have already been informed of this."

And that even made the captain look at her. He, too, grew paler by the second as he knew the entire gig was up.

"Those guards that have attacked me and tried branding me a criminal were in the pockets of these mercenaries. From the moment they took their money, their fates were sealed, and the same fate awaits any of you who have done the same. And I swear on the name of the Queen and the Ancestors that it'll be carried out even if I have to do so myself! Even if I fail, an army will come to take my place, and they will be even less lenient than I!"

"L-Listen to the shite she's spewing!" The captain yelled, "She's gone mad! D-Do the crown a favor and take her down before she hurts our citizens even more!"

But none moved. Their eyes were downcast, but their weapons still pointed toward her as if to keep both possibilities open. No matter the choice they made, they ran the risk of death. If they chose to listen to their commander, they had to go up against a knight of the second order. Lunarias was sure she would not stand a chance against so many, but neither did they once reinforcements would arrive in about a week.

If they instead chose to side with Lunarias, they would be forced to fight their comrades. That was a fight both testing one's physical prowess and mental resilience.

And either choice carried the risk of a higher power passing judgment. If they sided against Lunarias, the knights of Aurillia may judge their decision wrong, and then they would be charged and hanged for treason. Did they instead side with her and lose, there was a chance they faced the gallows, but this time for desertion and attempted murder of an officer.

To some, that may be an easy decision. They were paid to deliver a particular outcome. They did not have to think, just act. However, as she said, their fates were already sealed from when they received their first payment.

Lunarias felt they were at a tipping point. She may only have one or two sentences more before the fight broke out. Some had steeled their resolve, but many still looked to and from the captain, unsure what to do. She could not figure out how many allies she had. She could only hope she had enough.

"That's large coming from the one standing beside the mercenaries' leader."

All eyes were on the old man, who just exhaled as if it was time to remove the mask.

"To those of you that let all of this happen but did not drink from the poison themselves. Have you never felt strange about this man, always standing by the side of your captain? He's the root of this problem, and tonight, I intend to uproot all of it. I did not come to this city alone; I have friends, but I've also brought enemies."

All eyes were on her. A few took a quick peek at the smoke from the explosion. Even the commander now realized what it was that burned.

"I have been hunting a bunch of Abyssals for a while now, their destination suspiciously trained at Hybrik. Let me ask you, 'Commander,' did your regiment perchance partake in a campaign in the Abyss?"

It was nothing but a bet, but one with good odds. There were only two jobs for mercenaries: either they took care of local tasks, such as guarding certain villages or taking care of bandit encampments, or they campaigned in the Abyss.

Looking at the commander's face, this company fell into the latter category. He stared into space with a blank expression, white as a sheet. The captain was shaken, but he was closer to a breakdown and seemed ready to turn tail and run at the first opportunity.

"You must have kicked a hornet's nest back there because we've been following this group of Abyssals for months. Usually, hunting those creatures down would be my highest priority. Still, your treason to this nation's fair citizens has been so grave that I'm tempted to let the Abyssals carry out their dirty work for the betterment of Hybrik."

There were no brave faces among the soldiers. No one looked at their captain for direction. Each and every one of them was now forced to think of themselves and their own well-being.

"So, whose side do you want to be on? Mine, along with all the citizens of Hybrik and the Queen herself, or these common thieves and your corrupt captain? Now, those of you who still want to keep the citizenry safe, or those who've only just realized the true nature of your second employer, turn your weapons against the real opponent!"

She raised her sword, pointing it at the commander.

That was the spark in the gunpowder barrel. The circle of guards pulled back and reformed into two lines, one facing

Lunarias while the other raising their weapons against their previous comrades and captain. Seeing how people wore the same uniform fought against each other made her stomach churn, but she reminded herself that some of those fighting only wore the armor, not embodied it.

The first spear came at her, its point aimed squarely at her heart. She deflected it and stabbed her sword into the heart of her opponent.

Lunarias could not stop herself from saying a silent thanks to Astolphos for that sword. Any sword she had handled before could not pass through leather chest plates and gambesons in unison, while this one did so easily.

Seeing their comrade getting run through with such ease made her opponents hesitate. It must have been a godlike display of strength, a genuinely inhuman feat to stab cleanly through their armor and the entire way to the other side.

Another explosion happened in the distance. It was farther away, accompanied by a shower of splinters raining from the sky. It came from the Scaffolding, meaning Kennas completed her assignment. Along with it, the church bells rang aloud, signaling what no Aurillian wanted to hear. There was an official sighting of an Abyssal within the city, meaning all had to evacuate.

Those bells halted the battle as those who sided with the captain realized there, indeed, were Abyssals in the city. A few surrendered in that moment. They threw their weapons away and put their arms into the air. The rest still had some fight in them but were quickly dispatched. When everything was done, there were three surrenders and 20 bodies on the ground. Lunarias could not see who belonged to which side.

But she realized quickly that neither the captain nor the commander was among them. She barely saw both as they shut the door to the keep.

"Those of you who still have fight in you, follow me into the captain's building. They can't be allowed to escape!"

Only two of the remaining ten soldiers followed her. The rest collapsed from a mix of physical and emotional exhaustion. They ran through the courtyard. The battle still raged in there, soldiers against soldiers, each wearing the same armor with nothing to discern the sides apart. There was nothing she could do but wait for everything to be over.

The door to the captain's building was unlocked, and the building was empty. They ran up the stairs where Lunarias fought with the captain before and went straight for his office.

Inside, only the captain greeted them. He was on his knees, frantically shoveling fist upon fist of Merias from a hidden floor safe into a pouch. His expression was one of surprise as Lunarias' sword was pointed at his throat.

"Where's the Commander?" Lunarias asked.

The captain stuttered as he crept along the floor to escape her sword. His back soon hit his desk, and he raised his arms as if to surrender.

"He's on his way to the exit through the sleeping quarters. You'll never catch him before he reaches the headquarters."

"Then I'll take of him later. For now, you're under arrest for corruption and treason."

But then, for just a moment, the captain's eyes flicked to focus on something behind her, and a slight smile grew on his lips.

When she turned around, she saw one of the guards had slashed the other across the neck with his sword. That same guard now charged at her, his sword in front.

Lunarias parried the hit with her scabbard, but the sword chopped right through it. The wooden splinters flew at her like small projectiles, cutting and making blood trails wherever they found skin. The sword continued, but Lunarias leaned back, almost losing her balance, but making it so the sword only grazed her armor instead of cleaving her head. He was fast to make another swing, but without the moment of surprise, his sloppy technique made it easy for her to parry and make his sword slip out of his hands. She made ready to cut off his head when a hand grabbed her foot and pulled. She fell to the ground with a grunt, and when she turned around, the guard was already on top of her, his hands searching for her neck.

She tried to fight him off, but he was stronger than her and got a good grip on her throat before squeezing with all his might.

At that moment, she felt panic rise as her hands fumbled for her sword. It grazed the hilt of something, but then the captain swept it away. She beat at his arms, trying to just get the smallest amount of release as she gasped for breath, but he would not budge.

"Lunarias, push me into his chest."

At first, she thought it was her imagination, but then she remembered Glaucos was still affixed to her side. As her vision darkened, her hands found the metal wand and pressed it to the soldier's chest.

The wand was forced back into her breastplate, pushing the remaining air out as it made a dent in the metal, but the pressure around her neck vanished immediately.

Her throat was sore as she took some deep breaths and felt the scorching air rejuvenate her focus and burn her throat, giving her just enough to look at what had happened. The soldier had a large hole in his abdomen, but no blood seeped from it. His stomach was scorched away, the blood vessels cauterized, and its flames traveled up through the throat, judging from the look of horror in his eyes and the blackened mouth. Then came her own pain spreading from her hand holding Glaucos. It was red from where the flames had licked it, and blisters formed before her eyes.

"A-Abyssal!" The captain yelled, looking at Lunarias, "You're not a knight! You're one of those creatures yourself."

"Shit."

"We can't allow anyone to know the truth," Glaucos said, his voice abnormally cold despite what he had just done, "Point me at the captain."

Glaucos' voice had been audible to everyone as the captain looked at the wand in her hands.

"I was wrong! Please, anything but that!"

"Sorry," she said as she looked away and pointed Glaucos at his head.

***

When she left the captain's building, the fighting outside was over. She carried her sword in one hand, still covered in blood from her initial battle. She had bandaged her other hand using strips of the drapes from the captain's office. The soldiers took one look at her and approached. When she presented her blade to them, they took a step back and showed their hands.

"What happened in there?" One of them asked.

"One of the Abyssals was waiting in the office. It had already killed the captain when we arrived. I tried killing it, but it escaped."

"What now?"

"I'm taking command of this garrison, effective immediately," Lunarias said, "Your new orders are the evacuation of as many civilians as possible. Get them out of the city. Do not approach anyone who seems off; these Abyssals look just like us, and they are far too powerful for any of you to handle. I'll take care of them."

Chapter 51

Their plan was simple: each person had to complete their objective, then regroup at a small bar close to the scaffolding Lunarias introduced them to. Astolphos was the first to arrive, and back then, there was at least a measure of life inside, with the barkeep dishing out a few drinks to a huddled group looking around nervously. From there, rumors traveled fast; they soon heard of the being proclaiming to be an Abyssal that blew up a building in the craftsmen's district, and then the few guests went home.

With Astolphos being the only customer, the barkeep tried repeatedly to strike up conversation but was shut down every time as Astolphos placed an order.

Then, there was a loud crash and the sound of hail hitting the pavement outside, followed by the bells of the church making their foreboding tune. Even the barkeep and his wife left at that. They tried to wake Astolphos, but gave up as they thought he had drunk himself unconscious.

The moment their essences were out of range, Astolphos perked up once more and leaned back with his spellbook. It was the first time in decades he felt slightly peckish. The amount of life force he spent blowing the house up was too large, and even with the generous donations of the mercenaries, he felt that the decoy phylactery had run dry and a bit had been taken from the real one. It was not enough to be of any threat, but he had to stay in his lane and let Glaucos take care of the explosions and fire from now on.

Not long after, Kennas arrived. She seemed slightly out of it and went directly to the bar, grabbed a tankard, and filled it from a nearby barrel.

"Bad memories?" Astolphos asked but got no response.

He did not need one. He knew that was the case just based on her bewildered look. She needed time and distance, and Astolphos gave her both, coursing through the pages of his tattered book to refresh his mind on the rituals and costs of the spells that might become useful. Kennas just continued chugging down, the effect of the alcohol being slim to none and slow to mix, as expected of a being comprised of an unknown liquid. It would not surprise him if, underneath her disguise, there was a reservoir of free-flowing ale.

But they waited long for the third and fourth member of their entourage. It felt like hours passed, and there was no sight of Lunarias. Even when Astolphos looked for her essence, there was no trace of her. Frankly, besides Kennas, he could only see two other humans sitting at the opposite end of the plaza.

But before he had time to examine them, two new essences appeared in his periphery, and he recognized them instantly: Lunarias and Glaucos. He raised an eyebrow at their slow advance, its reason revealed as she entered the bar, breathing heavily. Her breastplate had a big dent right on her chest, and she had a black eye. But what caught his attention was the bandage on her left hand and her overall singed appearance. He knew instantly she was forced to rely on Glaucos at close range. She clutched her sword in her other hand, the scabbard nowhere to be seen.

"Are you alright!?" Kennas exclaimed, arriving at Lunarias' side almost as quickly as Astolphos, and helped her remove the breastplate. She immediately took a deep breath as it fell to the ground.

"Thanks," She said, "I couldn't get it off myself in this state."

Astolphos grabbed her hand and removed the makeshift bandage. It was red and swollen, with blisters the size of coins dotting its surface. He grabbed her wrist, hovered his other hand above hers, and let the essence flow between them. At first, she struggled, but then she looked on in wonder as the blisters disappeared in front of her eyes, and the redness receded, but not completely.

"It's still going to hurt badly, but you should be able to somewhat use it. Kennas, can you take care of the breatpla-"

And a loud clang sounded in the room as Kennas punched the dent back into shape. The rivets that held the crest into place could not withstand the pressure, and a few popped out and found a new home head-first into the bar. Lunarias groaned at the sight as the relief still held on, albeit with an unsupported middle.

"I'll fix it later," Astolphos said, "Do you want me to do anything about the eye?"

"...Please, but only because I need it for combat!"

She sat down on a chair, and Astolphos cupped a hand around her eye. He looked at Kennas, who put the breastplate on the table before Lunarias. However, her eyes were on rivets now embedded in the bar.

"Do you think we need to do something about that?" Kennas asked.

"You could put a note referring them to your business, but I think it's better to just ignore it. It requires less explanation that way."

His attention then went to Lunarias as he was done with her eye. The swelling and coloring were subsiding, but he could not do much more than to speed up the process. The body still had to take care of the rest.

"So, what happened at the garrison?" He asked.

Lunarias explained everything. How she turned the garrison on itself, how she followed the captain into his office, and the orders she gave the guards. She returned Glaucos to Astolphos, who quickly put him back on the scepter and threw the wand to Kennas. It then promptly vanished into her body for storage.

"Ready to continue?" Astolphos asked both of them, but Lunarias raised her hand, "Give me a few minutes. I suddenly feel very exhausted."

"That's natural. Your body is working overtime to process the healing. Give it a little, and it should even itself out. But if it's alright with you three, I have something I want to check out. I'll be back in a moment."

He had a hunch about the two beings outside, which was confirmed when he stepped outside the bar. More or less the same place he saw the parents sitting with their sick child before, he saw the parents once again. At first, he feared the worst as he approached, but they met him with a smile on their lips, and Astolphos eased up.

"I don't think it's safe for you to be here," Astolphos said.

"Something tells us that we're safe from the Abyssals," The father said, "Besides, we thought it was our best shot at meeting you again. We just want to thank you for everything."

"Our son is staying at the apothecary at the moment," The mother said, "we're told there's a high chance he'll make a full recovery. We couldn't have done that without your money."

"I just did what any decent person would've done. That's nothing to thank me for."

"Still, we're thankful for everything," The mother said, "Thanks to you, we can start figuring out a way to come back on our feet. And once this lout has gotten a job again," She slapped the father lightly on the shoulder, a light but mischievous smile on her lips, "We'll be able to get off the street."

But then their eyes looked behind Astolphos. He turned to see Kennas approach them, her eyes fixed on the husband, almost scanning every inch of him.

"How're your hands?" Kennas asked.

The father looked dumbfounded for a moment and looked at them.

"Besides a few callouses, they're working fine."

"Then meet me here tomorrow, then we'll see how well you'll be holding up as a carpenter. While in training, you'll only earn enough for a living and your son's treatment. We'll talk further after work, deal?"

"O-Of course. Thank you so much!"

But Kennas turned around, "Lunarias is ready, so sorry to cut this short."

And sure enough, Lunarias exited the bar and wore her breastplate and sword as if ready for anything.

But when they were outside of earshot, Astolphos had to satisfy his curiosity.

"Why did you give that offer?"

She turned around to look at him with a raised eyebrow.

"Glaucos told me you wanted to hear if I could employ that man."

They then both looked at the collapsible scepter, its crystal surprisingly still and quiet.

Chapter 52

Lunarias could not stop herself from raising an eyebrow as she realized their destination. Even from a distance, she recognized the brown building with its threateningly tilting upper floors. Its surroundings had changed drastically, as far as she could see from a distance. The remaining traitors hunkered down with their commander, hastily building makeshift barricades out of whatever they could get their hands on. Doors, carriages, tables, chairs, they must have broken into every house and removed everything not tightly nailed down. They had even built a raised platform where many soldiers stood ready with bows and arrows. And along with them, she saw the familiar bald head of the commander before he headed into the building.

Looking at her three companions, she realized she was the only one still surveying their enemy. They had gone down a side street, and Astolphos stabbed the scepter in between the paving stones while Kennas dissolved into the ground.

"Any ideas?" Lunarias asked, assured that their distance kept her voice from reaching their enemy.

He then raised his other hand, and several crystal pillars shot up from the ground, making a staircase leading them up onto the roof.

"Yes, but I need to get closer for it to work. Ladies first," Astolphos said as he gestured to the stairs.

As she walked the steps, Lunarias was careful with her sword. She knew that if it touched the stones, it would shatter just like her old one.

The steps were, however, wide enough for her to walk up with no problems, and when she reached the top, Kennas was already waiting for her. The steps dissolved as Astolphos stepped on them, leaving only a trail of side-swept paving stones on the ground.

They then kept low while walking along the rooftops. The houses were all connected wall-to-wall, and when there was the occasional gap, Astolphos was quick to bridge it. It only took a few minutes for them to reach the end, and in front of them was the headquarters.

Hidden by a slanted roof, they observed the soldiers beneath.

The soldiers were busy as ants, haphazardly throwing whatever they could find into their makeshift blockades. She even felt the building they were standing on occasionally shake as they ransacked its contents.

"Move faster!" A soldier on the platform yelled, "We don't know when they'll arrive, but the commander assures us that Abyssals will come here! If those knights can deal with them, so can we!"

Astolphos and the puddle of blue liquid snickered, "They certainly don't lack confidence."

However, the soldier's confidence was not reciprocated by his peers.

In the time she watched their opponents, Lunarias saw their nervousness manifest. It was visible in how they stumbled upon themselves and each other in and out of the houses, how they lost focus and lowered their weapons occasionally, only to quickly snap back and point them towards the shadows where they assumed their enemies would attack.

The archers had their weapons pointed to the streets, not even giving a gaze to the rooftops. After all, climbing the plaster-covered walls of the nearby buildings should be impossible.

"Our opponents are not just arrogant. They seem to be a bunch of idiots," Kennas said, "I've not seen such a display of incompetence since the war."

"Can't agree more," Astolphos said, "Just look at their equipment. Badly made and even worse maintained. My blades can slice through both their armor and weapons with ease."

Lunarias had to agree. She had already fought against them before and could, without a doubt, attest to both the strength of Astolphos' arms and the weakness of theirs.

But she also partly thought it was an unnecessarily harsh assessment. She could imagine that their clumsiness was partly due to rattled nerves due to realizing they were up against Abyssals, which were a problem to deal with, even for the knights. Not only were they going to battle against Abyssals, they had crossed the point of no return. The moment they went against their comrades at the garrison, they went from corrupt guards to traitors of the crown.

There was no salvation for those in their situation, only the hope of a quick death. She wondered how many of them thought they would end up like this. How many just saw another easy pile of Merias without another thought?

"Ms. Hewris, what fate awaits these men if they're captured by you and dealt with through due process?" Astolphos asked.

"They'll be charged with treason; the punishment is death."

"In that case," Astolphos' hand went into his belt pouch as he talked, "We'll save the executioner the hassle."

"Can't we just blow up the building?" Kennas asked, "We've already done it once today."

"I thought the same," Astolphos said, "But I need more essence to do that. I'll try draining enough of them to prepare the spell, but stand ready if things go wrong. Kennas, intervene if you see a cloud of essence."

"Ready at your word." Kennas' body changed form again, turning into a cone pointing at the sky.

Astolphos glanced at Lunarias and then extended his free hand toward one of the guards. He took a deep breath, and immediately, she saw the soldier swaying. At first, he stopped in his tracks and looked around. Then, he dropped his weapon and clutched his chest as Astolphos' fist clenched. Other guards ran to his side, yelling at him something intelligible. At last, Astolphos' fist closed entirely, and as on cue, the archer fell to the ground. The others tried shaking him awake; they even slapped him a few times, but nothing worked.

That display of power shocked Lunarias. She had expected that Astolphos had yet to show the true extent of his powers, but this one made her shiver. He did not even need to be close to his target. He could kill someone without a trace by just clenching his fist.

Before her shock subsided, Astolphos held the empty vial underneath his clenched hand. A crimson liquid dripped into the vial, slowly filling it drop by drop as the panic gradually encroached on their enemies. They yelled at each other but did nothing to find cover or protect themselves.

"It must've been a poisoned dart!" One yelled, "Search the houses. They must be in there!"

But the other mercenaries had stopped listening. Instead, they searched the barren streets. It did nothing but weaken their position.

Though the guards panicked, Astolphos took his time and ensured no drop went to waste. It felt like an eternity, but at long last, the last drop fell with only a fifth of the vial full. His attention then shifted back to the guards, picking out a target to repeat the process once again.

But their luck ran out as Astolphos emptied his palm for the fourth time. One especially eagle-eyed guard saw them and pointed at their spot as he drew an arrow from his quiver.

Astolphos cursed and loosened his grip, letting the drops turn into a light stream. The guard just managed to nock an arrow before he, too, clutched his chest.

Astolphos closed his fist instantly. The man fell like all the others, but Lunarias thought she saw a reddish cloud leave the body, making the nearby guards cough.

A powerful gust of wind shook the building they stood on. Kennas was gone, leaving only a blue stain where she had been. Then the building shook again, and the soldiers yelled as Lunarias fought to regain her balance. Kennas landed on the platform, passed right through it, and shattered the road underneath in a spray of mud and debris.

However, past the initial impact, nothing happened. Kennas collected herself into a glossy sphere that rested half-embedded in the ground like a giant cannonball. The impact caught everyone's attention; all guards raised their weapons against the seemingly innocent ball of mass destruction.

Perhaps it was because of the lack of a leader to talk sense to them. Maybe they simply did not know any better, but they all slowly approached the ball with cautious steps. Their weapons were pointed at the blob, and as the spearmen came within range, they poked and prodded at it, resulting in Astolphos shaking his head as he bore witness.

"What's Kennas doing?" Lunarias asked Astolphos, her curiosity finally winning.

"Waiting for them to get into position."

The guards continued stabbing at the blob as their comrades joined the fray. Kennas made no resistance. She let the weapons touch her without a reaction. Astolphos must have known from the start that Kennas had not been stabbed to death, for his response was so minuscule that he must have seen this before.

Then, there was an ear-piercing clash as countless spikes shot through the soldiers, instantly rending flesh, bones, and armor. The corpses hung limp in the air until the spikes withdrew as quickly as they appeared. The bodies collapsed, and the only one still standing was Kennas, still to regain her original appearance.

"How many of you are capable of that?" Lunarias asked, her eyes still on the guards slowly collapsing upon each other.

"Of transforming like that? That's something unique to Kennas. If you were asking for something similar in destructive capabilities, there were only the 30 Masters. Of them, only five of us are still alive." His expression grew grim, "Perhaps six."

That was the answer she feared. She only knew of two Masters, perhaps three, depending on what Glaucos was. It at least seemed these had no ill intentions towards the kingdom, but what about the others? Not that it mattered anyway, for she was confident that the Aurillian army would not stand a chance against one of these beings.

Kennas looked at her work and froze. She jumped back, hugging her body as she turned away from the sight.

"Are you alright?" Astolphos yelled, summoning a stairway down before running to Kennas' side.

"J-just give me a moment." But Lunarias saw it was a lie. Kennas did not turn around to look at Astolphos, as that would require her to also look at her work. He put a hand on Kennas shoulder.

"Bad memories?"

"No, more how easy it was for me to do this again."

"Staying out here is still an option,"

"...I need to do this."

"No, you don't." Astolphos' voice was now stern. He stepped before Kennas, "You've proven yourself more than enough. It's not going to be one bit better in there. I'm not going to risk losing you because of your pride. So go home now, or I'll make you."

"Astolphos is right," Lunarias said. Kennas turned her head to look at her but jerked it back to Astolphos as she got a glimpse of the corpses.

"We'll take care of it, so just go home."

"To where?" Kennas said, "They've taken my home away from me! I'm exposed; it just takes one of my apprentices going to the guards, and I'll have to flee. What then!?"

"Then you'll travel with us for as long as my ball and chain here permits it," Astolphos said, nodding at Lunarias. "But let's not jump to conclusions yet. We don't know what your apprentices will choose, and theorizing about it will do no good. Find somewhere to lie low, and meet us at your shop at midnight. Then we'll see their decision together tomorrow."

Kennas stood still, but Astolphos did not break eye contact. Eventually, she looked away and nodded.

"Now, Lunarias," Astolphos said, "let's get this over with. Are you ready?"

She regarded the building one more time. Its leaning stature once more gave her an uneasy feeling as she stared directly up and somehow still looked through a crooked window. It was both the best and worst hideout she had seen in a long time. On one hand, it was too eye-catching. The brown exterior in and of itself made it look apart from the otherwise white-to-grey buildings around it, and the entire leaning structure made sure for everyone who passed under it to have it ingrained in their memory. But that lean was also its saving grace since nobody in their right mind would call that place their home. It also looked like the slightest disruption would bring it down, instinctively making everyone avoid it as much as possible.

That would be their battleground; she did not know how the terrain would change once fighting commenced. The fact that she did not know anything about their enemy, other than they were somewhat skilled and had a severe advantage in numbers, made her uneasy.

But then there was that blacksmith. He was a wildcard. She did not know his plan, only that it would surely be devastating to their enemy. The question was just if it was enough.

Chapter 53

"I need you to keep the commander talking for as long as possible," Astolphos said, "The longer we can keep him occupied, the more of his men I can take down in one swoop."

Lunarias nodded, "Do we know what we'll encounter in there?"

"37 mercenaries on two different floors. Ten are standing on the top floor. Their stature indicates that they're wielding bows. Five are standing on a staircase in front of us, and the rest occupies the bottom floor. One is standing right beside the door, probably to ambush us."

She looked at Astolphos with a raised eyebrow, "So you can also look through walls?"

"Not exactly, but close enough. I think keeping my identity a secret for as long as possible will be in our best interest. Something tells me these rats will attack when threatened, but they're cocky enough to not regard us as a threat without that knowledge."

"Got it. You open the door, and I'll handle the ambush."

They both looked back at Kennas, who dissipated into the ground.

"You think she's going to return here?" Lunarias asked.

"She'll hang out close to here, but she will not enter the building. Are you ready? We're not going to get another breather before this is done."

"I'm ready."

Astolphos grabbed the doorknob and took a deep breath. Lunarias' body tensed, her grip on her sword hard and ready to spring into action. She held her breath and ran through the door as soon as possible, knocking the door wide open with her shoulder and turning to the right.

The mercenary swung a mace at her, but she parried it and went for a stab to the stomach. She hit, but it slid off, slicing apart the baggy clothes of her adversary to reveal a worn metal plate underneath. The mercenary readied his mace for another strike that never came as she grabbed hold of his arm, swept him off his feet, and aligned the blade with his neck. One down, 36 to go. As reluctant as she was at admitting it, Astolphos' healing helped her immensely, as it turned the act of using her left hand from excruciating pain into something that could be endured by clenching her teeth.

The room they were in came as a surprise to Lunarias. Her experience had told her to expect small rooms with convoluted layouts and messy appearances. This was more akin to the inside of a mansion.

It was one large and spacious room with a second floor held by wooden pillars. Clear lines were drawn on the ground, showing where the walls to the adjacent houses were before they had been knocked down. The second floor had also gotten a grand makeover.

It had been partially gutted to make room for a grand hall-like balcony surrounding the entrance. Its construction looked far from professional, with planks unevenly cut and nailed haphazardly around the underside. Support pillars were erected at times when it was sagging to a dangerous degree. It reminded her of the battlefield repairs her men had done on their carriages when campaigning.

Many pillars had also been placed on the wall facing the street, and she did not like the thought of those nailed-together planks probably being the only thing still keeping the building standing.

Astolphos looked at it with a raised eyebrow, muttering, "I'd like to have seen Kennas' reaction to this."

"Admiring our work?" The commander yelled as he stood halfway up a staircase. He had four guards around him, each having a tower shield in one hand and a spear in the other.

Their enemies followed their every move. The balcony was filled with archers ready to draw at every moment, and a veritable squad of soldiers stood at the foot of the staircase, clad in a mix of plate and chainmail. These men had given up on their disguises and showed off their old uniforms for everyone to see. There were no distinguishing marks, just a sea of plain brown gambesons and dented plates.

"I'm just surprised it's not collapsed yet," Lunarias said. She glanced at Astolphos, but he stared at the archers.

"Our carpenters have honed their craft on the battlefield. They know how to make things last."

"The lean on the building certainly shows that."

"Enough insults. I've seen through your tricks. You've come here with only your squire, but we know the rest of the garrison is waiting outside. How else would you've gotten through the first line of defense? Are you here to negotiate?" Despite the circumstances, the commander stood with a cocky smile. He thought he had the upper hand, and granted, with his knowledge, it would very well look that way.

"Leave Hybrik at once! Your place in this city is gone, and nothing good will come of you staying to fight."

"You say that, but we both know that's a bluff. Once your precious reinforcements arrive, it will be your word against the captain's. We'll be back where we started, with the city in our grasp."

"Even if the captain was still alive, my word is the word of the throne. It'll overrule that of a pitiful captain at every turn."

"You killed the captain?" The cocky smile vanished in an instant.

"The Abyssals hunting you and your men did it."

Silence befell the room as the commander looked at her, shocked. She glanced at Astolphos again, his eyes still on the archers, though it seemed he was working his way through them, whatever he was doing.

"And you just let it happen?" The commander asked, "Did you truly shirk your duty just to make him perish. That beast is still out there, and you're hunting us! Some knight you are!"

"The likes of you should never speak of shirking your duty," Lunarias shot back, raising her wounded hand, "And I bear this mark with pride, as it's proof of my attempt at bringing that creature to justice!"

The commander's smile returned, "So you failed your duty?"

"It's a testament to the creature coming your way. Your lives are forfeit. The only worthwhile thing you can do is leave the city so that the creature's flames consume no more of the city."

"We'll take that stand wherever we want. Besides, I've yet to see any proof of this creature you're speaking of. All I've seen is some burnt skin and a building in flames, nothing ground-breaking."

"Ignore my warnings at your own peril. This building will be your tomb if you don't run."

"But it'll also be yours," The commander said, "A wounded knight is not going to be a challenge. Men! Capture the knight and kill the squire. We can use the ransom to live like kings for years!"

The archers readied their bows, but the commander raised a hand to stop them, "Hold your fire! We need her alive. We can't afford you guys making her into a pincushion by mistake!"

Lunarias raised her sword at the advancing soldiers. Her chances of dispatching that many men were nonexistent, especially with a wounded hand. Astolphos still looked at the archers, seemingly not realizing what had happened around him. His support would have been greatly appreciated, but she could only believe that whatever he was doing would leave a greater impact than his fighting prowess ever could. She just had to defend both of them until Astolphos was ready, a task easier said than done.

She surveyed her opponents. Though a significant number of mercenaries surrounded them, only eight advanced in a threatening manner. Eight was still a lot, far more than what Lunarias could handle considering their armor, with most having complete protection of their torso, with a few also clad with solid helmets. She could not win a battle, but she could draw it out.

The mercenaries' advance was painfully slow. Despite their numbers, they feared Lunarias, one of the Knights of Aurillia, an organization whose members journeyed into the Abyss and faced the horrors as if it were just an ordinary Tuesday. That was, of course, just the rumors manifesting a larger-than-life image. It would not surprise her if some of these mercenaries had been to the Abyss just as many times as she had. But if that fear kept her opponents wary and away, the truth did not matter.

Three of the mercenaries attacked at the same time. Their attacks came from different angles. She had no other choice than to jump back. It was too much without backup; she had to split them apart and take them down one by one, but she could not see any way of doing that. At the same time, another two approached Astolphos.

Lunarias jumped between them and Astolphos and hit one with the pommel of her sword just to quickly follow up with a stab on the other. He dodged and ran back. She then felt something heavy hit her in the back. Another mace had struck her backplate hard, almost sending her to the ground. She quickly slashed at her opponent but had to stop as he jumped to the side to leave Astolphos between them.

This pause was too long, as she felt the grip of a hand reach for her left arm. She swung her sword around, cutting her opponent's hand clean off, but she did not have time to finish the job before she felt something sting on her shin. She fell to the ground, seeing another mercenary with a club trying to swipe her off her feet.

Still, she had a solid grip on her sword and stabbed ahead, connecting with the mercenary's neck. But it did nothing for her situation, as another mercenary just took his place. She soon felt the grasp of a hand around her wrist. It tightened and jerked until she let go of her sword.

At that moment, she knew it was over.

She looked at Astolphos just in time to see the mercenaries chop off his right arm.

"What is this?!" the one who did the cut yelled as he stepped back. The remaining mercenaries followed suit, not enough for Lunarias to be able to wrest herself free, but she was too stunned by the sight to even realize.

Despite the loss of a limb, Astolphos still stood upright. His eyes continued to follow the archers. Not a single drop of blood dripped from the wound.

And then he raised his left hand. He closed his palm quickly. All the archers collapsed together, and a large red cloud descended from the balcony. A few fell off the balcony and landed on the ground with a crunch as their bones could not withstand the fall.

"Sorry it took some time, Lunarias," Astolphos said, picking up his arm, "but the archers were the biggest threat. Now that I've dealt with them, it's time to take care of the rest of these insects."

He put the arm back on his shoulder; moments later, he could move his fingers once again.

"A-Abyssal!"

"She brought an Abyssal with her?!"

"She must be one too!"

The hands that pinned her down suddenly vanished, and their owners practically ran away from her.

"You're half right," Astolphos said, "I'm an Abyssal, but Lunarias here is genuinely an Aurillian. She's just tasked to be my escort.

"It's just a shame we couldn't keep their leader talking for longer, but no matter. It's time for plan B. But don't feel bad, Miss Hewris. There was nothing you could've done to avoid this from happening."

"What from happening?!" The commander yelled, his fear clear to hear.

"Apologies for not introducing myself earlier," Astolphos bowed,

"My name is Astolphos Auriolis. Many years ago, I was the right-hand man of The Abyssal King himself. You've threatened one of my friends and killed one of her apprentices. For that, none of you will leave this room alive."

He grabbed his scepter with both hands, raised it above his head, and slammed it down with enough force to pierce through the wooden floor. And then, the room was enveloped in a bright light.

Chapter 54

When his sight returned, the entire room was covered in a thick layer of crystal. Astolphos used the very same spell years before to create the tombstone of the Gifter, resulting in an entirely unimportant forest becoming the most treacherous terrain on the entire continent. Nothing of metal survived contact with the cyan crystal, and no person alive, who still had a body, could break through the layers of sharp corners.

This was a fact the mercenaries experienced instantly, as those wearing metal greaves suddenly fell a centimeter. The shock left them paralyzed, looking at their new surroundings with wonder and horror. It would not take long before they realized this would be their tomb, just like the Gifter before them. All doors were blocked, and all windows were sealed. Any attempt at hacking away at it left them without equipment, and fighting against it with their fists would only leave them with wounds that reached the bone.

This spell was the reason for Astolphos making his decoy phylactery. Having to fill the real one during a battle was not something he was going to experience one more time. However, with the limited area of the spell had to affect this time, he did not have to touch his own essence, thanks to using Glaucos' connection to the earth as a conduit.

The commander stood alone on the stairs, his guards having fallen flat as they lost their footwear and came tumbling down the stairs.

The commander knew what was coming. Not because he had experienced anything remotely like this before but because he had just now realized what he was up against. Astolphos knew well the effect his powers would have on the mercenaries. Aurillians feared the Gifted because of their power. Deep down, they knew that if the Abyssals truly wanted to take over the entire continent, all they had to do was actually try. Or that was what they thought. The commander had just realized a terrifying fact: one of the Hands was more than enough to turn the entire kingdom on its head. That was what he was up against: pure, unadulterated power.

And Astolphos was not going to restrain himself the least. He looked at Lunarias. The girl had seemingly reached the same conclusion. She stood as frozen as the rest, her hands shaking as they were clenched around her sword, not pointing in any particular direction. Her eyes, however, were squarely on Astolphos.

"Lady Hewris," Astolphos said, "I'd recommend you get behind me. I don't want you to end up in the crossfire."

But a light smile and a kind expression did nothing to wash away the worry painted on her face. However, she followed his suggestion, inching to the side until she was solidly behind him.

"And please make sure that sword doesn't touch the crystal. I'd hate to see my pet project turn to dust."

Ready for this?

"As ready as I'm going to be," Glaucos said telepathically, "Give me the order, and I'll take care of them all."

Wait a bit. I'll see how much essence I can get out of this.

"Is there anything I can offer for you to spare me and my men?"

The commander finally mustered the courage to say.

"And here's why I'm growing tired of you Aurillians," Astolphos said. His word made the commander stiffen up even more than Astolphos thought possible.

"You never stop to think before acting. All of this, and I mean ALL OF IT! Could have been avoided if you had stopped to think. If you had just not decided to turn to banditry, this wouldn't have happened-"

"But we had no other choice! Work dried up!"

"Bullshit! The Aurillian government always has work for you to terrorize my countrymen. You just eyed a quick way to earn a lot of money. But even then, you could've just stuck with burglaries instead of extorting business owners. And once more, if you had just stopped for a single moment, you might have realized that killing people would lead to someone seeking revenge. Well, HERE I AM! AND I'M TIRED OF ALL OF YOU TARGETING MY FAMILY!

"Your fates weren't even sealed when you attacked Kennas. That we might've been able to work through. But there is no way back when you killed one of her apprentices! I can't let you escape now that you know the truth. The only good any of you is now is as nourishment for me and my companions."

His speech collected all eyes in the room. Mouths were agape, and weapons fell out of their grasp, shattering on impact with the crystal. But no one moved.

That all changed when he took one step forward. The commander screamed as if he had seen a demon and ran up the stairs, screaming intelligibly until he was out of sight.

"Protect me! Don't let that monster come close to me!"

His troops were conditioned well, as such a suicidal command was obliged by one young man without hesitation. He charged at Astolphos, screaming as he plunged his sword into Astolphos' side. It went straight through to the hilt, but then the man realized there was nothing more he could do as

Astolphos grabbed him by the throat and drained the life right out of him.

None of these men deserved a peaceful death. They were the scum of the earth. They did not deserve to pass in peace. Just as Astolphos had learned to make the draining subtle and pain-free, he had also learned to make a mess of it.

The man screamed and flayed around frantically as the essence left his body. His gestures grew weaker by the moment until they seized, and he was thrown to the side hard enough to leave a bloody trail on the crystal floor.

Astolphos then pulled out the same vial he was filling before and let the red liquid in his hand drip into it, careful not to spill a single drop. He was in no rush. The crystal would stay in place as long as he wanted. The Forest was proof of that.

But his opponents were seemingly less patient, as another two found the courage to charge at him. Astolphos clicked his tongue, letting the essence flow in a steady stream instead.

One wielded a club, the other a pair of daggers. Astolphos picked the one with the daggers as his first target and punched him in the gut, only to kick him to the ground and pin him down with the same foot.

The other mercenary stopped in his tracks, the worst thing he could have done, as that made him easy to disarm. As-tolphos took hold of the arm wielding the mace and drained him, too.

That was when he felt a strange sensation in his leg. When he looked down, he saw the other mercenary screaming fran-tically, hacking away at his ankle with the dagger that had not touched the ground. It was a waste of essence, but he could not afford to be incapacitated. He raised his foot, only to stomp down hard on his head.The skull stood no chance against Astolphos' inhuman strength and petaled its content on the ground.

"One at a time, please," Astolphos said, "That was probably 40 years just wasted."

And they somewhat listened. One ran for Lunarias, his sword raised far above his head. He had probably thought that targeting Astolphos' companion was the way out of this situation.

Lunarias made ready to meet his blade head-on, but there was no need for it. The mercenary stopped abruptly as a pillar of crystal shot up from the floor and pierced through his chest. His breastplate sparked and fell to the ground in pieces, and the sword joined in when it fell from his dead hands.

"You know what," Astolphos said, "Just drop your weapons. I'm in complete control of this building. There's nowhere you can move to where I can't take you down. All exits have been sealed by a layer of crystal you will never come through. Just sit down and wait for the inevitable."

This was the moment they truly realized how hopeless a situation they were now in. A few decided then and there that there was no way they would let Astolphos get hold of them and ended the job themselves. But most dropped their weapons and ran screaming for the stairs. When Astolphos was done with the mercenary, the only ones left on the lower floor were part of the commander's private guard.

They stood firm at the foot of the stairs and blocked his advance with their bodies and weapons. Unfortunately, their tumble down the stairs had cost them some parts of their armor. But they still had enough on to be troublesome to drain, and it did not help that they seemed to have figured out Astolphos wanted to take them down one by one. They just waited for Astolphos to make the first strike.

"Glaucos, take care of them."

And without a word, flames erupted from within the metal plates. Their very armor killed them, as it contained the heat and roasted them inside out. What landed on the ground was nothing but charred corpses.

From there, it was just a quick stroll up the stairs until Astolphos saw a truly pitiful sight.

All the mercenaries were bunched up on one side of the balcony, scratching frantically on a door. It was stained red from the cuts they had received from the crystal, but it did not deter them at all. They only grew more panicked as they saw Astolphos at the other end of the balcony. They pushed and shoved each other to get a place at the door. So ferociously, in fact, that a few were pushed over the railing and landed head-first on the floor underneath.

"Thank you very much for lining up that nicely," Astolphos said. A crystal wall rose from the ground, blocking the way he had come.

Chapter 55

They never stood a chance. The scene in front of her was more than proof of that. Just like the mercenaries, the Aurillian kingdom should never have stood a chance against the might of just Astolphos. It should never have been a war, just a one-sided slaughter. She could not see what was happening, nor did she want to. What she had seen was already enough. Her eyes were caught on the mercenaries who had decided not to face Astolphos. She had never seen anything like that. Those men were driven off the brink by what did not even seem to be the start of the powers of that blacksmith.

She knew that the room she stood in was more than enough proof. The crystal around her told her of the limits of a monster. If one entered the Forest of Sorrows from the wrong angle, it would take four days to traverse, and even that might not show the upper boundary of that Abyssal's powers.

This was what the priest spoke of back at the church. He was right; there was no fighting such a creature.

And she had to bring it into the capital.

As Astolphos had said, it was in complete control of the room. And that made her wonder why that creature even bothered to keep her alive. She looked at the mercenary who had run for her and had gotten a pillar of crystal through his chest. Astolphos could easily do that to her at any point, and no one would be any wiser. He could escape his duty to the crown and live anonymously once more. What did that creature see in her that made it want to keep her alive? Was she just its plaything? An experiment to see what effect it had on the knights, the supposed hunters of Abyssals?

The cries of terror were dying with time, probably along with their originators, and soon there was silence. Astolphos was done.

There were no more mercenaries left. The question was just what was going to happen now. Was it all over? Or would they devise some way of checking the citizens for that one mercenary who knew the truth?

There was one last scream. She saw someone jump from the balcony and land on the stairs.

The commander's hands were leaving a trail of blood behind him. This was no longer the haughty bastard she saw at the garrison, only a broken shell rolling down the stairs. When he looked up again at the bottom, there was a deep gash on his forehead from where the crystal had cut him open. He tried getting back on his feet but could not force his broken hands to support him, instead electing to crawl to Lunarias.

She then saw something walk down the stairs. One step followed the clang of the scepter touching the ground. Astolphos was in no hurry. He walked down the stairs, intelligibly talking with Glaucos about something funny, laughing. Still, he stopped the moment he saw the commander crawling towards Lunarias. He raised his free hand towards the commander, but Lunarias shook her head. She wanted to know what he had to say.

"Please, save me," The Commander pleaded. He looked up at Lunarias, but almost no life was left on his face. He had given up, just going through the motions his body wanted him to, knowing full well that it would all end with his demise in this room.

"I-I can't," Lunarias said, feeling Astolphos' eyes on her, "I have no control. I'm as trapped here as you."

"Then please don't let it catch me. I want to join my Ancestors, not be part of what that creature is plotting."

Lunarias looked at Astolphos, steeling her grip on her sword. It looked at her questioning. The gaze was neither hostile nor friendly.

It was judging her. For what, she did not want to know.

But despite it, Lunarias raised her blade, and with one swing, it was over. The commander was dead, just like all the mercenaries.

She had succeeded; the citizens were safe from the menace inside their walls, but it felt nothing like a victory. It felt dirty. As if she defeated one monster by indulging another. One was a catastrophe waiting to happen, unstable at the best of times.

But the other was much worse. It was in complete control of its actions and executed them with an efficiency no one should be able to.

As it came closer, she looked at its belt. It was filled with vials containing the crimson liquid she had seen it gather on the rooftop. It was not content with taking lives. It wanted to extract as much as possible from them before finishing the deed.

This was not how she had wanted this to go.

The surroundings creaked as the layers of crystal cracked and fell to the ground in chunks, further shattering on impact into fine dust that fell through the rough floorboards. Despite everything that had happened, the building still stood, and the upper floors were still supported by the haphazardly placed wooden beams.

"And now that this is behind us," Astolphos said, "Perhaps we can finally get some solid progress on that carriage."

"How can you be so calm?" Lunarias asked, "Look at what you've done!"

Astolphos froze, looking at her questioningly. That just made her grow colder.

"I don't understand," Astolphos said, "This was the plan, right? Take care of the mercenaries before they had time to talk; wasn't that what we had agreed to?"

"I've never seen anything as brutal as this!"

"What had you expected? More than 30 one-on-one duels? All living up to the ideals instilled in you by your fellow knights? You felt it first-hand. They were not going to do this honorably. They attacked you in a group."

Lunarias remained silent. She did not know what to say.

"It was never going to be a fair fight. They never stood a chance, even if I had gone up against them with a sword. They could've hacked away at me until there was nothing but pulp left, and I'd still get back up. This way, their lives will at least continue serving a purpose. If it's any consolation, I made sure they felt nothing."

But Lunarias knew that was a lie. She saw how they writhed and screamed in his grasp, and she had heard it more than enough for a lifetime. Still, she did not say anything back. She wanted to, but the words got stuck in her throat.

"Come now," Astolphos said, "We have to show Kennas we were successful and figure out what to do back at the shop."

"I think I'll let that be up to you two. I'll be heading for the garrison."

"Could you possibly wait with that? We still have one loose end to tie up."

Chapter 56

They were back much earlier than Astolphos anticipated. When they first agreed on their plan, he had expected they would be back too late to stop Intros and Inaris from leaving. Now, dawn was still far away.

And still, they just stood outside the store, unable to move any closer because of Kennas. Their walk from the headquarters was silent, with neither Kennas nor Lunarias uttering a word. And though he knew the reason for Lunarias being quiet was how he had acted against the mercenaries, the reason for Kennas doing the same only became apparent once her home was in sight.

"Are you not going to go in?"

"What if guards are waiting in there? Waiting for us to return."

"Then I can fill up the remainder of my vials. Come on, it's been a long day for everyone."

She nodded and approached the door, only to stop her advance once more right in front of it. He could not blame her, even he was worried about what was waiting. He did at least know that the people inside were not guards; their essences were too small. But he did not know how many apprentices Kennas had, so he could not know if any had left. All he knew was that Inaris and Intros were waiting right at the entrance and that there were a lot of apprentices upstairs.

But eventually, Kennas took a deep breath and opened the door.

"You're back!" Inaris exclaimed. That woke up Intros, who had fallen asleep on a chair. The dim light of a candle showed their bags lined up on the desk. They were ready to leave the moment dawn arrived. Intros' hand went for the backpack strap even in his half-asleep state, and his skin was already hardened before his fingers got hold of it.

"Told you so," Intros said, yawning, "A few mercenaries aren't even going to be any trouble for us Gifted."

But Astolphos was sure he felt the slightest tint of uncertainty in Intros' voice. He did not want to dig at it, especially not at this time of the night, and instead elected to pick up their backpacks.

"I think it's been quite the day for all of us, so how about we get you two to bed?" Astolphos asked, realizing as he spoke that Cyrillys' body was still in the cellar.

Kennas seemed to have realized the same and stared at the backpacks with a mixed expression.

"You can use my room," Kennas said, "something tells me I still have a long night before me. But first, can you tell me if any apprentices have left the shop?"

The two young Abyssals looked at each other, "We've not seen anyone leave," Intros said, "but we've spent a long time in the kitchen cleaning everything up."

"But everyone was there for dinner at least," Inaris said, her expression grew morose, "though no one spoke a word."

"That's good news. Now, go to bed, you two. We'll figure something out tomorrow."

Astolphos was about to follow the two up to their room, carrying their backpacks, when Kennas put a hand on his shoulder and shook her head. Her message was clear: keep the backpacks here; they were not out of the woods yet.

And when the door to the upstairs closed behind the two, Kennas immediately went to work, almost marching towards the basement.

"Where're you going?" Astolphos asked.

"It's going to take a long time to get the blood stains out of the floor, so might as well start now," she said without slowing down a beat.

"And aren't you missing something important with that lop-sided priority?" Glaucos asked.

Kennas stopped and clenched her fists wordlessly.

"You're the only one here who knows if any of your apprentices are missing," Astolphos continued, "Wouldn't it be a good idea to go check?"

He turned to see if he had Lunarias' support, but she stared blankly at an empty workbench. She had been deep in thought since they left the headquarters. Her expression was blank, and though Astolphos could recognize the reason, he could not figure out what she was thinking. Still, there were more pressing matters to take care of right now. He could clear this up later, on their way to the capital.

"I'm afraid," Kennas said, "What if I go up there and realize that one has left? Would it not be better to just wait and see what happens?"

"Right now, we have the time to plan if someone has left. We can perhaps get everyone out of Hybrik since the garrison is in disarray. If we only do something when they come knocking, we have to improvise, and I've spilled enough blood for the next century, if not more."

"I agree with 'Stolfos," Glaucos said, "I'd like to know what we're up against. Besides, we must remember that we have to act like Lunarias is against us, which will only add complications if she has to be the first soldier storming in here."

Lunarias jumped at the sudden address, looking between each of the three Gifted.

"And that's likely to happen," Lunarias said, clearing her throat.

But no one said anything more. They all stared at each other in turn, except Kennas, who looked at the ground, her hands shaking as if in pain. In that unlit workshop, Astolphos saw something he did not think he would ever see again. From the edges of Kennas' eyes balled tears of blue liquid. They stained her fake skin as they tumbled down her cheeks. Kennas collapsed. A slight sobbing quickly turned to a river of tears.

"I don't deserve to know!" She yelled, "Not after everything I did today. I promised not to stain my hands again! I promised all of you to turn a new leaf and get a new, better life. I was so close to losing Control at that building." She raised her index and thump, barely keeping them apart, "I was this close to becoming the Devourer again! Do you want to know my first thought right after I killed those mercenaries? I thought that I didn't draw it out enough or make it as painful as they deserved! It was that thought that made me turn away from it."

Astolphos crouched beside Kennas and hugged her tightly. Her arms found their way around his slim body eventually. Her grip was slight as if it were to vanish at any point. It only got Astolphos to bring her in tighter. He had lost enough friends and would not lose another, no matter what.

"And the worst part is," Kennas said, "at that moment, despite everything, I still wanted to follow you into that building. I don't deserve to return here, so I thought I might as well go in there and lose myself once more and get exactly what I deserve."

"You more than atoned for what you did back then," Astolphos said, "Think about how many children you've helped get a proper and stable future throughout the years. More than 100 years of that more than covers the actions of the Devourer."

"Not even close. I remember everything,"

She buried her face in his apron, "I remember everything I did back then. There's nothing I can do to make up for it, much less what we did to the Gifter. No matter how much I try, I will never make up for all that!"

Only then did Astolphos hear the slight creaking of the floorboards behind him. He saw one of the Aurillian apprentices looking at them. Recognition flashed in the apprentice's eyes, and he darted up the stairs from whence he came.

"Do you truly want to keep such a danger alive?" Kennas asked.

"No other thought ever crossed my mind. What happened today was a collection of practically everything that could ever go wrong. Frankly, I don't think you're the only one that went overboard."He looked at Lunarias. She looked emptily at the scene before her, but still, her eyes saw nothing but her own thoughts.

"We should never be judged upon our worst days alone, but from the collection of it all. So why are you judging yourself on your worst?"

This time, he could not avoid hearing it. Those careful footsteps had evolved into what sounded like a semi-rushed stampede unleashed upon the stairs. The apprentices were almost pushing each other through the door to the workshop.

"Glaucos, since the secret is out anyway, can you give us some light?"

"No problem." All candles and torches lit in unison, enveloping the entire workshop in a light equivalent to what daylight would have given through the windows.

So many apprentices turned up that Kennas was unable to not notice. She tried to dry her eyes, but more tears just took their place. Then, she rose from the floor and looked at them all. She clenched her fists, and Astolphos heard her mumble the numbers. She finally counted them all.

"Y-You're all still here!" She said. A degree of happiness and relief rushed over her as Astolphos grabbed her before she fell to the ground again. "Why?"

"When you three left, we talked about what to do. We all decided to stay."

"What! Why? I'm an Abyssal! Your enemy!" Kennas yelled.

"You're more human than anyone else in this town," Another apprentice said, "You took us in when we lost everything. You sought us out when we had hit the bottom, intent on pulling us up. You gave us a home and a future. There is no way we would leave you."

"We're sorry we made you worry. We should've said something earlier," Another chimed in.

"But you're all risking your lives staying here!" Kennas shouted, more tears welling up in her eyes.

"You're not making us leave. We've already decided."

"A-are you sure?" Kennas asked.

Astolphos, too, felt the tears coming forth as all the apprentices nodded in her direction.

"Please, Kennas," The oldest apprentice said, bowing deeply, "continue being our master and lead us."

It took a few moments before Kennas could muster an answer through the tears.

"Of course I will!"

Chapter 57

Despite the time they saved at the headquarters, dawn was still upon them before Kennas got the apprentices back in their rooms. Both parties were excited to know that everything would be okay, which showed by the sudden burst of energy after midnight. Still, that energy dissipated eventually, and they all returned to bed just as the moon left the sky. Kennas went upstairs with the apprentices and stayed there for several hours.

As Lunarias had yet to return to the garrison and reported that the Abyssal was gone, none of the citizens had returned from outside the wall.

Still, Lunarias remained silent, which was something that surprised Astolphos. He had at least expected her to protest or complain about keeping the citizens worried just because of Kennas, but she said nothing.

Eventually, Kennas came down the stairs. Her tears were gone, but the blue streaks across her skin were still there. Still, the smile on her face told him everything he needed to know. Her doubt had been wiped away.

"Thank you for everything," Kennas said.

"That's perhaps still too early to say," Astolphos said, "there's still one more thing to do. Lunarias, how will the citizens react if you tell them that the Abyssal got away?"

"They'd probably return to the city, but they'll be wary and act like they did the last few days until they've got physical proof it's gone."

"That's what I feared. What do you mean by physical proof?"

"...A body."

"And we can't just take one of the mercenaries and say he was the Abyssal?"

"Absolutely not. We can't let it be publically known that Abyssals can take on human form. It'll start a level of paranoia never seen before."

"What about a public execution?" Glaucos asked, "We have a shape-shifter, after all. We can make Kennas transform into a sufficiently scary monster and just lob off her head in front of Hybrik. Then we just move the body out of town, and she returns to her old shape."

Lunarias grew silent but finally nodded, "That might work. If they see the Abyssal being executed, they'll feel much safer. But we'll need to get moving on this today, and you have to come with me to the garrison."

Lunarias looked at Kennas, who, in turn, looked at Astolphos, "Can I rely on you to keep an eye on my apprentices until I'm back?"

"Of course, but it'll mean you'll miss Cyrillys' burial."

"It's a small price to pay to finish all of this. So how should I look?"

"I might have a suggestion," Astolphos said, thinking once more if he should say it out loud. It would confirm something that had worried him since he came to Hybrik, but he might not like the answer. Still, it was the fastest way to accomplish both simultaneously.

"Can you take the shape of Balacastrys?"

Chapter 58

"Please, save me," The commander pleaded.

A sense of deja vu rose in Lunarias as she steeled her grip on her sword. The crystal layer cracked around her, but she did not care.

At the top of the stairs, Astolphos stared at them sternly. She could not take her eyes away from him.

"Don't do it!" Astolphos yelled. And then, her hand stopped moving. Though it would be difficult to prove, she was sure that none of Astolphos' abilities were involved. This was her body's own work. She tried wrenching her arm down, but all it would do was shake. It was futile, and the moment she gave up, she realized her entire body was shaking. Her whole being screamed for her to get away, but there was no way out, and there was no way to fight. All she could do was stand still as she saw Astolphos walk down the stairs. Two ringing foot-steps upon the crystal cover. In their wake, the crystal shat-tered behind Astolphos, and debris flew under the weight of Astolphos' steps.

"What're you waiting on!? Save me! It's your duty as a knight!" The commander yelled. He still lay on the ground as before. He struggled to stand up, but all it resulted in was him screaming in pain when he tried supporting himself on his flayed hands.

"Don't let it take me!" But she could do nothing. She truly was as trapped as he was, waiting for the creature to pass its judgment. She could not even mutter a word of apology as Astolphos seized the commander by the hair and lifted him off the floor.

And then he started draining. She could pinpoint the exact moment he began, as the commander started shaking like he had a fever cramp and shrieked. She had never heard anything like it before.

But despite this, neither the Commander nor Astolphos broke off their stares at Lunarias. They just looked on as the commander shriveled up from the extremities.

And she wanted to scream along with him, for she knew that the same fate awaited her the moment Astolphos was done.

There was a heavy knock on the door.

Lunarias suppressed a scream as she opened her eyes. Half of her face hurt from being in contact with the hard surface of her desk for the entire night. She rubbed her eyes to get the remaining sleep out, only to groan when she realized her hand was stained with ink. Even more infuriating was the part where she had fallen asleep on the order she had spent the entire evening organizing. Half of it was written immaculately, while the other had been reduced to a partial impression of her cheek.

For the last week, she had claimed the captain's room as her own. However, she had slowly stripped it for valuables and sold them off to pay for all the improvements she made. What remained was the carpet, the bed, the desk, and a mirror affixed to the wall, the latter of which she did not want to stare at too much at the moment.

There was another series of knocks on the door.

"Come in," She said.

The door opened, and a guard entered. He was young, probably around her own age. Not only that, he was inexperienced. At his own admission, he had never seen combat, nor had he been trained for it at the garrison in the six months he had been part of the guards. That was precisely why she picked him as her second in command. Unlike most of the remaining guards, he was a blank slate. Someone who could be taught the proper rules and conduct for taking over the position of captain someday, under the eye of the knights arriving in a few days, of course.

He stared at a bunch of parchment when he entered and was about to say something when he trailed off at the sight of Lunarias.

She raised a hand before he could say anything, "I know. After today's report, can you get me a towel and a water bowl?"

"Of course," He nodded, "Where do you want to start?"

"What about the number of recruits?"

He shuffled through the papers, a stack of which grew by the day, along with the countless projects Lunarias started.

"Here it is! The pay increase has resulted in 12 new recruits. Four conscripts have also agreed to become permanent guards under the new pay."

"Great news, that means we can release some of the conscripts. And what about the weapons that were to come in today?"

"The guild master is to arrive any moment with the order."

"And for the rest of the schedule?"

"After the weapon inspection, you have a meeting with the masonry guild for the repairs on the northern barbican and a meeting with the duchess about further funds for the restorations. In the afternoon, you have a training session with the recruits. A representative of the armorsmiths will also come to pick up the order and the advance. Then there is the execution of the Abyssal."

"So that's today, huh?" She had lost her sense of time just after a few days of taking the mantle of captain. Everything had just been so busy, with training sessions, rounds of conscription, and meetings with guild masters and influential traders to acquire the necessary materials for the complete restructuring and restoration of the garrison and the city's defensive structures. Those sessions were nothing but groveling and playing politics. Lunarias had, on more than one occasion, wanted to throw up from the drivel she had said during those meetings. At least she hit it off better with the duchess, which made all the other negotiations easier.

"And just to refresh my memory, the meeting with the duchess is about the economic impacts on the citizenry our bulk purchase of materials will have?"

"Yes, and about if it will affect the maintenance of the Scaffolding."

"...Perfect," She had completely forgotten that last part, "Alright, here's what we're going to do. You'll fetch me that water bowl and then cancel today's training session. Instead, you're going to gather up all the conscripts and make a lottery about which will be released from duty. Release 12 of them. After I meet with the guild master, I'll head to the prison for one last interrogation of the Abyssal."

She then looked down at the sheet of parchment on the desk and sighed, "And send a messenger to that representative and tell him he's going to wait one more day on the order."

***

Getting ink stains off was always tricky, a fact Lunarias could confirm after trying to wipe a large stain off her cheek and around her eyes. And though they were not completely gone, she was sure the remainder could not be seen from the podium she would be standing on tonight.

When she emerged from her office, the guildmaster had already arrived with her order and stood at the gate with several barrels of weapons strutting out of the top. Meanwhile, the guards were busy with their training regimens and patrols. She had never seen the courtyard as alive as today, with soldiers training both with swords and bows against the third pair of training dummies in two days.

Even more were getting ready to take over from the morning shift, and some were busy moving the old weapons stock out of the armory.

The weapons she had ordered were far from perfect, as expected from a giant rush order, but they would make do for a while. Once the guildmaster left happy and with a large, heavy pouch hanging from his waist, Lunarias headed for the prison tower.

Many arrests were made in the aftermath of that night, primarily of fences and other types of bribed officials. All of them awaited sentencing, something they would be waiting on for a while longer until the garrison had stabilized.

The guards on duty saluted as she passed them on her way to the top. Only one cell was on the top floor, and four guards stood ready in front of it.

"So, today's the day this monster gets dispatched?" One guard asked.

"Today's the day," Lunarias said, "Go take a break and something to eat. I want to interrogate it alone one last time."

The guards did not question her orders and left after one last salute. She opened the door and saw the most hideous creature she had ever seen, chained up on the wall. It was double the height of Lunarias, almost too wide to fit through the door no matter how they turned it. Even now, it had to crouch to not bang its head against the roof. It was a hulking monstrosity of bulging gray skin and scars. Its head was slightly better; it was still scarred and scaly, but one could at least recognize some barely human features. The creature melted into a blue puddle when Lunarias closed and locked the door to the outside. When Lunarias turned around, Kennas had already gotten her usual form back.

"Here to 'interrogate' me?" Kennas said with a playful smile.

"More or less, I'm still shocked that you can become that big."

"The secret is that it's just a shell, no more than a few centimeters thick. I just have to remember to make the neck solid tonight, or else we will have some problems, right?"

"I think it's going to be a good idea, but as long as you fall limp, the citizens will probably not care."

They sat down at a table. It was typically used to store the implements for torture and interrogation. Those tools were stacked in the corner instead, as Lunarias was the only one allowed to meet with the Abyssal.

"So, how's it going?" Kennas asked, "Still busy, I presume?"

"More or less, my workload has not decreased, that's for sure. This place is like an onion rotten to the core. You peel off some layers and hope things get better, only for it to look even worse."

"I don't envy your position. I remember how it was back in Lumina. I've experienced something similar back then."

"According to Astolphos, you never had any problems with corruption of this scale."

"That's right, but we encountered something similar. Once, we made some upgrades to a city's defenses and thought it was smart to get everything done in unison. The problem was just that it also meant that everything had to be renovated simultaneously. Just the scheduling of material delivery was enough to get me boiling."

"In that case, you shouldn't know how a renovation of that scale will impact other kinds of renovations in the city."

Kennas stroked her chin for a moment.

"That was always Heuristrys' responsibility. That guy could look at the weather and tell you how it would affect prices. But I did pick up a thing or two from him. Considering what we've discussed before, I don't think you'd have to think too much about the prices. It's the labor shortage, with a resulting pay increase, that's going to bite hard. I'd expect at least a 50 percent increase, with perhaps ten percent being rooted in materials."

"And you just remember those things on the top of your head?"

Kennas smiled, "It's just an estimate. You pick up a thing or two when you've lived as long as I have."

"You've been a great help till now, that's for sure. That duchess is way more economically considerate than I thought."

"You really came back morose after that first meeting."

"I'd just expected some girl who'd let her retainers take care of it all, not someone that hands-on."

However, as much as she disliked getting help from an Abyssal, Kennas was crucial in everything Lunarias did to the garrison. It was a coincidence that she brought up one of her many plights during a conversation. She just did it to vent, but then Kennas ran with it, telling her all kinds of details and warning her of things to look out for. Almost everything happened just as Kennas had predicted. Only then did the weight of the titles Kennas and Astolphos talked about truly hit her. Kennas was not just an Abyssal who coincidentally also was a carpenter. She had once been an advisor of a King and had a huge responsibility resting on her shoulders. There was no doubt in Lunarias' mind that if someone like Kennas were to become part of the Aurillian court, things might look very different in just a short period of time. And, however loath she was at admitting it, listening to Kennas had also made her reevaluate what Astolphos had told her weeks before. Could there really be some truth to the regrets Astolphos spoke of? But that was a question she could not get herself to ask.

"Are you sure you're going to be fine here alone?" Kennas asked, genuine concern painted upon her face, "I'd have no problem sneaking into the office occasionally if you need someone to spar with."

"I think I'll manage the last few days alone. You should just focus on getting home to your apprentices."

"You're right. How was it now that this is going to work?"

Lunarias leaned onto the table. The thought of the theatrics she had to put on in just a few hours washed away all other concerns. Along with it came a strange feeling of reluctance, as if she was to do something she was going to regret. But the strangest thing was that the feeling was not directed towards the citizens.

"Once I leave, some guards will come in here and put on a new pair of shackles. Then, in a few hours, they'll return and lead you out of the cell. You'll then be paraded through the city until you reach the podium at the market. Put up a bit of a fight when this happens, but not enough to make the guards draw their weapons."

Kennas nodded.

"Then I'll hold a speech, pick up the blade, and I'm going to cleave off your head. Once that's done, I'll instruct the guards to move your corpse into the woods, and you'll just return to the city once they're gone."

"Sounds simple enough,"

"And hopefully, there will be no mishaps."

"But Lunarias," Kennas said, her smile vanishing, "there's something else on your mind, other than all of this with the garrison, isn't there?"

"There isn't," Lunarias lied, "But why do you think there is?"

"You've been acting differently since that night at the headquarters."

"And you're sure it isn't just because we'd only met a few times before that night?"

"It's not a small change. You know you can talk to me, right?"

But this was not something she could talk to Kennas about. One thing was painfully clear: Kennas and Astolphos would go to great lengths to protect those they hold dear, and she knew that there was no way she would win if she ended up on their bad side.

"I know, but there isn't much to talk about. Sorry to cut this short, but I must return to my duties now."

Chapter 59

It was almost time to witness the execution, and thus also the end of the most stressful days Astolphos has had in several decades. The apprentices were much more of a handful than he had ever anticipated, and that was even when they apparently were at the best of behaviors. Of course, the mood in the shop was mixed because of everything that had happened. Those children were thrown from one unbelievable circumstance into the next. But taking everything into account, Astolphos would say they took everything in strides.

What surprised him the most was how autonomous they were when it came to their work. All his work entailed was to give his opinion if they were disagreeing on something. He did not even have to part out the work; they all knew where to find their tasks, and Kennas had helpfully already written who had to work on what far into the future. The stressful part was after work, when the apprentices had some free time. That was when conflicts and bickering arose. If not for the fact that he could measure it through his phylactery, he would have thought he had spent double the essence just mediating their conflicts.

But the atmosphere today was vastly different. Despite their work being done for the day, they did not peak up at the thought of free time. Instead, they looked at Astolphos with large eyes, pleading for something he could not give them.

"I hate this as much as you do," Astolphos said to answer the unspoken question, "But we all need to do this. Now, take off the aprons and wash off. We'll leave in an hour."

They knew why Astolphos had been in charge for the last week and a half. They knew that whatever shape was going up on that podium, it was their master who put their head on the chopping block. The fact that Kennas would still be fine afterward did not help lift the mood. But it was something they all had to do. They were supposed to be Aurillians. They were supposed to be cheering as the axe fell upon a vile creature, making them fear for their lives. If they did not go to the execution, the neighbors might suspect them to be sympathizers. That was the last thing they needed, as this ordeal was now under the watchful eyes of Lunarias' reformed garrison.

But despite their dislike of what they had to do, they still went to get ready without a complaint.

And soon, they were on their way to the marketplace. They thought they had left early enough to avoid the crowds, but that was not the case. The streets were packed, and moving ten steps meant shoving away twice as many bystanders. Still, they eventually pushed through to the market and could see the podium built upon the Scaffolding for this event.

"Intros, to me," Astolphos yelled, and Intros reluctantly obeyed.

"I still don't understand why you want me to stand beside you."

"You'll realize soon."

They all knew that Kennas was to walk upon the platform under a different guise, but he had not told anyone what the guise was to be. This was the second objective of this execution, to determine if Balacastrys was Intros' father. His reaction to the display would tell Astolphos if they had a swindler or a problem at their hands.

The crowd started to boo far before they got the sight of Balacastrys. They yelled obscenities and threw whatever rotten produce they had down the street. Then they parted ways as Lunarias led the proceeding, followed closely by a parade of guards. The hulking monstrosity that was Balacastrys was dragged along in chains.

"Just as ugly as I remember him," Glaucos said, but Astolphos gave no response. What he saw made him feel like he had swallowed a bag of rocks and was thrown off a pier.

Intros looked at the proceeding, his face twitched, and his hands clenched and shook.

"Is this a test?" Intros whispered.

"...Yes," was all Astolphos could say. His mind was already preoccupied with the implications of this.

"And what did you get out of this?"

"Something I had hoped never to experience again."

Chapter 60

The guards wasted no time locking Kennas' chains onto large hooks fastened into the platform. One week had not been enough training to instill some proper valor into them, as the guards did not even check if the chains were secured properly before scuttling away. They were too busy getting as far away from the creature as possible.

But the entire city watched, so she could do nothing about it without raising more mistrust between the citizens and guards.

Still, Kennas struggled against the chains. The platform shook, and planks complained under the strain, but nothing broke. Still, the sheer spectacle got the front row to step back and quieted the marketplace.

Lunarias took a deep breath and swallowed her nervousness.

"Fair citizens of Hybrik!" She yelled, "Look at this foul creature! This is the monster that dared disturb the peace of the Aurillian kingdom!

"It came here from the Abyss, far up north, on the hunt for revenge! A mercenary company had killed some of its ilk, and it wanted to pay them back! These mercenaries were the ones that had terrorized the entire city for months. Now both problems are laid to rest, and what remains is to punish this foul monster for its existence."

The citizens gobbled it all up. They believed every word as they looked up at her with starry eyes and at the monster with gazes of disgust. Despite looking back and forth at the sea of people, she saw no indication of doubt. All she saw was relief and happiness because now they could return to the everyday. She wanted to achieve this, even if the way to do so was through lies and subterfuge.Only when the crowd calmed down did she resume. She nodded to a guard on the ground to give her the sword. This was also the signal for Kennas to put on a show.

She struggled against the chains once more, thrashing about and testing the strength of every link. Then, one of the planks snapped, and the chain was flung into the air. The citizens screamed in fear as the creature started clawing at the chain to its other arm.

"Guards! Restrain it now!"

The guards ran up the platform again and grabbed the loose chain, stretching it and 'forcing' Kennas to give up. It was all a show to display the strength of the guards. To regain some measure of trust from the citizens.

"Disgusting creatures! All of you!" Kennas yelled, her voice deep and booming with an intensity Lunarias thought impossible. It was a foul voice, reminding her of the battlefield, of metal against metal and the screams of wounded soldiers, as if it carried the promise of the very same.

"I might leave this earth today! But my god smiles on my achievements in a way your false idols will never be able to. More will come, and let my death be the foundation of a new Abyss!"

The citizens murmured between themselves, and for a moment, Lunarias feared that they were a bit too effective at putting on a show.

She grabbed the executioner's sword from the guard presenting it to her. It was a hefty blade, weighing almost twice what she was used to. Practically, it was a rectangle with a handle and no guard. It was made to chop, nothing else.

"Don't listen to it!" Lunarias yelled, "We know it was traveling alone. There is nothing to fear, for it speaks of only empty
threats on its deathbed. Force it down!"

The guards grabbed both chains for its arms and pulled
them tight. Feigning resistance, Kennas tugged back but was
overpowered, presenting her neck to Lunarias.

She rested the blade on it and pulled it far above her head
before chopping down hard. The blade met no resistance on
its way through the thick neck. And then, the sword hit the
ground, the head landed on the podium and rolled down to its
resting place in front of the front row, who all jumped back
with a shriek.

"And with that!" Lunarias yelled, "The city is once again
safe."

The crowd cheered, and Lunarias bowed like a performer
who had just finished her play. But then it was back to work.
The crowd dispersed with stunning speed, but the atmosphere
of the entire city already improved significantly. As the crowd
thinned, she recognized Astolphos, along with a stunningly
large group of children at the back of the marketplace. But
there was something strange about him now, though she had
difficulties picking it out from such a distance.

"Lady Hewris," One of the guards said, gesturing to the
corpse.

"Get it on a wagon and drag it deep into the forest, then
dump it on the ground. It doesn't deserve a burial."

"Is there any reason not to burn it as custom dictates?"
Someone said from behind.

Lunarias turned around, expecting to perhaps see some
cocky guard, but was stunned for a moment instead. The
familiar man in front of her was of a stout build, and his beard
was gray from age.

He wore the heavy plate armor of the knights of Aurillia,
only that he had a gold trim around the relief and a sapphire

embedded in the wolf's eyes, signaling that he was a knight of the first rank, her superior. Both his hair and beard were gray, and he wore an eyepatch across the eye he had lost on one of his campaigns into the Abyss. Behind him were another five knights, all looked rather haggard, while he still beamed with energy despite being more than twice their senior.

"Gallados!" Lunarias said, hugging her old, grizzled teacher, "I thought you were still down south."

"I'd just returned to the headquarters when your messenger arrived. I told my troops their break was canceled, and all 400 of us headed for Hybrik immediately." He nodded at the corpse, "Though it seems like you have everything under control."

Lunarias looked at the small retinue of knights at the bottom of the podium, "So where are the rest?"

"I assembled a small team and rode through the Forest to get here as fast as possible. The remainder is taking the long route around but should be here in five days or so."

"Apologies, it seems my letter kicked up too much of a storm."

"Nah, it's probably more this old geezer who's kicked up a fuzz. But enough of that, what's the deal with that thing?"

"Can we talk about that a little later?" Lunarias asked, wanting to change the topic as quickly as possible, "I have a meeting with the duchess and have to get going if I'm not to be late."

Gallados got a mischievous smile, "So Ms. Hewris has had to begin politicking, huh? That I have to see that in person. Mind if I come along?"

"As long as the duchess clears it, you're more than welcome."

Gallados then turned to his men, "Crisis averted, boys! Go get something to eat, something to bed, and somewhere to sleep; the order is up to you. We'll meet at the garrison at dawn." The men made a half-assed salute and quickly got lost in the crowd. Lunarias and Gallados were then on their way to the largest building in the city. The crowd parted as they walked, and everyone laid out a greeting and their gratitude. The city had indeed returned to normal.

"So, how did you overpower that thing?" Gallados asked. The pause had luckily given Lunarias some time to think up an answer.

"Something tells me it wanted to be caught."

Gallados raised an eyebrow, "Now that's curious, and why's that?"

"When I arrived at the mercenaries' headquarters, I was too late. That creature had killed them all. It just sat on the floor, saying I could do my worst, it had already won."

"So, it has something to do with your special assignment, and you can't tell me the truth?"

Lunarias stopped and turned to look at Gallados, who was still brimming with mischievous energy,

"Don't look so shocked. I've known you since you were little. Of course, I know when you're lying."

Lunarias sighed, "How much do you know of my assignment?"

"All I know is that the order comes from the queen herself and that I'm under strict orders not to look into it. Nor am I to let you give the task to someone else."

She was relieved. That at least meant that there was no one to question why she was in Hybrik.

"And is that also connected to why you ordered the body to be dumped in the forest?"

Lunarias nodded.

"Some task you've gotten." He then continued walking.

"But I must say, a special assignment from the queen herself. I'm a bit envious of you."

"Trust me, if you knew the assignment, you'd swallow your words."

Chapter 61

"And then, Heuristrys jumped the fence, only to now stand face to face with a giant pig, and boy, was it angry," Astolphos said. The apprentices all listened intently, sitting at the breakfast table while Kennas was busy doing the final checkup of the carriage. This had become a sort of routine for them since the secret was out. Once Intros and Inaris were entirely accepted by the apprentices, the group's curiosity shifted to their Gifts. Then they seemed to recognize that they sat beside truly ancient Gifted and wanted to know what life was like back then. And that lasted more or less one day before Astolphos went on a tangent about some of their misadventures back then, and now that was all they wanted to hear. Luckily, Heuristrys supplied him with more than enough material to last for lifetimes.

"That thing was a giant bastard, the kind of thing able to tremble anything in its pa-"

"Language," Kennas yelled from the carriage.

Astolphos cleared his throat, "Anyway, here Heuristrys is, on the back and being stared down by this beast, frozen as if he was staring at death itself." He picked up a grape from his plate and put it on the table, "I had to act, so here's what I did."

Astolphos clenched his fist, and a small pillar appeared under the grape, launching it up and into a free fall. "I launched him into the air! But now he was coming down fast." The grape landed on the table, splashing out on impact, "Or that would happen. So here he was, screaming as he plunged to the ground. Luckily, Kennas was also there to see this mess, so she changed shape and jumped up to swallow him whole."

"Did he make it?" One of the apprentices asked. She had not touched her plate since he started his story.

"Heuristrys is like a cockroach. You couldn't kill him even if you wanted to. Frankly, we didn't even know what a fall like this would do to him, but we wouldn't take the chance. Kennas landed a fair distance from the pigsty and spit him back out. He was fine, but strangely enough, the blue color took weeks before vanishing."

He never did figure out how the color stuck to Heuristrys' skin, and there probably was no way of finding out. He could imagine how Heuristrys would scowl if he knew his deeds were used as a children's story, but then again, perhaps that would generate one more for the pile.

"Heuristrys got you into a lot of trouble, didn't he?" Inarias asked.

"They both did," Kennas said, walking out of the carriage with a smile that made Astolphos want to run before her next words, "He's just not telling you about his misadventures. Do you want me to tell you about the birthday surprise for your daughter?"

"Please don't. I finally repressed that one, and you've brought it back into the forefront once more."

"In that case, let me tell you about it tomorrow. I'm done checking the carriage. You've all done a great job. I'm so proud of all of you. I couldn't have done a better job myself. Now, please eat up. I've got to take 'Stolfos here with me for the final checks."

Astolphos followed Kennas to the carriage, or more accurately, carriages. There were, in total, two carriages drawn by the four horses. The carriages were made of thick oak planks so well put together that you struggled to see where one ended and another began. The sides were reinforced with thicker timber, and the slanted roof was tiled in reddish-brown cherry. The one in front had a stone chimney peaking above the roof. The stone made the carriage very heavy, and the wheels reflected this. They were large and thick, even by the scale of large cargo wagons, consisting of several rings of thick dowels connected by long square bars of Astolphos' Abyssal steel. The last and largest of the rings had a piece of iron enveloping it. This was a well-built carriage, able to take on practically everything besides being set ablaze, its design being perfected through many years of reconstruction and reiteration. This would be his and Lunarias' home for the foreseeable future.

"Did the tools arrive?" Astolphos asked.

Kennas nodded, "They've already been loaded."

Astolphos entered the first carriage. Despite being wide enough to fit at least three people side by side, the wall-mounted desks made it so only two people could pass each other, and with great difficulty.

The back of the carriage was one giant forge, with an anvil to one side and various tongs and hammers on a rack on the other. Right above it was the chimney, which could be closed off with internal shutters in case of rain. Rasps, files, and other non-heat-related tools were put on shelves under the desks, and the walls were free to display whatever wares he had available.

"Perfect as always," Astolphos said.

"Then you're going to like the other one too."

They moved to the back carriage, and Astolphos was immediately overwhelmed by nostalgia. This very layout had been his home on many journeys around Aurillia and the remains of Lumina. Two bunk beds to the sides, with a small fireplace and various cooking utensils strapped to the back wall. Kennas had even taken the liberty of moving his things to the lower-left bed he always took on their journeys.

"Can we sit and talk?" Kennas asked, her expression suddenly grave.

"Of course," Astolphos said, sitting down on his bed.

Kennas did the same and twiddled her thumps as if looking for the right words.

"I'm worried about Intros' reaction," Kennas said, then hesitated once more, "There's no way he could've been wrong, is there?"

Astolphos shook his head, his hands grabbing hard on the bed frame, "There isn't. There's no way another shapeshifter could've figured out how Balacastrys looked without seeing him in person."

"What if he wants revenge?"

"I'm afraid of the same. That's why I'm going to drive through the forest and check for myself."

"But 'stolphos," She grabbed hold of his arm, a certain tenderness mixed in with her worry, "What if he's waiting for that?"

"I don't think so. If anything, he's in Lumina, plotting either to start everything back up or to get revenge. Frankly, I don't know which one is worse..."

"Just promise you'll be careful and come back here if things grow tough. Then we'll get Heuristrys and Nitris to come, and we'll figure this out together, just like we did back then."

"I promise."

"What're you two talking about?" Intros asked, peering in from the outside.

"Nothing special, just some stuff from back then. What is it?"

"We just wanted to see you off before you leave," Inaris said.

Astolphos chuckled, "I wasn't going to just leave without saying goodbye if that's what you're thinking."

The two entered the carriage and sat beside Kennas, "This is a lot of space for two people," Intros said.

"That's because this is normally for four, but it'll serve fine for my trip."

"So, this is how you five normally travel,"

"More or less. We've practically spent years in here by now," Kennas giggled, "It holds quite a few memories by now."

"That it does," Glaucos said.

"What's the plan now?" Intros asked.

"Well, now I'll be waiting for Lunarias to arrive, and then we'll be off to the capital. Once done with whatever the queen wants, I'll probably head to Marados castle and wait for the rest of you. Something tells me I've gotten enough of Aurillia for a while after finishing this business."

"Does that mean we're never going to see you again?" Inaris asked, looking down at the planks.

"Probably, but who knows, perhaps we'll meet in the next cycle once we've regrouped and figured out where to head next. Remember, Kennas, ten more years, then you have to travel."

Kennas nodded, "I know, that's also why I've stopped taking in more apprentices."

The two looked at them in confusion.

"That's just how we do things," Glaucos said, "35 years, then we travel to Marados castle and wait for a few years, then we head to a new place, just to retread the cycle once more."

"But doesn't it get sad?" Inaris asked, "Just abandoning the life you've set up here?"

"You unfortunately get used to it," Kennas said, a morose smile on her lips, "That's why it's so important to know when to quit, when to close things down, and when to start pulling away so you don't get too attached."

"That's the curse of immortality," Astolphos said, "but it's a price we're all willing to pay. Though I must say that I sometimes envy those who aren't paying that price."

Kennas raised an eyebrow, but Astolphos could not meet her gaze. They both remember too well.

Chapter 62

"And this is what has to be done this week, right?" Gallados asked as he looked at the timetables Lunarias penned for him.

"No, this is for tomorrow. This is the one for the entire week," Lunarias said, pointing at a list several times longer than the one Gallados looked at.

"I'm getting too old for this..."

"Come on, you still have some prime years left, right?"

Gallados leaned back in his chair at the desk, looking for a moment as if he did not know how to continue. She might have stripped too much from the office, as Gallados had brought in a new table, some chairs, and drapes ordained with the knights' crest. This was no longer just a garrison. It had become a new outpost for the knights of Aurillia.

Nothing made that more evident than looking through the windows and out at the courtyard. Where it was practically barren when she had first arrived, it was now bustling with activity. Gallados' troops swooped in like a hawk and took the last remaining free spots in the garrison, freeing the remaining conscripts. So many knights arrived that more than half were asked to return to the capital for new orders.

Those that remained were kept busy by the new guards. They were trained by the top of the Aurillian military, and that was something that was felt. When a day was over, it truly was over, with the soldiers who trained being wiped out to a degree where it was difficult for them to sit up and eat. All the while, the knights took over the guards' duties and patrolled the streets day and night.

It all worked too perfectly. As they rounded up all remaining collaborators of the mercenaries, they filled up the prison to the brim, with most cells being shared by more men than they were designed for.

"Frankly, I'm not so sure anymore," Gallados said, suddenly the most serious she had seen him in years, "It's just that things have been more difficult as of late. I can feel it in my arms when I'm swinging my sword, and I can feel it in my mind when doing stuff like this. I just think it's about time for me to retire."

"But who's going to take your place?"

Lunarias was about to continue, but Gallados' stare made her uncomfortable, or more aptly, what that stare meant.

"You must be joking," Lunarias exclaimed.

"Far from it," Gallados said, stretching his arms and back, "This here is more than enough proof that you're up for the task. That, and of course, how you handle your meetings with the guilds and the duchess."

"You came along to evaluate me?"

Gallados nodded, "And you passed with flying colors. I'll file the paperwork when I get back from this, and you'll be tutored by me as soon as you're done with your task. Then, once you're ready to take over, I'll retire, probably move in with my children, and live the remainder of my life with them and my grandkids."

"That sounds lovely," Lunarias said, trailing off.

"What? Did you expect me to go down in battle?" He laughed, then pointed at his eyepatch, "I've already had one close shave with the Ancestors. I'm not going to test my luck anymore. So, do you accept?"

Lunarias was conflicted; there were many things she had pondered for the last few weeks, and this just added more complexity to an already unsolvable mess. However, she knew that there was only one correct answer for this one. She clenched her fist and hit her breastplate.

"I'll accept my new role with honor."

"That's great. I'd fetch a barrel to celebrate, but didn't you have to leave today? Letting your traveling companions wait is a bad habit, isn't it?"

***

As Lunarias approached Kennas' workshop, the first sight greeting her was Astolphos trying to rein in four horses with Kennas drumming her fingers and looking on with what could only be described as anticipation.

The horses did not like Astolphos, for every time he tried tugging the reins, they stood on their hind legs, forcing him to take several steps forward just to not lose his balance or grip. It seemed like all-powerful beings sometimes suffered the same banal problems as everyone else.

"Morning Lunarias, long time no see," Kennas said, smiling at her. She had not seen Kennas since the execution. Though Kennas seemed genuinely kind and had helped her more than once in the weeks of captivity, Lunarias had to remember that she was dealing with an Abyssal, a very powerful one even. Still, nothing could be gained from angering anyone at this moment.

"Morning," Lunarias said, flinging her luggage onto the ground, "Anything I can help with?"

Kennas pointed at Astolphos, "He's always been bad with animals. Been fighting with those four for more than an hour now.

Could you show him how it's done?"

"With pleasure,"

"That's not necessary. I've got everything under control!"

"You said the same thing half an hour ago," Glaucos said, "Give the reins to Lunarias so we can get going before sunset."

Now, with his pride on the line, Astolphos pulled on the reins one more time. The horses neighed and stood up on their hind legs. It seemed like the horses had the same mentality; they rose too quickly for Astolphos, and he was lifted off the ground, only to fall flat a moment later.

He let out a deep sigh and handed the reins to Lunarias without getting up.

"When you're done wallowing in your crumbling pride, go move Lunarias' stuff into the carriage," Kennas yelled to the defeated Astolphos, still lying on the ground.

"Don't worry, I'll take of it myself."

"That hurt," Astolphos said.

"So, you can take several sword strikes without batting an eye," Lunarias said, "but being thrown to the ground by a horse hurts?"

"I was expecting those cuts, but this came out of the blue."

"You were the only one who did not expect this," Glaucos said.

Astolphos finally rose from the ground and walked to the workshop, "In that case, I'm going to say my goodbyes now, if that's alright."

Lunarias approached the horses with a calm mind, looking directly at them without moving anything but the arm holding the reins. It only took seconds before the horses calmed, at which she slowly approached them. With a few caresses to their necks, they finally stood still long enough for Lunarias to fasten the leather harnesses. She had done so many times before when her knightly duties drew her fair distances away from the capital. Sometimes, it was to deliver emergency supplies. Other times, they returned with a wagon full of bound bandits who had been enough of a nuisance for the lord to request the knights to handle the issue.

But even as she focused on the task at hand, her mind was elsewhere. It was on the words of Gallados and to where her allegiance truly lay: to the crown or the citizens. If this assignment taught her anything, those two differed from what she initially thought.

"Astolphos can be a bit intense at times," Kennas said, "We've all been through a lot, but him especially. Though he's a bit secretive about everything, I'm sure he'll open up once you've gotten to know him better."

"You didn't see what he did to the mercenaries."

Kennas stepped even closer and whispered, "He drained every mercenary one at a time, keeping them in perpetual horror the entire time, right?"

Lunarias took a big step back and let go of the reins but then grew conscious of the many eyes now on them.

"Nothing to see here!" Lunarias yelled, "Back to business, everyone!"

She returned to Kennas and whispered, "Did you two talk about it?"

"No, but I've known him long enough to tell you exactly why he did what he did, but I don't think it will change anything. Is that not what has been on your mind all this time?"

The nightmares still persisted. It was the same thing almost every night. The commander's eyes would follow her for a long time, that much she knew. Along with it came her opinions of Astolphos and the reason for the difficult choice she had to make.

Kennas looked around to see if more people were watching and said, "He did what he did for me and the other's sake. The life essence keeps us all alive. If Astolphos doesn't get enough essence, we cannot continue living anymore."

"...I'll keep that in mind."

"What're you two talking about?" Astolphos asked as he exited the shop.

"I just told her to ensure you didn't cheap out on the food."

Astolphos cocked his head, and Lunarias saw a sense of realization dawn on him for a moment, but it was quickly washed away with a smile.

"Come on, it only happened once. Am I truly going to be reminded every time?"

"For as long as I'll remember. Now, have a safe journey, you two."

Astolphos sat down on the bench and grabbed the reins. This time, the horses did not complain in the slightest.

"Lunarias," Astolphos said, "there's both room on the front bench and in the back carriage. Your choice."

Lunarias chose to sit on the bench. She was forced to sit beside Astolphos, but at least she could take in the sights.

"Thank you for all of your help," Kennas said as she approached Lunarias, "Though it was a bit of a bumpy ride, I wouldn't have known what to do without the two of you."

She extended a hand towards Lunarias, who reluctantly shook it.

"You'd been fine without mine," Lunarias said.

"I don't think so. You took care of the entire garrison on your own. That was not something me or Astolphos could've done."

Kennas then went to the other side of the carriage and hugged Astolphos tight.

"Thanks for everything. I'll be able to continue like this for at least a few more years because of you."

"We have to stick together, right? Send my regards to Nitris and Heuristrys next time you see them."

"Likewise. Something tells me you'll see them before I do. I hear they're both in the capital."

"Then I have something to look forward to. What about that other thing?"

Kennas nodded, "All taken care of. The workers will meet with me in a week, and we'll get that church fixed right up!"

Lunarias turned to Astolphos with a raised eyebrow.

"Don't worry," he said, "I've already paid in full. I'm not going to straddle them with the bill."

He then set the horses off, and they were on their way. Kennas stood behind, waving her final goodbyes at them.

Despite its large size, Astolphos navigated the streets with that bulky carriage with no issues. It was evident he had done this many times before.

"We still have one last stop before we can leave," Astolphos said, "Remember the order of the food I paid for all that time ago? It's waiting for us at the market."

Lunarias nodded but did not look at Astolphos. Her mind was once again on the dilemma she was faced with. She had two options: she could remain loyal to the crown and become a knight of the first order or shirk her duty to keep the citizens safe from an unfathomable danger. She did not know what to do. No matter how she twisted and turned the problem, nothing seemed to line up straightforwardly.

What she needed was more information. She needed to find out what was the right way to go.

"I think we came out on the wrong foot," Astolphos said.

Lunarias finally turned around to look at the blacksmith. His usually easy smile was replaced with a sorrowful mien.

"I normally don't use my powers like this. I don't want to. This was just because they threatened one of my comrades. The agreement between the late king and I only permits me to use my powers under specific circumstances."

"Why do you follow that agreement?" Lunarias asked, tone overflowing with indifference.

He was at a loss for words for a moment but then shook his head and said, "You wouldn't believe me right now. That's one thing I am sure of."

And there it was, right back at all the secrecy and things Astolphos could not say anything about. It was the last thing she needed right now. There was something strange in his eyes as he said the words, but she turned her back on him, instead looking at the various shops of the craftsmen's district as they passed by on their way to the market. More than their fair share of people looked at their carriage. It was much bigger than anything else on the street, and her armor attracted just as much attention as usual.

"I respected Regios a lot. He was a great king. Ready to risk more than you could imagine securing our help. Such resolve deserves recognition, and is there a better way to do so than to honor your side of the agreement to the bitter end?"

"And what did that agreement entail?" Lunarias asked a bit of curiosity chipped away at the indifference.

And she was once again met with silence and a conflicted expression.

"Did it have anything to do with the form Kennas took?" Lunarias asked when she realized no answer came from her previous question.

Astolphos clenched the reins hard, and for a moment, she saw what could only be unadulterated anger on his face. However, it was followed closely by a wave of sorrow, and then it was back to normal after a deep breath.

"Yes," was all Astolphos said. Anything more would unmistakably stir up more painful memories.

"Who was this Balacastrys?" Lunarias finally asked when her train of thought halted.

"In your tongue, he was known as the Master of the Royal Guard. His duty was to lead the Abyssal King's personal guard detail."

That answer surprised her. A creature of that size and appearance was not what she expected to be a leader.

"Hopefully, such a creature died a long time ago."

"He's immortal. Like a cancer, you can chop him to pieces over and over again. He'll eventually find you, whole as if nothing ever happened. He doesn't age, and no weapon can pierce his skin. Getting on his bad side is a surefire way to end up dead."

"So, how did you two defeat him?"

"The four of us didn't defeat him, we tired him out long enough for me to encase him in crystal. But something tells me he's gotten out of it, and that's bad news for everyone."

"Escaped? How?"

"That's what I'd like to know. Once we've got our food, we'll cross through the Forest of Sorrows to check on it."

Lunarias looked at the wheels; sure enough, they were bound in iron. However, she saw a blue sheen mixed in once the sun hit just right.

"Don't we have to use different wheels for that?"

"That's not normal iron."

She did not want to dig any further at the moment. The marketplace appeared before them, and her eyes caught on to a familiar-looking tavern.

"While you take care of the food, I'm going to quickly take care of something," Lunarias said.

"No problem. I think it'll take half an hour to get everything loaded up."

The tavern was barren of life except for the barkeep, his wife, and two passed-out drunkards drooling on their table. It was the end of a busy night shift. Hours had passed since the last drink was served, and the couple was busy tidying the place up. What a mess the patrons left behind. More than a few drinks had their contents swallowed by the floor. It was a battle to simply walk around; the floor grabbed hold of her greaves with such intensity it felt like passing through a bog. The tables looked to have been tortured by the negligence of people under the influence. Spilled tankards, food remains, and unsightly spots of origins Lunarias did not want to know littered the worn-down tabletops. Amidst the chaos, the bar-keep was busy mopping the floors while his wife cleaned the tables and attempted to wake up the drunks.

It did not take long before the barkeep noticed her pres-ence. At first, he looked questioningly at her before he looked around his unruly establishment in embarrassment.

"Good morning, knight," The barkeep said, "Sorry to tell you, but we don't serve breakfast here. Might I suggest the Rusted Sword further down the street?"

"I'm actually here to talk to you. Do you have time?"

"Uhh-of course. Please, sit down."

He led her to the closest table that his wife had cleaned. It still reeked of booze, but it was manageable.

The barkeep sat before her, fidgeting as he looked around his tavern.

"I'm sorry you have to see the place like this," The barkeep said, "A stonemason ended his apprenticeship yesterday. Let's just say they bought their fair share, but most of it never came down the hatch." The barkeep lifted his foot, and the sound of the sticky floor releasing its grasp made both of them winch.

"Seems like you have your hands full," Lunarias said.

"It looks worse than it is. We'll be done before dusk. I hear you've been busy with, well, everything regarding the garrison. How's it going?"

"It's actually out of my hands now. One of my superiors is taking over, as I'm leaving today. But the city will be much safer for everyone, that's for sure."

"I hear you. This city is so peaceful since the knights are standing at almost every corner. But you should've seen the instructors rush when you announced training began the next day. They ran around the craftsmen's district, searching for anyone who makes new targets. The old ones had apparently grown moss and mold long ago."

"Trust me, the smell was the worst part of those."

"But at least they're getting into shape now that the knights are overseeing things," The barkeep said, "but what was it you wanted to talk about?"

"I'd like to thank you for your help in identifying the mercenaries' headquarters."

"What?" The barkeep looked surprised, but it was clear that he was playing dumb.

"Back when you told me the way to the church, you sent me on a route through the slums, right past their headquarters. That wasn't a coincidence since someone like you would probably have known about the quicker route around the market."

"..." The barkeep remained silent, looking at Lunarias, then back at his wife.

"I'm not here to arrest you. As I said, I just want to thank you. Nobody else knows that you knew about the mercenaries."

The barkeep finally exhaled in relief, "I'm in your debt. You guys have rounded up everyone who's involved in this. They came to me about a year ago, wanting me to use some connections to move their merchandise. What you saw that day was me trying to get them to back off, as they had accused me of taking more than my share."

"But why didn't you just tell me? You didn't even have to fear the dungeon if you became my informant."

The barkeep looked at his wife again. She scrubbed the alcohol out of the tables, an endeavor that seemed to require a lot of scrubbing. She blushed lightly as they both looked at her and went to another table further away from both.

"I feared for my wife," The barkeep said, "She carried our child back then. I didn't know if anyone was listening, so I had to be discreet, or else we'd end up like the carpenter last month. I've also paid for their protection, so having a guy here to extort me further was not unlikely."

"I see. I think you made the right choice then. They were a cutthroat bunch."

"But never mind that. I thank you for your help in bringing them to justice."

"What happened to them was no justice," Lunarias said, "Since I'm keeping your secret, I trust you can do the same?"

The barkeep nodded.

"I had the opportunity to bring the mercenaries to justice, but I let it go. I knew where the monster was going, and I could've stopped it, but I didn't. I was afraid of it. I failed as a knight that night."

Whether he thought the creature she executed was the one who did it or not did not matter. This was how she felt. She let Astolphos run wild. By not confronting him and his ways, she turned her back on the ideals she had held so high for many years.

"Did you?" The barkeep asked, "That thing was massive. It shouldn't be possible for anyone to take it down single-handedly, but you eventually brought it to justice. No one is going to look down on you for that."

"None of the citizenry, at least, but the other knights might use it to climb the ladder by using me as a rung."

"For all it's worth, I think it was the right decision. Their fate would be the same. You just spared the executioner the work."

When she exited the tavern, Astolphos was ready at the carriage.

He waved at her as if the two-wagon monstrosity were not enough of a hint. At that moment, she finally made up her mind. She did not want to feel this way ever again. So what if she was going to turn her back on the crown? The citizens were her responsibility, and that monster in front of her, that seemingly immortal being and the ilk it kept alive, was the biggest scourge upon Aurillia.

Even if she would be branded a traitor for it, she had to kill that Abyssal before they reached the capital.

Milton Keynes UK
Ingram Content Group UK Ltd.
UKHW020659180124
436254UK00016B/773